THE
MIDNIGHT
MAN

THE
MIDNIGHT
MAN

David Eric Tomlinson

TYRUS
BOOKS

Published by
TYRUS BOOKS
an imprint of F+W Media, Inc.
10151 Carver Road, Suite 200
Blue Ash, OH 45242. U.S.A.
www.tyrusbooks.com

Hardcover ISBN 10: 1-5072-0110-9
Hardcover ISBN 13: 978-1-5072-0110-7
Paperback ISBN 10: 1-5072-0109-5
Paperback ISBN 13: 978-1-5072-0109-1
eISBN 10: 1-5072-0111-7
eISBN 13: 978-1-5072-0111-4

Printed in the United States of America.

10 9 8 7 6 5 4 3 2 1

Library of Congress Cataloging-in-Publication Data
Tomlinson, David Eric, author.
The midnight man / David Eric Tomlinson.
Blue Ash, Ohio: Tyrus Books, 2017.
LCCN 2016031743 (print) | LCCN 2016039473 (ebook) | ISBN 9781507201107 (hc) | ISBN 1507201109 (hc) | ISBN 9781507201091 (pb) | ISBN 1507201095 (pb) | ISBN 9781507201114 (ebook) | ISBN 1507201117 (ebook)
LCSH: Public defenders--Fiction. | Choctaw indians--Fiction. | Basketball players--Crimes against--Fiction. | Murder--Investigation--Fiction. | Child witnesses--Fiction. | Capital punishment--Fiction. | Family secrets--Fiction. | BISAC: FICTION / Crime. | FICTION / Mystery & Detective / General. | FICTION / Sports. | GSAFD: Mystery fiction.
LCC PS3620.O565 M53 2017 (print) | LCC PS3620.O565 (ebook) | DDC 813/.6--dc23
LC record available at https://lccn.loc.gov/2016031743

Cover design by Frank Rivera.
Cover images © GettyImages.com/OceanFishing; GettyImages.com/aetb.

This book is available at quantity discounts for bulk purchases.
For information, please call 1-800-289-0963.

for my dad and his brother

We're perched headlong

On the edge of boredom

We're reaching for death

On the end of a candle

We're trying for something

That's already found us

—The Doors, "An American Prayer"

FALL 1948

The cowboy is shorter than you'd expect, chisel-chinned and sun-dried, and when he walks bowlegged onto the basketball court the jingling of his spurs rings clear and true. He's pushing ninety years old but you'd never guess it, with still-bright eyes and a handlebar moustache shaded by the Stetson resting on his head. The hat hides his fabled silver mane; the old man still braids it Indian-style, long locks coiled beneath the felted crown. And as he takes the microphone a murmur rolls through the crowd, the breathy whisper of people reconciling the sawed-off figure standing here to their collective imaginings. It's a familiar reaction, this undertow of grudged wonder. The sound now part and parcel of the man's status as minor local legend.

It's a sweltering fall Sunday in Stillwater, Oklahoma, and former frontier lawman Frank "Pistol Pete" Eaton has come to introduce the Harlem Globetrotters for a goodwill exhibition against Hank Iba's Oklahoma A&M Aggies. A pair of pearl-handled Colt .45 revolvers are holstered at Pete's hips, and at the sight of them the play-by-play jockeys up in the press box pause in their prattling, dumbstruck by this caricature on the court. The lexicography of basketball seeming insufficient, somehow, to describe the moment.

Curt Gowdy, the twenty-nine-year-old AM 1520 sportscaster, interrupts this break in today's broadcast with a gruff chuckle.

"Would you look at that," Gowdy says. "Ladies and gentlemen . . . I'm looking at Pistol Pete. Walking right out onto the court here in Stillwater. Plain as the nose on my face. Rumor has it he was faster on the draw than Buffalo Bill, back in the day."

You can almost hear the tongues of the newsmen untying in the warm, wheeling banter that follows. Gowdy's here to bring them all along, ready and able to give gravelly voice to their muted sense of muddlement. He's a fresh face on the Oklahoma sporting scene, on loan from somewhere up in Wyoming, with the relaxed, seen-it-all delivery of a well-seasoned uncle reflecting on the weather. Nobody expects him to stick around for long. A voice like that? No, this Gowdy fellow's got the big leagues in his future.

"I always pictured Pete taller," Gowdy says. "People around here tell us he's half native. Choctaw, I think. Cherokee maybe. Smokes a peace pipe, I hear. I am *not* kidding. It's rumored Pat Garrett gave him that six shooter just before Pete was all shot up in Lincoln County. Gunning for Wyley Campsey. The Campseys killed Pete's daddy when he was just knee high to a grasshopper, if I recall correctly. A posse of outlaws. Pete got himself deputized so he could track his father's killers. Fifteen years old and already he was working for that hanging judge. Judge Parker. Wyley was the last of them. Over there in Albuquerque. No, not *that* pistol—the other one. That's right, eleven notches in the barrel. One for every sad sack Pete sent to meet his maker."

Pete thumps the microphone, trying to be heard. He feels at home among these people, these fine folks still filing, damp-browed and wilted, into the muggy bleachers of Gallagher Hall. Earthbound men in shirtsleeves and bolo ties, hand-rolled cigarettes idling absently on blistered fingers and generous lips. Their crisp wives in floral-patterned cotton pique, fanning back the heat with straw hats or colorful paper fans folded from the Sunday circular. Crewcut boys preening coolly for the attentions of one or more sad, blank-faced young girls seated nearby. These plainsmen, who approach their games with a kind of reverence. As if every win validates some shared aspiration to greatness.

One of the A&M athletes stops short at midcourt and spouts off about Pete's getup, nodding at the bandolier slung below his belt.

"Those things really loaded?"

Pete peers up at the player, flat-topped and towering in his A&M colors, pumpkin orange and charcoal black. Then a quick finger flick and he's tossing the microphone to the kid, pistols whipped skyward, firing both guns at once into the vaulted ceiling. A thunderclap roar tears a hole in the heavy air, sounding then resounding madly in the empty spaces above the boards and below the bleachers with a tailbone-jarring judder.

The high squeaking scrape of shoe-rubber frictioning to full stop over the polished hardwoods. The sober pall falling over the spectators. The players at both ends of the court halting mid-motion in their drills.

"Son," Pete says, "I'd rather have a pocket full of rocks than an empty gun."

A light misting of plaster rains down on Pete as he holsters his guns, the barrels trailing thin wisps of smoke.

Gowdy says, "Well, there you have it folks. Pistol Pete living up to his name."

Pete collects the mike. "They wanted me to come up here and say a few words before this game today," he says. "This *basket* ball. But I'll shoot straight with you. I haven't seen a goofier sport played since I was a kid."

Someone coughs.

Pete says, "Used to watch those Choctaw men down the way play stickball before their stomp dance. That was a good game. Though I don't feel qualified to talk about this. This *basket* ball. But I was just watching these young men out here on the floor, everyone getting along just fine, it seems to me, on both sides. And it reminded me of something."

The Globetrotters' clown prince, Goose Tatum, saunters over to Pete with an Afro-hip pep in his step, looking like an oversized American flag in his bright blue jersey and peppermint-stripe shorts.

Pete says, "I've lived in these parts a long while. Used to be the armpit of the world, Indian Territory did. Crawling with rustlers and bandits. Just as soon slit your throat as give you the time of day. I'd smoke the worst lot from their hideouts over in Nigger Gap, out near

Bartlesville, then herd them over to Fort Sill so Judge Parker could hang 'em proper."

Goose is palming a basketball, grinning. With a fluid snap of his wrist he launches the ball into a controlled spin atop the tip of his finger.

Pete says, "After the land run I staked my claim south of Perkins. Stayed there ever since. Sheriffed for over thirty years. You want to know the hardest part of being a lawman?"

Goose slaps the air tangent to the rotating ball, nursing the spin.

Pete says, "Learning how to talk with the aggrieved."

And then Goose does the unthinkable. With a stealthy swipe of his free hand he reaches over to lift the ten-gallon hat away from Pete's head.

What follows is part pratfall performance art, part Buffalo Bill's Wild West comedy theater, as the referees enlist a handful of farmer-tanned A&M players to try and retrieve Pete's hat. Goose dishes the still-spinning ball to a referee, passes Pete's Stetson to a fellow Globetrotter, and soon we've got a quorum at center court and the game clock is starting and Robert "Showboat" Hall—he's flaunting the cowboy hat now, if you can believe it—has taken possession.

The A&M marching band, ambushed by this unscripted tip-off, responds with a rushed rendition of the school fight song. Dressed head to toe in western gear, their black cowboy hats dip and twist in time to the booming beat of the giant spirit drum parked in the endline aisle bordering the student section. The biggest drum in America, approaching seven feet tall in its custom-made pushcart, is manned by a petite coed swinging a felted mallet with $\frac{4}{4}$ fervor.

"Trotter Ermer Robinson wearing the cowboy hat now," Gowdy laughs. "Look at those socks. Loudest uniform I've ever seen."

An atmosphere of congenial bedlam permeates the clapboard stands, the crowd clamor swelling suddenly under a large white sign reading COLOREDS in black block type. A not unimpressive turnout of young Negroes hoots and hollers for the Globetrotters, now goofing and hamming their way to the first basket with practiced pizzazz, sleek-skinned and glistening like circus seals.

❧

Three rows back from center court, in the white section, a strapping young Cecil Porter leans down to his kid brother Ben and says, "Boy these niggers can handle the ball, can't they?"

Ben straightens his shoulders and nods. He's a pocket-sized twelve-year-old, red-cheeked and rounded at the edges. Standing next to Cecil, who's already six-foot-eight and only four years his senior, Ben feels half-handicapped in comparison. He strains his neck to see over the surrounding field of taller heads and shoulders. The people are all on their feet, cheering for their Aggies. It's understood that they'll remain standing until A&M scores its first basket.

"Help me out down here," Ben says. "I can hardly see."

"What can I do about it?"

"You tell me. You're the biggest one here."

"Help your own self."

Aggie forward Jack Shelton inbounds to the scrappy J. L. Parks. Two Trotters press Parks hard at half-court. Parks is in trouble. He lofts a baseball pass downcourt to Bob Harris, now loping for the basket with loose-limbed resolve. Globetrotters Babe Pressley and Ducky Moore move in, doubling down on Harris, who bobbles the ball, spooked. Just long enough for Babe to bring off a steal and force the turnover.

The crowd moans.

Babe weaves past an ambitious Aggie defender in the backcourt, juking him with an impossible crossover dribble, then cruises by Robinson to claim the Stetson, which he fits onto his own head with a feel-good flourish.

Scattershot laughter lifts into the rafters.

"If they ever let these coloreds into A&M," says Ben, "you'll have to work harder to keep your spot on the team."

Cecil dismisses Ben's barb with a swipe of his oversized hand. He's the star center for his high school basketball team, the Perkins Demons, with an unstoppable jump shot that's taken the Demons to the Division 4 finals for two years running. On track to break the state scoring record in the first half of next season, if he keeps it up. He surveys the Aggie sidelines for Hank Iba's scouting manager, who has all but promised him a full ride to A&M after graduation.

"Stay healthy, and keep making baskets," the man had said, clapping Cecil on the shoulder. "And eat plenty of spinach. Grow another two inches and you can write your own ticket."

Cecil had promised to work on it.

Ben wants to take his seat but doesn't. Someone in the student section claps twice and stomps a foot on the floorboards, kicking off a percussive, rhythmic chant that cascades throughout the hall. It's clear the Aggies are outmatched. But these Okies are nothing if not stubborn, and won't stop fussing until their boys are on the board. Goose reclaims the hat from Babe. Ben watches Harris seize the moment, cutting into the paint for a lay-up and a quick two points for A&M.

The marching band pounds out a celebratory song.

"Aw, come on," Cecil says. "That gets my blood up."

"What?" Ben says.

"It was a damned handout. They gave us that basket."

Cecil eases his huge frame into the bleachers. Others are following suit, the wave of spectators breaking into whorling tidepools of people, everyone eddying down into his seat, ready for the show. Ben's grateful to the Globetrotters for finally opening up his line of sight.

Hank Iba twists a crimpled paper program in his fists and rocks on his heels. They say nothing happens on his court unless he's first thought it through on the blackboard. Iba closes his eyes at night and dreams in chalk talk, geometric vectors boxing the other side into a predetermined course of action. Strongside offensive flows outlined in tightly drawn X's and O's.

He'd never admit it, but the coach can't help marveling at the Globetrotters. He's searching for a word to describe them, this effortless cadence of theirs. *Fast-and-loose*, maybe. Goose's every movement occasions a rippling readjustment from the other players. Let's air things out here, their bodies seem to be saying, so everyone can breathe a little easier. It's like some multi-tentacled sea creature. Watch it twist and curl through the deep ocean drift.

Symbiotic. That might be the term.

Aggie Harris steps out of the lane, hedging Goose in his drive for the post. Without slowing, Goose skips a no-look pass back to Robinson in the elbow, who pump-fakes his defender Parks, then lobs the ball into the empty air under the basket. And here's Goose, sneaking in the back door behind Harris, boosting the basketball up-up-and-away until it's kissing the board for a bank shot, effortless and silky smooth.

Iba's thinking, *In a million years I can't diagram this play.*

No. It's *soulful.* That's the word.

Ambling for the frontcourt, Goose detours by Pete's seat near the A&M bench, stooping down to mouth a private confidence in the old man's ear. He returns the hat. Pete allows a gap-toothed chuckle, complicit in his role as comic relief for these characters on the court, and installs the Stetson in its rightful place on his silvered pate.

Ben says, "You think he was in on this from the get-go?"

Cecil shakes his head, uncertain.

At the buzzer's howl the Globetrotters lead the Aggies, 28 to 12.

Gowdy says, "Iba leads Oklahoma A&M off the court to regroup for round two."

People yawn and stretch into the lull, waiting for the Globetrotters' slapstick halftime show. Showboat Hall starts things off, wowing the crowd with a stupefying display of dexterity, juggling four, no six . . . make it seven balls all at once, in defiance of entropy or gravity or whatever short-sighted law tends the world to disorder.

Gowdy says, "Look at that. I'll have to think twice next time I want to say something's not possible. What a thing."

Showboat spins like a top, flipping each juggled ball out to a different player, purling back-bounce passes and blindside feeds with centrifugal efficiency. The other Globetrotters launch into stunts of their own, dribbling and passing with madcap pomp, courtside jesters playing to the peanut gallery. After a few more minutes of flamboyant fun Showboat takes the microphone, assuming his duty as master of ceremonies.

And here comes Goose, sailing over the heads of two dribbling Trotters, slamming the ball two-handed through the hole.

Appreciative whispers riffle through the gallery.

"In Harlem we call that the *dunk*," Showboat smiles. "Before we go starting the second half, I wanted to ask for a volunteer from the audience."

Ben tugs at Cecil's sleeve. "You should get out there," he says. "It could be your chance to impress Iba."

"Iba's still in the locker room," Cecil says.

"Who wants to help us out?" asks Showboat.

Ben nearly upends a neighbor's chili-soaked boat of Frito pie as he leaps to his feet, shouting to be heard through the hullabaloo. The Globetrotter spots Ben waving his arms and aims his microphone at the boy.

"What in Sam Hill are you doing?" Cecil asks, watching his little brother scramble down the steps, through the spectators, out onto the hardwoods.

"What's your name, little man?" Showboat tilts the microphone down to Ben's level.

"Benjamin Porter."

"You play ball, Ben?"

"No sir," Ben says, puffing out his chest. "But my big brother Cecil can shoot circles around any man in this room."

Ben's bravado, standing in such stark contrast to his stature, draws a smattering of chuckles from the fans.

"Is that a fact?" Showboat says.

"Yessir. It is."

"Is this brother of yours here today, Mr. Porter?"

"I'm glad you asked, mister Showboat." Ben points to Cecil. "He's sitting right over there."

The bleachers creak as rubbernecking faces swivel round to size up this Cecil fellow. Cecil rises slowly, as if perched on stilts, long legs pushing and propping him up from the stands. Though taller than most, Cecil still has an unfinished look about him, prominent hands and feet sprouting wildly out of proportion to his trunk. His spit-polished boots (sized seventeen, special-ordered with a little extra "room to grow" by his mother Ida, who fears another spurt in her son's future) clomp a wooden tune on the hardwood floor as he walks onto the court.

Ben grinning like a shot fox. Cecil thumps him square on the skull.

"This will do just fine!" Showboat says. "Surely *you* play basketball, Mr. . . . Cecil, is it?"

Cecil nods down at Showboat.

"Okay then!" Showboat says. "Here's the deal Cecil. I'm going to give you one minute to shoot as many baskets as you can from the free-throw line. How many can you sink in a full minute, do you think?"

Cecil shrugs, noncommittal.

"Okay. Don't worry. It's no big thing. Because we're going to have Goose Tatum out here shooting from the other charity stripe." Showboat pauses, addressing the arena now. "How many of you think Cecil can score more free throws in a minute than Goose?"

The locals, wary of rising to Showboat's challenge, answer with a lackluster flapping of hands. The Globetrotters have been hypnotizing everyone with their hocus-pocus horseplay for the better part of an hour now; they're a known quantity. Cecil on the other hand . . . he is tall—we'll grant him that—but only the dedicated prep school fans have ever seen him in action.

"I've got to be honest with you people," Showboat says. "I'm not *feeling* it. I don't want you going home today with the sense you've accepted a raw deal. I'll tell you what. I'll go ahead and *blindfold* Mr. Goose," Showboat brandishes a red blindfold from some squirreled hideaway in his jersey, wags it like a flag between chocolate fingers.

"How do you like Cecil's odds now?"

The crowd cries out in good-humored glee. This is something they have got to see.

"Now that's what I'm talking about!" Showboat says.

Gowdy feels his second wind coming in.

"The young Mr. Porter removes his boots. Giving them to his little brother for safekeeping. Goose Tatum sizing up his opponent. The Globetrotters wheeling a ball cart out to each of the players. Cecil Porter warming up. Look at that, ladies and gentlemen! This young man *can* handle a basketball. But Goose doesn't look rattled. He's confident out there as Ermer Robinson ties the blindfold in place. And here's Hank Iba and his Aggies returning from the locker room. Just in time for the shootout."

Showboat wields a silver stopwatch and says, "Ready?"

Cecil crouches into his stance, eyes on the rim. Licks his lips and nods twice.

"Get seetttttttttt . . ." Showboat says.

Beneath the wine-dark swath of the blindfold Goose lets loose a hundred-watt smile.

"Go!"

Cecil senses everything sliding away, fading to background noise, eclipsed by the task at hand. He's deaf to the reflexive awe percolating from the spectators every time Goose scores one of his blind baskets. He's unaware of Hank Iba sizing him up from the Aggie bench, the way a cattleman might buy beeves at auction. He doesn't register the slow-burning spark of wonder his own free throws begin to stoke in these gathered bodies.

Because it appears that Cecil simply cannot miss.

A good fifteen seconds have elapsed before the Globetrotters realize how quickly Cecil will empty his basketball cart. Babe and Ducky quickly form a human resupply line, Babe beneath the bucket firing rebounds back to Ducky near the top of the key. Ducky offers Cecil a fresh ball every few seconds. Cecil spins it once in long fingers before unwinding, piston-like, knobbly knees feeding the elbow's fulcrummed snap, to send it sailing through the hoop.

People are chanting, "Thirty-one. Thirty-two."

Ben watches Iba's mouth hang open on the opposite sideline. Even Goose is gaping now, having removed his blindfold, after shooting just fifteen baskets, to see what the hubbub is all about.

"Thirty-seven. Thirty-eight."

Showboat blows a whistle at the one-minute mark and all at once everyone has forgotten how to breathe, waiting together for Cecil's last lobbed ball to breeze through the net with an effortless *swish*.

"Thirty-nine!"

Cecil surfaces from his minute-long reverie into a shower of praise, a laudatory cloudburst drowning out the basketball's hollow slap upon the floorboards. Ducky pumps Cecil's fists with inspired delight, head bobbing with encouragement.

Showboat is talking into the microphone but nobody can hear him over the Babel-crash din.

Cecil tries and fails to keep a straight face, mouth screwing into an aw-shucks grimace. Ben hands him his boots.

Showboat pretends to eat crow into the mike. His voice cuts, rich with mirth, in and out of the roar pouring forth from the crowd. Cecil's performance sure has humbled the Trotters, he could be saying, we'll have to be more careful of you Aggies in the second half. Didn't think you had this kind of fire in your bellies.

But secretly he's pleased. Winning is a foregone conclusion for the Globetrotters, easy as apple pie. Then there's the hard part, the thing Showboat and Goose and Ducky and Ermer and the rest of them labor so mightily to deliver, one workday gig after the next, to the well-ordered burbs sprawled, sea to shining sea, across this land. How to remove the sting of a loss from the equation altogether? How to make everyone feel like a winner? Not just the losing team, but their fathers and mothers, too. Their brothers, sisters, friends . . . no matter if they're red-faced or pale, high yellow, cinnamon brown or ink-dark ebony, for that matter. Just like some of Showboat's own colorful soul brothers—each and every nappy-headed black Sambo nigger one of them all.

How can everyone walk out of this auditorium with the high-stepping gait of a champ, feet lighter than the air in his very own lungs? It's a kind of magic, Showboat thinks, when it does happen.

And Cecil's homegrown shtick has just done the trick.

"Mr. Cecil Porter, ladies and gentlemen," Gowdy says. "Keep your feelers up for news about this boy. I have a feeling everything will be coming up roses for him soon."

Cecil and Ben retreat to their seats. Hank Iba trots over, follows the boys into the bleachers, proffers a puff-knuckled hand for Cecil to shake.

"That was quite an impressive display, Cecil," says Iba.

Iba's hand is soft in Cecil's grip, like a heifer's teat.

"Thanks."

Iba barks into the air and the Aggie scouting manager appears at his side wielding an overstuffed clipboard. The man nods knowingly at Cecil and awaits Iba's orders with arched eyebrows.

"Let's have Mr. Porter sit in on practice with the second squad," Iba says. "I think our second stringers might could use a few pointers on the free throw. How does next week work for you, Cecil?"

"Just fine," Cecil says.

"Perfect," Iba says. "We'll be expecting you."

Iba jogs off, leaving his scout jawing on with Cecil about the particulars, his height and age and position, home address and whatnot.

Ben elbows his big brother in the ribs and winks hugely. "You can thank me later."

The Aggie players are chomping at the bit, prepped and ready for the second period. But before the officials can clear the court Pistol Pete commandeers the microphone, stirring up quite a commotion at the scoring table.

"Hold your horses," Pete says, tottering out to center court again. "I've got something else to say. I hope you all enjoyed that little charade we played earlier. With the hat. Mr. Tatum and I worked that out in advance."

Goose Tatum bows low and smiles.

Pete says, "But in our hurry, we've forgotten the pledge."

Pete places a hand upon his heart and turns toward an immense American flag suspended from the rafters, its guylines glinting in the dust-mote sunbeams leaking through the windows. People peer fixedly at the flag, floating there over the arena, as if seeing it for the first time. A stillness settling over the room.

I pledge allegiance, to the flag . . . Cecil mouths the words from memory, eyes glazed . . . *of the United States of America* . . . He doesn't see the edgy cluster of basketball players, anxious to get out there and test their mettle once again, or hear the humdrum litany issuing from the mouths of his neighbors. He's not registering Ben's earnest recital of the pledge at his side. He doesn't even see the flag, though he's staring straight at the thing . . . *and to the Republic, for which it stands* . . . Instead he's remembering those free throws, shot after shot after shot after shot, every one of them bounced once on the packed earth drive behind his house in Perkins, spun in his fingers then lobbed for the makeshift hoop his dad had nailed to the side of the barn.

Gowdy shouts into the mike, "Let's play some basketball!"

∽

Despite the A&M loss the Porter brothers are in high spirits after the game lets out. Wonder-struck, the both of them. They gallivant the

quarter-mile gauntlet of empty and idling cars, zigzagging, momentarily
lost in the choke of gravel dust clouding the arena's unpaved parking
acreage, and when they finally find Dad's pickup truck Ben jogs for
the driver's side door to affect a profound nonchalance.

"Want me to drive?"

"Like I want a chapped hide," Cecil says.

"C'mon. Home's barely ten miles."

"Nope."

"I been driving longer stretches this summer on the farm."

"City driving's different."

"Do your chores this weekend?"

Cecil finds a cigarette.

"A whole week?"

Cecil lights the smoke, takes a quick squinting toke.

"Two."

"Dad would get pretty hot, he knew you was onto those."

Cecil walks around to the Chevy's passenger side, he's whistling
tobacco shavings from his tongue, and says, "A week then. Plus you
get to polish my boots."

"Brother, that is a deal!"

He tosses Ben the keys and they each climb up into the truck.
It always takes him a few tries, but eventually Ben gets a sense of
the clutch and soon he's steering guardedly through the pyrotechnic
haze, following a pink blinking trail of taillights, everyone swinging
out into the street, headed for home. Cecil reels his window down,
rests an enormous forearm on the door frame.

"Turn right."

"I know it."

"It's right again at Perkins Road."

"I know it."

"Two lights down yonder."

The two-lane highway running south to Perkins is crackling
with post-game traffic, brake lamps and headlights and high beams

blazing in the hot summer night. Wind wallops through the open window as they pick up speed: rhythmic, physical. Ben shifts into third then gooses his big brother on the thigh.

"Pretty fine driving, right?"

"Stay in the right lane," says Cecil.

"I know it."

"Go the speed limit."

"Jesus, Cecil."

Cecil draws off the last of his smoke and flips it out the window. The brothers watch the butt skitter askance the asphalt like a fuse. Ben's managing pretty well there in the southbound lane, he's working the clutch like a pro, like a real cross-country trucker, shifting the clunky steel heap down into fourth. His legs might be a little short but it's not stopping him getting the job done. A string of cars crowding behind the back bumper, impatient-like, but Cecil says don't worry about it, let them wait.

A queue jumper pulls into the unoccupied northbound lane, a tanker truck tearing south toward Cushing. It blows by the bottleneck and then Ben's window, going way too fast.

He senses the tanker's wake suck sickeningly at Dad's truck, drafting them, drawing them like a magnet.

"Ben . . ."

Ben yanks the wheel hard, panicked, pulling right, away from the big barreling rig.

But he's gone too far, he's overcorrected.

"Cecil . . ."

Then Dad's truck develops a head all its own. It's bucking from the road, ducking down then up then over a ditch, they're clipping through a barbwire fence, cotton branches clawing at the chassis, a ghastly *screeeeeeeeeeeeeech!* and everything shake bang rattling, Ben's arm jerking like a rodeo champ's and Cecil's cursing him *Goddammit brother what in Hell* and now they're rolling, dizzying end-over-end spins that just keep on turning, on and on into that cartwheeling dark.

∽

When he comes to there's a scorched-earth stench haunting Ben's nostrils. He's curled stock-still in the dirt, peaceful-like, and thinking: *Is this how Heaven smells?*

Ben pulls himself back into the world, his fingers digging for earth, clawing for something substantial. He is painfully, miraculously, alive. Not a scratch on him but this goose egg on his forehead. He's been thrown from the cab. And a good thing, too, because Dad's truck has been crumpled like a Coors can, its engine block wild-firing there in someone's cotton field, not fifteen feet away. Cars have pulled off the main highway, are slowing to a stop atop the rumble strip. Horns are trumpeting. People climb out to investigate, looky-looing, concerned citizens hollering above an insatiable wind: *Is anyone there? Hello? Is anyone hurt? Hello?*

Burnt and burning cotton bolls, despondent fireworks, tendril down from on high.

Ben hears something howling for help.

He makes for the sound, crawling at first. Then stumbling. Skipping. Running. More hollering. A child's voice, he thinks. Then realizes the voice is his own. Eventually Ben finds big brother, rag-dolled and unconscious—*oh dear Lord in Heaven thank you for that*—twenty yards beyond Dad's truck.

Cecil's big limbs are twisted about a fencepost, his spine bent nearly in half.

Cecil's hurt.

Dear God.

Cecil's hurt bad.

∽

Cecil?

He's waiting for the show to begin. But where's everybody gotten to? Cecil's the only one here. And this chair seems unnecessarily cramped. He tries shifting in the seat but it doesn't help. He's stuck smack-dab center of a big picture-frame stage, confronted by an immense curtain.

Cecil.

It really is a beautiful curtain. Familiar somehow. A pleasant human sound purring from the opposite side of it. A mumbling. Generous, heartfelt laughter. Cecil recognizes several of the voices: Dad, Mother, and Ben. There's Ellen's. Even old Doc MacBride. But Cecil's is the only chair here on the stage. There's a floodlight baking his neck, warm as a second sun, somewhere behind his shoulder. But before the performance can start Cecil's got to get up from this chair. They're expecting him. They want him to walk out there and address that crowd. He's cribbed a good joke, saved it for just such an occasion. And now they're calling him, whispering his name. But this chair's more awkward than a cross-hobble. He can't get free of the thing, no matter how he twists.

Cecil tries standing, but his legs won't work.

Cecil.

⌘

"Cecil?"

It's Dad talking at him this time.

Open those eyes. One after the other.

"Easy now, son. Careful out of the gate."

See and hear and feel, if this is still the word, the where and when and how of this thing. But he can't quite fathom the why. Every breath is an effort, as though he's been freight-trained by a fighting bull. The hospital cell smells of bleach and laundered linen and Mother's pacing the narrow strip before the window, looking caged, and his insensate legs have been screwed into some horrible science fiction superstructure drawn straight out of Ben's funny pages. It's impossible not to see them, these cables and weights and pulleys gluing him together after that first surgery. The doctors said there'd be a few more operations like the last, said he'd be wired to this rig for months. Said he'd never walk again.

He'd rather be back in the dream.

"Morning," Cecil croaks.

From his overnight pallet in the corner Ben sits up from the floor, stretching, peeks out at a sky sectioned by thin orange clouds.

"Night," says Dad.

"What?"

"That's a sunset."

Dad's eyes have got more red in them than blue, something Cecil's never seen before.

"There's a policeman here. He's got a few questions. You feeling up to it?"

Cecil mumbles that he's not feeling much of anything. But he's got nothing better to do and agrees to speak with the man, one officer Dobrowski, a burly bullhorn of a man, broad as he is long.

"Saw you throwing that ball with those Globetrotters the other day," Dobrowski booms upon entering the room. "You got some talent, son."

"Yessir."

Flipping open the notebook in his hand, Dobrowski nods at Ben and says to Cecil, "I've already spoken to your little brother here. Ben says your dad's Chevy lost control after that big rig passed everyone on Perkins Road. Says he remembers you talking about sticking to the speed limit. It makes me wonder how fast that tanker must have been moving? To pass you like that, I mean."

With those outsize eyes Ben looks like he's trying to hypnotize Cecil.

"I wouldn't know," Cecil says.

"Course. Of course. Neither of you was wearing those lap belts?"

Cecil clears his throat.

"No."

"You see any markings on the truck? Who owned it, maybe?"

"No."

Ben comes over to the bedside table—the nurses have set up a little water station here—and pours a glass for Cecil. Little brother has developed the jimjams, those pudgy little hands trembling something fierce.

Dobrowski flips his notebook shut. "Just as well. If you two hadn't been ditched from that truck, if you hadn't been driving, Cecil, I'm not sure either of you would have lived. Those quick reflexes saved you both. You probably don't like to hear it, son, but you were lucky."

Cecil accepts the cup of water from Ben.

"I was driving?"

"Doctor said they was worried you mightn't make it through the week," says Dad.

Cecil sips his water, trying to find Ben's eyes. But baby brother has lost all interest in hypnosis.

So this is how it's going to be. Everyone would assume it was Cecil behind the wheel. And, knowing the consequences—Ben would catch holy hell if Dad knew the truth—Ben would be too timid, at first, to correct that popular misconception.

"Then they said you was stronger than an unladen mule," Dobrowski laughs.

Dad tries to smile.

"He sure is more stubborn."

Mother walks sobbing from the room, heels clapping.

"Said they wouldn't have been able to put you down even if they'd tried," Dobrowski says. "You keep those spirits up. I know it's hard to see right now, with that injury and what all, and this is a bad one. Bad as I've seen. But God's got a plan for you. And this is all part of it. It'll come clear to you one day, you just wait and see. You'll be walking again soon, I'm certain of it. Maybe even running."

Cecil laughs, he can't help it, at Dobrowski's awkward gospel. But the slight motion it provokes in this traction contraption pretzels what's left of him into painful knots and the sound quickly contracts into a pathetic, childish whimper.

Ben takes the glass, concerned, reaching over to fluff Cecil's pillow and mutter, "Let me help."

Cecil closes his eyes, licks his lips, tries sighing through the spasm.

"Leave off," he says. "I don't want your help."

GHOST DANCE

SUMMER 1994

1. DEAN

Along the dawn-lit tracks of the Santa Fe railroad line the big Indian comes running. The man is quicker than his bulk implies, fleet feet flying over the splintered wooden ties. But he's breathing heavy, thick shoulders and ropy legs stippled with beads of sweat, dark stains pooling about the neck and arms of his patchwork gym shirt.

Dean Goodnight skips over the polished steel rails, hopscotching into the bombed-out neighborhood east of Oklahoma City. He lopes across the warehouse district, gaining ground under a cat's cradle of sagging telephone wires, partway done with his morning run. Power lines shimmer in the half-light overhead.

In the pooled glow of a distant streetlamp, two teens are tagging five-point crowns on the broadside canvas of an abandoned storefront, marking their territory with hissing bursts of acrylic. Latin Kings, real go-getters from the looks of them, decked out early in the team colors. Black and gold.

Dean detours down a side street, trailed by the rattle-crack shake of spray cans being primed. The two-toned tantrum of a police claxon sounds down the alley. A few blocks ahead an OCPD police cruiser, gumball lights strobing the street in official reds and blues, has T-boned an old Plymouth sedan. Two of OKC's finest are busy putting the hurt on some poor, enormous mope, wrestling the giant shirtless kid to the ground and into a rear chokehold. A second black-and-white is curbed a half block from the action, front doors flung wide, and behind it, a safe distance from the bust, a well-intentioned badge counsels an emaciated woman and her hysterical, yammering child. The boy looks to be about four, maybe five, years old.

Intesha.

Dean stops running.

His hands raised—everyone needs to know he's unarmed—Dean walks slowly in the direction of the disturbance. The fourth officer on scene, a marbled fellow overseeing his partner's interaction with the woman and child, invites Dean to join them with a terse wave.

"You live around these parts?"

Dean lowers his hands.

"Yes."

"Where?" A veined palm rests on the man's gun butt.

The younger officer is staring across the roof of his cruiser at Dean, ignoring the woman and her kid. His face is vague, almost apologetic, under a hard night's growth of stubble.

The boy is sobbing, *"Inki!"*

"Twenty-fifth," Dean says. "Near Hudson."

"What's the name of that park there? The one with the playground?"

"Andy," says the badge interviewing the woman.

"Goodholm Park."

"Hold up, Andy."

"The hell, Paul! I'm interrogating here."

"Andy. I know this guy."

"What's your name, son?"

"Dean Goodnight."

"That's him."

Officer Andy unbuttons his holster and crowds in close.

"Collared him before?"

"I wish. He works for Paxton."

Officer Andy steps off shrugging. He leans against the trunk of the black-and-white, the car's shocks popping audibly, and settles into a more comfortable skin.

"You're a public defender?"

"Investigator," Dean says. "Mostly capital cases, these days."

Dean recognizes the officer taking the woman's statement, Paul, and nods.

Officer Paul doesn't return the favor.

"That's the guy I was telling you. The one got Williams off."

"Williams?" officer Andy asks his partner. "The skell? Williams the spitter?"

Paul nods, directing his attention back to the woman, a tweaker type painted into acid-washed jeans and a Rage Against the Machine T-shirt.

"*Inki!*" the child is shouting, face knotted with anger. "*Chim achukma? Sa yoshoba!*"

Officer Andy admits a rough smile, as if recalling an off-color joke.

"So you're playing for the other team. We lock 'em up . . ."

"He sets 'em loose," officer Paul finishes.

Dean shifts his weight from one sole to the other.

Intesha, intesha.

"What's going down here tonight, guys?" asks Dean.

Officer Andy pops a thumb over his shoulder, in the direction of the ongoing scuffle. "Gigantor over there killed a meth dealer name of Carl Jefferson. No mean feat, if it's true. Jefferson was a six-foot-eight homeboy. Used to play college basketball. Didn't just kill him, either. Tortured the guy. Drowned him in bourbon, I hear. We get a tip he's been living in the Plymouth, pimping out the missus here, and it's on. Bad guy collared. Case closed."

"Murder one?"

"That's for the D.A. to decide."

The two more distant officers, amped from the arrest, have hauled their collar to his feet and now have him spread-eagled before the Plymouth's headlights. The guy's a real leg-breaker, standing six-foot-five if it's an inch, and one of the badges is whispering at his head, nose to nape. He's reading the man his rights in a tone that says you have no rights, in a tone that says you're mine, shitbird, when the suspect's head jerks back to butt the officer in the face, breaking his nose.

Everyone watches the policeman, blood flooding into his lips, chin-check the collar into a prone position. His skull tattoos the Plymouth's hood with a metallic *whoomp!*

"You know, I've heard a little bit about you, actually," officer Andy says to Dean. "That bartender girlfriend of yours, what's her name?"

The little boy babbling and the dispatch crackling from inside the police cruiser: *That's a ten-six. Please stand by. Over.*

"Sam," Dean says.

"Right. Sam. Sam from behind the bar at Flip's. You're a lucky man, Mr. Goodnight. She is one hot smoking blonde on . . ."

Dean risks three steps away from officer Andy, in the direction of the arrest.

"Stop right there, public pretender." Andy hauls his girth from the black and white's trunk. "Unless you're looking to spend a night in lockup, too?"

"For what?" Dean says. "Contempt of cop?"

Intesha, intesha, intesha.

Dean walks around the police cruiser, he's breathing hard again, approaches the skinny woman and her child.

"My name is Dean Goodnight. I'm with the public defender's office. Don't talk to any of these guys until someone from our office comes to help. Tell your husband the same. We'll get a lawyer down to the jail today, if at all possible. Though it could be tomorrow . . ."

"Billy ain't my husband," the woman interrupts. She's really soaring this morning, jaw working, her mouth sounding that sick clicking meth-head music.

"Boyfriend then," Dean says.

The girl grinding what's left of those molars.

"Pimp?" officer Paul asks helpfully.

"Don't answer that," Dean says to the woman. "What's your name?"

"Willa."

"Billy's Choctaw," says Dean. "Am I right? Part of the Nation?"

Again with the teeth. Willa is exceedingly disinterested in her circumstances.

"Alright Willa," Dean says. "You make sure Billy doesn't talk to these policemen, got me? Here or at the jail. I'll get somebody over there to help him just as fast as we can manage. Do you understand?"

Willa snorts, says, "Do I look like a halfwit to you?"

Officer Andy is laughing.

"You know when you first walked up, Mr. Goodnight, I thought you were just one of these porch monkeys. Out jacking hubcaps in the wee small hours."

"Just out for a run," Dean says.

"Have to make our quota some other way then, I guess."

"I hear there's a code seven at the donut shop this morning."

"Haha! Hear that Paul? Goodnight's a real smart guy. Next thing you know he'll be arguing cases."

Stepping from the curb, heading back the way he came, Dean accelerates into a dogtrot. The graffiti crew has moved on, spooked by the police cruiser. The outlines of a wildstyle burner shine from the storefront, the unfinished pattern dripping dry in the morning light.

Sun's up. Time to work.

◌◊◌

His skin is the color of cinnamon. His boss jokes that Dean sports a sort of sixth sense. Put Tonto on the case, he says, and his bullshit detector will sniff out the truth. During gaps in the small talk Dean's coworkers wonder if he might be tapping into the things they've left unsaid, plucking secrets from the depths of those uncomfortable silences.

He runs five miles every day—*rain-or-shine* is what they say—and has yet to reach the end of himself. If he pushes hard enough, Dean believes, the world might still give way.

They call him Tonto at work. Dean plays along.

Intesha is a Choctaw word describing the snare-drum thrum from a rattlesnake tail.

Intesha: stay away.
Intesha: there is danger here.
Intesha: keep your distance.

2. AURA

Aura Jefferson sees the man surging up from the crush of bodies in motion but, too late, she's airborne, free-floating, the ball curling from her fingertips for the backboard. Nothing to be done but give in to gravity and here's the midair collision and now she's falling, sprawling, sliding on her backside to a sweaty rest out beyond the baseline.

The twitchy white kid with the peach-fuzz moustache, Van Something-or-Other, blows his whistle and cries "Foul!"

The basketball bobs into the bleachers.

"Sweet Jesus," says the man standing over her, "I'm sorry about that." He extends a helping hand.

Aura ignores him. She hauls herself from the floor, heavy-grunting. The gym swims.

"Two shots," Van says.

Aura says, "I need a few."

The man follows her to the sidelines.

"That was a pretty rough tumble," he says. "Are you okay? I sure didn't mean to floor you like that."

"And yet," Aura says, "here I am. Floored." She takes a seat in the bleachers.

The man offers his hand again. "I'm Nate Franklin."

Aura looks up at him, shakes the hand.

"You're the new preacher over in Langston. How are you liking our little midnight league?"

Nate smiles, jocksure of himself, white teeth bright against skin a few shades darker than Aura's own.

"It's a wonderful thing! And you must be Aura. Your style on defense . . . it reminds me of Carl's. You know, I used to watch him play. Back when he was at Oklahoma State. Seems like I'm up against your brother out there tonight."

Aura covers her head with a towel and mops her face dry.

"He was . . . wow. Carl Jefferson was talented. A natural-born swingman."

Her hooded stare.

"*Was.*"

Nate pulls a face. "I heard about his . . . his murder, Aura. I am so sorry."

Aura puts on her shrug, tries to ignore the spasm in her heart, looks out from the safety of her shroud.

"They caught the boy who killed him a few nights ago," she says absently. "He was living in his car."

The corners of Nate's mouth turn down. "It's all so awful. Is there anything I can do?"

"Get back to your team Nate. I'll be back in the game soon enough."

It's after midnight on a slow, summer Saturday and the regular kids have scattered, back to Guthrie and Cushing and Perry and Drumright. Just a few stragglers left hangdogging around, latchkey types with no place to be, cutting up in the dim and bleachered gym perimeter. The adults have ventured out onto the court now, Aura and Nate and Waldrop and the other coaches, winding down the night with a good-natured game of pick-up. Worn joints crackle and pop like kettle corn as aging cagers jostle and whoop under the hoop, everyone moiling away at some strained muscle memory, searching for the glory days.

This midnight basketball is a good program, one of several bright stars carried over from the original thousand points of light. Aura's been volunteering here every weekend without fail since her brother Carl died, herding packs of thin-limbed hoop dreamers about the court for a few hours of fun. Bullet-skulled aspirants to the NCAA, CBA, USBL. The NBA. USOC. *Dream Team.* Large-lettered initialisms spelling out bigger and brighter futures than are written in this place. The backwatered suburbia known as home: Stillwater, OK, *U.S.A.*

She stands a sixteenth-inch shy of six feet tall, with a slick jab-step crossover drive that hasn't failed her yet, even at thirty-three. She plays the one spot some nights but mostly the two, point or perimeter, depending on the need. The only woman on staff. And a registered nurse, to boot. Proud member of the esteemed *RN* league.

The guys tried pigeonholing her as mother hen at first. Mender of skinned knees and bruised egos. But after a week spent tending the weak and wounded Aura's got no patience for frailty come Saturday night. It's the ex-cons like Van over there, the ex-cops like Waldrop, who seize onto the teachable moments. Any night now and Nate will be out there with them, extolling the benefits of sober living and goal-setting. Faith and forgiveness and redemption and the like. Like half-drowned men clutching at flotsam. Waldrop—Stillwater PD, retired—says his nights here make the days go a little easier for his buddies still on the force.

"Life doesn't forgive the big mistakes," Waldrop likes to say before dismissing the kids. "That's God's job. So don't screw up out there this week. I'll see you all next Saturday."

She convinced Carl to tag along with her once. A few years back, it must have been. Midwinter. Some snow-white Saturday night. There'd still been something of him worth salvaging then. Some pure and sapient slice of her brother would surface from the front he'd assembled, the signs and the tics and the doublespeak. *Slangin' and bangin'.* For a moment they'd talk, in plain and simple language. The way real-live people do. Then Carl saw the rinky-dink facilities here, the fledgling talent, the blank and needy faces.

"Amateur hour," he'd called it.

Aura's burnout brother laughed and fell back into his pusherman front. End of conversation.

But Carl was playing at an altogether different game. The rough and tumble rhythms of midnight basketball are sufficient for Aura's needs. Tomorrow she'll wake in a body writ with bruises, a blue-black play-by-play of the night before. But she'll keep coming back.

For that sense of escape from the steady festerwork of time. For that feeling of being absorbed.

Aura comes up from the bleachers for her frees and when the second shot clips the rim a crowd of ballers go elbowing for the rebound. Van calls a jump ball and now she's bent into the whistlestop bustle at center circle, players spreading fanwise in expectation of the tip-off. Aura crouched into pistol position, hipshot and ready to run. Nate Franklin swats the rock above the scrum but she lays hands on it midair and now the ball is hers. Whipsawing goalward through the brick-footed bunch of them all, Waldrop and Nate and the rest, dribbling out and around and through, the basket beckoning. Nate trundles slantwise into the paint but Aura's ready for him this time, twisting 'round high-shouldered to draw the foul now *there's* the release, the ball sliding down the glass and into the net for two plus one, everyone plunging, reckless and giddy, toward the floorboards.

Nate trips, stumbles, falls. Falls hard. Van blows his whistle and cries foul.

Aura extends her hand, helps the man to his feet.

"Don't worry about it," Nate says, rubbing at his elbow. "Probably my . . ."

"Shake it off," Aura says. "It won't hurt long."

The preacher looking a little dazed. He smiles and nods, shuffles back to his teammates.

She comes here to forget.

3. BEN

Big Ben Porter bounds into the Sheraton convention center ballroom like a man dancing. Though he tipped the scales at close to three hundred pounds this morning, Ben carries his excess weight with pride, as if it's the punch line to some joke he's just told. Something about mass as a correlate to power. *If it doesn't have mass, it doesn't matter. Ba-dump-bump.* Ben struts, his calfskin wingtips cutting a crowded rug for the buffet table, where he helps himself to a hefty wedge of Key lime pie because, why not, Becca's not here to tell him no. Ben forks a bite into his mouth—it's a goddamn great slice of pie—and reads the room.

Today is the Greater Oklahoma City Chamber of Commerce summer meet-and-greet. The event's been billed as a party-neutral luncheon, a networking opportunity for up-and-comers. But the midterms are only a few months away, and everybody knows it's just an excuse to listen to a few stump speeches. Auction a few votes off, maybe, to some enterprising pitchman trying to buy his way into the Beltway. Poker-faced staffers thread like guided missiles between the tables, where pockets of people have already positioned along party lines.

The event planners must have been aiming for an understated kind of refinement, an atmosphere that would highlight the Chamber's reluctant support of the New Austerity washing over the electorate. From the barebones decor here it appears they might have overshot the mark. Just a few delightfully tacky flower arrangements, plastic peonies and paper wildflowers girdled by giant doilies.

In the room's far fringes a dapper black man is taking the klieg-lit stage. It's former Oklahoma University quarterback J. C. Watts behind the lectern, all gym-chiseled angles and custom-tailored lines.

"Good afternoon, Oklahoma City!" Watts says in his downhome drawl. "Do we have any Sooners out there?"

A Boomer-Sooner *ooh-rah!* muffles up from the tables. The Oklahoma State fans in the room, Ben among them, stew in customary, put-upon silence. After earning his diploma in Stillwater every Aggie begins a kind of lifelong sentence—in football and in life—playing second fiddle to the better-known, better-financed, better-performing, often better-looking graduates from Norman.

"I hope you're enjoying your meal," Watts says. His crimson-and-cream tie burns bright under the spotlights.

From his place near the punchbowl Ben can see Oklahoma City mayor Terry Giffords pressing the flesh, wading among his constituents the way a game-show host greets his studio audience. Ben takes another bite of pie and bides his time.

"As a fiscally responsible Republican," says Watts, "I was glad to see there wasn't an ounce of pork on today's menu."

A more bipartisan laughter spreads among these meat-and-potatoes conservatives.

"I'm here today to talk about trimming the fat from our federal budget. About incentivizing pro-business behavior with our tax laws. About the crime bill floated by the 'man from Hope,'" Watts adds, framing the mike with thick-fingered air quotes. "And when I'm done speaking, well, *I hope* you'll lend me your support in my bid for the U.S. House seat being abandoned by President Clinton's own Dave McCurdy."

Giffords glimpses Ben from across the room and waves. A staffer is dispatched. Ben follows a pinstriped, acne-scarred kid to the mayor's private table, still palming his pie plate, feeling like a contestant called out on *The Price Is Right*.

Big Ben Porter . . . come on down!

Ben shakes the mayor's hand and takes his seat.

"Have you tried the pie?" Ben says.

"Carol has me dieting." Giffords pats his stomach. "Re-election season."

"Too bad." Ben forks himself a big bite of Key lime.

Onstage, Watts is wondering why Clinton has set aside forty million dollars in his new crime bill for—more finger quotes now—"midnight basketball."

"It's pure, social pork," says Watts. "Might as well fry that program up and serve it with your grits for breakfast."

"The tent gets bigger every day," Giffords says, watching Watts.

"They're eating him up," says Ben.

"Mr. Watts goes to Washington."

"Who'd have thunk it."

"It's beyond imagining."

"The future always is."

"I hope McCurdy's Senate grab helps us," Giffords sighs.

"It already has," Ben says with a smile. "Good old Boren. You've got to love a liberal who goes AWOL. Resigning the Senate to run the University of Oklahoma. Now McCurdy's eyes are getting bigger than his stomach. Abandoning a surefire seat in the House to try and fill Boren's shoes in the Senate. Jesus. Why'd the Democrats want to go handing us two vacancies like that?"

"Don't look a gift horse in the mouth," Mayor Giffords says. "Who do you like to replace Boren in the Senate?"

"Jim Inhofe by a nose. McCurdy doesn't stand a chance. You should see the polls."

"I see the polls three times a day. It doesn't help me sleep at night. Did you hear?"

"Did I hear what?"

"Charlton Heston's endorsed Watts for the House," says Giffords. "And, get this. Jack Kemp."

"It was bound to happen. Kemp's probably showered with more blacks than you've shaken hands with, Terry."

"That's Newt's line."

"Tell him to take it up with me on that corrections day of his."

Both men watch Watts talk.

"How's the Metropolitan Area Projects oversight committee getting along?" Ben says.

A more beleaguered mayoral sigh this time.

"Did you read what that newspaper mogul Gaylord called me in *The Oklahoman* the other day? Said I was a new species of Republican. A tax-and-spend conservative, he said. Now that bleeding-heart, wannabe mayor Gould can't go anyplace without dropping the tax-and-spend soundbite."

"You got off easy. He could've called you a socialist."

Giffords fidgets.

"This is an important election for us, Ben. I can't lose to Gould. It would mean the end of everything."

"Frontier politics," says Ben. "It's more fun than watching a game of musical chairs."

"I don't want to be the last man standing when the music stops come November."

Ben feels it might be time for a little "let's make a deal." He puts the pie aside.

"What's your sport, Terry?"

"What?"

"Football? Basketball? Table tennis?"

"If I had to pick . . . basketball, I guess."

Ben sizes up the mayor.

"I wouldn't have guessed."

Giffords lets this sink in.

Big Ben tells tall tales with a disc-jockey's delivery. He's mastered the dramatic pause, the just-between-us whisper, the big baritone reveal. He's got pull here. People gravitate to his Huckleberry charm, the unselfconscious presence Ben brings to the Grand Old Party. That and the piles of cash Ben tends to hand out during the election cycle. And so as Big Ben Porter starts talking, Terry Giffords leans in to listen.

"A good campaign, it's like a basketball game. Say your team has got the ball. You're playing man-to-man. The other guy slaps up a two-three zone. What do you do?"

The mayor doesn't bite. He's waiting to see where Ben's headed.

"You adapt. Move to your zone offense. Back-screen the weak side, if your team can get away with it. Defense dictates the offense. Now. Downtown's on life support. Hell, Terry, downtown is *dead*. You and I both know it. Gaylord knows it. Your opponent, that liberal whatshisface, Gould, knows it. Leonard Cohen said it best. Everybody knows."

"Sometimes I wish we could just bomb everything east of the railroad," Giffords says. "Rebuild from scratch."

"Well, look here. Your Metropolitan Area Projects redevelopment plan will do that very thing. Three hundred million dollars. A riverwalk rivaling San Antonio's. A ballpark. Hotels and restaurants and art galleries galore. High-end condominiums filled with kids who like to spend a night or two on the town. It's a businessman's promised land, Terry."

"My problem," Giffords complains, "is that businessman's selective memory. The voters, they're like amnesiacs. They remember I've promised a neat new downtown. But they won't see the new skyline for, what? Three years? At best? Meanwhile they're complaining about the pinch in their pocketbooks. We have to pay for it somehow. Riddle me this, Ben, how come it takes so long to demolish a few rundown warehouses? What have you done for me *lately* is the question I'm hearing. Speaking of which . . ."

"The environmental impact study," Ben says, "is ahead of schedule, Terry. You'll have your book report by Christmas. Maybe sooner. I've got my engineers at Dirt Devil Construction running models this very minute. You won't hear of any problems on my end."

"It had better stay that way."

"It will. Which is why I'm asking you to consider Dirt Devil for the project coordinator appointment."

"I've bet the farm on M.A.P.S."

"So let it ride, Terry."

Giffords goes blank. Still not getting it.

With the knuckles of his right hand Ben bumps the mayor playfully on the thigh.

"What has Gould done? Nothing. Doesn't even hold office yet. He can only attack you for raising taxes. You're wondering, what's my play? Turn it back at him. Defense dictates offense. M.A.P.S. will," now it's Ben's turn for air quotes, "'incentivize pro-business behavior,' like Watts just said. You're the businessman's best friend. You've just got to remind him of it. Remind the amnesiacs what the future holds. It's time to start shouting M.A.P.S. from the rooftops. Until the old town has been torn down, that is, and your oversight committee has named me the project coordinator for the rebuild."

Giffords grins.

"An advertising campaign like that," says the mayor, "requires airtime. TV. Drive-time radio. Column inches in *The Daily Oklahoman*."

"Those things cost money, Terry."

"You took the words right out of my mouth, Ben."

4. CECIL

Cecil Porter swings wide the front door to Riley's Café, drops the Sunday headlines in his lap and, in a move he's spent more than forty years perfecting, pops a wheelie and roll-hops his wheelchair over the saddle sill to glide coolly down the little concrete ramp leading to lunch. The door hinges shut behind him with a wooden *slap* as Cecil turns into his corner-table two-top, built two inches taller than the rest to accommodate his rig, leafs over to the crossword puzzler and waits for someone to start giving him grief.

Libby Riley waddles by swirling a carafe of coffee. "Help you, Cecil?"

"What's the special?"

"Coffee and snails." Libby brims Cecil's mug and leans on his chair, resting her new titanium hip.

"Cinnamon rolls?"

"Don't even get me started."

"Those are slim pickings."

"Sounds like you might need more time, Cecil. Let me know when I can be of assistance." Libby limps away, looking harried in black hornrims and hairnet. An outfit that came into fashion, if memory serves, when Truman was in office.

Motormouthed Carter Burrell, would-be farmer and fair-weather Sooners fan, moseys over.

"Cecil."

"Carter."

"I tell about that time my great-uncle Earl had his crick-neck fixed by a twister?"

"The one lives in Wichita?"

"The very soul," Carter says, hooking thick thumbs in his overall braces and swelling up into something resembling a horned toad. "What happened was, Earl was stretched out on his La-Z-Boy watching Gary England foam from the mouth about a supposed supercell whirling toward town. He's been having neck problems chronically for more than eight or ten years, you see, which is why Earl's supine. Doesn't want to aggravate his crick. So there old Earl is, hoping like hell the storm will hop over him altogether, when he hears a holy terror of huffing and puffing out there. I mean it's *blowing.* Earl's got no other choice now. He has *got* to seek shelter. So Earl makes a run for the neighbor's cellar across the street. But the tornado, this is an F-3 blew through Kansas in sixty-five, it's directly overhead. Earl's looking straight up into its green and grinding gizzard. The pressure's so low—*slurp!*—it pops the hood *clean off* his truck. Just sucks that hood spinning up into the sky."

Cecil swallows the better portion of his coffee in a grim and merciful way, as if trying to spare the drink any further part of Carter's balderdash.

"Well as you can imagine, Earl's not having much success getting across the street. So this twister decides to help him out. Picks him up off the ground. I mean, lifts him up and *whips* him about like a rag doll."

"I'd like to meet this uncle of yours sometime, Carter."

"Well, next time he's in Perkins, Cecil, I'll be sure and arrange introductions. But wait till you hear the best part."

"I am on the edge of my seat."

"The best part is . . . After the wind has had its way with Earl. After it lays him in the middle of that road. Flat on his back . . . he crawls to his neighbor's storm cellar and waits out the weather."

"That it?"

"Cecil. I am hurt. Would I be taking up your valuable time if *that* was it? This tornado did what years of quack chiropractors couldn't. It set old Earl's spine straight as an arrow. He hasn't suffered a day of neck pain since."

"You might be onto something, Carter." Cecil repositions his deadweight legs and says, "Think the spine doc should refer me to a cyclone?"

"Just talking on it has me itching to enlist with those funnel-chasers down at OU."

But Cecil's consulting his crossword now.

"I need a six-letter word means the same as *imbecile*."

"Imagine scouting the state with one of those big video recorders. It'd be like looking down the barrel of God's very own shotgun, you got close enough."

"I have it," Cecil says, producing a pencil from his shirt pocket and mock-scribbling in the paper. "*S-O-O-N-E-R*. Lacks the sense God gave a barnyard dog. Normal people get wind of a storm like that, Carter, they take cover."

"Well," says Carter, walking away. "All those national championships must have addled our brains."

The greasy spoon is filled with old men who loiter here every morning of the world but Monday to nurse coffee, dissertate on the weather, and tell lies. Libby closes the restaurant on Mondays, so by Tuesday dawn everyone in Perkins has had ample opportunity to polish his fictions to high, bald-faced gloss. Then the coffee cups get topped, the grill begins spitting, and the yarns start spinning. The stories grow more outlandish as the week progresses, such that by Sunday afternoon the air is so smogged with hogwash Libby has to shutter the place just to catch her breath. The good whoppers have a hand-me-down implausibility thwarting all attempts at verification. The better ones include a little twist at the finish giving the lie to some newfangled perturbation, reconciling so-called *progress* with the more homespun folkways stitching these modest farmsteads together.

Libby looms.

"Has mister particular made up his mind?" she says.

"I'm waiting on my baby brother. But I'll take another dose of that belly wash."

She refills Cecil's cup and scuffs over to greet a just-arrived family of five. From behind the safety of his father's trouser leg a towheaded toddler examines Cecil's wheelchair with brazen-faced skepticism. Cecil bugs his eyes and winks but the kid won't blink.

Having now made the rounds and found Cecil to be his most attentive listener, Carter Burrell comes to roost on a nearby counter stool. "You hear about these boys over in Elohim City?"

"Wingnuts," Cecil says.

"First there's Ruby Ridge. Then Waco. Michigan. Now Adair County. This is our doorstep, Cecil. It's end-of-days, I tell you."

"You're puzzling together pieces from different boxes."

"Then explain April nineteenth to me."

"Partly cloudies, mostly. My perennials are in full flower. About ten months off."

"That standoff between the CSA and ATF? April nineteenth. It's what got Ellison to move from Missouri to Elohim City, Cecil. The Waco siege? April nineteenth. Shot heard round the world? April nineteenth."

"Come off it, Carter."

"Patterns like this don't happen coincidental."

Cecil cockeyeing his crossword again.

"Here's another word for you," Cecil says. "Twelve down. Eight letters. *P-A-R-A-N-O-I-A.*"

"Time's running out, neighbor."

Cecil siphons another impassioned inch of coffee off his mug.

They both hear him before they see him, the unmistakable timbre of that chest-register laughter clapping in from the sidewalk. Then big Ben Porter saunters through the café door, dispensing handshakes and hugs to Cecil's neighbors as if he was Slick Willie himself.

"Hold tight to your little ones," Cecil announces. "Ben's in baby-kissing mode."

Ben appraises the carrying capacity of the empty seat next to Cecil and says, "Brother."

"Brother."

Ben lowers himself in timid installments onto the chair.

"Big Benjamin Porter," Carter says.

The chair holds.

Ben relaxes. "Carter how in hell are you?"

"I am well and good, Mr. Porter! Your big brother and I were just palavering on political matters before you arrived and it's got me thinking. You're in bed with those political types down in the city, aren't you? What's the consensus on this whole Contract with America proposal?"

"Like him or don't," Ben says, "but that Newt is one shrewd shark. Everybody is wondering if these guys are already bought and paid for. Whether they'll turn Judas come January. He's flipped that doubt around. He's saying, 'Sure, we're up for sale. Get in on the deal! Send your check or money order today! You too can own your very own congressman.' The stroke of genius is that it's all aboveboard. Laid down in a legal-type document for the whole world to see."

"Make sure you read that fine print," says Cecil. "That's where they'll stick it to you."

Libby Riley lumbers up and fills Ben's coffee mug.

"Time to order, Porters. Lunch rush is starting. I'll be needing this table double quick."

Ben takes Libby's free hand, makes a show of kissing it, says, "It's good to see *you* too, Miss Libby."

Libby reclaims her hand.

"Don't you be getting fresh with me, Benjamin Porter."

"I'll have the chicken-fried steak and potatoes," Ben says.

Libby scratches Ben's order in her notepad.

"What about daddy longlegs here?"

"Chicken club," Cecil says.

Libby turns to Carter at the counter.

"How about you?" she says to Burrell.

"Can't I just sit for a spell?"

"I don't have space to water a wallflower who's not eating."

Cecil laughs and says, "You're running out of time, Carter."

Burrell glowers into his menu.

"Did Becca add chicken-fried steak to the list of approved foods?" Cecil asks.

Ben pats his stomach.

"What Becca don't know won't hurt her."

"Going to the football game Saturday?"

"Gave my seats to a client."

"I hope he's worthy."

"He's not."

"The Aggies are going to embarrass us on the gridiron this year."

"I can't even watch."

"You can and you will, brother."

"I know it."

"I keep hoping another bulletproof buck like Thurman Thomas or Barry Sanders will just walk on and surprise everybody. Damn those niggers could run."

"My daughter in San Francisco says it's not, how did she phrase this? *Politically correct* to talk that way, brother. She told me we should be saying *African American*."

"That's made up."

"It absolutely isn't."

"It's funny, don't you think? Your hippie-dippie daughter wanting to limit my freedoms of speech."

"Never mind."

"It's like, blackwhite."

Ben admires Cecil's nut-colored Lucchese ropers.

"How are the new boots fitting?"

"This is the last time, Ben. Next pair I'm refusing delivery."

"Who says there'll be a next pair?" says Ben. "Those soles sure are holding up."

"And here I was about to thank you."

Ben lifts two basketball tickets from his pocket.

"The alumni committee finally sold you on the box seats?" says Cecil.

Ben slides the tickets across the table for Cecil to inspect.

"You didn't."

"Floorside."

"Lord." Cecil whistles. "That team better get their act together come November."

"By then it'll be too late."

"Season won't even have started, brother."

"They're doing the important work *now*. They just don't know it yet. The do-or-die streetball games. The card-playing and double-dating. The study groups. The grudges and adolescent cliques and the drunken pledges of *bros before hoes*. Those boys believe it's all just horseplay. It's anything but. This is serious stuff. It sets up the whole year. By the time they step on the court for that first exhibition the post-season has already been decided."

"Becca's diet has made you a poet."

"I'm deeper than I get credit."

"I'd say you were wider."

5. BECCA

Ben will be home in seven minutes, give or take, and if her sole's not perfect by then Becca Porter will be waiting in the garage and tell him keep away till dinner's done. She whisks thyme in with her sauce, garlic-peppered oil and lime juice, adjusts the phone receiver balanced at her shoulder and advises her daughter Sarah.

"All they need is love, honey."

"*Love, love, love,*" Sarah is singing from sunny San Francisco.

"That's right."

"*All they need is love, love.*"

"Who is that?"

"*Love is all they need.*"

"Patsy Cline," Becca guesses.

"John Lennon."

"I'm expected to know this how?"

"Mom. The Beatles."

"Oh, right. The hippie band. Your father never preferred them. We like Johnny Cash. Do you remember seeing him sing that time? The supper club in Tulsa."

But Sarah's chiding her own children now, Josh the terrorist toddler and his older sister Heather. Becca can hear her grandkids laughing on the other end of the line. The two get so gleeful sometimes they'll forget to breathe. Then Becca's reduced to giggling, she can't help herself, and soon everyone's doubled over, red-faced and gasping, like land-stranded fish. The nonsensical babbletalk burbling from the phone pulls at Becca's heartstrings. It's a feeling more bitter than sweet. Similar to the inner stirrings from her two pregnancies, those little butterfly flutterkicks tickling inside her tummy that warned: *big changes are on the way.*

The soup kettle clatters, cream of mushroom bubbling and troubling above the burner.

"I'm only saying. Give them too much and they'll spoil," Becca says.

"They're not avocados, Mom."

Becca dials down the fire and stirs the pot.

"It certainly wouldn't hurt either of them to eat more of *those*."

Sarah chooses not to hear this. She's on about ear infections now. Josh keeps bringing them home from daycare, and her husband Hank, the ophthalmologist, thinks they should install tubes in the boy's ears but this is a real *operation*, with general anesthetic and everything— Josh will be unconscious for a half-hour, maybe more—and she's heard there's an inherent risk in these so-called *simple* procedures and she's not so sure, herself, what to do so what does Mom think?

"Tubes?"

"He comes down with one of those ear bugs," Sarah says, "Josh just isn't himself. The tubes air him out. My friend Laurie's daughter got them last summer. You remember her. She hasn't had a single ear infection since. Not one."

"Tubes. Like, plumbing?"

"Tubes. Yes. To flush out the gunk."

"I am at a loss, dear."

Becca calls Sarah several times a week to offer counsel, one mother to another. Last week Sarah asked her what the secret to good parenting was and Becca said, "Retail therapy."

"We'll probably go through with it," Sarah says. "Hank is hammering on me to make the appointment."

"I don't know where you find the time, honey."

Becca was double-booked for the better part of twenty years, holding down the home front while Ben was out digging in the dirt. Ben called it her pink-collar career. She would wake before dawn to sip coffee and map out the day. Which diversionary tactic would buy enough time to pay bills? Which educational program would the kids watch while she folded laundry? Could she spot-clean the house *and* make dinner during second naptime?

But just listening to Sarah's schedule makes Becca want to put her feet up. Her daughter is one of those super-moms Oprah likes to crow about, a high-powered attorney married to a higher-powered physician. The two of them vacation in the sun twice a year, at high-priced places like Fiji and Bora Bora. Both of Sarah's children had stamps on their passports before they could walk.

"We'll need to keep Josh away from the water in Cancun."

"Cancun?"

"Hank's parents are springing for the trip."

"How nice!"

"Over Thanksgiving break."

Becca counts ten.

"Mom. It will be tight at your place this year. What with the remodeling. And Reese's family. The four of us. It's Hank's turn to show the kids off during Thanksgiving."

"Well."

She worked so hard to fill them up, their bellies and their heads and their hearts and their hours, with everything she knew. And it was *work*. All the livelong days. As though the hours might just stretch on forever. But Becca would give almost anything for the chance to go back. To have that time with her babies ahead of her, rather than behind.

"It sounds like a laugh and a half," Becca says.

Now her children have gone away into the world. And Becca's left to wrestle with this aggressive, expanding emptiness. How is it that she feels crowded by their *absence?* Pushed aside by a thing that's not even there?

"How's Dad's diet?"

"He jokes. Says he once lived to eat."

"And?"

"And now I only let him eat to live."

"Hank said he could develop diabetes."

"He's shrinking before my very eyes, Honey."

"That's good."

"It makes me sad."

"I know it does, Mom."

"Don't worry about a thing, dear."

"I love you, Mom."

"Love you back, Love."

∽

She's alone in the kitchen when the garage door motor begins growling. Ben blows the car horn to announce his arrival. Becca constellates the sole with two pinches of parsley, ladles the soup into a serving bowl, and practices her smile. She always tries to cultivate a steady state of awareness throughout the day, to collect tidbits of trivia for dinnertime table talk. Sense memories, plucked from all context and ambered in her mind's eye. All of it speaking to her of some deeper current below the circadian flow.

Then Ben comes bouncing through the door and her tongue, weighted by the urgent catalog of these experiences she needs to share, thickens to lead in her head.

"Tell me something I should know," Ben says later, over dinner.

She smiles and waits for the words to come.

He takes a bite of sole. Closes his eyes and makes muted murmurs of pleasure.

"I've been noticing doors," she says.

He opens his eyes.

"You feel a need for more involvement in the world."

"Or less involvement in this remodel."

He has this trick, a sort of emotional scrying. He can intuit her moods before she has even identified them.

"There was a bright red one," she says.

"Fire-engine red."

"That exact color. A hundred years old if it was a day. Paint shavings flaking from the panels."

"Open or closed?"

"Not quite open."

"You're hiding something."

"Dessert, you're not careful."

"Ah-hah!" Ben smiles. "*Sugar!*"

"*Sweet'N Low.*"

"You're on the threshold. Tempted to embrace some new . . ."

". . . husband," she jokes.

". . . passion."

"The possibilities are limitless."

"We're still talking doors."

"For the new addition," she says.

"Which will magically fill our empty nest with grandchildren."

"Sarah's not coming this year either, Ben."

His hand touches hers. She can see the pulse pounding in his milk-blue veins. Isn't it peculiar how the color is an exact match for the tablecloth she's chosen to cool the room?

"Hardwood or veneer?" she recites. "Solid or windowed? Fire-rated for twenty or sixty minutes? Hand-carved or cut from a lathe? Made in Mexico or Monaco? Or Chile? Morocco?"

"What about America?"

"Tell me what you think."

"Oh no," Ben raises both hands, fending her off. "This is your baby. I'm wrapped up in the redevelopment bid."

"We have time. The contractor said he won't install the door until everything else is said and done."

"He doesn't want the wetbacks to steal the door off its hinges. Smart."

"You know I hate that kind of talk."

"I'm sorry."

But she has already forgiven him.

"The possibilities are limited by the budget," he says. "Start there."

"The *possibilities* aren't limited in the slightest," she says. "The *decision* is limited by the budget."

He takes another bite of fish and replays his murmurous, shut-eyed ritual.

She is easing by degrees back into the Becca she needs to be.

She can't imagine a future without him in it.

6. DEAN

"Lookit."

"What?"

"Tonto's here."

"Hi-ho Silver—awaaaay! Come bend an elbow with us."

"Nice one, Wolfman."

"Call me Kemo Sabe tonight."

"Rack 'em, Kemo Sabe."

"Shut the hell up, Staples! I won the last one. You rack. Better yet, let Tonto here rotate in. And get me another beer, long as you're up."

Friday nights the indigent defense team converges on a rundown watering hole north of downtown Oklahoma City known as the Cock O'the Walk. Cheap beer and cheddar fries draw a happy hour horde of twentysomethings hell-bent on blacking out the work week—muscle-shirted college kids and shaggy, oversexed slacker types, white-collared professionals and the large-haired southern girls who always end up drinking for free.

The gangly office intern "Staples" sidles around the pinball machine, pauses backlit before a big-screen TV blinking game five of the NBA finals.

"Who's winning?" Dean asks.

"Knicks," says Staples. "Who else? You want a beer, Dean?"

"Still on the wagon. Girlfriend's orders. Get me a burger. And iced tea."

Staples disappears into the shuffle-bump queue mobbed at the bar.

Dean flips a wooden triangle onto the felted bed of the pool table.

"Name the game," he shouts to his boss, Trent "Wolfman" Paxton.

Wolfman seems hypnotized by something on the television set.

"Nine ball," Paxton finally answers.

Dean plucks nine numbered balls from the well, assembles them into a parallelogram on the velvet tabletop. He lifts the triangle away with a twirl, grabs and chalks a heavyweight stick. Wolfman leans his weight into the break and a rifle-crack report cuts sharply through the hubbub, each ball ricocheting repeatedly against molted bumpers.

"There's not a better sound I can think of," Wolfman shouts.

"Not a bit of ambiguity in it," Dean agrees.

"I'm looking for a word."

"Clean."

"No. Quick?"

"Quick has zero gravitas."

"Pure?"

"How about true?"

"What?"

"True."

"That's the word."

"True has gravitas."

"True's got gravitas out the ass."

All nine balls have rolled to a halt.

"Pushout?" Wolfman asks.

Dean sizes up the state of play, shaking his head.

"Call it."

"One in the corner," Dean says. "Off the rail."

Paxton, the Capital Trial Division Chief in the public defender's office, is a bearish trial attorney who cut his litigation teeth doing a twelve-year stint as Judge Advocate General for the U.S. Marine Corps. The man's swollen forearms are etched with tattoos paying tribute to a history still being written: one arm sports the faded USMC eagle, globe, and anchor emblem; the other is decorated with a catchphrase inked in bold and elaborate script: "What you ~~kill~~ .SAVE is yours forever." Wolfman had an ink pusher cross out "kill" and replace it with "SAVE" when he left the Corps.

With an imposing courtroom demeanor and a tendency to howl theatrically behind closed doors, Paxton earned the handle Wolfman early in his tenure with the Public Defender's office. Every staff member earns a stage name, eventually. There's Staples, who can usually be found imprisoned in the sixth-floor copy room. Ethan Podesta, the ex-police officer heading up defense investigations, has been dubbed Dragnet. Dean, a Choctaw Indian, is known as Tonto.

"Nicknames are like bellybuttons around this place," Wolfman told Dean on his first day, almost fifteen years ago. "Everyone gets one. Some are prettier than others."

Nobody wants a name like "Kevorkian" there, the mousy attorney melting into the pinball machine, drowning the day's trials in yet another perspiring tumbler of rum and Coke. She boasts the worst winning percentage in the office—eighty percent or more of her clients have been sentenced to death. "If your client pulls Dr. Kevorkian," the saying goes, "nothing can save him."

Dean misses his shot.

"I heard about Payton Taylor," he says.

Wolfman ignores Dean, eyes welling. The big man is prone to blubbering, the hard-as-nails exterior harboring a heart soft as butter. Payton Taylor was his latest case. Last night a jury handed the boy a death sentence for a home invasion gone horribly wrong.

"You have this idea about an argument before it's made," Wolfman says, wistful. "This is the case you were put on earth to defend. It's predestination, you're thinking. This one I can win. This one makes up for all those losers."

"Your hands were tied," Dean says.

Wolfman sinks the one ball in a side pocket, clean. He straightens up, dries his eyes with the back of a fist.

"Spilled milk. Let's talk about this client you stumbled across in Bricktown the other morning."

It's considered poor form to use the word "defendant" in Wolfman's presence.

"No rest for the wicked," Dean says.

Wolfman lines up another angled shot.

"Billy Grimes," says Dean's boss. "Injun. Choctaw or Cherokee. I can't remember which."

"We all look the same."

"What I'm always saying." Wolfman misses the two ball. "Grimes says he was mixed up in a drug deal gone bad. Filed for indigent status Tuesday. The judge bound over at preliminary hearing yesterday. Drop by and pay your respects next week. I've got to warn you, though, he's a hard case. Not too chatty."

Dean nods. "Two off the seven."

The two glances from the seven to fall clacking into a side pocket.

"Thanks for this Grimes, by the way. I hadn't had his name and the particulars, the kid might have sat in county a few weeks waiting for us. First time I can remember we've been this far ahead of the district attorney on murder one."

Dean lines up the three.

"So we won't be playing catch up with Macy," he says.

"We'll see."

Staples materializes from the bar scrum, scarecrow-thin limbs wobbling a tray brimmed with pub grub. The intern is welcomed with convivial catcalls from his coworkers.

Dean misses the three ball. He finds his food and bites into a greasy burger. Wolfman scans the table, thinking.

The giant television display has abandoned the basketball game to broadcast the pixelated feed of a low-speed car chase unfolding along some crowded coastal freeway. Someone shouts, "Turn that up." The bartender spikes the volume.

The CNN anchor's punchy enunciation, ". . . was scheduled to turn himself into the Los Angeles Police Department this afternoon. LAPD spokesman David Gascon called a press conference earlier today to announce this unusual development in the highly publicized murder investigation." A telegenic Gascon addresses the media with deliberate precision: "Mr. Simpson has not appeared. The Los Angeles Police Department right now is actively searching for Mr. Simpson."

An almost ecstatic gasp from the assembled press corps. Someone in the media gallery whistles, long and low and slow.

A hush diffuses by degrees through the bar. Something is happening out there. An event captivating in its total lack of production value. Blurry and immediate and awkward and real. The screen cuts back to the chase. Filmed from the belly of a hovering traffic helicopter, the pan-and-scan picture jerks queasily about the San Diego Freeway, where a white sport utility vehicle cruises slowly down the highway, emergency lamps blazing. An ordered wedge of police cruisers follows from a respectful distance, pale rollers whirling red and blue through the vivid twilight. Cars slow and stop at the roadside, making way for a carnival-like conflux of satellite trucks and news vans, sports fans and taxicabs and rubbernecking Angelenos. Everyone nosing along in dazed disbelief behind their fallen gridiron idol.

"An anonymous source within the LAPD tells us they have a detective negotiating with Mr. Simpson right now," the news anchor is saying. "We're getting word that O.J. is armed, and might possibly be suicidal."

A lone police car swerves lane-to-lane behind the phalanx of LAPD cruisers, holding the helter-skelter throng at bay. But the people refuse to be denied. They're scaling concrete barriers to spill openmouthed into the road. Cheering pockets of pedestrians puddle in the medians, gawk from the overpasses, huddle in the thin threads of shoulder fronting the freeway.

"He's going home," someone says.

"They always do," Wolfman adds.

"Guilty as sin."

"He'll get off with the best defense money can buy," Dean says.

The procession passes the Los Angeles International Airport. Dean sees passenger jets landing beneath the chase choppers, wings twinkling silver against the gilded skyline.

"Two thousand yards in a fourteen-game season," says Wolfman. "I'll be God-damned."

Dean and Wolfman are perched watching upon the pool table, their game all but forgotten.

"Listen. I mean . . . Really. Pay. Attention," says Wolfman. "Do you hear that?"

"What?" Dean says.

"Silence."

Someone sneezes.

"It's . . ." Wolfman says. "Reverential. We're paying tribute. All of us. Bowing down before the primetime pedestal of race and violence and celebrity and death."

A bar stool scrapes complaining across the floor.

"You're talking to yourself again," Dean says.

"So what if I am?" Wolfman frowns down the field of felt at Dean. "I think I've earned the right."

Dean wants to look away but he can't.

A queer game of chicken breaks out in Simpson's wake, as a trio of police motorcycles ride herd on the pedestrian swarm, the hulking machines revving and braking, revving and braking, over and again in irregular rhythm up then down the shoulder, cowing everyone out of the freeway and back to the sidelines in skittish, sluicing waves. O.J.'s white Ford Bronco steers for the Sunset Boulevard exit.

A woman bouncing in the median clutches an orange poster begging Simpson to "Run Juice Run."

"I met him before," someone says. "Got his autograph, his picture. The works."

"I think maybe I dreamed this once," Staples says.

The white Bronco is rolling slowly through the California gloaming.

7. AURA

Sunday mornings Aura rises early for the drive to Langston. She takes her time with it, rolling through the vacant Stillwater streets, dew runneling up the car's hood. Skirt the university, over and across the railroad tracks, then right at Perkins Road, past the junkyard and the western dancehall, the tractor dealership and the high plains cemetery, its headstones leaden in the dawn. Another right at the T-junction onto Highway 33, the seedy roadhouse there looking like a cardboard cutout in the wind. Light poles fall away behind her into pink-bellied clouds.

Aura feels more substantial in the open, reassured by the widening horizon line, the fixed and rugged nature of the countryside spooling by. Her Sunday morning homecoming. Hints of new-turned earth and manure and fresh-cut alfalfa waft in through the open window and start her mouth watering. She dips her forearm into the slipstream breezing by outside and remembers schooling her little brother on the essentials of aerodynamics from the back seat of their grandmother Opal's Chevy Nova, his little brown hands flailing.

"Watch me," Aura had said over the windbluster, demonstrating a corkscrew roll with her hand. "This is flying."

Aura was older than Carl by nearly seven years, and provided she could keep him in line the two of them were given free rein to roam.

"Look after your brother now," Aura's father would say. "You're his keeper. Anything happens to that boy, it comes out of *your* hide."

Sometimes they'd leave at sunup, take turns playing the good guy in Cowboys-and-Indians. Dry-gulching one another from the switchgrass with makeshift rifles or spears salvaged from the underbrush. They shared a tin-plated sheriff's badge and when the day was done they'd trudge back home slathered head-to-toe in red clay war paint, ready for supper and bath time and the cool comfort of crisp bedsheets.

They outgrew the shoot-em-up games. And after Mom died, after their heartsore Dad had abandoned them to Grams, Aura embraced basketball. She was decent. Quick on her feet, quicker with her hands. Good enough to play point guard at Langston University for four years. She showed some of her moves to Carl and soon it was her little brother giving the flight lessons, tongue lolling from his head as the ball lifted him through the air for the basket. Like a puppet on kite strings. Carl stood six feet tall at the age of ten, and it was clear by then his future rested with the game. She'll never forget the day he first beat her in a game of twenty-one. That grin high-beaming forth, as if from some radiant nuclear core of him.

Furrows of cotton flashing past the quarter glass. She crosses the rust-watered Cimarron River over a steel-truss bridge, the road curving down into Coyle, Langston's sister city. Black clots of Angus are huddled amongst the scrub oak. Orderly columns of mature maple and twist-limbed elm overhang Main Street. Aura slows the car to a crawl and rolls up the window.

She drives two miles under the speed limit and counts three at the stop sign: *one-Mississippi-two-Mississippi-three.*

Sundown town, they'd called it. Block-lettered signage posted at the city limits here used to warn: *NIGGER DON'T LET THE SUN COME DOWN ON YOUR HEAD IN COYLE.* Aura's father had still been in the picture. He'd huff and puff as they idled through Coyle, batten the car windows against the spittle that sometimes flew into the windshield with a viscid *thook.* And in college, when Aura and her teammates caravanned into Stillwater to watch the Oklahoma State basketball games, they'd detour all the way round to I-35 after sunset, loop into Langston from the west to avoid any trouble.

The day that sign came down—she must have been five years old at the time—Aura and her father sat watching from the Chevy's hood as a lupine field hand uprooted the signpost with his winch. He'd pause once in every while to stare up-road and spit, pale hands fingering at a twist of chaw stashed in his bib pocket, mirrored sunglasses winking under a pale straw Stetson. Carl wouldn't be born for two more years.

Leaving Coyle, Aura accelerates into the quarter-mile home-stretch along Sammy Davis Junior Drive. The window cracked again, sunlight warming her face. A lone Hereford lows thickly at the thinning sky. She blows past the spot where that sign once stood. They'd parked, where was it, *there*, to watch it come down. Unremarkable little landmarks now, both smaller than she recalls. Aura sees them shrink, shrinking, shrunk into the cracked rearview.

The car rolls over the Indian Meridian and Aura is home.

Her brother's been dead eleven Sundays.

∽

"Tell me about the hairdo," says Aura's grandmother Opal.

"I'll have to beat the widowers away with a stick."

"Not too plain?"

"Not for where we're going."

"I can't find the walker."

"Next to the armchair," Aura says. "Here."

"Well."

"Are you ready Grams?"

"Ready. Child. I's born for Sunday mornings."

"Let me help."

"Don't paw."

∽

The red oak pulpit of the Gracefield Baptist Church wasn't constructed to contain pastor Nate Franklin, a man who routinely inspires visions of heavenly ascension in his congregation. The bachelor inspires even more romantic visions amongst Langston's single women. Skylit by a polychrome stained glass window set back of the chancel, the pastor cuts a colorful figure behind the lectern, in chalk-stripe worsted wool and a bright orange bow tie, his shaved head buffed to a deep brown polish.

"People walk around, bellyache about *tomorrow*," pastor Nate is saying this Sunday morning. "Fret over the *rent*. Wonder about the *weather*. Afraid of *cancer*. The days go by pretty quick, what with all that worrying. Pretty soon . . ." amplified crackle of the Bible thump-thump-thumping at the mike, ". . . *BANG!* You've up and *died*. Got so caught up worrying about the *future*, you done forgot to take time out for *living*."

Pastor Nate sidesteps the pulpit. He rolls the broad beam of his shoulders and quick-skips down the steps after his words. He has an almost physical relationship with these sermons, these rhythmic syllables echoing above the packed pews. He's left the microphone behind but still holds to his Bible. The preacher cradles its thumb-worn pages, parsing the phrases like a child working at a tongue-twister. Most everyone knows he can recite the scriptures from memory. But pastor Nate doesn't like to preachify.

The good word can't be heard from a soapbox, he likes to say.

"Psalms tells us 'This is the day which the Lord hath made. We will rejoice and be glad in it.'"

We've got a go-ahead *Amen!* from Mrs. Thurston in the back corner.

Pastor Nate steps deeper into the aisle, paging to the New Testament.

"And Matthew says we needn't worry about tomorrow."

But Mr. Wilson, who can always be counted on to play devil's advocate, blows out a *Say-what?* raspberry.

Pastor Nate retreats to the pulpit, taken aback.

"I hear you, Mr. Wilson," the preacher says. "I do. 'Don't worry, be happy' won't pay the cable bill. Unless you're Bobby McFerrin. Mr. McFerrin—are you sitting out there today? Raise your hand, please, if you're with us."

Wilson laughs.

Pastor Nate takes this as a good sign.

"Mr. McFerrin has left the building," he says.

More laughter.

This new preacher won't be bridled and this is why they love him.

Pastor Nate advances into the aisle, reclaiming lost ground.

"But I'm not so sure Matthew was telling us to be care*free*. I think he's saying: Be care*ful*. Let's read it: 'Be not therefore anxious for the morrow. For the morrow will be anxious for itself. Sufficient unto the day is the evil thereof.'"

A sober-faced queue of Gracefield Chorale Singers stands crisply by in burgundy stoles, ready at the slightest signal to choir into ecstatic, four-part harmony.

"Matthew wasn't saying let your guard down. No ma'am. Sit around in front of the television set all day. Nosirree. I believe he's telling us: 'You've got enough work cut out for you, just figuring how to get through *this* day.' So don't worry on tomorrow today. Worry on tomorrow *tomorrow*." Pastor Nate advances further. "Worryin' on a thing that's out of your hands is a waste of your God-given time. And this is why I think forgiveness is so important."

Pastor Nate treads ahead. He's among them now, puzzling through the parable of the unforgiving servant. His free hand grips and lifts and dips, shaping the air there to a fuller articulation of God's game plan.

"Peter asked Jesus, 'Lord, how oft shall my brother sin against me, and I forgive him? Until seven times?' And Jesus says: 'not until seven times; but, until seventy times seven.'"

That's right, says Mr. Harper.

The ayesayers grow louder as he reads, more sure of things. A restlessness is rolling through the pews.

The preacher says, "Jesus tells of the servant whose master forgave him a debt of talents. But then this selfsame servant runs out into the fields, demands payment from one of *his* coworkers. 'He laid hold on him, and took him by the throat, saying, Pay what thou owest!'"

I can't believe it, Miss Young says to her neighbor.

"Well now. As you can imagine the servant's master wasn't too pleased to hear about this development. 'Shouldest not thou also have had mercy on thy fellow-servant, even as I had mercy on thee?'"

Say it one more time, son. Mr. Wilson says, back on the bandwagon.

If the Bible this man's holding is a road map to their salvation, these sermons are the journey itself. Sure, the bright young preacherman can lose them at times. It happens. There are dead ends and detours aplenty on this trip. But with everyone pitching in to course-correct, sooner or later they're holy-rolling down the highway once more. Bound for glory.

"Forgiveness is the flip side to God's command not to fret over tomorrow," pastor Nate says.

Another curtsy of approval, this time from Opal.

"It's His way of saying: Save your energy for more pressing concerns."

Pastor Nate claps the Bible closed, signaling Deacon Fanning and the Gracefield Chorale Singers to begin the hymn. Everyone stands, bodies and voices rising together into song.

What a Friend we have in Jesus, all our sins and griefs to bear!

Aura's grandmother warbles at top volume. Opal's holding her hymnal upside down but, no matter, eighty-odd years of repetition have burned the words onto the tip of her tongue.

O what peace we often forfeit, O what needless pain we bear, All because we do not carry everything to God in prayer.

Aura can feel her own lips mimicking the music, the breath blowing in her hollowed cheeks. But the verses themselves fall to her feet, like stones in still water: *Plunk.* The hymns have been giving her trouble for some time. She keeps hoping, one of these Sundays, she'll stray upon her old voice, somewhere here among the hymnals where she last left it. But it keeps not happening.

The Gracefield Chorale Singers stand down. Pastor Nate takes stock of the congregation one last time, making sure his message has sunk in, his eyes lingering for a moment upon Aura, who is studying her hands.

She's forgotten how to sing.

"Let's pray," says Nate.

8. BEN

The tractors are trawling the middle distance. From the comfort of his air-conditioned trailer Ben watches his men reshape the landscape, heavy machines muscling tons of topsoil in the dog day afternoon. Bright orange bulldozers strain mightily behind blood-colored berms of clay, the dirt curdling, cresting, spilling in thick waves before the scalloped blades.

Everything quivers in the radiant shimmer lifting off the earth.

He's always dreamed of striking black gold. After graduating from Oklahoma State with a mechanical engineering degree, he tried his hand wildcatting with the rest of the roughnecks. But Ben lacked the essential prophetic knack. He'd tap into the bedrock, shooting for a seismic bright spot, only to hit brine. A few dry holes in a row and you were done developing petrochemicals back then. Everyone was looking to be the next Diamond Glenn. So Ben retooled. He saw a need for more specialized equipment, took out a loan, and launched Dirt Devil Drilling. He sold drill bits and backreamers custom-made for directional boring into hostile soil, the chunk rock and cobble that wore traditional bits down to nothing in no time at all.

But the real money wasn't in oil. It was in commercial construction. Mini-malls and tract-home developments were springing from the ground thick as milkweed back then. By the '80s Ben had diversified, expanding his operation to include equipment rental and subcontractor services for developers and engineering firms who didn't want to get their hands dirty. Dirt Devil Drilling was reborn as Dirt Devil Construction. Now he owns a fleet of big rigs—hydraulic track loaders and pipe-layers and articulated dump trucks and trenchers to dig every conceivable category of ditch a man might want. All of them coated in three loud layers of atomic orange paint and decorated with the diabolical silhouette of the devil Ben lifted from his high school alma mater, the Perkins Demons.

He's made a Texas-sized fortune off people's need to dig in the dirt.

Beyond the trailer's windowpane Ben can see his right-hand man Ken Vincent, hardhatted against the heavens, tiptoeing through the track-worn worksite. Eight minutes late and counting. And Vincent is never late. One of the reasons he's the right-hand man.

Ben pours himself a cup of stale coffee and waits.

A sweat-soaked Vincent comes blustering in, face afluster.

"Sky falling?" Ben says.

Vincent removes the hardhat.

"Tell me," Ben says.

"What do you want first?"

"Surprise me."

"The Metropolitan Area Projects oversight board has thinned the herd to two possible coordinators. Dirt Devil and New Horizons."

The coffee has the consistency of toxic sludge.

"New Horizons will go long," Ben says. "On everything. Materials. Budget. Timeline. Oswald, over at New Horizons, he can't even get kickbacks right. He'll leech the city coffers dry and come begging back for more."

"It's a fifty-fifty chance, Ben. I'll take those odds any day but Sunday."

"What's the bad news?"

"There's a guy on the M.A.P.S. oversight board. Gary Chambliss. Oswald's a close personal friend of his, he says. They go way back, he says. And Chambliss has got pull with the other board members."

"He says."

Ben tosses the Styrofoam cup at the wastebin and commences cracking his knuckles. He's at that phase in his career when people have started guessing about the lines of succession. Sixty years old. The lame duck years. Ben's son Reese, the surgeon, can't hardly stand to set foot in the state of Oklahoma, much less take over the business. Young Vincent could be the heir presumptive. Or Ben could auction the company off to Oswald, the cocksucker. But just thinking about it gives him heartburn. Not if his life depended on it.

"We have to win this, Ken. Little city like this, it doesn't see a second chance like this very often."

"Chambliss is going to be a problem."

"Handle it. Anything he wants. Sooners tickets. Box seats at Texas Stadium. Pussy. Anything."

Ben cracks the knuckle on his ring finger.

"How did your sit-down with the mayor turn out?" Vincent asks.

"Well, we're still in the running for this project coordinator spot."

Vincent waits.

"We reached an unspoken agreement," Ben eventually says.

"How much?"

"You tell me. Re-election campaign advertising. Run the spreadsheets and give me a number."

Ben knows that M.A.P.S. represents the best leg up from here. He's always wanted to go out with a bang. Some illogical, lateral leap. A green-built residential community in the Texas Panhandle. An alternative energy project, maybe, overseas. Someplace exotic. Becca's never been to Asia. Nor has Cecil. Some late-stage sendoff into the sunset. A thing worthy of their wonder.

"When Dirt Devil bags the M.A.P.S. bid, Ben," says Vincent, "it will be time to talk about my future."

Outside, a backhoe blade plows into the ground.

"Yours and mine both, Ken."

The trailer trembles.

9. CECIL

It's come undone.

This is the thought carried over from the sweet side of sleep into the half-broken dawn. This idea that things are unraveling in nonspecific but significant ways. The weather-sprung square of linoleum in his entryway implies consciousness. He has slept on his back. He feels for his legs beneath the sheets, finds and straightens them, elbows himself up into a sit.

Easy now. Careful out of the gate.

He has left the television on again and the talking heads inside of it are sounding out the previous day's violences in appropriately sober tones. The Draft-Dodger-in-Chief has invaded Haiti. On the bedside table are a pack of Marlboro Reds and a Zippo lighter, three Louis L'Amour paperbacks, two different egg timers, and a box of suppositories. He unwraps an ass bullet and slides the slug home. Bull's-eye. Dial four hours on one timer and twelve minutes on the other. Untangle from the quilt, scoot to the edge of the bed, swing down into the wheelchair waiting there.

A talking head says "moral imperative."

He sleeps on a king-size mattress set flush against the partition wall dividing his living room from the little galley kitchen opposite. Wheel in and wash the hands and get the coffee brewing. A quick breakfast of buttered toast and the alarm is ringing time for morning ablutions.

On the television set an armored tank bulldozes through a building, crumpling wall siding as if it was construction paper. Someone says "police state."

Dawn brings a whole checklist of somatic subroutines, the dirty and probing hygienics that keep him clear of the hospital bed. Twelve minutes until the suppository kicks in. Twenty-eight more and the enema has flushed his bowels. Another thirteen-or-so hosing down in the shower then he's back in the chair, toweling dry before an array of ointments and vanity lights and Anglepoise makeup mirrors fit to flush a beauty queen green with envy.

He drapes his shanks in the towel and sips his coffee. Not quite naked before the full-length mirror like this you could almost believe he was whole. Everything above the ninth thoracic vertebrae still fit as a fiddle. He's proud of his working parts, sticks to a strict diet and dumbbell regimen to keep the parabelly at bay. Under the towel his dead dick rests like a spent balloon between the corpse-thin limbs. He studies his skin for signs of trauma with one of several custom-built hand mirrors, the type of telescopic, articulating tool a SWAT team might use to defuse a car bomb. He begins with the feet, proceeds upward from there as the spiritual dictates, foot bone to leg bone to knee bone and so. No cavity is left unexamined.

He hears an announcer say "angry boys with guns."

He has to become a kind of deductive gumshoe in this room. Skincare is life-or-death business. At the first hint of pressure sore Cecil smears antiseptic cream around the suspicious area. The location of the rough patch or hot spot or induration is recorded in a little notebook. If you cared to listen he could rattle off more about your pores than an internal medicine resident. A seeping wound can lead to traction, toxic shock, death. Worse. Gooseflesh on his right side might hint at a stage two fissure in his limp left foot. A sudden case of flop sweat could mean an impacted bowel below the injury. This phenomenon is called *autonomic dysreflexia* and it has made Cecil a skeptic regarding the possibility of free will.

When he can feel fingertips spidering up his abdomen Cecil knows he's done. On his way into the bedroom his tires catch on a raveled seam of carpeting in the hallway. He makes a mental note to get this fixed and dresses himself with care in the wheelchair. Wiggle slowly into his diaper, blue jeans, and T-shirt. Slip the condom catheter on. Snake the leg bag into the Wranglers. Now the cowboy boots. He chooses from a dozen-and-a-half pair of shop-mades custom-tooled to suit any occasion: square-toed stockmans in honeyed caiman crocodile, snub-nosed ropers in distressed goat hide, filigreed exotics in cream-colored calfskin. On game days he wears full-quill ostrich Tony Lamas stitched with the orange-and-black frown of OSU's mascot, good old *Pistol Pete* himself.

His property sits at the dead end of a dirt-top lane leading into town, a four-room rambler that Mother willed to him when she died, on three flat acres of pecan and drooping dogwood. The rooms are stacked with literature, swaybacked Britannicas and novels and VHS movies and sleeved LPs and *National Geographics*, a whole microhistory of Western culture compiled in the decades since the accident. His walls seem to bow beneath the weight of all these words.

Cecil refills his coffee and accelerates down the garage ramp, zooming past sawhorses and power tools and the black velvet curtain draping his workspace. Momentum brings him up the opposite ramp and out onto the wraparound porch.

Getting dressed has taken longer than he would have liked. Seems his whole body is aching for a cigarette, even the petrified parts. Doc says the lung darts are pure poison but Cecil doesn't put much stock in the man's opinion. When they first predicted he wouldn't live to see twenty Cecil said if anyone was taking wagers he wanted in on the action.

He's been swallowing twelve pills a day for forty-six years now.

He lights a Marlboro and blows a blue plume out into the yard. The sky has blushed past pink to a chalky yellow that leaks through the leaves. Cigarette smoke drifts amongst the tree trunks, scaring up peekaboo shafts of slanted morning light. His pickup truck is parked on a slab of poured concrete that doubled as a basketball court when Ben's kids used to stay over. A rust-blackened backboard is nailed to the light pole there, but it's been a long time since he's tried shooting anything at that hoop.

The four-hour timer will be sounding soon, reminding him to get horizontal for two more hours of bedrest. But first he's going to sit and smoke in this slow breeze. Listen to the pip-squeaking scissortails and rustling leaves and crackling cigarette ash and buzz-bombing horseflies and the stammering television. All of it sounding at cross-purposes or maybe the same purpose if you listen long enough. He anticipates the brief bridges of small talk the talking heads will use to introduce the next hearsay, sipping his coffee and mouthing the meaningless phrases and blowing concentric smoke-rings which melt away in the gathering day.

He hears "leave-me-alone coalition."

A crop-duster drones slow chandelles out above the far-flung fields.

He hears "new world order."

10. BECCA

In the event of apocalypse, if God doesn't step in to save the worshippers at First United Methodist Church from calamity, district attorney "Cowboy Bob" Macy will have to suffice. The silver-haired lawman sits stoic as a statue across the aisle from Becca and Ben, two pews up, the white Stetson he wears on TV cradled in timeworn hands. A pearl-handled pistol pokes from Macy's coal-black suitcoat. Rumor is he can shoot the tail off a rattlesnake from two hundred feet. That he sleeps with one eye open, in nothing but boots, his guns hung from a holster on the bedpost.

He has sent more men to death row than any other prosecutor in the country.

"If I had half the enemies Bob Macy does," Ben likes to say, "I wouldn't count on the power of prayer to protect me, either."

The preacher plays to Macy in his closing.

"People are always asking me for proof of God's existence," he says. "I tell each and every one of them the same thing. I tell them I won't give witness at a jury trial."

Macy smooths his silk colonel bow tie and allows a ministerial grin.

"What will they do with this . . . *evidence?*" the preacher says. "Sit in judgment of the Lord's divine grace?"

The word reverberates above the hollow *thock* of hymnals sliding into pew-back pockets. The flock can sense the imminent burst of wisdom before benediction, and many are ready for deliverance unto the heavenly promise of a summer's Sunday brunch.

The preacher says, "Faith is not a verdict, my friends."

First Church held its first service the first Sunday after the land run in 1889. It was the first Christian congregation assembled in Oklahoma Territory, the first official house of worship in downtown

Oklahoma City, and the last place Becca ever imagined she'd be bending her head in prayer. She was raised Church of Christ by her mother's sister after both parents drowned trying to ford a low-water crossing, their truck washed away in a freak flash flood. Aunt Mabel used to joke that the only difference between a Methodist and Baptist was that the former would tip his hat to the latter when they met in the liquor store.

The post-sermon scatter has the frenetic feel of a fundraiser. But Ben's not here to be moved by the heavenly spirit. He's here to mingle, to mine for gold in the more mundane strata of this city's movers and shakers. An earnest "Amen," then Ben's off and running at the mouth, rubbing shoulders with this councilman and that judge, nodding to a previous deacon's mistress, clapping the broad backs of oil barons and businessmen and at least one leathery television personality.

Becca doesn't wholly approve of the man Ben becomes in these moments. Nevertheless she loves to watch him work. There is a visceral physicality to his charms, a whole touch-and-go stratagem underlying the charismatic hands. The knuckles brush an arm, the fingers squeeze an elbow, and before long Ben has broken into that close-guarded personal space where luck is made. Ben thaws district attorney Macy's cool front with a joke he's been perfecting, some blue bit about an Amish emergency brake. Soon Mayor Giffords has dropped in to listen and the three of them are cracking wise like truant choirboys.

Becca abandons Ben to his devices. It's her turn to teach Sunday school, the grown-up kind, and it wouldn't do to be late. She navigates the colonnaded church campus, with its warren of intersecting hallways and quiet, cloistered spaces architected to encourage awe, heading for the bunkered atmosphere of the lower-level lecture halls. She is already picking apart the pastor's sermon. Faith might not be a verdict, she'll give the man that much. But it most certainly *is* a trial. Or *trying*, might be the better term. She feels *tried*, trying to keep her faith.

She has been teaching here for over a decade, down in the dry-walled classrooms where the real tests of faith take place. This particular group is marketed as *Solid Start* in the sanctioned church literature. But the members, mostly young married couples, jokingly refer to themselves as "the Teamsters" because, really, they're just trying to stay together despite the union-busting thrust of these modern times.

A few new faces today, so Becca has everyone sit in a circle, group-therapy style, and introduce themselves. First there are the regulars: Helen and Dale Baker, Gloria Pickering (who always comes alone), and Stephanie Kehoe (her husband Albert is out with the flu today). Then the newly minted Wilcox family, young Tripp and his blue-eyed bride Brenda, both of them still bronzed and glowing from the honeymoon in Hawaii. And a whittlestick-thin woman who runs the battered-women's shelter up the street, Joanne Perry.

"I'm scouting for reliable support networks that our clients can fall back on after they have left the facility," Joanne says. "If you don't mind, I'd like to just sit and watch."

"Are you usually S.O.S., then?" Gloria, the outspoken black woman who is always trying to keep it real, says to Joanne.

Joanne looks tired. "Esso . . . ess?"

"Single on Sundays. Like me, unless I can raise my man from off the couch. He's like Lazarus, that one."

"Yes," Joanne says. "I am S.O.S. for the foreseeable future."

Nobody takes issue with Joanne's presence, so Becca opens her Bible and reads from Genesis: *"Therefore shall a man leave his father and his mother, and shall cleave unto his wife: and they shall be one flesh."*

Brenda Wilcox smiles and laces her well-manicured fingers in with Tripp's.

"How can this passage help the Teamsters?" Becca says. She has spent very little time preparing, having learned that the more spiritually instructive discussions take on an animated, wandering character beyond her jurisdiction as mere class moderator.

"I don't get it," says Helen. "Doesn't *cleave* mean *split?*"

"*Cleave* also means *cling*," says Becca.

"It means once you're married you have to reprioritize," says star student Tripp Wilcox. "When conflicts arise, your new family takes precedence over the old one."

"I'm pretty sure that's not right," says Helen. "*Cleave* means *cut.*"

"Just take my word for it," says Becca.

"Does anyone think it's funny we mostly talk about when things will go wrong?" asks Gloria.

"This from Gloria," says Stephanie. "African queen of the worrywarts."

"Funny *ha-ha* or funny, you know, sad?" says Helen.

"Watch it, Stephanie, with the whole African queen thing," Gloria says.

"Morbidly funny," Dale says.

"I don't like this word," says Helen. "This word makes me feel fat."

"I didn't mean it that way, Gloria," says Stephanie.

"You're thinking morbidly *obese*, Helen," says Dale.

"Am I, Dale?" says Helen. "Is *that* what I'm thinking?"

"I'm saying," Gloria speaks up again, "we exist in reference to a negative, rather than a positive. As a group, I mean. Our purpose seems reactive. Or defensive. Something."

"*Ironic*," says Dale.

"I'll say," says Helen.

"You're overthinking it, Gloria," says Stephanie.

"Someone has to," says Gloria.

"Instead of *funny*, I mean," Dale tries to explain.

"Go to hell, Dale," Helen snaps.

This last exchange sends Joanne, who has been observing with diplomatic aplomb, into hiccup-fits of laughter. Brenda Wilcox has squeezed the tan clean out of husband Tripp's poor little hand.

Becca wants to warn the Wilcoxes that time won't abide their newlywedded bliss for long. *Don't let go!* she wants to shout at Brenda, or twenty years from now you'll be trying to reach him across an uncaring chasm of children and jobs and rote daily routine. The mindless drudgery of honey-do-this lists can have a more corrosive effect on devotion than infidelity.

The only constant in life is that you will be changed by it, Becca wants to say. *And your love will need to keep pace.*

But instead she says, "Everybody say this with me: *Leave* and *cleave*."

The class drones the words in dutiful singsong.

"This rhymes," Becca says. "The rhyme makes it easy to remember. When you're at the end of your rope or, wits, whatever, you can repeat it like a charm: *Leave and cleave!* Then make the right choice and, like Tripp said, focus on siding with the family you've *chosen*, not the one you were born into."

"But this doesn't get us any closer to understanding the text," Helen complains. "*Repeat after me!* It's child's play. I want to understand how the Bible can help Dale and I stay married, Becca. Not just recite nursery rhymes."

"It doesn't matter *how* you find intimacy," says Becca. "Just that you do it."

Dale begins laughing but chokes it short after a sharp look from his wife.

"Commitment won't come from the Bible," Becca says.

"Where will it come from then?"

"From . . ." Becca hears herself start, before she's even had time to think. ". . . listen. It's from . . . it takes time. Time and independence. Elbow room. You've all heard the saying. If you love someone, set them free. If they come back, they're yours forever."

"Oh this is rich!" Gloria slaps her knee, cackling. "I can't wait to tell this to my sister's husband's girlfriend!"

Becca is no longer so enamored with the whole notion of mystical redemption, this take-it-or-leave-it ticket to paradise. "Doubt is the fastest route between Heaven and Hell," Aunt Mabel used to say. But any backsliding on Becca's part has occurred at a more glacial pace. Which is why she keeps volunteering here, to slow the slide. She has seen marriages brought back from the brink by the power of a tender word or two. It's a more wonderful vision than any of the biblical miracles she can imagine.

And shouldn't this count as a kind of faith?

11. DEAN

"War's coming," says the killer.

"This red power bit isn't helping, Billy," Dean says, drained.

"Better get back to the blanket."

They have been at it for almost three hours, Dean and Grimes have, faced off across a metal-topped refectory table in one of the County Jail's interview rooms. Billy Grimes is built for prison, six-five and not a neck in sight, with the puffed-up profile of a true goon. When the guards walked him in their slapsticks were at the ready. Dean asked them not to restrain his client but apparently Billy hasn't been behaving, so Grimes is chained hand and foot to a steel eyebolt sunk into the concrete slab floor.

"I get visions," Grimes says, rattling his chains. "Waking dreams, like."

"Let's get back to your parents."

"There's still time," Grimes says. "That race war starts, though, and you're still trying to pass as cracker, nothing can save you. Nothing but the language, *hatak nahollo*. Back to the blanket. Choctaw's the only way we'll know which side you're on."

"I'm sitting here talking to a ghost," Dean says.

"What?"

"I can do futures too." Dean's done with nice. He finds Grimes's eyes. "Let's do yours. After the trial. After you're found guilty, after you're sentenced to death row. They will put you in a windowless seven-and-a-half-foot by five-and-a-half-foot box in McAlester State Prison. H-Unit, Billy. That's the supermax wing. The warden likes to joke the H in H-Unit stands for *Hell*."

Grimes doesn't look away. Duly noted.

"Have you ever been to the stockyards?" Dean asks. "H-Unit smells exactly like that. Like the funkiest locker-room you've ever stepped foot in. This is the fear you're smelling. And while some down-on-his-luck lawyer appeals your death sentence, you'll be waiting there, in this concrete shithole, for decades. A decade is ten years, Billy. You're, how old now, twenty? Twenty-two? Double that in your head. The hearings and motions and paperwork have gotten you nowhere. You are forty-two years old, give or take a few, and it's time to die."

A universal sort of *hiss-boom-bah* hums from somewhere beyond the interview room, the dismal plainsong of men under pressure. The hydraulic slide and crash of a security gate, belligerent shouts echoing over snatches of barked horseplay.

"One day they take you to a holding cell. Nobody who's slept in it has walked out alive. You'll be bunking there about a month. Now this new cell of yours has two doors: there's the regular one, the one you entered through. Then there's the other one, the one painted yellow. The yellow door opens onto the death chamber. The anticipation is building, Billy. One morning they wake you up and say it's time. Your whole life has been building to this day. That big yellow door swings open. Your knees might give out, so maybe they have to carry you. Or maybe you'll put up a fight. But eventually you will find yourself strapped to a gurney. There's a big shatterproof window here but you can't see through it because of the blinds. People are sitting behind the blinds, waiting for the show to begin. They'll be dressed up like for church. A medical technician punches a bunch of tubes into your veins. This might hurt a little. Your heart, Billy," Dean pounds his chest several times in quick succession, "is jackhammering."

Billy scratches his face and the jangle of his chains is lost in the ambient noise.

"Don't worry though, because the drug cocktail is about to put a stop to all that. It's supposed to knock you out first. So, theoretically, none of this should hurt. I say theoretically because who knows, right? But many veterinarians are switching to more—get this—*humane* drugs."

"Chahta Okla imanukfila achvfa."

"No. Billy. We are speaking English."

"Chahta imanumpa ish anumpola hinla ho?"

"How do you say *sodium thiopental* in Choctaw?"

Grimes finally looks away.

"How do you say *temporary insanity* in Choctaw?"

"Fuck you."

"You're locked in a box, Billy. They have you in chains here. How do you expect to get out if your language can't even describe the box? No. We speak English."

Billy examines his ankle restraints.

"Let's get back to the courtroom. The judge, you see, can't get elected without district attorney Bob Macy's endorsement. So the judge and the district attorney are on the same page, sentencing-wise. Hell, Macy would shoot you on sight if they'd let him." Dean begins ticking off fingers on his left hand. "So on their team is: the judge, the district attorney, the twelve people in the jury box who—and this is important—elected them both. And behind the witness stand we have your girlfriend Willa, and your son Caleb."

Grimes jumps as if stung.

"That's right. If Bob Macy can get your son to testify without looking like a bully, he'll do it. Now after all is said and done, if nobody comes to claim the body they'll wheel your corpse out back of the prison for burial. The cemetery at McAlester is called Peckerwood Hill. I'm not kidding here. I'm not smart enough to make this cornball kind of stuff up on my own. Guess how many visitors that cemetery gets in a year?"

Dean curls his fingers into a donut.

"Zero," he says. "Now this is your future. It's all going to happen. It's *happening*. You are going to die in prison. At this point it's just a question of how. Do you want to die of old age? Or the way I've just described?"

Dean stops talking.

After a long while Grimes says, "What do you want?"

"First, talk to no one but me. Bob Macy is already putting pressure on your cellies, hoping they'll rat you out. I'm the only person in the world right now who cares about William Grimes." Dean slides his business card across the metal table. "If someone from the outside comes calling, give them this. Don't tell them anything but to contact me. I'll handle it. Second, if you did this crime, plead guilty. Tell me everything. I maybe can help you get life in lockup instead of a lethal injection."

"I'm not pleading guilty."

"Then let's talk about your parents." Dean picks up a legal pad and readies his pen. "And Billy?"

His client seems deflated. Dean's getting through.

"I need the truth."

12. AURA

Having decided that Gracefield needed a midweek wing-ding to celebrate its new preacher, Deacon Fanning promptly forgot the whole affair, leaving it for the choir to arrange today's potluck.

Aura watches Opal chatting and laughing with her longtime neighbors in the sunlit church cafeteria, her walker parked with the other assistive contraptions in a kind of handicapped loading zone nearby. Over paper plates piled high with home-cooked fixings, they talk food and sports and family and politics. There are ham steaks glazed in brown sugar, fried chicken sliding from the bone, baked macaroni casseroles and breaded okra and green beans simmered in bacon grease. More experimental dishes too, like the radioactive, pink-jellied dessert freckled with marshmallows, or the various mystery pies, each overbursting with some strange and fragrant stuffing.

Aura walks the wall of fame, eavesdropping on the chitchat. The wallpaper is merely hinted at, overrun with framed and matted tokens to Gracefield Baptist's role in the history of Langston and its university, everything from early incorporation papers granted by the Indian Territory court clerk, to sun-faded portraits of past and present parishioners. She never gets tired of seeing civil rights legends like Bessie Coleman, Ada Fisher, Clara Luper. Gridiron icons like Mo Bassett and "Hollywood" Henderson. Marques Haynes, of Harlem Globetrotter fame. They say he could dribble the ball half a dozen times in one second.

one-Mississippi . . .

"Did you watch the preliminary trial on Court TV?" asks Mrs. Thurston. "That Johnnie Cochran is one fine-looking, sweet-talking piece of black man."

Aura lingers over a sepia-toned print of Langston's very own Delta Rhythm Boys, crooning together in the fieldhouse gym.

"Now they've got Shapiro and Cochran *and* Dershowitz. How can they lose?" says Mr. Wilson.

"They're calling it the Dream Team," says Mrs. Thurston.

"It's some kind of dream," Opal says.

Aura finds her own college graduation photograph, a smile stretched tight across her face, just after nursing school commencement exercises. Aura had been a good student. She'd asked the right questions, learned quickly how to snake a Foley line and draw blood. How to run an EKG. The tricks to sponge-bathing a big-boned patient. She'd wanted not just to learn, but to matter. Carl towering behind her in the picture, all of fifteen years old.

She tries touching Carl's face but her fingertips catch on a greenish fracture webbed across the protective glass. When she got the call he'd been murdered Aura realized she'd only spoken to her baby brother a handful of times in the last two years, all of them on the phone. If he was standing beside her right now it would be hard work deciding whether to hug him or kill him all over again.

"They planted that glove on O.J.," says Opal.

Mrs. Thurston agrees.

"He's a strong, proud black man. We don't have enough of those to go round. There's bigger things at stake here than a dead white woman."

"Berta! For shame!"

Pastor Nate breezes in from no place at all to wrap Aura up in a teddy-bear hug. "How's it going, bruiser?"

Aura hurries a smile into her eyes. "How's the elbow?"

"I'll live." He peers at Aura's graduation portrait. "That's a pretty lady you're looking at."

That smile's feeling almost genuine now.

"Is our new pastor already flirting with his congregation?"

Nate's cheeks are dimpling.

"You know the closer you are to pastor Nate, Aura, the closer you'll be to God."

Aura swats the preacher's thick arm.

"Do you always talk about yourself in the third person?"

"This could be a first."

"Well. This lady here is ready to whip you in another game of pick-up. How are you finding Langston?"

Pastor Nate dares a double take in the direction of his geriatric welcoming committee.

"You want to know the truth? These potlucks scare the bejeezus out of me. I don't try a bite of every dish they offer, these women suspect me of the most incredible spiritual turpitudes."

Aura laughs.

"For me? A potluck tends to feel like a breather."

"Why's that?" Nate asks, seriously this time.

"Opal gets to gossiping, she forgets to forget things. It never lasts long. But for a moment, or an afternoon, I sense that whip-smart little old lady who raised me and Carl."

Pastor Nate lowers his voice. "How has she been getting along?"

"We're managing. We've been making lists. To try and cope with the memory loss."

"That's good. Lists can be helpful in these instances."

"They help me more than they do her."

"And how's the new job? You've left the hospital to do rehabilitation, I hear, in people's homes?"

"Yes."

"Do you enjoy it?"

"There's more freedom."

"Take all of that you can get," pastor Nate says. "You're doing the Lord's work, Aura. Keep it up."

"Thanks."

"And let me know how I can help."

"Better put in an appearance at the buffet table before our choir starts searching for another pastor."

Then the preacher is gone, as quickly as he came, to shepherd the rest of his flock on their weary way through the workweek.

Aura watches him go. This pastor is some puzzle. Playful where he should be profound. Handsome where he should be holy. What would it look like, she mulls, the African-American Amazon settling down with a honey-tongued preacherman like that? It would stew up some kind of scandal. She can already hear the gossip.

Miss Young is saying, "O.J.'s not black. Not on the inside at least."

"If he ain't black, what is he?"

"He's not purple," Opal says.

"He's O.J."

"That'd be, what? Orange."

"Plenty of pulp for everyone on *Hard Copy*."

Opal's brittle-boned fingers flutter mouthward, trying to contain her elastic laughter. It's a child's gesture, this reflex of hers, learned and polite. Something a schoolgirl might do.

"Color's got nothing to do with it," says Miss Young.

"Girl . . ." Mrs. Thurston hikes a penciled-on eyebrow. "You and I are living on two different planets."

13. BECCA

The lean and hungry-looking workers in Becca's backyard blast *Banda* music noon to night, big brass rhythm sections blowing country-and-western polkas over a *bajo sexto* backbeat.

Oom-pah-pah-pah, rum-pah-pum. Oom-pah-pah-pah, rum-pah-pum . . .

She should have approved the add-on blueprints three weeks ago. But Becca can't seem to stop reworking the renderings. Two beds, two baths, and a great room for the grandkids to run rampant. What's to decide, right? But once she signs that dotted line the future is fixed. The contractor, a friend of Ben's, is ready to pour the foundation. He's given her two more days to finalize the footprint. Otherwise he'll have to regroup and send his men elsewhere.

She tapes onion skin over the scroll paper and reimagines the entryway. Something about the door. Under the table, as she draws, Becca's toes tap a tranquil Cotton-Eyed Joe.

Oom-pah-pah-pah, rum-pah-pum . . .

A shadow eclipses her plans. Becca looks up and sees a stubbled face behind the bay window, peering in from the patio. A gaunt Mexican, one of hers, sweating bullets in the unholy heat spell. Her feet freeze. The man cocks his head. Runs ravaged fingers through blue-black hair. He says something in Spanish.

It takes her a minute: he's preening. He hasn't seen her. Is he here legally, Becca wonders? Or is he some kind of alien?

She tries the word on for size, says: "*Alien.*"

She savors the "*l*," rolls it on the tip of her tongue.

The man grins at his reflection and disappears. Becca is left squinting into the brain-searing sun.

. . . she is alone at the breakfast table, spreading strawberry jam over hot buttered toast. Her feet don't reach the floor. She slides down from her

chair and clears her plate and walks into the bathroom. Already dressed for school, her hair pulled into pigtails. These are harder to do by yourself than she had imagined. She should brush her teeth. But they're not here to remind her and so she decides to forget. She takes her lunchbox from the refrigerator and shoulders her book bag and unlocks the front door. She has seen them hide the key under the mat and this is where she finds it now. She locks the big red door behind her and replaces the key and walks to the corner where the school bus will be waiting. She can hear it idling even now, honking for her to hurry, oom-pah-pah-pah, rum-pah-pum . . .

The music delivers Becca into the present.

She blinks away the after-blindness blotting her vision.

She does not understand what is happening to her.

∾

The mercury is twitching in the triple digits when one of the contractor's hired hands demolishes the air-conditioning unit with a forklift. Becca calls up every HVAC repairman in the yellow pages, but summer in Oklahoma has them all working overtime. Three more days before the cooling can be put back to rights. Despite the ceiling fans helicoptering in every other room the heat permeates the house in a mean and implacable creep, and by midday the master bedroom thermostat reads ninety-two degrees.

Ben has a two-hundred-pound ice block and a galvanized tin washtub delivered. He jury-rigs a poor man's air conditioner at the foot of the bed, a pair of portable fans blowing tepid zephyrs off the melt, and they lounge there in stupefied torpor, half-dressed, watching *The Maltese Falcon* with the sound turned down.

"Could you eat?" Ben says.

"Don't," Becca says, "talk."

"I could eat."

"*Too hottttt.*"

"I brought ice cream."

"The diet."

"The diet. The diet is a psychological double cross. It instills a Spartan sense of self-control enabling, coincident, the wheedling mindset of the hedonist."

"You have no idea what's about to happen when that mouth of yours starts moving, do you?"

"If it feels good to enforce the rules, why, how much better it must feel to break them! This is the bipolar reasoning of the diet."

"It's a kind of superpower you have."

"The diet is a flimflam philosophy that can't hold up in this kind of heat," he says. "I say we jettison the diet for a day."

"You are a bad, bad man, Benjamin Porter."

"I stand accused."

The ice cream comes in wacky packaging, neon pints painted in psychedelic swirls of purple and green and pink and bedecked with mock-poetic flavors like *Cherry Garcia* or *Chunky Monkey* or *Dublin Mudslide* or—and this one earns a belly laugh from the both of them—*Chubby Hubby*.

"Pick your poison," he says.

"You should know by now that *Chubby Hubby* is the only one for me."

They spoon illicit scoops of ice cream straight from the carton, watching the hardboiled gumshoe onscreen pursue his wasp-waisted femme fatale through the deliciously shifting trickeries of a mystery.

"Do they never remove the coffin nails from their mouths to, you know, breathe?"

"Movies were more fun before we discovered lung cancer," Ben says. "Christ. I think . . . yes I do. I actually want a cigarette."

"Benjamin Porter if you take up smoking I will divorce you this instant and send you packing back to Perkins and bunk with Cecil."

"*Winston tastes good like a cigarette should,*" he sings. "Remember?"

"Oh! The Flintstones."

"Right. Fred and Wilma lighting up after another long day in Bedrock."

Becca remembers, when she first left for college in Stillwater, being bowled over by the sheer sprawl of it all. Oklahoma A&M in 1954 seemed bigger than life itself. But then she returned to Antlers one weekend and her hometown seemed to have shrunk. Her childhood room in Aunt Mabel's house had been replaced with what looked like a model done in miniature. As that second semester started, everything seemed to be in a perpetual state of contraction. Becca would watch the clouds at last light and imagine she could see the world curling back upon itself.

It was in this diminishing landscape that she met her future husband. He was canvassing the campus, recruiting Young Republicans. Ben was commanding and good-natured and well-made, even a little dreamy in his beefcake shirtsleeves, never mind the slide-rule always holstered at his side. Taller than Becca, which seemed important at the time. And still is, now she thinks about it. She bought a diary later that same day from the Student Union bookstore and lay in the grass by Theta Pond and recorded her first secret and feminine insight which was, she remembers word-for-word: *Today I passed out pamphlets for the boy I'm going to marry.*

The sentence still sends a little thrill along her spine.

After Ben had talked himself into Aunt Mabel's good graces their meetings took on an aura of inevitability. She had landed her man and wasn't this the goal back then? To sally forth into polite society and secure that golden ring around your finger? Once she was pulled into Ben's ambitious orbit, Becca didn't stand a chance of escape. She was quickened by his country-boy charms, her collapsing world buttressed by those big-boned arms.

She takes another bite of ice cream.

"I had a daydream the other day."

"Good or bad?"

"Hard to know."

"Must have been good."

"It was like a lost memory. Or a deja vu. I was small. I didn't like being so little. Helpless. This must have been before my parents died. Before I went to live with Aunt Mabel? Anyway I was making myself breakfast. But the cereal was so high up on the shelf I had to stand on a chair. The house was deserted. Nobody was there to help me out. Then I left through the front door. But this wasn't a house I remember. It was someone else's. I locked the door and walked to the bus stop and then I woke up."

His dead-mouthed expression says Ben is worried.

"It's nothing." She touches his tummy. "I'm getting a little stir crazy lately, is all. Being all alone in this big empty house, it makes me feel . . . I don't know . . ."

"Have you called your aunt?"

". . . not so safe."

"Mabel will be able to explain some of this. You should get out of the house more."

"I'm already volunteering at the Sunday school."

"Take up a hobby. Something."

When she doesn't reply, Ben turns back to the television set.

"That's a nice fedora," he says.

"He's got her cornered, I think."

"No way. She's too tough for mister milquetoast here. Deadlock at best."

"Why milquetoast?"

"Look how thin he is."

"Thin was in back then."

"I don't remember thin being in."

"You don't remember my birthday."

"You will always be twenty-nine to me, my dear."

There's something a little off-limits in these tender nothings passing between the two of them. Kind of lower-class and dirty-sexy all rolled in together. Becca and her big bad Ben eating sweets in rumpled sheets, each trying to best the other in the sultry summer smother. Ben leans in for a supersized kiss and she wonders if he's thinking the same thing but before Becca can wonder for long they have uncovered the answer together which is . . . oh, *my* . . .

Oh . . .

Yes.

14. DEAN

"How was your night?"

"Another intellectually stimulating evening working as a cocktail waitress. And yours, Mr. Goodnight?"

"You know. Unicorns and rainbows and shiny happy people holding hands. The usual."

Samantha laughs, a succession of short chuckles building gradually to a big, artless, cackling finish. This is the sound that drew Dean to his girlfriend in the first place, this infectious, snowballing laughter. A sound so sure of itself Dean thinks he might burst into bits just hearing it.

"You think I'm funny," Dean says. He feels himself smiling.

"I do."

Laugh lines fade into faint tracework around her grin.

"I went to the library before my shift," Sam says.

They sit barefoot at the small moonlit table, passing a dimpled silver spoon back and forth, dissolving stubborn cubes of sugar in steeping cups of tea.

"I sat on a big yellow beanbag in the children's section. The tables and chairs were doll-sized. I looked like a giant next to it all. Funny though. I felt small on the beanbag. Swallowed up by it. I read Shel Silverstein and when I was done I couldn't stand. My legs fell asleep. I had to ask the librarian to help me up."

Sam taps the spoon on the chipped rim of her teacup and a string of bright chimes rings cleanly through the muffled quiet.

"I don't know Shel Silverstein."

"Oh he's great." She hands the spoon back to Dean. "I used to recite *Where the Sidewalk Ends* over and over when I was a girl." Sam closes her eyes, palms outspread on her knees, like a faith healer working at miracles, and leans into the headwinds of some remembered breeze. The poem she reads has the abstracted quality of myth, calcified flowers and black smoke billowing and compassionate, oracular children, wise beyond their years.

Sam's fingertips drift up Dean's forearm, linger there a moment, courting.

"It sounds sad," he says.

"I never thought so."

Dean douses the edge of a sugar cube in his tea and the pristine crystals darken in a flash. He reels the tea bag up by its string, squeeze-drying the sodden lump over his cup. Muddy runlets silt down his fingers. Dean tosses the spent bag into the wastebin, where it bickers against a half-empty birth control pillpak.

They have agreed to stop talking about having kids. And yet the subject persists, an almost physical presence in the silences between the things they say. More and more lately, when they talk, Dean feels crowded against the contours of Sam's burgeoning maternal urge.

"What are we talking about?" he asks.

She takes the dark, damp cube from Dean and lifts it into her mouth, sucking the sweetness hard between white teeth. Sam stands, she's still not answering, rolls the sugar on her tongue, walks away smiling.

Dean finishes his tea.

She's waiting for him in the bedsheets, windows flung wide to the star-spangled night.

"Dean," Sam calls from the bedroom. "It's late. Where are you going?"

But he's already changing into running shorts, retrieving his keys.

"For a run."

15. BEN

By ten minutes to five o'clock Oklahoma City's mainline highways and arterial avenues are stop-and-go, clotted with cars. Everyone flees, riding the brakes in one last dash for home, like some slow-motion replay of the land run. The rush hour crush reveals the essential loneliness of this city, which by six has been abandoned by all but the most industrious denizens. But right now, at twelve minutes past quitting time on a Monday in September, ninety-three degrees in the shade, flushed faces are boiling in Ben's rearview. The road is a parking lot, gridlocked with thousand-yard stares, brows twisting and scowling in reflective, cartoon rage.

Ben signals his intent to merge onto the interstate. He checks his blind spot, steers the big black sport utility vehicle into the lane, gives a quick wave of thanks into the wing mirror. He's never been ticketed. Drives four miles faster than the speed limit, surrendered to the flow, like a retiree soaking up the sights.

He dials the stereo to the AM band and waits for his favorite talk radio show to start.

So much of his life is whiled away in this car. He's done the math and it comes out to almost two full workdays a week. There's the forty-five minute commute bookending his day, into the city and back again. Several trips to the sticks, remote places like Canton or Antlers, up to two hours each way. The Sunday lunch with Cecil in Perkins. And during basketball season the midweek road trips to Stillwater can last hours if he doesn't judge the traffic right.

Ben fell asleep at the wheel once. Gentled by the amniotic drone of Firestone rubber whining over the road. He awoke to the sound of plastic safety stanchions *slap-slap-slapping* at his front bumper. Had to stop the car on the road shoulder and catch his breath.

He still dreams about that night Cecil was hurt. A pitch-black highway. He's conscious of watching two distinct selves, each sleeping in different places: asleep in the car; asleep in the bed next to Becca. There's a seeping feeling, a steady diminishing of control. But the Bens won't wake up. The car and bed both drifting slowly off course, diverging into a double darkness.

Ben cranks the A/C in his SUV. He read somewhere that warmth is a soporific, and now he won't drive anyplace without a vent blasting cold air at his face. Becca says it calls to mind a dog with its head stuck out the rear window, jowls flapping in the wind drift.

A funky bass guitar lick leaks from the speakers. The Pretenders are wondering what's happened to Chrissie Hynde's hometown back in Ohio.

Crash Lambeau, "the most dangerous man in America," ramps onto the airwaves. "Be *afraid*, ladies and gentlemen," Crash says, tongue-in-cheek. "Be very afraid. Chrissie said it best. You just heard her. Our cities are in danger. But it doesn't end there. Oh no. It's much more insidious than that. The freedoms guaranteed to you by the Founding Fathers are disappearing. Every minute of every day that Slick Willie and his feminazi shadow president Hillary occupy the White House."

Crash isn't buying what big government's selling. He sucks down a big breath and launches into an incredulous riff on recent developments. "I mean, if it wasn't for all of you *real* Americans listening out there right now, this socialist Hillarycare bill might have actually squeaked through Congress. Big Brother would be stealing money from your paychecks to fund a government takeover of one-seventh of this country's economy. And in return for your hard work, 'Billary' and their fascist intelligentsia would be dictating which doctors you're allowed to see."

Ben's no dittohead. But he can't stop listening. There's something fascinating about the Lambeau phenomenon. At the very least, it keeps Ben awake on these long hauls home. Here's a guy, not a single marketable skill other than his mouth, talking to himself from some soundproof studio. Earning millions and influencing elections.

What Ben wouldn't give for that kind of clout.

Crash riffs on.

"Now. Fascism is a word thrown around on the left by people too dumb to understand what it means. In deference to these idiots, I'll be doing the rest of this show with half my brain tied behind my back, just to keep things fair. Because I have talent on loan from God, people."

Crash's soundman gives up a *badum-tish!* rimshot.

Crash laughs, a rich, chocolate chuckle.

"Let me simplify it for the intellectually handicapped. The Merriam-Webster dictionary defines fascism as 'A political philosophy, movement, or regime that exalts nation and often race above the individual and that stands for a centralized autocratic government headed by a dictatorial leader, severe economic and social regimentation, and forcible suppression of opposition.'"

Crash wields words like a martial artist. No one can touch him. Threatened by an argument, he redefines the battlefield, dodging the attack altogether. He turns terms inside-out, obliterates entire lines of reasoning. Fact is fiction. Logic is passion. Reason is propaganda. Meaning is irrelevant. There is only the freewheeling tickertape of Crash's inner dialogue.

"Don't let these cosmopolitan, so-called . . . *intellectuals* confuse you with their convoluted logic and statistics. This is how they win. Misdirection and obfuscation. In a society where state-run media and liberal universities indoctrinate our youth into the idea that speech should be 'politically correct'—a term worthy of George Orwell if I've ever heard one—ignorance isn't just bliss. It's essential to our survival as a democracy! Ignorance, my fellow Americans, is downright *patriotic* in this day and age."

He's fashioning language from whole cloth. A new school of thinking. An otherspeak.

Crash returns to the defeated healthcare bill.

"Know how you can tell if a Clinton is lying? One of them is talking. I saw you all infiltrate Hillary's stump speeches to drown out her lies. And when *Herr-Doctor* Clinton stood up in that town hall to stump for Hillarycare, we were ready with our secret weapon. How can Slick Willie argue with a fellow soul brother like Herman Cain? He's the poster boy for Clinton's demographic. And there Cain was, in Technicolor, taking Bill to task on national TV.

"We engineered a bloodbath ladies and gentlemen. You, me, Bill Kristol. My man Newt. What a team. Oh. It was beautiful. There's not another word for it. The bill was dead on arrival. Mitchell just won't admit it yet. Give yourselves a pat on the back.

"But don't rest on your laurels. This war is just getting started. There are more important battles ahead. Like *Generalissimo* Janet's crime bill. What a piece of work. A ban on our second amendment freedom to bear arms. You saw what happened down in Waco. This crime bill passes, you'd better get used to seeing more of that kind of thing in the news. You want my honest opinion? Every man, woman, and child in this country should own a gun. The Founding Fathers knew we'd need to defend our freedoms against jackbooted thugs like these Clintonistas."

Crash fires one last volley over the bumper music before giving up the bully pulpit.

"Freedom is *not* a crime, ladies and gentlemen," Crash says.

The Pretenders are back again, still trying to find Hynde's version of Ohio.

"Not yet, anyway."

Ben hears a big rig Jake-braking in the traffic up ahead, sees it *burp-burp-burping* black palings of brume into a blue-swept sky. The exhaust spirals heavenward, thin dieseled rifts in the moment. And why does this feel like a premonition, of a sudden, or a memory, these fissures? As if the world's been broken.

16. CECIL

Second daypart and he's parked at the garage workbench hid back of the black curtain, cutting streamer glass into patterns cobbled together from borrowed picture books.

Cecil is feeling good about this stained glass window. It's his most ambitious work yet, a panoramic slice of Americana done in opalescent earth tones: Lakota Chief Sitting Bull admiring the last sunrise of his life as Lieutenant Bull Head and his horsemen ride in from the east. A tight-faced Catch-the-Bear looks on, shouldering the breechloader that will spark the whole history of miseries to follow. A surrounding circle of Sioux have just dropped into the fateful Ghost Dance.

The glasscutter slides over the pane with a grainy *whiiiiiish*.

Soon the cutting will be done and he can start soldering pieces into the larger design. Cecil mallets the fresh-etched grooves and a shard falls away from the scrap glass. He polishes the splintered edges, sets the feathered shape into Sitting Bull's war bonnet, consults the reference book cracked open at his elbow.

Kicking Bear said to his army of Ghost Dancers: "Our fallen ancestors will rise with the spring and drive the white man back over the big water from where he came. Sing and dance with true belief and prepare for the spirit war to come."

Outside his workshop window the tree leaves have whisked the afternoon into a dither, dappling an overturned wheelbarrow in brilliance. He could spend a lifetime trying to capture this commonplace play of light. He can hear the egg timer ticking off the hours in the other room. The *plip-plip-plip-plip* of urine dripping down his leg bag. The tinny spank of the refrigerator fan straining to life in the kitchen, *slap-slappity-slap-slaaaaapp-pppuh*.

He doesn't talk about his hobby and might not even if someone asked. The Porter boys weren't encouraged to nourish anything like an inner life. When Dad said action equals character he meant it as a kind of putdown, a hedge against either son becoming intellectual or, God forbid, some kind of aesthete.

He cuts another feather and lets himself drift.

He's in church, watching the stained glass skylight rainbow down on the severe profiles of his parents. He used to stare up at that window and blink, think he'd been lit from within by the afterimage of the Holy Ghost itself. Praying. The pebbled hide of the basketball under his fingertips. That double-action zing ringing inside the thing and the way his feet felt *rooted* at the free-throw line, a very part of the living earth underneath. Slopping the hogs in the sodden dawn. The heavy dread of the wreck and how it wedged between him and little Ben. Dad's coronary and Mother's long decline and the steady falling away of the faith he once held so tight. His wife Ellen, the vanilla-cream taste of her tits on his tongue and those electric fingernails stroking his scalp. He couldn't please her the way she needed. Or wouldn't, might be the better word. His body seemed willing enough at times. There were a few erections Cecil could see. See but not feel. But Ellen didn't care about all that, not really. It was Cecil's own bullheaded pride that finally pushed her away.

Anger is a young man's emotion. Regret, though, seems to have a longer half-life. He just folded. Gave up, or in or out. Any way you want to say it he ought to have been a better man. For Ellen, for Mother, for Ben. For every one of them.

"The Earth has grown old and must again be made new. Go then, my children, and tell these things to all the people and make ready for the coming of the ghosts."

Cecil cuts another feather, remembering.

17. BECCA

To Becca's mind the produce aisle at Homeland is the best barometer of the times. The moment she glides through the pneumatic sliding doors—*whooosh!*—her troubles are obliterated by the refrigerated veneer of eternal spring. In *this* future the temperature never rises above sixty-four degrees, the flowers are always in bloom, and the white noise of faintly familiar show tunes is occasionally amplified by someone named Suzie at register three.

"Cole, this is Suzie on three. I've got a code blue for you up front," Suzie says. "Cole, code blue please."

If you step back from it all, give a little tilt to the neck and allow your eyes to trail along the failing depth of field, the displays cartwheel into a cubist kind of inconsistency, Plasticolored islands overspilled with manna. Vine-swollen tomatoes bleed into citrine speckles of lemon-lime. Pastel pyramids of honeydew melon are undercut by collard or some other species of greenery.

"Wendy, I need a price check on Mom-to-Mom Kiddie-Ups," Suzie says. "Wendy, price check at three please."

Becca rights herself and rolls her shopping cart toward the shiitake mushrooms, marveling at the bioengineered bounty surrounding her. Sweet potpourri of apple and onion and mint, with a bitter bit of earth mixed in for good measure.

"Cole, cancel the code blue and send a mop to aisle fourteen. I need a cleanup on aisle fourteen, please."

A red-aproned young man pushing a mop bucket wheels by Becca in the dry-goods aisle. Cole is on the case, apparently.

She is reaching for a box of oat bran when the hollow shock of a slamming door sounds somewhere back of the store, *ker-whoooomp!*

A gooseflesh tremor prickles her in place.

. . . starving but the pantry shelves are nearly bare. She sees something up top. Climbs tippy-toe up the chair back trying for, what is it? Cornflakes, if she's lucky. Just . . . a little . . . higher. But it's no good, like trying to walk a seesaw, so she chickens out . . .

Becca trips witless down the aisle and past the cash registers, fleeing the market. The heat hits her like a fist out here but at least she's in motion, breathless yes but moving, driving now and crying too in the slamming-down sun.

. . . they went away too long this time . . .

She steers quickly through a lazy-daisy snarl of streets, aimless, imagining she can outrun the waking dream that has managed to stalk her here from the house.

. . . worried. Something's gone wrong . . .

She comes to her senses waiting on the stoplight at some unfamiliar intersection. A steeple creeps skyward just ahead. She is downtown, somewhere near First Church. She turns left, drives by the dark-mirrored Murrah Building, impenetrable as a frontier fort there beside the YWCA, turns onto Tenth Street and into the Passages Women's Shelter parking lot.

There is some confusion at the reception desk. Becca can't seem to summon the words necessary to explain why she has come.

Becca is holding a clipboard stuffed with intake forms and saying, ". . . help."

". . . the help you need," the girl behind the counter says. "Just fill these papers out and we can get started."

"Don't understand."

"I do," the girl says. "I know you're feeling alone right now. But it will pass. We're here for you. Only for you. Our counselors have years of experience helping women through these troubles."

"I am . . ."

"He can't hurt you here."

"I want . . ."

"Don't worry . . ."

". . . to help."

". . . everything will be fine."

Becca closes her eyes.

"I need to see someone named Joanne Perry."

With each beat of her heart the light needles across her lids.

She opens her eyes. "I'm here to volunteer."

18. DEAN

"Picture a cowboy," the girl says.

Dean is sitting with Billy Grimes's girlfriend Willa Busby in a dim-lit observation room at the Passages Women's Shelter. In the see-through expanse of one-way looking glass behind them Willa's wiry reflection pantomimes a cattleman with amped, ants-in-pants dramatics. A half-dozen children are at play on the brighter side of the mirror.

"Let's call him Roy," Willa says, red-shot eyes roving. "Roy's roaming the wide blue yonder. Amber waves of grain and such. Yodeling, playing his harmonica. Some kind of cowboy shit. Suddenly he's surrounded by Indians. Big red *badmen* like you and Billy. These natives are ornery. They're in this killing kind of drought. So the braves decide to sacrifice Roy to the rain gods. Spirits. Whatever."

A discordant swirl of hoots and hollers from the opposite room. Aggrieved, high-pealing howls and extravagant, cackling laughter. Willa's five-year-old son Caleb sits cross-legged on the playroom floor, immune to the chaos, absorbed in a Rubik's cube. From her seat by the door a middle-aged brunette observes the boy's every gesture, a clipboard balanced on her ample lap.

"That's right, the savages intend to kill poor Roy. But first the chief tells him: 'We grant you one last request.' So Roy says, stoic-like: 'Bring me my horse.'"

Caleb has almost solved the blue side of the cube. The little boy's lips move as he works. The woman writes something on the clipboard.

"The chief brings Roy his horse. We *have* to call him Trigger, right? Old Roy whispers in Trigger's ear and that mount is off like a shot."

Dean doesn't have time for this. But he can't find the heart to shut her down. Willa's funny, emotive. She's got the pressured eloquence of the stand-up comic down cold.

"Well just before sunset Trigger comes trotting back with—get this mister Dean—a nekkid lady perched in the saddle!"

Willa cups both hands beneath her breasts and squeezes.

"She's packing some guns herself. So Roy looks at this painted lady and shrugs. He takes her into his tent. Teepee. Whatever. And proceeds to shag that girl like there's no tomorrow. Roy and this strumpet *go to town*. The earth, it literally moves. Well and you know how drafty these teepees can be. Everyone in the *tribe* can hear what's going on."

Willa's knee bounces manic pumpjacks beneath the table. She's geeked to the gills.

"So the next day the chief comes to Roy's tent. 'Cowboy strong like bull,' this chief says. 'It is good for my warriors to see. We give you one last chance, mister paleface. One more request. Then tomorrow you die.' So Roy says again: 'Bring me my horse.' Same thing: Roy whispers into Trigger's ear. Trigger takes off into the sunset, brings another nekkid woman back to camp."

"What about the first woman?" asks Dean.

"Don't overthink it."

"The one with the guns?"

"She doesn't matter. Like I was saying. Roy and his new dish head back into the teepee for some sexy time. The stars align. Lightning crashes. Et cetera. The tribe gathers round the tent to wonder at Roy's exploits in the sack."

"She matters."

"Jesus lumps-of-fat-fucking-Christ."

"You need to think about what happens to this woman the next day," Dean says. "The day after that one."

"Well, day after *this* one, Roy comes from his tent. The Indian chief bows down. He might even be blushing. It's hard to tell, get me? 'You make big love last night,' says the chief. 'I will give one more request. But come sunrise tomorrow, nothing can save you.' Again, Roy calls for his horse. But the cowboy's done whispering.

Trigger isn't listening. Roy's shouting now." Willa gooses Dean's leg and yells, "I said *POSSE*, you idiot!"

Dean tries not to laugh but can't help himself. Eventually he says, "Tell me about Billy."

"Billy Grimes was an unholy terror."

"I'm looking to help him."

Willa summons a strangled sort of croak. When she understands Dean isn't kidding she says, "We were in that hot-sheet motel for months."

"You and Billy and Caleb?"

"Plus the goddamn cat."

"Billy was rolling johns," Dean says. "With you as bait."

"A girl's gotta work," Willa says. "That night, he was five days in on a drunk like to . . ."

Dean lifts a finger and presses it against Willa's cracked lips. She stops talking, dark-rimmed eyes going wide. Good. The girl is seeing him. "I don't need to know about that night," he says, lowering the finger. Her lips are softer than they look.

She folds a bruise-blued arm over her chest and draws away from Dean. "You're certainly a first."

"I only want the high points."

"The happy days."

"You said it."

Willa examines her fingernails, knee jiggling. "He was a pretty good father."

Dean leans in, listening. He's not taking notes.

"No shit, mister Dean. When he wasn't just blotto, Billy spent all his time with Caleb. They spoke in code."

"Code."

"It was *hah-lih-toh* this and *umm-bih* that and *mih-hah-moh-mah* all the time."

"*Miha moma*," says Dean. "*Umbi. Halito.*"

"It was like living with two retards," Willa snorts. "But it grew on you."

Caleb has forgotten the cube and is now staring through his playmates with the X-ray gaze of the truly traumatized. The brunette and her clipboard have left the room.

"This deal with the D.A."

"What of it?"

"It doesn't mean you're off the hook."

"This is some kind of news."

"You're still on parole."

"Some kind of news, mister Dean. This deal is my get-out-of-jail-free card."

"Let's say, just for the sake of saying it, let's say you piss a dirty U.A." Dean snaps his fingers. "It would be straight back to jail, Willa. Do *not* pass GO. Do *not* collect two hundred dollars. And CPS would dump Caleb to live in a foster home."

Her knee freezes mid-jerk.

"This is no joke. You pop positive for meth, for coke—for anything—it turns into some kind of sob story." He stands and says, "Your parole officer, what's his name?"

"Sampson?"

"Sampson. Right. Sampson and I are tight."

"I'll tell you, mister Dean. You sure can ruin a mood."

"Get your head straight."

"Downcast Dean," she says. "Dean the downer."

"Wait here."

He leaves through a green door, searching for the brunette who had been observing Caleb. He finds her talking with Joanne Perry in the shelter director's office. Dean knocks on the aluminum door frame and both women look up.

"How did it go with Willa?" Joanne asks.

"It's still going," Dean says. "How's the boy?"

Joanne defers to the brunette.

"I think he needs to see a psychologist, psychiatrist. Something," the woman says to Joanne. "He's pretty well shell-shocked. Caleb doesn't make eye contact. He speaks nothing but gibberish. He's so . . . sad."

"He was in the motel room," Dean says, "when it happened."

"I don't understand how people get into these life situations," the brunette says. A plastic ID card clipped to her blouse reads VOLUNTEER.

"Well if you ever figure it out," Joanne laughs, "let me know."

"He might be talking Choctaw."

Both women look at him.

"Can you translate for us?" Joanne asks.

Dean plays dumb but promises to fax them the number of a Choctaw translator. He'd been putting Willa's interview off for this very reason. Beyond the strict scope of his duties at the public defender's office, beyond this deep dive into Billy's background, he'd rather not get involved. Too much work, too little time in which to do it. A few days ago he reached out to the victim's grandmother in Langston, one Opal Jefferson, and has just learned that Carl's older sister, a nurse, rents an apartment in nearby Stillwater.

Dean extends his hand to the brunette woman and says, "I didn't catch your name."

The volunteer lowers her clipboard to shake Dean's hand.

"How rude of me! I'm new around here. It's Becca," she says. "Becca Porter."

19. AURA

Grocery Store: BUY:
- *bread, milk, eggs, cheese, ham, pudding, trash bags, peas, soup, salad-in-a-bag*

Bills: PAY, STAMP, and MAIL:
- *OG&E, water, cable bill*

Bank: WITHDRAW:
- *$10 cash for lawn boy*
- *SEAL money in envelope*
- *WRITE "Lawn" on envelope*
- *PLACE envelope under doormat on front stoop*

Repairs:
- *Dishwasher fan belt—(405) 555-0122*
  - *Maytag, Serial #S-989732-25*
  - *Sears Home Insurance Policy #782913*
- *Weatherstrip under back door*
  - *TOM fixed it last time*
- ***Phone Call****: (800) MED-CARE*
- *APPEAL MEDICARE DENIAL*
- *NAPROSYN (arthritis)*
- *Claim #J87-0213-537*

Pharmacy: REFILL:
- *Niacin, Coumadin, Glucophage*

Phone Call: (800) 555-0183
- *PRE-APPROVAL REQUIRED*
- *Neurology visit with Dr. Cronin*

Phone Call: (405) 555-2368
- *DISCOVERY for Carl's murder trial*
- *DEAN GOODNIGHT, Investigator*
- *Oklahoma County Public Defender's office*

When you struggle to get through any given today, like Aura's grandmother Opal, someone else has got to step in and worry about tomorrow for you. So they work through the list as a team, seated side-by-side at Grams's kitchen table. They pay the bills and stamp the envelopes. Drive to the grocery store for the milk and the eggs, the bread and the pudding. They cook the pork chops and the rice, the beans and the stew. They seal the meals in airtight Tupperware containers, stack the tubs neatly in the fridge for Opal to reheat during the week. Then Aura bathes her grandmother, tucks her tight in the crisp, laundered bedsheets, just as Opal did for Aura when she was a child.

They've come full circle.

It's dusk when Aura locks her grandmother's front door. That blue-gray hour of the day when things feel torn. Daybreak or nightfall, it could go either way. Flip a coin and the light might leak right back into the sky.

Aura drives west out of town into a towering cloudscape. She turns north at the interstate, trailing a neon-red caravan of taillights headed for Stillwater. She's driven this route so many times, sometimes Aura doesn't even see the road. She'll find herself suddenly home, dazed and wondering: *How'd I end up here?*

It doesn't hit her until full dark.

She's gone the long way around, steering clear of Coyle after sundown.

20. BECCA

Becca finds herself haunting the women's shelter three times a week, sometimes four. She could volunteer night and day and nobody would object. Today she's here to play with the cute little Indian boy again. After dropping in briefly on the mother, Willa, Becca finds the Indian investigator, Mr. Goodnight, sitting alone in the shelter's darkened observation studio. The lamp-lit playroom past the one-way looking glass casts the man's face in a goldenrod glow. Inside, Caleb Grimes and the translator Dean has found, a barrel-bodied American Indian woman named Abigail, are both lounging on a mound of green beanbags lumped upon the floor.

"How's mom?" He doesn't look up.

"It's hard to tell," Becca whispers. She takes a nearby seat. "Willa can be so magnetic."

"More like bipolar."

"You should hear the way she makes Caleb laugh. Other times it's as though he's taking care of her. She's erratic. Inconsistent, at best."

Dean pulls a pained face. He is twirling a yellow pencil up then down the knuckles of his right hand. The big Indian is quiet, a dispassionate gentle giant, but even in this ulterior half-light it looks like he could use a hug.

"A kid needs routine," Dean says to her. "He'll pick boring over crazy any day."

Becca takes in the dark-rimmed eyes and sallow skin and wonders if the man is getting enough to eat.

A glottal string of *tuks* and *toks* and *pops* comes clipping over the observation room's speaker system. Caleb's hands flap excitedly about his mouth as he chatters in what must be Choctaw. The translator is all ears: smiling, nodding, drawing the boy out.

"How's it going in there?" asks Becca.

"She's almost done."

"How can you know?"

He holds a finger to his lips rather than answer and, sure enough, before too long the translator has distracted Caleb with a connect-the-dots puzzler. The ample woman lifts lightly from the floor, buoyant as a soap-bubble, excusing herself through the blue playroom door.

"Well?" Dean says when the translator lets herself in.

"Slow down, big guy." She practically floats over to Becca, pulling her from the chair and into a soft, motherly embrace. "You," she announces, "are Becca."

But Becca is too hypnotized by this unexpected intimacy to answer.

The translator holds Becca at arm's length. "I'm Abigail Whistler."

Becca wants to say something smart or at least charming but all she manages is "Yes."

"You were right," Abigail says, transitioning back to Dean and to business. "He is speaking Choctaw. Or something similar, anyway." She falls into a chair and the caster wheels grate a plaintive, metallic complaint.

Becca finds her seat. She can't help but notice these Native Americans are so shamelessly self-contained, so unapologetically *at ease* in their outsized bodies. Where Dean is tall Abigail is wide, not fat so much as quilted, with pillowed rolls of flesh spilling from her lilac-print muumuu. Her chestnut cheeks are stretched so tightly across her face Abigail's eyes seem pleated in permanent, guileless glee.

This woman, Becca thinks, she *glows*.

"Can you get him speaking English?"

"He's communicating, Dean," Abigail says. "Let's don't push him too far too fast. You say the mother doesn't speak Choctaw?"

Dean shakes his head.

"Billy was his teacher."

"It's unfortunate. In the absence of his father Caleb is freestyling. He's teaching himself the language now. Inventing portmanteau words and phrases. Compounding, blending, back-forming the phonemes he does know, trying to describe his world. And his tenses are a mess."

"How do you mean?" Becca says.

"In Choctaw," Dean answers, "you think and speak in the present tense."

"Yes," Abigail adds. "My mother used to say the future, the past—they can't ever bite you in the ass. But don't ever turn your back on the present."

"Seems like a healthy worldview," Becca says.

"It has its drawbacks," Dean says.

"Caleb talks about remembering things that haven't yet happened," Abigail says. "Going to see his father in jail, for example. Has he visited Billy there?"

Dean shakes his head. No.

"And he seems to believe this horror at the motel—he keeps calling it the *big burning*—has yet to occur. He's terrified of it. Honestly I don't understand half or more of what the boy tells me."

"Can't you tutor him?" asks Becca.

"I would dear, but," Abigail smiles, "it would take more time than I have to give."

"Abigail's work is pro bono," Dean explains. "As a favor to me."

Becca stands and approaches the window. On the other side of the mirror Caleb's fist is curled around a red crayon. The boy has abandoned his puzzle and appears to be frozen in place. Becca sees him squeezing, straining, tighter and tighter until the crayon buckles into cherry-colored chunks.

"He talked about that night?"

"Yes," Abigail says.

"Well?"

"I don't know how much to give you, Dean."

"I'm on his dad's side, remember?"

"He said it was a game. Between the—he said something like *midnight-man*—and his father."

A wooden *crack!* and Becca looks back. Dean has snapped the pencil in his hand.

"Do you think he could testify?"

"Too premature to tell."

"But what's your gut?"

Abigail won't answer. Instead she says, "I didn't know you were left-handed."

"I'm not."

"The watch is on your right wrist."

"Oh, that. It's a little protest of mine."

"Protest against what?"

"It's a private protest."

"What good is a protest nobody hears about?"

"Call it a reminder, then."

"Abigail," Becca interrupts, "what if we could find a way to fund your time?"

"I love the optimism," Abigail chuckles. To Dean, "She's so *new!*" Becca presses.

"But would your schedule open up? Could you tutor him then?"

"Sure I could. Sure it would. But this kind of thing just doesn't happen, Becca."

"Let me worry about that," Becca says. "Can I go see him now?"

"By all means," Abigail says. "He's been asking for you."

21. CECIL

Mold has set in under the foundation. Funky rills of rot blistering beneath the linoleum tiles, under the entryway carpet and on down the run of his hallway. A buzz-cut shaveling from Sears drove all the way from Stillwater and quoted Cecil a price to fix the mess but Cecil told him the extra eighty-five dollars to pull up that old shag was some kind of boondoggle. The kid's bringing his crew back tomorrow and so Cecil is wheeling around the hallway perimeter, box cutter in hand, trying to save some money. He'll jew that boy down yet.

Cecil cuts along the baseboards, bent double at the waist and yanking. A half-yard of carpet and staples and drywall chunks come dusting up and he moves on.

It looks as if the previous carpet-layers earned a good deal of their wages around this bathroom doorjamb. Cecil tugs at the woven backing there but nothing gives. He braces himself on the door casing and folds farther over for better purchase on the piling. He gives a good heave-ho and before Cecil knows what's what, he's getting cold-cocked by checkerboard tilework.

"Christammfffff," Cecil says into the bathroom floor.

He has capsized and is now pinned ass-end up like a lassoed calf beneath his chair. His right eye is blood-blinded and he's wrapped around the door frame, the feeling half of him pressed against the bathtub grouting while the rest remains knotted in the hallway.

The wheels on his rig spin round-and-round making a rickety racket.

Every room in Cecil's house is wired with a phone line for just such an occurrence. The bathroom phone jack is wall-mounted within easy reach of his toilet. He'll have to untwist himself before crawling over and call someone. Cecil tries sizing up the damage.

It's not looking good. The chair is anchored somewhere out there beyond his sightline and from this angle it's holding fast. If he can . . . just . . . shimmy . . . out . . . from . . .

Cecil hears a *crack!* that turns his stomach.

He's not in any real position to feel if something's broken. Cecil elbows forward across the bathroom floor. Pinlets of blood drip from the cut on his forehead and smear red, unsettling brushstrokes beneath his clothes as he pulls past the toilet bowl. He claws for the dangling phone cord and dials that new 9-1-1 code.

"Perkins Fire-Rescue," says the switchboard operator.

"Betsy, it's good to hear your voice."

"Well Cecil, you old hound dog. I hope nothing's amiss over there."

"Betsy, I'll admit it. I'm a little jammed up. Ralph might need to send a car."

Cecil describes the particulars of his predicament. He can hear Betsy muffle the receiver and shout, "Sheriff, Cecil Porter has fallen . . . No, Ralph, he can *not* get up. That's in poor taste . . . Yes I *have* seen the commercial." A rustling. "We're on the case, Cecil. You sit tight, now. Try and tell me how you're feeling, darling."

This last bit leaves him speechless.

"Cecil?"

"What."

"How you doing?"

"I'm laying practically in the shitter, Betsy."

"Well there isn't any call for that type of language, Cecil."

"I'll be sure and wash my mouth out after someone comes set me straight."

"Help is on the way. You just keep talking now, okay?"

The hook-switch is too high for Cecil to hang up and so he suffers Betsy's interrogations as best he can.

"Betsy . . ."

"Ralph is making an attempt to be thorough, Cecil."

"I only need a hand getting into my chair."

"Don't worry. Says here your fire subscription has been paid in full so you aren't getting charged a dime for any part of it."

Excepting Betsy and Sheriff Tippins, Perkins Fire-Rescue is staffed by two paunchy deputies named Neddy Burdett and Rowan Udall, each of them abetted by a despondent posse of paramedics and firefighters who always seem to be grousing about the lack of real action occurring within city limits. Ralph has apparently contrived to piggyback a little teambuilding drill on top of Cecil's mishap, broadcasting the call like it was a three-alarm disaster. Within minutes a caterwaul of different sirens is dueling its way to his property from the firehouse.

The first responders arrive only to be foiled by Cecil's deadbolt.

He overhears some discussion about an axe coming from his front stoop.

"Betsy, you tell those boys not to go busting down my front door. Back patio's unlocked."

Neddy and Rowan have soon sardined themselves inside, side arms drawn, marveling at the carnage. Rowan strokes his bald spot.

"Lord Cecil. You been attacked?"

"Lost my balance."

"Clear the house, Neddy," Rowan says, holstering his pistol. "Won't hurt to be safe."

"Why'n't you clear it?"

"*Because*, Neddy. I am the senior officer on scene. Means I get to give orders."

"Betsy, I'm going to let you go now," Cecil says into the phone. "Tweedledumb and Dumber are here."

"Alright," Betsy says sweetly. "You call again anytime, Cecil."

"Well," Neddy decides, putting away his own gun. "I ain't doing it, Rowan." Neddy hikes his trousers and rests his arms across the broad swell of his belly.

Cecil holds the phone receiver out for Rowan to hang up. A pimple-faced paramedic in the hallway has assembled Cecil's wheelchair and Neddy wheels it into the bathroom. Everyone looks down at Cecil, pondering how best to proceed.

He can feel their eyes on him. The awful weight of all that good intent.

"Which one of you Keystone Cops is going to get me off this blasted tile?"

The three men bend to help him up.

"Don't wrench, Neddy," says Rowan. "You've got to lift it thisaway."

"Those sure are some pretty boots Cecil."

"Thanks Neddy."

"Now you've did it."

"Okay thataway then."

Cecil is lifted into his wheelchair with slightly more care than might be taken to toss a bale of silage. He pats himself down, feeling for fractures, but everything seems to be in working order.

"Mister dadgum knowi-tall," Neddy says to Rowan, wiping both hands on his uniform.

Cecil's bathroom floor looks like someone's just been murdered on it. Bloody boot marks and tire tracks and handprints smirched every which way. Even the walls are begrimed.

"It's more gore in that head of yours than a swelled-up tick," says the paramedic, slapping a bandage on Cecil's forehead.

What with all the mouth-breathers crowding him, the air in here is getting scarce.

"Neddy, push me out to my pickup," Cecil says.

"Where you got to be getting?"

"The hospital."

"We can't have you *driving* under these circumstances, Cecil," Rowan says. "Lookit your face."

"I'm not paying the city for an ambulance ride to Stillwater," Cecil barks. "I've been making that trip my own damn self going on fifty years now."

The other paramedic is out front, a jimberjawed chainsmoking fellow named Quince Ingram. Seeing Neddy help Cecil up into his truck sends Quince into a state of bug-eyed dudgeon. With one hand Cecil grips the steering wheel for balance and, in a fluid and practiced maneuver that wreaks hell on his left shoulder, leans out to fold his rig closed with the other hand. He strong-arms the chair up into the Chevy's passenger seat.

Ingram looks like he's enduring a brain embolism there in the driveway.

Cecil disengages the parking brake and revs the truck's engine with his hydraulic cripple controls until Ingram throws his cigarette in the pea-gravel and steps aside. Cecil steers around the ambulance and police car. The four figures are still arguing in the rearview mirror when he turns onto the roadway. But soon the ambulance lights are whirligigging in his wake and Rowan's cruiser has howled past on Cecil's left.

In this way they all caravan the ten miles or so to Stillwater Medical Center, Cecil and this well-meant troupe of utter fools.

∾

Cecil's entourage escorts him to the Emergency Room reception window, where they are greeted by a crag-faced old battle-axe. A plastic name tag on the woman's periwinkle scrubs reads "*Call me Robin!*"

"Which of you is hurt?" Robin says, wrinkled fingers shuffling a sheaf of intake forms.

Everyone starts talking at once. Robin regards them silently, waiting. But the men may as well be speaking Swahili for all the headway they're making. Finally Neddy Burdett pushes Cecil's wheelchair parallel to Robin's desk. He is admitted under his Medicare policy. Robin records his vitals, runs through her triage checklist, retrieves his chart. She flips through his medical history.

"Complete T9 CSI?" Robin says, crozzled eyes floating up from Cecil's chart.

"Yes ma'am."

"When?"

"Forty-eight."

"*1948?*"

"Yes ma'am."

"Well for someone who's been sitting on his hind parts for so long you're looking pretty good to me," Robin says, closing the chart. "Blood pressure's elevated, but that's to be expected after all the excitement. Why don't we get you inside and clean up that head and have the doctors take a closer look?"

Once inside the hospital bay he is lifted onto a gurney by two athletic-looking orderlies and then draped in a lead vest. The X-ray technician doesn't want to ruin his patient's pants by scissoring them off, so the kid just rolls the jeans up over Cecil's knees, scanning the exposed shins for any evidence of internal violence. Cecil stares up at the foam-paneled ceiling as that big machine moans above him.

His skin is cold and clammy as chicken flesh.

A toothy doctor finally arrives, the developed X-ray plates tucked under his arm.

"Mr. Porter, I can't find a thing wrong with you that's worth worrying on," he says, holding the X-rays up for Cecil to inspect.

Cecil knows something is off but doesn't know how to get this across and so he just nods. The doctor cleans Cecil's head wound, whistling softly, and an orderly helps Cecil down from the gurney into his rig.

"Next time you feel the urge to do some home improvements, why don't you call a handyman," the doctor says, shaking Cecil's hand and smiling.

Cecil promises to do that. His left leg looks crooked in his chair, so Cecil bends forward to reposition it, reaching beneath his thigh and lifting.

His femur snaps in two with a wicked-sounding *crunch!*

Okay. Keep your head. Okay.

The orderly runs yelling into the hallway.

There is more blood bleeding out of him than Cecil is comfortable with, a quick stigmata staining his Wranglers. Thank heavens he can't feel that thighbone tenting his pant leg like a teepee. Looks like it would have smarted something horrible. His eyes have focused on a faraway place which nobody but himself seems interested in witnessing.

"You're lucky we caught this before you got home," the doctor says, urgently. "That might about have killed you."

Everything is resembling some other thing. His chest feels as though it's being pressed in a vise and a hot fury of hurt has him blinded in one eye.

"You know doc," says Cecil, pressing a palm heel against the tormented eye socket. "One thing I've always been is lucky."

He blacks out, seeing stars.

REVOLUTION

FALL 1994

22. DEAN

Idling in a southside parking lot, watching students arrive for school. Show-muscled jocks and dye-job Goths pile out of fastbacks, awkward and invincible with youth. The children mass in self-selecting packs that range over the asphalt for class.

Dean's wristwatch reads 9:01 but it's wrong, he forgot to fall back. He has an appointment with the Southeast High custodian of records to review Billy Grimes's transcripts. Dean visits several times a semester on other official business and could probably walk in unannounced. Best, though, not to squander Marla's good temper. Dean spins the watch crown around and time unwinds. A few seconds ago he was running late; now there's an extra hour to kill.

He cruises south Oklahoma City in the primer-paneled Oldsmobile Delta 88 that once and future clients call a *hoopty*. The gunmetal streets are glutted with unexpected light.

When he first moved to the city Dean lived four years in a cracker-box shack just beyond the school's catchment area. The deadhead pursuits of the old stomping grounds have yet to present, but it's early. Flatfooted maids are already following top-heavy housekeeping carts from one flophouse room to the next, restoring order. The wastoids will start crawling out of the woodwork soon enough, huffing gas in back alleys, queuing up before riot-gated liquor store doors. Then Oklahoma City's finest will badge up, ready to serve and protect, and the whole batshit game of crazy will pick up right where everyone left off last night.

Dean's seen enough evidence to know their client is likely guilty. He hasn't pushed Billy too hard, hasn't let Willa tell him too much about the night of Carl Jefferson's murder. Macy's got the burden of proof, the reasoning goes, so let's let sleeping dogs lie a little while longer.

If Dean is right, too much truth too soon could put Wolfman in a tight spot.

Most murderers aren't so different from the rest of us. Quick to laugh, maybe, or tell a good joke. But Grimes is one of these chip-on-the-shoulder violent types. Hypersensitive. He likes teasing Dean. Likes bragging right up against the edge of confession. Sympathy for this poor devil will be a hard sell. What jury is going to buy the line that this big Indian—the one who tortured Carl Jefferson for forty dollars worth of crank, the one who thought it might be a good idea to have his five-year-old son watch as he drowned Carl in a litterbox swamped with Wild Turkey and cat droppings—that this dumb chug shouldn't die on a gurney?

Dean drives back to Southeast High, parks his beater in the visitors' lot and steps smiling into the records room. The wall clock points straight at nine. Right on time.

"Marla, it's like you're aging backwards," Dean says. "You get prettier every week."

Marla's wise to his Eddie Haskell act, but Dean doesn't care. He has learned to appreciate the emotional economies governed by the golden rule. There is a cheesy teambuilding poster hanging in his office downtown which outlines, in seven sentences, everything a man need know about human relations. It boils to two words: *Be nice.*

He hands over the standard packet of release forms and follows Marla down to the basement-level file vault. New coat of color on the walls but the carpet hasn't changed. Marla leaves him with the fresh paint fumes, acrylicized air burning at his throat. Dean sifts through stacks of cardboard boxes looking for report cards, hall passes, detention slips, attendance records—anything he can find on Grimes.

He is trying to wrap his mind around the chronology of a life gone horribly off-rail. If Billy had his bell rung in football practice, Dean needs to know. What's this two-week absence in April of his sophomore year? Did the kid have a part-time job? Clock in five minutes late? Break a bone? Get busted for fighting? Ever come down with lice? Mono? Shingles? Was he bullied in grade school? Teased for bad body odor?

He used to get a kind of shot in the arm from this job. Some wrong thing was getting set right. Or so he told himself. But not all things want righting. These kids come stumbling through lockup like the undead. Numbed-out, imprisoned in the present tense, they break bad with adrenal spurts of violence and jinx all the tomorrows to follow.

Bad juju, Wolfman calls it.

Then somebody gets his ticket punched and everyone goes grasping at the past for answers.

There are references in the paper trail to separate medical records administered by the school nurse. He asks Marla if he can see these, please. She could demand an additional privacy release but it hardly ever hurts to ask. People don't know what they don't know, which is a lot, and the net effect of these unknowns is that Dean has room in which to work.

Marla marches into the nurse's office and returns with Grimes's file. Dean remembers to thank her. He scribbles names on columned foolscap for future follow-up: *Authority Figures, Friends, Family, Other.* Everything is photocopied twice, filed inside a bulky accordion-file box labeled: *Grimes, William (Billy, Male)—DISCOVERY.*

"The Public Defender's office really appreciates your help, Marla."

The next-to-last maxim on that teambuilding poster over his desk reads: *"The least helpful word to know in any language is: 'I.'"*

Dean smiles and waves goodbye and says, "We'll see you soon."

23. AURA

She is onboarding a new physical therapy assignment in his private room at Stillwater Medical Center. Her patient is strung up like a marionette, his mangled left leg tractioned in a tangle of wires tensioned above the bed. They have trued the break with a steel rod implanted into his femur, and an angry fluid seeps slowly from the wound site.

Aura reads the third question on her intake form.

"Do you smoke?"

The man looks to the window.

"No ma'am."

Number three gets them every time.

"Nice try," Aura says. "I can smell it on you."

"Old Spice," he says.

This guy's a liar alright—and a big one at that. He must be— Jesus—six-ten? Seven feet? Aura walks around the electric bed and sifts behind a giftshop-bought pot of sunflowers lodged on the window ledge. The cellophane complains, a sunlit crackle. She comes back holding a cardboard pack of Marlboro Reds and a Zippo lighter.

"This must be that new fragrance I've been hearing so much about. *Eau d'ashtray.*"

"That's my property, missy."

"What happened to ma'am?"

"Guess who it was thought up the first-ever no-smoking campaign."

"Don't hate the player, Mr. Porter." Aura pockets the cigarettes. "House rules."

"Mister's for bigwigs," he says. "It's Cecil. Guess."

"Cecil, I believe we need to start over. My name is Aura Jefferson, your new nurse. Your insurance company has hired me to help you recover from . . ." Aura waves to the web of weighted cables, ". . . whatever it was that happened here."

"It was the Nazis."

"We're already to the Nazis, Mr. Porter? How original."

"A nurse. Pretty sure of yourself for a second stringer, aren't you?"

"I'm pretty sure of myself," she says, "period."

She has learned to live with this kind of flippant disregard. White folks in this corner of the world will let themselves get into pretty bad sorts before asking a black woman for help. It's why she drops in on them here, interrupting the autocratic clockwork of the hospital to make that essential first impression. Aura can't always command their respect. But the setting sometimes coerces it, and when she's lucky this semblance of authority carries over to the in-home therapy.

"Not everyone gets a private room," she says. "Somebody must have pulled some strings for you, Cecil."

"Was that a joke?"

Aura tries not to smile.

"Not if you have to ask."

Cecil flares his palms, petitioning the surrounding machinery.

"I feel like a damn meat puppet here."

He says this with an air of injured pride, as if the hospital bed is yet another letdown on a vicious and infinite regression from some remembered height.

"Well I'm here to see if we can keep you from getting into a similar pickle in the future. Once that bone is healed we can start rehabilitating your leg. How long have you been paralyzed?"

"Since before you were born."

"We don't have much to work with." Aura examines the man's lower body. Cecil's musculature isn't just hypotonic; it has atrophied almost to nothing. She can trace the hints of individual bones beneath the paper-thin skin of his legs, the femur and patella and tibia and fibula. The twiglike toes of his right foot have contractured into a simian curl. "Have you been doing any range of motion exercises over the years?"

Cecil shrugs.

"We'll revisit those. It also helps to reduce the friction between your body and its habitat."

"Habitat?"

"What sort of bathtub do you use?"

"I don't pay property taxes on a *habitat*."

"Are you able to wheel your chair directly into the tub or do you use a mechanical lift?"

Cecil ignores her. "Must've had a good basketball team at that nursing school," he says. "What spot did they play you?"

"Cecil, I am on the clock."

"Point."

"Point and two guard."

"Shooting guard. Where at?"

"Langston."

"Langston. There was a redshirt out of there, if I remember. Played swingman for the Pokes a few seasons ago."

"Carl Jefferson."

"You know him."

"It's a small town."

"He flamed out right quick."

"How about you?" Aura says, deflecting. "Surely Mr. Porter played center. What's your alma mater?"

"Oklahoma State," Cecil says. "But I retired at the top of my game, before Iba could get his hands on me."

"Just like Magic Johnson."

"You're pulling my leg now."

"How can you be sure?"

This earns a raspy smoker's laugh.

"Magic made quite a comeback," Aura says. "If you'll allow it, maybe I can help you do the same."

"What ever happened to that Carl Jefferson?"

"Heaven only knows."

As lies go it's a good one, quick and painless, and it has put an end to a conversation she'd rather not have. But it has cost her something. They are both guilty now—each of them equally—of some small and needless deceit.

"A whole mess of Jeffersons over in Langston, are there?"

"You'd be surprised."

She taps three Marlboros from the box, lays them alongside the Zippo on Cecil's bedside table.

"I didn't think you looked German."

"After these it's cold turkey for you, Mr. Porter."

"Don't call me mister."

She can already tell he's going to be the backseat-driver type.

"Why don't we get back to the assessment," Aura says, fieldstripping the remaining cigarettes over the wastebin. "How many of these things would you burn through in a given day, before your recent decision to kick the habit?"

24. BEN

When people dream of Easy Street there is usually a view, some imagined elevation from which things can be more capably overseen. A view like this one, from Ben's offices on the twenty-seventh floor of the Oklahoma Tower skyscraper. He can think, up above the world like this. On a clear day the rustic prairielands south of town threaten to stretch directly down to Texas. The vista packs such punch it has a belittling effect upon even Oklahoma City's vaunted sprawl.

Take the capitol building there, with its two functional oilrigs thirsty-birding crude out of the earth. The workmanlike statehouse, still waiting on its dome after the raw materials were diverted to support the first world war, presides over an ordered urban gridwork reminiscent of Ben's first Erector Set: a scale-model boomtown populated with scale-model buildings and industrious, scale-model citizens and their going concerns.

He is waiting, again, for his right-hand man. And Vincent is running late. Again.

Ben waves a remote control wand at the flatscreen television mounted behind the wet bar and the display surges to life with a plasmatic purr. The smug mug of Crash Lambeau takes shape. The habitually camera-shy radio host is strutting his stuff on some distant soundstage. Trying out a new format, apparently. Look at that Rorschach-blot nightmare of a necktie. Crash pauses in his virtual victory lap to bask in the dittohead war cry bellowing from his well-heeled fans: *ooh-ooh-ooh, rah-rah-rah, Crash!*

"Is this the best-looking audience on television or what?" Crash croons.

A soft knock at the door and Ken Vincent slides quietly in. Ben pours two fingers of Maker's Mark, raises his glass in greeting and says, as if they've been discussing the subject for hours now: "But you know what Columbus's biggest problem was, Ken? After stumbling onto the new world?"

Vincent slumps humpbacked into a chair, looking like a man who's just come through a minefield.

"What in hell to call every damn new thing under the sun. How do you know a jaguar's not just some spotted tiger, first time you see it? Newt and company are in the same boat. They're making such an airtight case against big government, the public is about to send half of Washington packing. But our soon-to-be-anointed Mr. Speaker and Senator Dole and . . ." He wags his head toward the television screen, ". . . mister Majority Maker Lambeau here—in this new world they *are* that big, scary government specter. Crash and Newt are tying their own silver tongues. The situation demands an entirely different vocabulary."

"I'm not sure your analogy holds. Though I see . . ."

"Mr. Bright-and-Early's feeling awful feisty today."

". . . what it is you're trying to say."

"Doesn't hold how?"

"Columbus was trying to describe an entirely new experience. To name the truth. Newt has a simple labeling problem."

"Simple my ass," Ben says. "In war and politics, truth's the first casualty."

"What's the phrase? *In times of universal deceit . . .*"

But Ben waves him off. "Holier-than-thou doesn't suit you, Ken. Spit it out. What's got you spooked?"

"Chambliss has thrown a spoke in our wheel."

"You were fixing it."

"Fixing it." Vincent's mouth withdraws into a pained rictus, the way a dog smiles against the heat. "Fixing it is a few notches above my pay grade, boss."

"How many notches are we talking about?"

"You're looking at a hundred thousand," says Vincent. "Cash." Ben whistles.

"How worried should we be?"

"I think this is real. Something you'll need to deal with, one way or another, before the oversight committee votes next month."

There is a disturbance of some sort onscreen. Crash has ceded the floor to a middle-aged black woman, and she proceeds to give Lambeau an earful.

"Bully!" she shouts. "You are nothing but a big bully!"

Lambeau's having trouble grasping the dynamics of the moment. Here he is, live, on national television. And he's being taken to pieces. Crash blanches. He blinks twice and opens his mouth but nothing comes out.

Vincent worrying at a hangnail.

"Can you take it to the mayor? Have Chambliss kicked off the committee?"

"This close to the election? He'd shoot me as messenger boy. Probably ask us to walk back our own bid for the project coordinator spot, just to play it safe. Terry's not taking any chances with M.A.P.S."

An element of partisan paranoia is playing among Crash's spectators. They're getting involved. Someone shouts down the black woman, saying *how dare you.* Saying *keep it to yourself.* The situation is degenerating. The crowd convulses, a muscular shudder. A woman screams. Lambeau looking like he's seen a ghost.

"Hold on now, folks," Crash is saying, praying for calm. "Let's just settle down."

The studio cuts awkwardly to commercial. On the plasma screen a sexy pitchwoman touts gold as the best hedge against an uncertain future: "Secure your future," she says, "today."

Vincent looks to Ben. "What are you thinking?"

Ben mutes the television set and walks to the window.

"Stop doing that."

"What?"

"Saying *you.*"

Vincent makes eye contact. It seems to take a great deal of willpower.

"Ben. Where this is going . . ."

"You know what I want most of all? The dam. Look at that sad little backwater down there. Just hardly piddling along at all. It took millions of years for the North Canadian to carve its way through this state. In a matter of months we could dam the riverbed, flush it out, fill it up. Give this city a riverfront to be proud of. A dam represents human ambition in the purest, most elemental sense. Earth and air. Fire and water. Working with the soil, it does something to your soul."

"I can't follow, Ben. Where you're taking this, I mean."

Crash has returned to the tube. But the radio jockey is talking to himself now. He's had to dismiss the entire studio audience. The camera closes in on Lambeau's face. A black-box, stenographic typescript creeping across the mute screen, several seconds behind the movements of the man's mouth. But there seems to be a bug in the broadcaster's voice recognition software.

"I HAVE ATTACKED PERSONALY . . . KNOW ONE HERE TWO DIE . . . ," the closed-captioning reads, "TRYING TWO DISCUS . . . INTELLIGENTLY THESE SHOES . . . IS IM POSSUM ABLE. I DONUT . . . THINK ANY ONE SHOULD BE EXPECTED TWO WITHSTAND THESE AND SULTANS . . ."

Ben savors the bourbon's perfect burn. He looks past the plate glass at the flat-line horizon outside. The sun trundling down a wall of dead blue calm. There is this desperado thing building inside of him and nothing in the landscape to argue against it.

"I want to get my hands dirty, Ken."

25. CECIL

Cecil's not even done with traction when that negro nursewoman sets to hounding him.

"The stronger you can be when the doctor lets you down from this trapeze," Aura says, "the faster your rehab will go."

Two-three times a day she's breezing by and high-pressure him into one or another sissified form of toil. Deceptive chores, like tugging at a rubber band or holding a golf ball, each of which reveals some secret defect in Cecil's constitution.

Today she has him holding both arms up. Nothing more. Even so, after almost two minutes of grabbing air Cecil's really sweating it, both arms and his shoulders and entire torso joggling like a bowl of Jell-O.

Aura checks her watch and says, "*Tustenugee.*"

"What?"

"*Tustenugee.*"

"Is that a candy striper's way of saying stick 'em up?"

"You're working hard, so . . . *tustenugee.* It's a compliment."

"I must not be hearing you."

"I used to date a trainer who stretched out the Cowboys basketball squad . . ."

"You date a lot of guys on that team, do you?"

"With a mouth that fresh, Mr. Porter, it's a wonder your breath smells so sour."

"It's Cecil," he breathes through his teeth.

"My diagnosis is those cigarettes. I'll see you clean of them yet."

Cecil doesn't answer. He's really hurting now and doesn't care to show it.

"Anyway. *Tustenugee.* It's a Creek Indian word Coach Sutton throws around," Aura explains.

"I can tell you *all* about Eddie Sutton."

"It's supposed to mean *warrior*. But it's just Sutton's way of conveying anything about the game that isn't easily communicated. If Reeves winds up with a triple double, that's *tustenugee*. If Rutherford takes a flying leap into the stands, inbounds the ball so someone can convert for a three-pointer, that's *tustenugee*."

"*Tustenugee*. Never heard that one. I'll tell you a thing, though. Eddie Sutton is the goofball spawn of Will Rogers and Yoda."

"He's a good coach."

"He's a great coach. But great's not good enough by half and old Eddie knows it. He needs someone like a Reeves, someone like a Rutherford, to pull it all together. I heard him on the radio one time. Eddie said he tries to stack his squad with as many thoroughbreds and as few jackasses as he can find."

Aura laughs and, sensing an opportunity, Cecil lets fall one of his noodling arms.

"You know Sutton has a body language teacher prep him for those press conferences?" Cecil offers. "He's even got a competitive research firm that goes skulking about undercover before the big games. They file scouting reports on the tougher opponents so Eddie can fine-tune his strategy."

"The team has a different game plan for every opponent?"

"Pretty near. Sutton's talking Final Four this year."

"That must be, wow. A lot of work. When I played basketball it wasn't so . . . Machiavellian."

"Eddie doesn't put much stock in the happy accident. He'd probably like to loosen up a bit. Let the kids off their leashes every now and then. But the man came up under Iba. And Iba didn't believe in the concept of free will where it concerned the game."

"That trainer I mentioned, he told me the first thing those kids do when they roll out of bed in the morning is twelve jumping jacks, twelve burpees, twelve sit-ups. Repeat after every meal."

"Those guys eat like seven times a day."

"It adds up," Aura nods.

"Why twelve?"

"Twelve's the biggest number with one syllable. Easier to remember."

Cecil is nodding in agreement.

"Eddie's always wanting to simplify," he says. "He's got this defensive concept. The umbrella. Anytime the other team penetrates the paint, all five men on D are to collapse to the ball." He splays the fingers of his right hand, closes them into a quick fist. "The way you shut an umbrella."

"That makes sense."

Aura still hasn't noticed his sandbagging, so Cecil lowers the other arm.

"It does," he says. "Simple. But it took a few years for them to figure out how to sell the idea. Sutton kept yelling from the sidelines, 'Collapse to the ball! Collapse to the ball!' But it wasn't sticking. Eddie sounded like Louis Armstrong after those games. Plus more days than not the kids were forgetting anyhow. So after a few years of this, one night Eddie brings an umbrella to practice. He's standing under it, looking like Mary Poppins on the basketball court, while the players scrimmage around him. First time the ball bounces into the paint Eddie screams 'Umbrella!' and starts flapping it about like a crazy person."

"I imagine it would be a difficult image to forget," Aura says.

"Watch any of those game tapes and you'll see. Half these boys are mouthing the word 'umbrella' when they collapse to the ball."

"Umbrella?"

"Umbrella."

"Alright, Cecil. Why don't you stick 'em up once more. Then I'll be through with you for today."

Cecil obeys the woman and after a few grueling seconds his arms and shoulders have again fallen victim to that disgraceful quaking.

Aura smiles and watches her watch.

"*Tustenugee*," she says.

"What say we talk English from here on out?"

26. BECCA

She's hand-washing the good china, suctioned to her elbows into pink rubber dish gloves and warm soapy suds, when Ben wanders glumly into the kitchen, checkbook in hand, seeming stumped.

"There's this check in the register . . ." he starts.

"Oh, right . . ." Becca interrupts. "I meant to tell you about it. There's this little boy at the women's shelter . . ."

"Has it cleared?"

". . . and we need a translator to help him . . . wait. Has it what?"

"Has this five-thousand-dollar check cleared the bank yet?"

Becca stops scrubbing and reaches for the dishtowel.

"Why?"

"Because, Becca. This is one sizeable sum of money. You could have given me a heads-up, at least."

"This boy needs our help, Ben. You should see how lost . . ."

"Becca, I'm chasing every red cent to land this deal with Terry. And I wasn't expecting to be ambushed like this. We can't go handing out freebies to every Tom, Dick, and Harry who wants it, or . . ."

"What are you? *Ambushed?* We have oodles stashed in the accounts."

"You'll be dipping into way more than just the walking-around money."

"And since when do you allocate personal money for chasing new business?"

She must have hit him where it hurts because Ben's diplomatic grin comes off strained.

"It's *all* personal, Becca," he whispers. "Every bit of it is."

"Ben, I need this from you."

"Is this, translation—whatever—a one-time disbursement, do you suppose, or an ongoing commitment?"

"I'm not certain. Not yet anyway."

"Well, tell me when you are."

Becca watches him lumber toward his office.

She submerges both hands in the dishwater. Beneath the surface the heat squeezes agreeably around her fingers, an elemental embrace.

27. DEAN

Dean and Wolfman have taken the elevator one floor down to the district attorney's conference room. Cherrywood wainscoting and plush leather wingbacks. Granger, the assistant D.A. on this case, has done the stunt where he shows the victim's family in along the wall of shame, a floor-to-ceiling memento mori wallpapering the outer hallway, mostly push-pinned snapshots of the murdered or missing but the occasional personal effect, too—gold-plated chains and earrings and crosses, laminated student IDs and keychains and other trinkets. Found objects, collaged together in ad-hoc tribute to the unadjudicated dead. Macy calls this "walking the gauntlet" and it gives his team a sizeable home-court advantage.

Opal Jefferson is still trying to absorb the body-shock of seeing her grandson's face taped to the memorial outside. The brittle little woman has settled down for the most part, but every now and then a whimper works itself from her lips. Opal is flanked on one side by Robert Granger and on the other by her granddaughter Aura. Wolfman and Dean sitting across the table from them. Dean's boss wishes Granger wasn't here but the Jeffersons wouldn't take the meeting unless the assistant D.A. was sitting in.

Even dressed in drab nursing scrubs Aura Jefferson is beautiful, tall and dark and lithe. She stares into the air above the D.A.'s veined marble conference table, looking tired. Wolfman has tried to tread lightly so far but Dean can see his boss wants more than he's getting from the women.

"Aura, is there anything else you can tell us about Carl?" Wolfman asks.

"I loved my brother," she answers.

"Of course you did," Wolfman says. "Can you tell us a little about what he was like?"

"He was like a brother," Aura says. "Like himself."

"That wasn't . . ." Dean starts to interrupt, but Wolfman reins him in with an evil-eyed scowl.

Granger drums a ballpoint pen on his legal pad, *rat-a-tattle-tat*. Wolfman goes for it.

"Did you know he dealt drugs?"

Opal weeps, gives herself wholly over to grief. Aura looks at the tape recorder blinking on the table. Her brown fingers are steepled so tightly together the tips have paled nearly to taupe.

Granger pulls a tissue from his herringbone suit pocket and offers it to Opal. The assistant D.A. kills the tape recorder with a finger stab.

"We're done here."

Granger shows the women out, his florid face grave. Dean and Wolfman hang back, and when Granger returns to talk shop he affects a square-john swagger, elbows hiked, high-stepping like a bandleader. His loafers look more expensive than Dean's car.

"Billy Grimes's dream team isn't quite as big as O.J.'s," Granger says, smiling.

"Little pecker like you should've learned by now size doesn't matter," Wolfman says.

"There's still time to cop a plea."

"Our client won't admit to murder."

"That's not what he's telling everyone else."

"Bullshit."

"A little jailbird told me Billy Grimes likes to talk."

"Go fish, Robert."

"You sure about that? Have you interviewed his cellie? What about the other perps in his pod? His detention officer? Trent? My guys have. And Barrett's hair and fiber evidence is going to point right at your boy."

Wolfman cracks his big bull-neck.

"It must be nice," he finally says.

"What."

"Having that black magic to fall back on when you can't take time to stick your case."

"Billy Grimes is going to H-unit and get put down like a dog."

"Under what aggravating factor?"

"Heinous, atrocious, and cruel."

"Kind of a catch-all, don't you think?" Wolfman looks at Dean. "Tell me, if Macy goes on vacation how does forensics know who to finger? Do you clowns take turns? Or is it just Macy gets to play God?"

"There's still time to deal," Granger says, collecting his things. "But our patience is wearing thin."

Back upstairs, in Wolfman's office, Ethan "Dragnet" Podesta is already waiting for them. The liverspotted ex-cop has strewn the Billy Grimes discovery file about the room. Paper covers most every horizontal surface. Dragnet paces meditative laps over the carpet, hands on hips, bloodshot eyes blown big behind Coke-bottle lenses, trying to take it all in.

"So," Dean says, "whodunit?"

Dragnet gathers his evidence.

"I'll show you mine if you show me yours."

Wolfman has established certain procedural safeguards against perpetrating a fraud upon the court. Dragnet's still popular with the rank-and-file police squad and gets the dirty work of determining what has happened. Dean only wants to see mitigation testimony. Dragnet often says Tonto wears blinders. The defense wants to preserve Dean's bright-side mindset long as possible, so until Wolfman gives his blessing the two investigators aren't to discuss their findings. Every bit of data is classified as *attorney work product*, a bureaucratic parking lot protecting it from discovery by the D.A., until Wolfman has had the chance to review it.

Wolfman sidesteps a pile of paperwork to sit groaning behind his desk. The decor is decidedly different down here. Dog-eared bubbles of wallpaper peel from water-damaged baseboards. An assortment of threadbare men's clothes hangs from a coat rack in the corner—navy blue blazers and button-down oxfords, khaki slacks and clip-on neckties. In a pinch this communal wardrobe can civilize an indigent client before his big day in court.

Wolfman swivels his chair around to face the window. Directly across the alley, not ten yards away, the County Courthouse climbs into an ashen hover of cloud cover.

"What's the weather forecast?" Wolfman asks.

"Who's wondering?" Dragnet says.

"Billy Grimes."

"Then a shitstorm is imminent."

Wolfman gives Dragnet plenty of leeway when deciding if something is relevant to his defense. If a sketchball like Grimes wants to play innocent, the men can speak in this crude kind of cant for weeks.

"How'd it go?"

Wolfman mimics the sound of an explosion, big mitts lifting. "Crash and burn. Tell him, Tonto."

"Granger's bragging about a jailhouse confession," Dean says.

"Goddamn."

"Dragnet, I want statements from everyone Grimes has talked to since he's been in County," Wolfman says. "No stone unturned."

Dragnet writes while Wolfman talks.

"I heard a different rumor," Dean says.

"What now?"

"Granger's offered the girlfriend immunity."

Wolfman slumps in the chair. "The flannel-mouthed . . ."

"Maybe Granger's just trying to throw you off his trail."

"We won't know until we do the legwork," Wolfman says. He turns to look at Dean. "How's business on your end?"

"Still tracking down some missing medical records," Dean reports. "Still looking for the parents. Grimes was absent from school a few weeks. Might have been a concussion. Abuse maybe. Both, if we're lucky. I should know soon."

"Our client needs to shut the fuck up. If he's not admitting this, Billy'd better get wise post-goddamned-haste." Wolfman slams a palm on his desktop and howls "Fuck!"

"Jefferson's family?" Dragnet asks.

"We take a self-defense stance and go gunning for Carl Jefferson in trial, it will be hard on them," Wolfman explains. "But we're lucky. No way Grandma can handle the stress of a victim impact statement. That leaves Jefferson's sister."

"Did you see what she did?" Dean says.

"What."

"There at the end. What she said."

"So she loves her brother. So?"

"That wasn't the question."

"I said Aura is there anything else you want to tell us *about Carl.*"

"Then she says, I love my brother."

"You know," Wolfman says, "a perp does that."

"That's something a perp will do," Dragnet says.

"Miss Jefferson has got the qualms."

"What's she hiding?"

"Aura doesn't want to speak ill of the dead," Dean explains.

"It's an opening," Dragnet says.

"It's something," Wolfman agrees. "I swear Tonto, you get any better at this we'll start hiring you out as a dope dog. The narcs sure could use the help. Dragnet, stay away from the Jeffersons until Tonto's done his thing." Wolfman shoots Dean a look. "Don't go it strong."

"Kid gloves."

"And Dean," says Wolfman. "I love you like a kid brother. But don't ever interrupt my interview like that again. Now go get 'em."

Back in his own office Dean fires up the Selectric to transcribe his notes. The type ball whiffles round kissing the page in a staccato series of mechanical snaps. A bumper sticker pasted across the typewriter housing quotes Woody Guthrie: THIS MACHINE KILLS FASCISTS.

Dean has some maneuvering to do.

The head of forensics is a Negro woman named Jane Barrett. Her expert witnessing for the prosecution tends to go above and beyond both the call of duty and the capabilities of modern science. Thus the nickname *black magic*. Even so, the D.A.'s overconfidence is strange this early in the game. It has spooked the boss. The way he went after Carl Jefferson like that in front of Granger. Wolfman tends to wait before doubling down on the murder victim. It smells of desperation.

Wolfman told him once you only win a race to the bottom by refusing to run in the first place. Dean likes the sound of this saying but can't figure how it fits with his daily life.

28. AURA

Anger trims the fat from a man's vocabulary. Diction gets edged, syllables sharpened, subtleties of speech shaved away until all that remains is the flensed thrust of a thing being said.

It's the Sunday before midterm elections and pastor Nate is no longer pretending to parse phrases. The light has gone out of the window over his shoulder. What is left of the stained glass panel there has been battened with naked planks of plywood, a partitioned morning leaking weakly through the board seams. The preacher wears white from neck to toe and as he talks his hands rest in odd blessing on a pair of bricks bookending the pulpit before him.

"Words matter," says the pastor.

From the back pews where Aura and Opal are sitting it is difficult to make out the expression on Nate's face, but his pale summer suit and tie glow with an almost ghostly light against the chancel's variegated darknesses.

"Two little white boys went missing last week in South Carolina. You might have heard of it. Woman name of Susan Smith said a black man stole her babies. Just rode off in her car, she said, with her children still buckled in the backseat."

Opal's eyes have fluttered shut. The old woman's chin nods in an attenuating, trancelike wilt until it has bobbed to a stop atop her breastbone.

Aura removes the hymnal from her grandmother's lap. Opal has been acting puny since her breakdown at the district attorney's office. Aura was practically rabid afterward, angry at that good-ol'-boy public defender and his skyscraping Indian sidekick. Angry with herself for even agreeing to the meeting. Angry at Carl's ghost for getting Grams into such a state. For dealing drugs and for getting away with it for so long and for getting not just killed but tortured.

152

For every boneheaded blunder her brother made since the day he was born.

Before she could drive Grams back to Langston, Aura fled to the district attorney's toilet, hid there whispering a blue streak for ten full sacrilegious minutes, trying to compose herself. Just remembering it Aura feels her pulse knocking fast and loud against her insides. So loud it's a wonder anyone can hear the preacher speaking.

"Now I've been around the block a couple three times," Nate is saying. "You can stir the rhetoric with a stick in that last run-up to election. Who remembers Willie Horton?"

The pews shake with unanimous, grumbled complaint. Nate raises his voice above the fray.

"That was a lowdown dirty shame. Just a hateful perversion of free speech. They trotted out Willie Horton and his weekend pass I thought: There can't *be* a thing worse than this. But I'll tell you what," says the pastor. "I was wronger than wrong."

The preacher's teeth catch and release the light, a Cheshire-cat flash.

"There's people will say *anything* for a shot at running this country. Let's take this Newt character. The one's been hawking his Contract with America on all the talk shows. The one who looks at a big, beautiful crowd of black people like we have sitting here and sees instead a bunch of *welfare queens* on the *dole*. Driving their *Cadillacs* down to the corner store for more of that *barbecue*."

The general sense of bedlam intensifies. Nate turns it up a notch.

"Now when Mr. Gingrich heard about Mrs. Smith's loss he was understandably upset. We all were. So maybe Newt wasn't in full command of his faculties when he opened his mouth. Said this tragedy was caused by a *sickness* in society. A sickness, he went on to say, that he could cure. But here's the catch: everyone has to vote Republican on Tuesday!"

Someone says, "Oh no he *didn't!*"

The preacher is almost shouting now.

"Or maybe mister Newt was taken by fear. Fear of that big black *bugaboo* carjacked Mrs. Smith. That'd scare any man. Maybe this dismay made Newt start speaking in tongues. So when he said this whole thing was the fault of Lyndon Johnson's Great Society—everyone here knows it—social security, war on poverty, Medicare, Medicaid, the civil rights acts."

Nate grips the bricks with thick fists.

"Might be that was just some confused bit of word soup Newt was serving up. Maybe Mr. Gingrich would tell us he's *sorry* if he were here today. But Newt can put his sorries in a sack. It's not the thought that counts—it's the deed. Mr. Gingrich's words make waves here in the real world. Some concerned citizen heard those words. Then decided to launch a brickbat or two through our stained glass window."

Pastor Nate lifts the blocks overhead so everyone can see. A name is chalked across each brick face: one reads SMITH, the other SIMPSON.

"I figure this person watches too much Court TV," pastor Nate says. He lowers the bricks with a kind of tenderness, the way a father might handle an infant, and when they are laid back to rest the pulpit resounds with a subdued *bukka-boom*.

"A few days back Mrs. Smith admitted killing those boys. All by herself. Said she popped the parking brake and rolled that car into a lake. Wanted to make herself more appealing to some fella didn't want a ready-made family." Pastor Nate draws a breath and says, "Mr. Gingrich is using your grief, ladies and gentlemen, to advance his own career. Newt's taking you for a ride. Just like Susan Smith took those policemen for a ride. Just like she took those two little . . ."

The preacher's hands whip away from the bricks as if he's passing off a hot potato. He retreats into the deeper shadows backgrounding the pulpit and whispers something no one can hear. Opal is breathing soft snores beside Aura.

"Lord help me," Nate says, wringing his fingers. "I haven't been this angry in I don't know. Feels a little like dying. Please forgive me.

Please . . ." He returns to the pulpit and says, "Let's all bow our heads in prayer for those poor boys. Michael and Alexander Smith."

A hypnic jolt lifts Opal awake in time for her to hear the preacher's call for prayer. She utters a heartfelt "Amen!" and starts to stand. Aura hands her grandmother the hymnal and guides her smoothly back into a sit.

The whites of pastor Nate's eyes cut to Opal.

"That's right, Mrs. Jefferson. Amen doesn't have to mean we've reached the end." The preacher smiles, bashful, as if embarrassed by the simplicity of his epiphany. "Sometimes it means we're just getting started."

29. BEN

"People think action equals character," the preacher is saying. "But action isn't the half of it."

This is one of those earnest sermons, the kind with typewritten notes and drawn-out pauses, and it is threatening never to end. The topic is Babel Tower, and deep down Ben knows he'd better be listening or Becca will have his hide. But he has other things on his mind. Like where's the mayor gone to ground?

"If we read Babel closely, we find that character is the product of three things: community, communication, and yes . . ." yet another pregnant beat from the preacher, ". . . imagination. Imagination precedes action. You can't *do* a thing without *imagining* it first."

Ben scans the nave, head-hunting the assembled congregation for Giffords's distinctive salt-and-peppered pate.

"But Babel also serves as a warning of sorts. Someone has this idea: let's build a tower straight to *Heaven!* Let's make *a name* for ourselves! This same someone brings everyone together. He explains his scheme. He makes things *happen!* But the original plan behind this whole enterprise, it isn't a group kind of concept. It's some-*one's* idea. A selfish idea. And this is the sin."

Bingo. Terry has parked himself by the side exit doors opposite Ben's own column of pews, four rows up.

"Mankind's divinity is implicit in collective action. Listen to what the scripture is telling us. At Babel we were organized: one people, one language, one purpose. *Godlike.* The Lord took notice. He was impressed. But what did we *do* when we all gathered together at Babel? Did we cure cancer, or hunger? Did we press for world peace? No. We idolized ourselves. We tried one-upping our Creator."

Ben tries flagging down the mayor on the sly but a preemptive pinch from Becca sends tears to his eyes. He suffers the preacher's speech in compliant silence.

"Babel says expand your perspective. Don't just think about your future. Take your neighbor's future into account. Don't just imagine. Imagine together." The preacher thumps his notes and proclaims, "None of us is as powerful as all of us."

Ben is on his feet almost before the benediction has been uttered, sidling through the pews in pursuit of Giffords. The mayor and his wife have already slipped out. Ben bobs and weaves through the throng of fellow well-to-doers, begging off the small talk, hot on Terry's trail. As he elbows through the crowd Ben can hear himself making excuses: *Let's talk next Sunday, Chad. Karen, you're looking good enough to eat! Give Becca a call and we'll all get caught up. Larry, where have you hidden your better half?*

Ben finally buttonholes Terry alone on the church steps. It's a sullen Sunday morning, cool and misty and close, and the mayor is shivering as he unwraps what looks like a lollipop.

"You did not," Ben says.

"Carol keeps finding ways I can be bettered," Giffords explains.

"Big Tobacco will miss you."

The mayor rolls the lollipop on his tongue and the stem pinwheels crazily about his mouth.

"What did you think of the sermon?"

"I thought it wath thwell," Terry says through the candy.

"He was getting awfully Eastern Bloc on us today. I hope the preacher isn't switching sides on us just two days before the election."

Giffords removes the lollipop. "I haven't yet had the chance to thank you for that 'turning the tables' campaign, Ben. When those TV spots started running it was as though I'd shot Gould with a silver bullet. He and his liberal monkey-wrenchers still haven't recovered."

"Glad to hear it, Terry. So then, after Tuesday, there's nothing standing between the mayor and his Metropolitan Area Projects?"

Giffords laughs.

"Something always rears its ugly head."

"I hear your oversight committee is getting closer to making its recommendation."

"You heard that, huh? I wish someone would keep me in the loop."

"Any idea where they're coming down on this?"

Giffords chipmunks the lollipop in one of his cheeks. He crosses his arms and bounces on the balls of feet.

"You think it might rain a week from Thursday Ben?"

"What?"

"I've never been very good at forecasting the weather, myself."

The mayor curls both eyebrows, putting on a look of such dedicated ignorance Ben almost wants to console the poor guy. He has seen the expression before. These types learn it in civil servant finishing school and it means the discussion is done.

"We're not so different, Terry," Ben pushes. "I don't know much about the weather. But I'd bet money you had some doubts about that sermon today. A little esoteric for people like you and me. When everyone has a say, nothing worth hearing ever gets said. Maybe I ought to be talking with Gary Chambliss."

"Simmer down, Ben. I can't go gabbing about M.A.P.S. until after the committee makes its recommendation. It wouldn't be seemly."

Ungrateful prick.

"Especially with our lovely wives here to fetch us home," says Terry.

And here they are, Becca and Carol Giffords, whispering intimately down the church steps for their men, a perfumed vision of pink taffeta and white cashmere that seems to lighten everything about this grayscale day but Ben's black mood.

"Don't forget about me, Terry."

"Church is out, Ben." Giffords claps Ben on the nape of the neck and gives a collegial squeeze. "Let's pick this up over lunch next month."

Giffords greets Becca with a kind of curtsy before spiriting his wife off to the parking lot. Ben and Becca watch them go.

"You left me in there all by myself," Becca says. "You know how I feel about that."

"I'm sorry. I needed to talk with Terry."

"Promise me it won't happen again."

"It won't happen again."

Becca balls her fingers into a fist. She punches Ben in the shoulder.

"Ouch!"

"Promise me, Ben."

Ben rubs his shoulder. "I promise."

30. CECIL

"Where does it hurt?" Aura asks.

Cecil touches his breast just below the collarbone. "Here."

He's been home two days now, sorting junk mail, and the task has kinked an indispensable muscle in Cecil's chest. He'd arranged for a few things to be forwarded to him in the hospital: the bills, his *Orange Pride* alumni newsletter, *Sports Illustrated*. The important stuff. But yesterday, after some nurse forklifted Cecil down from the cripple cart his insurance company made him ride home in, they ended up having to put considerable effort into prying open his front door, what with the weeks-deep drift of paper piled below his mail slot.

Aura walks around his rig and wraps him up from behind in a kind of chokehold, pressing her palm upon the offending spasm.

"Here?"

Cecil hisses.

Aura has her answer. The fingers of her left hand play along the ridges of Cecil's spine, wander to the hollow below his shoulder blade, gently prod at a golf-ball–sized knot there.

"Think of pain like a stick of dynamite," she whispers. "A fuse has been burning for a little while before the thing blows. The real source of your problem . . ." Aura's prodding grows more aggressive, the hand on his breast bearing down, until a circuit of grief arcs from the bother above Cecil's heart clear through to the tic in his back, ". . . is here."

Cecil doesn't want Aura to see him flinch but he does it anyway.

She eases up, her fingers by turns feather-light and a merciless firm. He can feel her breath blowing hot in his ear as she rubs out the knot.

"You're all catawampus," says Aura. "In the front, your chest and arms are overdeveloped. This pulls everything forward and stresses the

160

superficial muscles in your back. The weak link is your infraspinatus muscle . . ." another rough embrace, another shot of pain thrilling through him, ". . . right here."

Cecil groans.

"What's so superficial about my, inter-fera-spin-whatsit?"

She laughs beneath her breath and releases her hold on him.

"Not a thing that can't be fixed. We'll get you back in balance, strengthen your deltoids, your lats, your traps. And Cecil," she's standing over him now in her hospital scrubs, wiry arms akimbo, "you'll need to stop it with the cigarettes. I won't waste my time coming here if you keep lighting up behind my back. You smell . . ." Aura fakes a frown, a brown hand batting back the surrounding air, "like a roadhouse. Where's your stash?"

Cecil adjusts his good leg—the other one's still braced—and rolls to his window to study what remains of his basketball hoop. A slow skein of geese winging silently south under a soggy sky.

"Do you still play?" he asks.

"I do," Aura says. Then, almost as an afterthought, "It's a way to forget."

"It's the opposite for me. I haven't held the ball in a coon's age." Cecil shakes his head. "Makes me remember."

"Tell you what." Aura moves to the window and stands beside his rig, staring out at the driveway. "Let's shoot for it."

"For what?"

"For Cecil Porter quitting smoking. Cecil wins, Aura stops henpecking. Aura wins, Cecil goes cold turkey."

"It's the little end of the horn either way. And cold turkey's no good for me."

"Then we'll work something else out. But you'll quit."

"Assuming I lose."

Aura laughs.

"Oh, you'll lose alright."

"Someone doesn't mind strutting her okra."

"You'll be wanting some time to train."

His sly smile.

"Not too long, if we're shooting free throws."

"Free throws it is. Why'd you stop practicing?"

The smile slides from his face.

"Do you have brothers?"

"One." She eyes him sideways. "One little brother."

"A little brother's tricky. Tricky to know. I can remember feeling responsible for mine, even after this," Cecil gestures at his legs. "Then Ben, this is my little brother . . ."

"Not *so* little."

"So you've met him then."

"This is the great big one who arranged your private room?" she asks. "I've heard the other nurses chatting about him."

"Funny because all I see is the chubby little nosepicker Ben used to be. A kid, who's always trying to care for me. Or always trying to want to. But the big lunker's too blind to see things as they are. Which is that he's the one has his priorities mixed up. Which is that he's the one needs help. Not me."

"Why don't you tell him?"

"It's not so simple."

"Someone told me once it takes two men to make one brother."

"I like that."

"Yours might require a few more, big as he is. Though I always wondered why they don't say the same thing about making a sister."

In all his born days Cecil hasn't spoken to a black woman like this—at length, and with such emotion—and the experience leaves him feeling impoverished. As if Aura has accepted, maybe even taken, something that wants giving back. "You're about to tell me to stop being a hater and such," he says. "Forgive and forget. That kind of thing."

"Not at all." Aura's own faraway grin. "Hate away."

31. BECCA

Caleb's mother has been arrested after testing positive for crystal methamphetamine. The boy isn't exactly processing it well. What's worse, he'll be taken into custody by Child Protective Services in less than an hour. Becca hears all of this while standing in the doorway to Joanne's office. She is looking for a safe place to set these four bags of leftover Halloween candy, but Joanne and Dean won't stop talking at her.

"Maybe you could play with him for a while until the woman from CPS gets here?" Joanne asks Becca.

But, she thinks, but wait this can't be right because I haven't even taken off my pea coat.

". . . sneaking around and lushing out, probably, with her old set."

"Dean, she doesn't look well. Becca?"

"She'll be fine. Where's Abigail?"

"How should I know?"

Becca drops the candy atop the deranged paperscape of Joanne's desk. She shrugs the pea coat from her shoulders and hugs it into a bundle.

"I'm fine."

"There you have it." Dean looks fit to be tied. "Is Abigail coming in?"

Joanne *yawps!*, her entire face tautening into a Phyllis Diller grimace.

"She's *your* colleague, Dean . . ."

"Friend."

"So can your friend be here inside thirty minutes?"

"I need a phone," he says, storming out.

Joanne relaxes.

"I don't know why he won't just go in there and talk to the boy himself."

"Dean speaks Choctaw?"

"I'm sure of it."

Becca fishes through her purse for the five-thousand-dollar check. "I found the money to pay Abigail."

"Wow, really? How? Where?"

She's drowning and this coat is her only hope. Becca's clutching it like a life raft. "Does it even matter now?"

"You're only partially right, Becca, to think that. Things do get more complicated after today. Any access to Caleb will have to be approved through the state-appointed guardian. And we'll need Willa's explicit permission. Prison doesn't take away your parental rights. But these are just speed bumps. The money was the real hurdle."

Becca shuffles from Joanne's office in search of Caleb.

They play Candyland in the conference room so no one will be watching. But no matter how hard she tries Becca can't find a graceful way to let him win. She defers at first, skipping whole turns or tiles, but Caleb is too attuned to her every move and won't have it. After being on the receiving end of one too many mute little frowns Becca stops sandbagging and plays the game for keeps. Guess he'd rather earn the defeat than be given the win and who wouldn't? She beats him five times in a row before the woman from CPS arrives and for several days after Caleb has vanished through that door Becca can still feel the tug of him, going.

32. DEAN

"They should sterilize these dirtbags at birth," Dean says.

"This is your idea of foreplay?" Samantha asks.

"Or make them take a test."

"Oh . . . *my* day? It was *fine*, dear. Thanks so much for asking."

"The parental fitness exam, they could call it."

"How do I love Dean?"

"With a multipart essay. Letters of recommendation. All of it. Like trying to get into college."

"Let me count the ways."

"*Tell us, in one thousand words or less, why you feel qualified to reproduce.*"

"I love him most of all when he's angry." Sam screws her face into a pout. "That cute wittle face he makes."

"Euthanasia could work."

"His fighting face."

Dean rolls onto his side and rests his head on the pillow.

"Tough problems call for tough solutions."

"This is how the big man fights," Sam says. "Not realizing he's already laid out. Flat on his back."

Dean waits for her to take the bait.

"We've been together awhile."

If she takes the bait he gets the upper hand.

"And we will be together a long time from now, too."

But she's going to keep him waiting.

"You will stop grousing around about this. We will have babies and . . ."

"Babies."

". . . and we will grow old together. Old and gray, as they say. We will die in *this* bed," she scoots in close to take both his hands.

"Like this. Holding hands. Creaky, arthritic hands. Surrounded by our babies. And our babies' babies."

"Babies plural."

"There will be lots of babies."

"One little two little three little Indians?"

Dean tries rolling away but she straddles him, pinning his arms under her knees.

"Do you want to argue the pros and cons, Mr. Goodnight?"

"Not really."

"Then do we want the angry sex now?" she says, bussing him roughly on the lips. "Or the makeup sex later?"

They pick the angry sex, urgent, bent only on the goal. But some sort of wonderful happens partway through and it turns into the makeup sex anyway. The shape of her desire softens under his touch. Yielding, melting, taking him in. The apartment breathes curtains out into the chill, the pale fabric dancing in the November dark. Dream-slow, indistinct, like the memory of how curtains ought to move. A train whistles in the mournful distance and in those final trembling moments Dean finds himself stifling an urge to cry out.

Afterward they lie tied together in the sheets, zebra-striped by streetlights banding in through the casement panes.

"So we've come to an understanding, then," he says.

"Speak for yourself. I came to three of them."

33. AURA

Aura surrenders her ballot to the lockbox and steps down out of the polling station into the sparkle and fade of freshly fallen twilight. A row of streetlamps stutters to life, freckling the OSU Family Resource Center in weary spheres of light. Just a few faces remain queued at the doors, the last of the body politic waiting to get inside and get out the vote. She slow-walks the parking lot for her car, skirting the floodlit ground in a sidewinding path, making a game of it. A cold front has moved into town and the air is tanged with woodsmoke and ozone, leaf mulch and diesel. The deep-nasal burn of synthetic rubber and pigskin. It's a smell outside of time, pensive and prescient in the same instant. The smell of basketball season, just around the corner.

She's reaching for her keys when a voice calls "Aura!" and jumps her heart up thumping someplace behind her throat. Nate Franklin steps out of the night, looking good in faded jeans and a camelhair sport coat. A DayGlo orange sticker stuck to his lapel announces: *I VOTED!*

"You even dress down nice," Aura says. She pops her jacket collar against the chill, pretending everything's copacetic. "How about that turnout?"

"Looks like folks are voting early and often. You look hungry."

"Sneak up on me like that again and I'll show you what angry looks like."

"I could eat a horse all by myself. Let me buy you dinner?"

"It's the least you can do after giving me such a fright."

"It's a date, then."

"Call it what you like, long as you're picking up the check."

They decide on a seafood place hard by the university, one of those gimmicky franchises where the chef fishes your dinner still wiggling out of a bubbling showroom aquarium, and as they consider the merits of the various lobsters waving from the display tank all she can think is: *We who are about to die salute you.* She lets the preacher in on the joke and they share a not-so-guilty laugh about it, deciding finally on the bug with the biggest claws of the bunch because, packing a pair of pincers like that, surely he's done something to deserve it.

The booths are jam-packed with belt-buckled cowboy types and farmer-tanned college kids, many of them sporting the same over-bright sticker as Nate, who does his best with the topical small talk—who d'you like tonight and so on—as if either of them could vote for anybody but Keith, the Democrat, whom they both admit doesn't stand a snowball's chance against Istook.

After a second awkward pause, which extrudes a few too many beats into her comfort zone, Nate lowers that bottomless voice of his even further and asks, in a gleeful whisper, "Do you feel it?"

"What?"

"That spark."

"I don't believe in all that."

"You don't go in for love at first sight?"

"Only in fairy tales."

Nate sizes her up a moment.

"Yep. You're feeling it alright."

"Is this why pastor Nate left his last church? Run out by the womenfolk who got tired of being pestered?"

"This has nothing to do with my being a preacher. Nothing to do with religion or faith or politics or any other abstract philosophy found on God's green earth. Unless it's chemistry. Because this right here is about a man and a woman fixin' to fall in love."

"You certainly cut straight to the chase, Nate."

"On a date, see, a pastor's always guessing how long he needs to fake interesting."

"There's a concept you don't seem to be embracing. When you are paying for the meal . . ."

"Right."

". . . you don't need to."

"Got it."

In the neighboring booth a mutton-chopped beanpole of a man and his grade school–age daughter face one another across their food. She is perched with perfect posture at the very edge of her bucket seat, baby blues combing the sundry surfaces of the dining area. The man does not wear a ring. He is hunched over his clasped hands with the fatalistic patience of the single parent, resigned to yet another evening utterly lacking in adult conversation.

"I-spy-with-my-little-eye something that begins . . . with . . ." the girl says.

Nate watches Aura watch their game, listening.

"P-T-O-T-N."

The girl turns to her father and waits.

"That's cheating," he says.

"No!"

"Too many letters."

"Daddy. Get real."

"I cry uncle."

"People. Talking. On. The. News."

She performs a self-satisfied flourish, finger-pointing to the television cantilevered over the bar's mirrored liquor display, where Wolf Blitzer and a crack team of CNN newscasters are offering close-captioned commentary on the election-night tidings.

Intrigued by the preacher's nerve, Aura turns back to Nate.

"Why me?"

"Well, I tried hitting on your grandmother first," he deadpans. "But Opal informed me she was too young to be dating a pastor."

His smile is tremendous, contagious, delicious.

"I think you're beautiful, Aura. Why not lay it right here on the table?"

"So this—*spark*—you're feeling. Where have the symptoms been presenting?"

Nate laces his fingers above his heart in a hopeful and supplicant way.

"I know a decent cardiologist at the hospital," she says. "I'll introduce you."

"You're dismissing this as just another facet of handsome pastor Nate's quirky personality."

"The preacher has reverted to the third person again."

"Don't dismiss it."

Though the pastor's diagnosis is accurate, Aura still finds herself wanting to object.

"I'm here, aren't I?"

"And I'm glad of it."

"Let me try to understand this spark of yours. You think I'm pretty and . . ."

"You can say that again."

". . . that this equals some basis for a romantic relationship?"

"It's more than physical."

Aura laughs.

"You don't even know me."

"I most certainly do. You are a kind and caring and attractive woman who worked her way through college and then nursing school." The preacher ticks off traits on his outstretched fingers as he talks. "You drive thirty minutes every Sunday to care for your elderly grandmother Opal. You help people cope with the worst injuries of their lives. You help people back into the world. You set a pick like nobody's business."

"You heard all of that at the potluck."

"Right before Opal told me one day I'd make some lucky lady a good husband."

Aura slumps her head in mock mortification, mumbles into the tablecloth, "Nobody knows anybody, Nate. Not really."

She can tell from his voice that Nate's grinning again. "You're a healer, Aura. Don't try and deny it."

A waitress delivers their dinner of hard shell lobster and king crab splayed on a bed of rice pilaf and steamed Yukon potatoes. They crack into it one heat-blushed extremity after the other and before long their hands and faces are greased with a sheen of clarified butter. When Nate sucks the meat from a demolished crusher claw Aura says, "You're not showing any mercy."

"I maybe should have played the first date a little safer," Nate confesses. "There's really no way to eat crab claws and come off looking like a gentleman."

"Don't worry." Aura licks her fingers clean. "You're looking just fine from here."

Aura's having a good time and why shouldn't she be? Nate is funny. Gainfully employed. And tall. She could probably get away with wearing heels. Plus that ass in blue jeans looks like it's been chiseled from a block of granite. Aura imagines taking him home. The things she could do to pastor Nate Franklin. A single word and he's hers. But it's never so simple as all that, is it? Being a woman. In the awkward choreography of the first date—and they both understand this on some unspoken level—Aura's dancing lead. That one little word might invite him into her bed, but it also initiates a whole sequence of stumbling evasions. All those morning-after missteps.

Her gut says take it slow.

When the hostess shows a lumbering threesome of midnight basketballers along the well-trafficked path to the bar Nate excuses himself to drop by and say hi.

The father in the opposite booth has signed the check. As he reclaims his credit card the man's eyes wander up from the wreckage of dinner, surveying the room one last time.

"I-spy-with-my-little-eye," he says to his daughter, "something that begins with . . . ess."

"S?"

"Yes."

The girl leans back into the booth's button-tufted headboard, pale eyes tightened to slits. She cranes her neck up and around, searching. "*Seiling.*"

"That's *see*, not *ess*," the man says. He notices Aura watching and offers a complicit wink. "C-E-I-L-I-N-G," he spells to the girl.

The girl looks to Aura. Back at her father. Over to a poster hanging on the wall.

"*Seafish*," she spurts. The poster shows two fishermen netting a catch of salmon from a roiling sea.

"Close."

"*Sailor.*"

"No."

"*Sailors.*"

"Nice try."

"*Sailboat.*"

"No."

"*Ship.*"

"No."

"*Storm.*"

"No."

"What are those black fish called?"

"That's not black."

"Do I know what they're called?"

"I don't know," he says with a slow smile. "Let's find out."

"That's black."

"It's not," he chuckles. "It's some shade of gray. Or silver. But not black."

The girl points at Aura and says, "What color is she?"

The smile fades. The man straightens in his seat, gives Aura an apologetic shrug of the shoulders, says, "She's brown."

"How come everyone says she's black?"

The man reddens. "Let's talk about this in the car." He scoots from the booth and says, "Time to go."

But Nate has just returned and for the briefest of blundering moments the three of them end up tip-toeing around one another in the too-cramped gangway between tables, left then right, back then forth, everyone trying not to intrude on someone else's personal space, until Nate finally beats a retreat back to the bar and the family has enough room to pass.

Nate settles into his booth with a riled-up sigh.

"That guy was keyed up, now."

"It was nothing, really." Aura sneaks a peek over her shoulder. She and Nate watch the man stoop into a whispered caucus with his daughter.

"What's going on there, do you think?"

Aura turns back to Nate.

"They're teaching each other how to see."

34. CECIL

In the beginning she visits three times a day. Don't mind me, Aura tells Cecil, I'm just here to observe. She watches him dress, follows him round the house. Watches him eat and shit and brush his teeth. Watches, even, while he washes and inspects his flimsy body parts. He sets the egg timer as always, tries getting about the day as if she's not there. But everything takes more time since the latest mishap. There are new textures under his fingers, a braillework of wounds he hasn't yet learned to read.

His days are measured in lunkheaded therapies. She works him over with a set of industrial-strength exercise bands. Shows how to tie the rainbow-colored hoses around his doorknob and use the handle grips for resistance training. She demonstrates wall climbs and overhead stretches. Installs a horizontal bar in the garage and has him do self-assisted chin-ups from the safety of his rig. She puts a journal by his bedside table, expects him to record his calisthenics for her review. Fixes that carpet, tells him stop trying to be an interior decorator.

They play basketball every third day. She watches his pathetic attempts at shooting and doesn't say a critical word, thank God.

"Forget everything you know," she tells him, "because we're starting over."

Get your shoulders under the ball, she reminds him, something Cecil knew from before but hadn't remembered to do. She makes him shoot left-handed. When he complains she tells him this isn't just fun and games.

"We're trying to build both sides of your body," she explains. "Just do it."

She grocery shops, stocks the refrigerator with foods he'd rather not eat without a clothespin on his nose: broccoli and fish and liver

174

and onions. They fall into a workable rhythm. There are reverse fly pulls and arm raises. Shoulder rows and pendulum swings. Those girl pushups he can still accomplish, plus dips and curls and a crossways endeavor called partial wood chops. She helps clean the bloodstains blackening his bathroom floor. Says you're lucky, people your age don't get many accidents like this. Helps him order a robotic swing set of sorts for the bathroom, the better to get him into the bathtub. But he puts a foot down, so to speak, when she recommends a motorized wheelchair.

He aches in places that don't have names. She lays him out flat on his back, kneads at the knots in his arms and neck and shoulders and chest. Fixing one gripe only seems to aggravate another. She is remarkably careful with his legs, lifting and twisting and tugging and pushing, trying to build a cushion of muscle mass back into his paralyzed limbs. These are slow and difficult stretches and he knows he'll never be able to accomplish them on his own.

"The hook," she pronounces, "is your best chance from that chair."

But he won't give up his set shot so easily.

She turns the house inside-out looking for his cigarettes. He says his every move doesn't want superintending. She tells him it does until she says it doesn't, or until his insurance runs out, whichever comes first. He asks when do I get time off for good behavior and she says first you'll have to exhibit some. When she leaves for the day he rolls down the ramp into his garage, sits smoking behind the workshop curtain there, his hands playing over sheets of textured and colored glass, thinking how good it is to be home.

He begins to anticipate the sound of her car coming down his driveway, the crunch and pop of tires over gravel.

If you ever suggested he'd be taking orders from a woman—a black woman, no less, and under his own roof—Cecil wouldn't have been shy about recommending where you shove the opinion.

Yet he gets a little better every day.

35. BEN

He's being tested. Half past two on Thanksgiving afternoon and Becca's making Ben take a test. Or rather, she is grading a test he has already taken. One of these chronically empowered types from the women's shelter has imposed a self-help book upon them and Becca's been behaving strangely ever since.

Becca looks around the edge of her book.

"What did I just say?"

Ben fingers a sky-blue table runner spilling out of the cardboard box resting on the end table.

"There's something about this color that brightens my spirits."

"That's not an answer."

"Blue improves my mood."

"Most people would disagree with you."

"You want me to be like most people?"

"You're stalling."

"You said the Choctaw translator woman thinks this little boy has some sort of speech impediment or oral retardation. Hopefully he's just messed up after seeing what he did. You said if the shelter would allow it you'd bring him home and live with us which, by the way, don't even think about it. You also said you'd be driving down to Antlers and visit your Aunt Mabel to talk about these daydreams."

Ben beams, pleased with his performance. Thirty-nine-odd years of marriage has perfected this capacity for instant recall. No matter how far his mind might have wandered Ben can stop, rewind, and parrot back every word Becca has uttered in the last thirty-or-so seconds. The skill has saved his skin more times than he cares to remember.

"I almost had you."

Becca buries her nose back in the book: *The Five Love Languages—How to Express Heartfelt Commitment to Your Mate*. She is lying on the couch in her reading glasses, scoring Ben's answers to a quiz which—the dust cover promises—should solve the various problems plaguing her marriage.

"I'm liking this whole hot-for-teacher thing you're working today," he says.

"Shush."

"How'd I do?"

"The jury's still out. Go upstairs and get the next box."

Ben does as he's told, traipsing up the staircase and along the hallway to the attic. Beyond a narrow plywood landing where the holiday decorations are kept, rafters rise in shadowy crosshatch out of a pink blanket of insulation delicate as spun sugar. The kids, when they concede to make the long trek home, still call this the unfinished room. Ben's breath comes hard and fast in the cotton-candy quiet. Five more boxes to go and he's not glad about it. Turkey Day in the Porter household has always promised a brief amnesty from the diet or exercise decree of the moment. After a guilt-free day spent stuffing himself with sweetmeats, Ben looks forward to an afternoon in front of the fire watching America's Team grunt the football down the field in Dallas. Maybe get his glow on with a nice single malt. Until this year, that is. After lunch, when Becca asked him to unbox the Christmas decorations, a sinkhole opened in his gut. Talk about gluttonous interruptus. He'll be lucky to tune in for even the last quarter of the ball game.

Normally Ben would already have started needling her, wheedling his way out of anything resembling a chore. But Becca isn't herself today. Or lately. What with the Neverending Remodel From Hell going on in the backyard and the kids away and this new internship at the battered women's shelter.

It was odd the way she wrote that check without even asking.

Ben knows he's being evaluated. She's using this relationship test as an excuse to get things off her chest and so, at least for now, he's leaving it lay.

He wrestles a box down the stairs and into the kitchen, reminding himself not to bellyache. But when he sets it on the granite countertop a St. Nick statuette breaks through the cardboard to poke him in the kidney, provoking a wounded whimper.

"Don't hurt yourself."

"Too late." He walks into the living room. "So did I pass?"

"Your love language, Benjamin Porter, is *words of affirmation.* Which, as you refuse to stop talking, makes perfect sense."

"And yours was . . ."

She frowns.

"*Touch.*"

"Okay, so this one's easy. We just need to make like rabbits and have lots of sex. Then you tell me how great I am in the sack."

Her laugh tells Ben he's still got it.

Back in the kitchen, he pours himself a drink and, despite the pain in his side, indulges a shit-eating grin. The midterms were a rout, and a Pokes fan doesn't get to revel in an utter skunking like this very often. For the first time in four decades the *Geeee-Oohhh-Peee* is calling the shots in the House. The morning after the election Ben was glued to the tube. He couldn't look away. Gingrich and Dole on the Capitol steps with their fabled contract, Republican lawmakers fanned out behind them in a human victory rip so poetic Bob Dole broke character and betrayed something approaching actual, human emotion. D.C. is even lauding Crash as some kind of right-wing rock star. Word on the Hill is, come January, he'll be inducted as an honorary member of Congress.

But the best part—the most important part of all—is Terry Giffords's landslide of a win over that push-button liberal Gould. After Ben manages this situation with Chambliss, he should practically have the mayor in his pocket.

He had damn well better.

Back in the living room, ready for a break from manual labor, Ben hoists Becca's bare feet, slides under them onto the couch beside her, starts kneading those toes.

Becca closes her eyes and allows a relieved sigh.

"Go easy on Cecil tomorrow."

"Becca. It's the Great Alaska Shootout. The first real basketball games of the preseason. Cecil won't let me in the door if I don't come bearing a six-pack. I hope that nurse of his isn't there. Cecil says she's tough as a drill sergeant."

"Your brother's not as strong as you think."

"He's stronger."

"He's only just home."

"You remember that time Cecil hurt his shoulder?"

"Ben."

"Hold up a second. Remember it? They had to give him surgery. Well he never would tell me how it happened. But I finally got it out of the doctor who operated on his arm. Turns out Cecil's low on firewood. But he doesn't want to hire some kid to rick it for him. So he rolls that chair out into his field, starts chopping down scrub oak with his axe. Now I have seen Cecil's axe. It's hard lifting that thing with two hands. But Cecil was out felling trees with it one-handed. I swear I'll never . . ."

"Ben," Becca's eyes are open. "Don't talk."

He doesn't.

Becca's toes wiggle in his lap, teasing, closer.

"*Touch.*"

Ben does as he's told.

36. BECCA

She had forgotten about the prison, erased any trace of the place from her memory. But the roadside sign brings it all back:

NOTICE: PRISON FACILITIES IN THIS AREA.
DO NOT PICK UP HITCHHIKERS.

The Oklahoma State Penitentiary in McAlester. Her forgetting it hasn't made the jail any less of a fact. Straightaway she remembers being driven by the site as a child and asking Mabel why that big white castle had so many fences around it.

"This is where they put the badmen down," her aunt had said. "That tangled-up razor wire might look like tumbleweeds but it's called *concertina*, it's what keeps the convicts from running too far."

There had been that school field trip. And the social studies report on *Crime and Punishment*. Then those awful riots in the seventies. The state pen.

How was a lapse of this magnitude even possible?

She might have misremembered about the prison, but the saw-tooth profile of the Ouachita Mountains is too picturesque to forget. You just can't see this kind of scenery in the city. All the motley colors of creation spilling like a cornucopia across the earth. Rolling foothills lined with pine and high cedar. A ghostly smolder of mist lifting off the river in the precise autumn light.

Becca is driving this morning to her old hometown of Antlers in southeastern Oklahoma. Paying a visit to her aunt Mabel to discuss this recent rash of strange memories. Becca had brought them under control for a time, the spells. Or so she thought. Until Willa Busby was arrested and Child Protective Services took custody of Caleb. Then the daydreams came haunting, even worse than before.

She has yet to see Caleb since they took him away. So far Abigail is the only visitor CPS will allow.

She decelerates down the off ramp and hooks a left onto Main Street. Three years since the last visit. Her aunt was always a collector of gimcrack and as Becca pulls into Mabel's breezeway it is a snug comfort to see how little things have changed. The house still has the higgledy-piggledy sprawl of a chawbacon pawnshop, with gilt-framed objets d'art and reclaimed furniture shrapneling out the front door to bunch on a covered sunporch. The yard is contained by a sagging chain-link fence hung with antique farm tools arranged according to one of Mabel's ever-evolving taxonomies: hog tamers near the sheep shears, muckrakes commingled with monkey wrenches, branding irons beside hand scythes.

The blue-haired woman who answers the doorbell seems creased beneath the weight of her eighty-some-odd years. Becca holds up a bow-tied cakebox filled with homemade sugar cookies.

"I brought your favorite."

"Becca! You were always such a wizard in the kitchen. Come in here and sit a spell."

Her aunt plods inside with the periodic deliberation of a wind-up toy, drawing to frequent stops so that she might recharge her aging motor and chart another decrescent vector through the house. In this inch-wise way Mabel leads them from the foyer to the hallway niche to the hat rack and finally on to the kitchen stove, where she begins boiling water for coffee.

Becca slides into her favorite seat, catty-corner to the head of the dining table. The view from here has the same backdated appeal as that from the curb. Every shelf teems with odds and ends: spineless cookbooks, miniature porcelain figurines, a rusty pair of tinsnips. A family of hand-lacquered Russian nesting dolls waits patiently on some imagined breadline; a Betty Boop wall clock vamps above Mabel's microwave.

"It give me a fright when I heard the door chime," Mabel says. "How could you be sure I was home?"

"How far could you go?"

Mabel laughs.

"At least I've avoided needing the walker."

Her aunt dismisses with the standard palaver—the *oh dears* and *let me get a gander at yous* and *you haven't aged a days*—and Becca realizes she's as quick-witted and sharp-tongued as ever. Even so, Becca has to stifle an urge to offer assistance as Mabel carefully ferries each steaming mug of coffee over to the table. Before eating, Becca says the prayer aloud, the version she and Ben have adopted, and when she gets to the bit about *forgive us our debts* Mabel clucks her tongue.

"You ought to spend more time worrying on your trespasses than your debts, dearheart."

"Oh Mabel," Becca says. "It's good to be home."

They share a laugh at that while sweetening their drinks with Becca's sugar cookies, dipping the holiday designs incrementally into the bitter brew until the surface is crumbed with colorful floaters of frosting. When the talk finally falls off Mabel fixes Becca in one of her full-frontal look-sees.

"I owe the pleasure to what?"

"Well, it's like I said on the phone," Becca starts. "I haven't been sleeping. Nevertheless I've had dreams. There is this door, an enormous red door. And I'm alone in a house. It's a horrible, sudden type of lonely feeling. But it's not this house, though, in the dream. It's a strange one. And . . ." Becca grasps her aunt's hand. "Tell me again about what it was like before my parents died. Did we ever own a house with a red front door on it? There's something . . . I'm hiding from myself, or not remembering properly."

"We always agreed your parents died in the flash flood," Mabel says.

"Eli drove over that low water crossing," Becca nods. "The truck was washed away, with him and mother in it."

Mabel does this queer little fidget, retrieves her hand and sits back to gather up the neck of her housedress, cagey.

"Your mother Deborah would have fawned over you, eventually. I'm sure of it. She would have changed. But when it came to his heart, your daddy was some kind of Indian-giver. A pretty new thing caught Eli's eye, he'd let her have more than his affections. I know for a fact there's bastards all over this county on account of ole' Eli's wandering eye. I can't count how many times I told her throw that man over! But does Deborah listen?"

It was a rhetorical question, but apparently Mabel requires a response.

"She doesn't listen."

"That's right. She never does listen."

"What about the red door?"

Aunt Mabel reaches back across the table to press Becca's fingers into her own. "Your parents were in love, honey. At least in the beginning they were. Your daddy charmed the bobbysocks right off my little sister. Eli Cain was a handsome devil, that's for sure." Mabel laughs but there's little mirth in it. "All her friends were crushing on him. He was older by three or four years. Deborah was a junior in high school when she had you. Dropped out after they'd eloped. But they were just kids, Becca, much too young to handle the stress of a newborn. Understand?"

There is a paralytic dread spiking up Becca's spine. Because she's not crazy after all. Because her visit hasn't been for nothing. Becca says that, yes, she does understand.

"You were born in, what, thirty-five? Prohibition had only just ended. And your parents, they were wild, dearheart. Yard dogs running loose from the chain. Eli had it bad. Worst I've ever seen. He'd get lost in the bottle, disappear for days on end, come awake two counties away in someone's drunk tank. Sometimes he'd be bloodied and bruised for weeks after a bender. Pretty soon Deborah was drinking almost as much as he was. It breaks your heart, doesn't it?"

It does.

"Sometimes they'd let you stay over at my house so they could head out of town and get roostered. Everybody here was wise to Eli. That pair'd show up Sunday morning looking just absolutely torn to pieces. This city's mighty tightknit, and when the people in it peg you for a certain sort of person, well, that's who you are and there's no changing it. Eli and Deborah were always pushing the limits, always talking about getting out of town. But he couldn't hang on to a job any longer'n a few months. They tried cleaning themselves up plenty of times. Went to services at the Church of Christ. But he couldn't stay on that wagon."

Tick—Betty Boop blinks—*tock.*

"I should have been more forceful. Gotten some help for your momma. But I didn't." Mabel looks trapped. "This doesn't make me a bad person, does it?"

As Becca consoles her aunt she realizes there is a point to these seemingly pointless rhetorical pauses. Mabel isn't soliciting input on her story but rather trying to recruit Becca, somehow, into its performance. Hoping it will become *their* story in the offing.

"One night Eli and Deborah borrowed Yardley's old pickup—Yardley is Eli's brother and he didn't have any use for that truck. Anyhow he was out of town. They drove over to a honky-tonk bar in Idabel. This was a school night, you were in kindergarten, must've been six but only just. They tucked you snug in your bed then went out. Deborah didn't even call me to babysit. Eli got guttered up enough he crashed that pickup truck into a creek on the ride home. Flipped it upside down. They only found the bodies after Yardley came home six days later and went looking for his truck. I guess he thought Eli had stolen it because Yardley called the sheriff. Your parents drowned that night, Becca. But there wasn't any flood."

"Why didn't Yardley come by the house first?"

Mabel draws a deep and trembling breath.

"He did."

"But, where was I?"

"You were at school, honey. By the time the sheriff found you, Becca, you'd been bathing yourself, feeding yourself, walking down to that bus stop on your own for nearly a week. Just going about your business as though nothing could be more normal than this . . . *waiting*. You'd wake up, make some cereal, close the big red door of that damned rat trap your folks called home, take the bus to school. Spend all day just normal as could be. Then bus it back to the house and make yourself some kind of dinner. Wondering when Deborah would get back home."

Aunt Mabel is crying.

"Six days you did this. Yardley came by, the door was locked, he figures you and your parents have left on a road trip. But you must have been at school when he came by. So you've been cooking practically since you could walk. I'd just graduated from college myself and was teaching math over at the school. It made sense you should move in with me. After that, whenever anyone talked about it, we left out the bit about Eli flipping his truck. We just blamed it on the flood."

"The flood that never was."

Mabel's head lolls, a mea culpa bobble. "I hoped you'd forget. It's why I never left any photos of Deborah lying around the house. I wanted you to put this horrible mess behind you."

Becca retrieves her hand. The coffee has gone to slush in her cup. Mabel scoots her chair back from the table and totters into the study. When she returns it is with a framed print depicting two teenagers happily baffled by a sepia noonday sun. The boy is cadaverously thin, with a scrimpy peach-fuzz moustache and a sidewise smile. The girl could be a younger version of Becca. Or her daughter Sarah.

"This is the last picture of your parents." Mabel relinquishes the picture frame. "It was taken a few months before the crash."

"They're so young."

Mabel sleeves her eyes dry.

"I've always dreaded this conversation. But I feel relief, now it's here. I do. A secret, especially with a child, it's easy at first. A baby asks about Deborah, I can just go on about how my sister used to make me cry with laughter. Talk about the good times and hopscotch over the bad. But something like this, it only gets heavier with time."

Betty Boop's infernal tattle: *ticktock-ticktock-ticktock-ticktock*. Becca swallows a compulsion to hurl her parents at the wall clock.

"Thank you for telling me."

"Love is the four-letter word spells 'the end' for many a good woman."

✤

The pressurized drive back to the city Becca can hardly see the highway for all the crush of memory. Everything comes pummeling back, every pent-up moment vivid as life itself. The whiskey on mama's breath and papa's sandpaper stubble. Mama in her pajamas dancing a foxtrot along the dry-goods aisle. A muffled ruckus after bedtime, that out-of-whack laughter and the bottles going *clink!* in the night. The glassy-eyed smiles and the brushfire smell of a smoking cigarette and the pink, blinking solace of her nightlight. The loneliness of that bus stop and the front door of her old house, closing.

That red damn daydreamt door. Always closing.

It isn't safe to drive in such a punch-drunk state and so she stops in McAlester to find a tenable center for her thoughts. She parks near the jail and it is exactly as she recalls, not a whitewashed brick out of place. The helical tumble of barbwire on the prison lawn shimmers so sharply under the sun she wants to avert her eyes. She imagines the fence as a swirl of tinsel, it's not so large a leap, decorating one of Mabel's antique doll houses.

Concertina wire.

What a pretty name for such an ugly thing.

37. DEAN

Opal and Aura Jefferson have stopped returning his calls. It's time the kid gloves came off. So they're making a shoe-leather trip to Langston, on through Stillwater, Dean poring through the Grimes file while Dragnet drives. Hoping to scare up statements in assist of Billy's defense.

After the Guthrie turnoff Dragnet quiets the car stereo and says, "How'd you get into this, Tonto?"

Dean has been thumbing through birth certificates and hospital records, affidavits and school transcripts, job applications and time sheets. Eyewitness testimony and circumstantial evidence dredged from the misbegotten world. And the thought dogging him, as he rifles through Billy's life, is that fate has a certain dumb momentum to it. That we are simply vectors of raw power and possibility, hurtling along the edges of a few numbered days. Always in danger of crashing headlong into some opposing force and getting bounced out into the void.

"You know these kids we defend," Dean finally answers, "sometimes it's like watching one of those nature shows on PBS. Every one of them born into fucked-up families. I mean. Every. Single. One. Parents high or gone missing. Neglectful. Or feral. Like those bears that eat their young. And our clients with their spindly little legs and big doe eyes, trying to keep up with the herd. Let's bet on who gets to the end of the episode without getting eaten for lunch."

Dragnet clucks his tongue. "That's some kind of answer."

Dean folds Billy's case file closed and watches the world glide by the window.

"Wolfman stopped me from killing someone."

With one thick finger Dragnet adjusts his retro G-man spectacles, nudging them farther up that gin-blossom nose of his.

"*This* I have got to hear."

"I'd been on a two-day drunk."

"I can't even picture that. Honest."

"I was leaving some honky-tonk south of town, walking across the parking lot, when this cowboy gets in my face. When the fight got going, I hit him in the throat. He dropped like a sack of meal. But I wasn't done. I hit him again. And again. Again. I was maybe two beats shy of killing the poor guy—and he was just a kid, hell, we were both kids—when Wolfman tackled me. A few drunk punches away from winding up just like Billy Grimes."

"No way, Tonto. No way you're anything like that punk. I've seen into him."

"Wolfman gives me his card. Tells me come visit when I get sober. Which I do. Second time I see him Wolfman's offering me a job."

"Killers are made," Dragnet begins.

"Not born," Dean finishes.

"Wolfman recites it like catechism."

Dean cracks his knuckles and stretches his arms above his head. "Any luck on your end of discovery?"

"The case is crow bait. Let's just say Wolfman will need to lean on your mitigation findings. Any luck finding the parents?"

"None."

"Friends?"

"None."

"Well. Our boy is pretty well fucked."

Dean reopens Billy's discovery file. In it are photos of Carl Jefferson's mangled and naked body lying upon the coroner's slab. Snapshots of assholes and pubic hair and cloying, blue-black hemorrhages. A strained death grimace preserved in 35mm precision. These images tend to linger in the mind's eye. Seeing them, Wolfman's doctrine can be a difficult one to get behind. Dean feels complicit, at times, in the crimes of his clients, eyeing these pictures. As if he's violated some private trust.

"You want to know a funny thing?" Dean asks.

"Always."

"On my life, I can't remember what that cowboy said to set me off."

38. AURA

Aura locks her front door and takes the apartment complex steps three at a leap until she's made it down to the street. It's hard to imagine better weather for a run, a brisk-but-not-bracing forty-three degrees beneath a blue flight of sky and not a cloud in sight. As she stretches her legs on the Bermuda-grass devil strip fronting the sidewalk Aura can sense a certain pulse in the December air, an exhilaration. Tonight the OSU Cowboys basketball squad will tip off against Texas–Pan American in Gallagher-Iba Arena, one of the first home games of the season, and the neighborhood is charged with that infectious, hive-mind kind of hopefulness particular to a college town on game day.

"Miss Jefferson?"

It takes her a few seconds to place the big Indian standing curbside. Jeans, gray sweatshirt, threadbare running shoes. From the public defender's office. The quiet one. Dean something. Inside the sedan idling a few feet behind him sits a potbellied, salty-dog type in thick plastic glasses, napping under a partially read newspaper.

"It's Aura."

"Aura, right," he says, coming closer. "Dean Goodnight. That's my colleague in the car. Ethan Podesta. We met at the district attorney's office? Would you have a minute . . ."

"Mr. Goodnight, I'm . . ."

"Dean."

"Dean, I'm on my way out." Jogging away, her words trailing behind, "Why don't you give me a call?"

"I've been . . ."

"Maybe we can find a better time to talk," she shouts over her shoulder.

Aura carries a miniature spray-tube of mace threaded to her keychain, and easing into her gait she swings the thing noisily against her palm like a metronome, keeping time: *ka-jingle, ker-skrrink, ka-jangle, ker-plink.* Before long she hears an irregular footfall approaching from behind. Dean Goodnight pulls alongside, matching her stride-for-stride, breathing easy even in blue jeans.

"Persistent," Aura says.

"Might as well kick out the frost before driving all the way back to the city."

"Tell you what. See if you can keep up. We'll talk after."

They run. She steers east, away from the university. As they cut past the railroad tracks a siren grieves above the cross-town traffic, a diminishing shriek, and in the subsequent stunned silence all Aura hears is the mechanical regularity of Dean's shoes crunching gravel at her back.

"Your team is doing pretty well so far this season," Dean says.

"You try not to get your hopes up. They manage to throw the big games pretty much every year."

She admires the way this guy moves. He's a brawler type. Headstrong. Like a boxer only bigger. But, all that bulk, surely she's fleeter of foot? Despite the stitch in her side Aura picks up the pace. They cruise past a strip mall scattered with fast-food restaurants and hardware stores, out into the flatland expanse of copper-toned farm tracts surrounding Stillwater. Aura leads them in a roundabout loop away from town. The distant phonics of the city serve as a kind of soundtrack to their own private contest: a train's homesick whistle and she seems to be running out of gas; four impatient foghorns from an eighteen-wheeler and her second wind comes kicking in. At the cemetery she digs deeper, giving everything she's got, but Dean just keeps keeping up, plugging away beside her with efficient, blank-faced grace.

After four or five miles they have come full circle. When her apartment complex hoves into view Aura decelerates into a walk, hands clasped over her head, sucking air.

Behind the wheel of the idling sedan Podesta seems to have risen from the dead. The investigator sits smoking a cigarette and reading the newspaper. When he spies Aura and Dean a practiced concentration warps into his brow. Podesta lowers his paper, watching.

"So," she fills her chest with breath, "you're," another lungful, "a runner."

"Off and on."

Dean's sweatshirt sags with a damp choker of sweat and his jeans look drenched a darker hue of blue, so why does she get the sense the big man seems hardly to have exerted himself?

"Let's walk," Aura says, leery of Podesta's intense surveillance. "I need to cool down."

She leads him to a grade-school playground where a couple of coltish kids are playing HORSE on the blacktop basketball court, all lanky legs and gangling elbows. Aura sits on a park bench to check her pulse, fingers behind her jawline, and says, "Shoot."

Dean sits next to her. As Aura watches the children play she can sense Dean reading her, deciding how to proceed.

Ninety-seven, ninety-eight . . .

"I'm sorry for your loss, Aura," Dean says. "But I have a job to do. We were in Langston today, Podesta and me, and I . . ."

The very thought sends Aura's jugular spiking.

". . . was hoping to talk with you or your grandmother about the trial. But Opal wasn't home."

"Anything you want to ask Grams," Aura seethes, "I can answer. Leave her out of it."

"Normally I would. But someone needs to start returning my calls."

"Fine."

"Okay. I'll call that progress. After the trial, before sentencing, the district attorney is going to ask you and your grandmother to give a statement describing your feelings about Carl. What his life and death meant to you, personally. This is called the victim impact statement."

"They've already asked."

"It's the last thing the jury will hear before the prosecution rests."

Aura removes her fingertips from the breakneck cadence at her throat.

"When was the last time you spoke with Carl?"

Aura doesn't answer. From behind the three-point line one of the boys looses an arcing sky hook and when it sails cleanly through the hoop he launches into a robotic sort of breakdance, popping and locking his joints in incremental, slow-mo celebration.

"Why do you think your brother chose to be in that motel room?"

The other child on the basketball court tries and fails to re-create the break-dancer's sky hook. The first boy stops his gyrations to sign a giant letter *O* with outstretched arms.

"Listen, I get it," she says. "You have a job to do. You're looking for answers."

Dean's body language changes. He leans in, hunting.

"Why are you still angry with your brother?"

Aura rests both elbows on her knees. She looks at her feet. Her shoelaces are peppered with sandburs.

"I saw you in that conference room. You and your boss staring knives at the prosecutor. Him glaring right back across the table. You know what I think, Mr. Goodnight? That this is just a pissing match between boys. Why don't you all just get it over with? Pull them out and see whose is bigger?"

Dean relaxes back into the park bench.

"Billy Grimes deserves an impartial defense."

"You really believe that."

"A life spent in prison is no picnic."

"He killed my brother, Dean. Tortured and murdered my baby brother."

"Thirty years in McAlester and Billy Grimes will be *praying* for the death penalty. Kids like Billy don't adjust well to life behind bars.

The ugly in this kid's heart is going to grow and grow and keep on growing. It will eat him from the inside out. And trust me, Billy doesn't have what it takes to kill himself. I've met him. Death's too good for Billy Grimes, Aura. You tell the jury this and they will listen."

"What if he gets out?"

"There's no getting out."

"All you care about is winning."

"Maybe. But if I win, someone lives. If they win, someone dies. From where I'm sitting, picking sides is simple."

"Is it?"

It's Dean's turn to keep quiet. They watch the game of HORSE.

"I've got to be honest . . ." he starts.

"How big of you."

"My boss is going to make Carl look bad in that trial. Anything he can do to save our client."

There is a sudden uncertain . . . she doesn't know what or why . . . compulsion to fight or flee that keeps her from answering, and this conversation has jammed that cheerful frequency she felt earlier, wrung the vitality clear out of the day.

But the boys laughing on the playground couldn't care less as they bang tirelessly away at the backboard, lost in the moment.

"Killing Billy won't bring back Carl," says Dean.

Aura stands and walks away. It's everything she can do not to run.

39. BEN

The river ribbons through the bottomland shadow, dusk-lit, a quicksilver sliver. A slushy squall blew through Canton this afternoon and the dark-dripping trees now seem crouched against the failing daylight. Hint of winter in the air. Ben pulls his overcoat close, cups his hands, blows a bird whistle to warm his fingers. A songbird sounds from across the sandbar, then another, a territorial call-and-response ringing cheerily among the idle earth movers hulked nearby.

No chance they'll be spotted here. After kickoff on a Sunday in December? Forget it. He told Chambliss the drive to the construction site would take an hour but it's really closer to two. Ben wants his councilman unbalanced for the meet. He is thinking, for some reason, when Chambliss's white Seville pulls into the Dirt Devil yard, he is thinking about carte blanche. *Rick's Café Américain* and those all-important letters.

The package in his coat pocket dragging on him like a sinker weight.

The storm was a real clodbuster and the worksite is now gluey as flypaper, swamped with standing water and syrupy red clay. Ben has parked his SUV near the front gate and hiked to a rise overlooking the cut-bank drop down to the waterline. Chambliss parks his Cadillac and waves but Ben ignores the councilman, who tries lightfooting it through the mud to Ben, hoping to keep his composure. But despite his contortions the man ends up sinking and sliding and sucking through the muck anyway.

"Have you ever watched *Casablanca?*" Ben asks, by way of greeting.

"What?" Chambliss pants.

"The movie. Humphrey Bogart, Ingrid Bergman. The bug-eyed guy, whatshisname . . ."

"Peter . . ."

". . . Lorre, right."

"Sure. Who hasn't?"

Chambliss burrows into his coat, hunkering against the wind, and kicks the clay from each of his feet with a fastidious, wet-dog shimmy.

"So, these letters of transit. There's a movie term I think, means the strawman at the heart of a good mystery. That offscreen thing worth killing over. Unknowable. And ultimately irrelevant to the real story we're paying to see, the human drama. Hitchcock coined the word and on my life I can't remember what it is."

"Wish I could help you there."

"It's not important."

"But I will say this. I don't appreciate getting called out onto the prairie."

"And I don't much like having the bite put on me."

Chambliss smiles.

"What's that you got in your pocket?"

Ben breathes in the peat-bog stink. His passions produce a somatic sort of residue: anger inflames his joints, anxiety tends to bunch in the tendons of his neck, gloating bloats his balls. Right now he's experiencing all three emotions at once and the result is a ropelike twist of gut pangs approximating hunger.

"We'll get to that soon enough. First I want you to explain to me why we're standing out here in the mud when we could be sitting at home watching the football game."

"Ben . . ."

"Gary, I'm working with a delicate trigger today."

Chambliss straightens into his salesman's stance, really turns on the charm.

"Say there's a man in this town wants to make his mark. Wants to be a public figure. What's the first thing he does? Well if he's a student of history maybe he decides to go into government. But let's just say the government this man studied over at university is a far cry from the government he ends up working in. Statecraft . . . in a textbook statecraft makes sense. But bureaucracy, government by and for the people . . . it's like driving the short bus in a NASCAR race. Because the people, Ben, is a goddamn retard gone off its Ritalin. The people wants one continuous show, debate and discussion ad nauseum. Nothing is too inconsequential for its gaze: Earth Day resolutions and keys to the city and sister cities in darkest Africa and meanwhile nothing—nothing of real import, anyway—is ever getting done. Can you imagine? Day in, day out, for twenty-three years?"

"You're dancing around it. I want you to call this what it is."

Chambliss ignores him.

"Well let's say this man wakes up one day. Looks around at who's making moves in this city and spies someone like yourself. Here's a guy sees something he wants—he goes out there and gets it. And doesn't just get it. Takes it! Well. *This* man standing before you is impressed. Moreover, this man can help. He happens to be holding something you desperately need. The veritable golden ticket. And he's willing to surrender it. In exchange, all this man's asking is an anonymous cash donation into his new exploratory committee . . ."

"Exploratory committee."

"The time is ripe for my moving up from city council. I've had my eye on Giffords's seat."

"You'll need to chew that a little finer for me."

"Listen, Ben. It's simple: you scratch my back, I scratch yours. This donation . . ."

"Donation?" Ben spits. "Donation's just another dodge."

"It can't be your first time to this rodeo! Twenty years from now, look, this whole town will be brand spanking new. Nothing will be the same here after M.A.P.S. All because of you, Ben. Because of Dirt Devil. You're about to make hatfuls of money here."

Ben makes a fist and releases it. The night is falling hard on what remains of the silver-plated day. There is a bit of eternity happening all around him. No matter how many times he witnesses it a sunset still commands his awe. Something in that folded brightness, something about second chances.

"And no mistake," Chambliss says, "I want in on the action."

Ben mines his pocket for the package. But his brow must be etched with some sinister tell because Chambliss suddenly retreats furiously through the mud, slip-sliding away, backpedaling in actual fear.

Now he remembers: *MacGuffin.*

Ben lifts the shrink-wrapped brick of cash from his overcoat.

"Fifty thousand," he says. "The rest after the vote."

Chambliss re-collects himself. He crabwalks to within spitting distance, dares a closer look, extends his palm for the payoff.

"It's been a pleasure doing business with you, Ben."

But Ben is already tugging back the package.

"Just one more thing Gary."

"What's that?"

Ben turns sharply back to the river, away from Chambliss. One last fuse flares along heaven's edge and then, just-like-that, the light is gone. He stands pat, shoulders held high and wide.

"I want you to scratch my back."

40. CECIL

"You're taking notes?" Aura asks.

"Criminy," says Cecil. "We're really doing this part of it?"

She bounces the basketball on his concrete slab driveway and bends into a frigid wind.

"Because school's in session."

He puffs into his cupped hands, warming to the trash talk.

"Don't go choking now. I can't do the Heimlich on you from this chair."

Releasing the free throw she suddenly freezes, arms upraised, trophied with anticipation against the treeline, as the ball falls threshing through the net. Then she's boogying back to earth, hands a-clap, dancing a celebratory hip-hop slide step.

"Stop, drop, and roll . . . Aura's on fire!"

"Good for you." Cecil lights a Marlboro. "Only twenty more of those to go."

Aura retrieves the ball, incredulous.

"What do you think you're doing?"

"Free country." He blows a hot fog of smoke Aura's way. "You haven't won it yet."

High noon under a sky flanneled with low-floating snow clouds and they're both suited up in sweatclothes, playing for keeps, trying to decide whether today's the day he gives up the habit. A boom box bleats folk music from his porch. Cecil tried tuning to talk radio earlier but when Crash got rolling Aura complained of psychological warfare tactics. So she dug a Tracy Chapman cassette tape from her car and now they're listening to this hippie woman warble on about civil disobedience.

"This revolution business sounds like a lot of work," Cecil says about the song.

Aura ignores him, prepping the next shot. She air-balls it, missing the backboard entirely, and the ball skitters to a stop in the driveway's graveled approach.

"Did someone leave the barn door open?" Cecil asks. "There's a draft in here."

She jogs laughing to the basketball, bends and scoops a bounce pass over to Cecil.

He snares the ball with his left hand and flicks the still-burning cigarette into the ice with his right. Rolls for the throw line, dribbling timidly. Licks his lips against the cold, leans back into the rig, empties his head of everything but that hoop.

Nod twice and shoot, wait to hear the crisp whisper of nothing but net.

Goddamn that feels good.

She is waiting for the ball beneath the basket.

"How long have you been licking your lips like that?" Aura passes back the rock.

"Long as I remember." Cecil twirls the pigskin on his palm, seeking the sweet spot with his fingertips. "Back when I was playing, when I was *good*," he offers, unsolicited, "I remember thinking this game was as close a kid would ever get to flying."

She's staring hard at him now, funny-like.

"It reminds me of someone."

He dribbles once and tries going empty again. But Cecil can't resist the opening.

"Is it your mama?" he says before firing the free throw.

The ball flies way wide, walloping the concrete slab and ricocheting sky-high with a shrill, vulcanized peal. For a delicate second or two they stand stunned, the both of them, wondering if his last joke has gone too far.

"You keep laying down bricks like this you'll have built another house before we're through," Aura cracks back.

"You talk a mean game, missy. Sure you're not related to Reggie Miller?"

"I've got your number, old man. See Cecil thinks he's fly, like Larry Bird."

Aura's slowing her breath and toeing the line, bending into her stance, surrendered to preparatory rituals committed to muscle memory since childhood.

"But this white boy right here can't even jump," she says.

Aura dribbles, shoots, scores.

"Pretty slick. For a girl."

"Oh no you *didn't*." Aura rolls her head and shoulders with a put-upon, homegirl swagger.

"You get tired of throwing like the big boys do it just let me know. I'll allow you to fall back on granny shots anytime you need the rest."

She rebounds her own ball and tosses off another quick bucket. Three more—she's getting into her groove now—then it's his turn. When he misses, Aura mimes the international sign for choking, eyes bugged, clawing silently at her throat.

Cecil lights another defiant Marlboro, happily fuming.

"That's right, smoke 'em if you got 'em," she says. "It's almost quitting time."

A storm is fussing up when she finally beats him hollow, twenty-one points to his twelve. But even those paltry goals have fagged him out more than normal. Gripping both wheels and rolling hard for the house he is forced to pull up short when a fresh tension grips his right shoulder. Aura notices, coming over to take his chair by the handle grips.

Steering him up the ramp, she is blessedly, respectfully silent.

"I may have overdone it," Cecil admits.

"It's my fault," Aura says, pushing him inside. The house is warm and still, a meditative counterpoint to the endless, blowing ruction out under the sky. "Let's loosen up the kinks and ice you down before I go. You'll heal faster that way."

She helps transfer him into the unmade bed. Cecil sits awkwardly, trying to wriggle out of his sweatshirt, but even the simple act of crossing his arms seems an extravagant form of torture.

"Lay back and let me help," Aura says. "You're only making it worse."

Grudgingly, he gives himself over to her expertise. She undresses him slowly, completely, taking care with the injured shoulder, the recovering leg, the catheter. He was shy the first few times she saw him like this. But his frequent disrobing is a kind of prerequisite to the physical therapy—Cecil jokes he drops his drawers more than a Playboy bunny—and they have reached an unspoken agreement not to be fazed by his promiscuous nakidity.

Aura gives him a quick sponge bath, spot-checking he hasn't hurt himself during the game. His femur has healed past the point of needing a brace, but the upper thigh is now girdled by a purple, ridged scar. Aura covers his privates with a bedsheet and begins manipulating Cecil's rotator cuff, draping the forearm across his brow, probing into the soft tissue of his armpit with dark, tenacious fingers.

Her thumb explores a sore spot.

"Your leg is looking better."

"Looks like roadkill from where I'm sitting."

"Only because you haven't seen worse. Try to relax."

"If you'd leave off tormenting me . . ."

"Close your eyes," she orders. "Imagine you're in flight. Like you said outside."

"Where did this come from? The Jonathan Livingston Seagull school of new-age medicine?"

She probes again, cruelly, hard enough he has to suppress a flinch. "How about the Black Panther school of shut your trap and let me do my job."

So he does, closes his eyes and surrenders to her knowledgeable hands, and soon he's daydreaming, listening to the increasingly inclement wind tick and scritch and scratch among the bare tree branches out of doors. Aura's inquisitive fingers pressing, prodding, compressing the corded muscles in his back and neck and scalp. She clasps his temples and squeezes. A red starburst of discomfort blooms behind his eyelids, followed straightaway by a pin-prickly, bittersweet relief.

He is remembering Ellen. Those long hot naked showers. How she'd soap him up and tease every inch of his skin with her genie fingernails.

"Looks like you might have some . . . ah, Cecil . . . swelling here."

"Okay, well," still shut-eyed, "take care of it then."

A flurry of nervous laughter.

Cecil opens his eyes. The coverlet draped across his crotch has swollen straight toward the ceiling.

"Is that . . ." he asks.

"It is."

Cecil peeks beneath the sheets. His dick is huge—a happy, quivering tent pole. He can't remember the last time he saw an erection.

"Look at the size of it!" he says proudly.

"It's not the size of the knob . . ."

"I know, I know. It's how you handle it."

They laugh so long and hard Aura starts fretting he might fracture a rib.

41. BECCA

Having made up her mind, the first thing Becca does after walking into Passages—she's not even on the schedule today, it's Christmas Eve after all—is drop by Joanne's office unannounced.

"Holy cow! Becca," Joanne says, rising from her chair, "you look great! Did you get your hair done?"

Becca jumps in with both feet.

"How would one go about adopting Caleb Grimes?"

Joanne sits down frowning.

"Why don't you close the door."

"I'd rather to leave it open if that's okay."

"How would *one?*"

"This isn't an entirely hypothetical exercise."

"It hadn't better be. You'll need to be absolutely sure before getting into something like this. There's more red tape than you'll see on a Valentine's Day float. What does your husband think?"

Becca hasn't felt so strong in years.

"Let's worry about Ben later."

There's no way to know the future, Becca thinks. But she can know this, she can and she does: there's no going back.

BIG COUNTRY

WINTER 1995

42. DEAN

The barroom windows are steamed with excess body heat when Dean finally arrives at the Cock O'the Walk. He shoulders through the tail end of happy hour, baby-stepping through the carousal. Inching closer to the pool tables he can see the last minutes of a basketball match glowing slowly from the big screen, Oklahoma State at Kansas State. Staples and Dragnet are pressed against the jukebox, waiting to quarter into a game of doubles, but the boss is nowhere to be seen.

Penned in amidst the table-squatters, thinking about leaving, Dean feels something tug at his coat sleeve. Wolfman is drinking alone at a two-top trashed with empty beer bottles and shot glasses, not six inches off Dean's elbow, wide mouth working.

"Say again?"

"Justice is a blind, mother-loving-goddamn-bitch," Wolfman yells.

Dean wrestles the sole remaining seat in closer to his boss. He drapes his coat over the chair back, sits, and barks into the din.

"Have you ever defended a client that was innocent?"

"I've never defended one who deserved to die," Wolfman barks back.

"Negative pregnant."

Wolfman signs V-for-victory with two thick fingers. There is a high-wire kind of stiffness in this gesture, the inebriated vigilance of a man determined not to fall out of his chair.

"Two?"

"I am sure," says Wolfman, "only of two."

"What I wouldn't give to pull an innocent. It would make the rest of it seem bearable."

"As it turns out, the experience tends to have the exact opposite effect." Wolfman sips his whiskey. "Because when John Q. Patsy is eventually put down you're standing there, dick in hand, watching the entire system perpetrate murder in the first."

"Was Osborne innocent?"

But Wolfman won't answer. Last night in McAlester the state executed its first death-row inmate of the year, one Allen Osborne: teenage gangbanger cum war veteran cum wounded warrior cum drug addict cum double murderer. Osborne was one of Wolfman's dearest clients, a genuinely good kid who came back from Iraq afflicted with traumatic brain injury and a concomitant paranoid psychosis, and Dean has come to see if his boss needs anything. From the looks of it he could do with a ride home.

"You're going deep tonight."

Wolfman drinks. "Where's the Grimes case?"

"I'll need to go on the road. Still haven't found the parents."

"You'll do it on your own nickel. My discretionary funds are," Wolfman laughs, "running low at the moment."

"About your two patsies. You said the verdicts were tantamount to murder in the first."

"Both those boys were somewhere else at the time of the murder. Both were muscled into bogus confessions. Both got put down. Even if they had done it, which they didn't, both were incompetent. And everybody in that courtroom knew it. Or should have."

"And Macy?"

"Macy fuck. Macy knows one thing."

"Which is?"

"Which is Macy's never wrong. And he'll screw our beloved, blind, murdering, mother-loving-goddamn-bitch Justice in the ass every business day of the week just to prove himself right. That white Stetson of his might as well be a halo. Second you start arguing against him people in this town assume you're some kind of devil."

"Ironic."

"It is dramatically that."

On the big screen a buzzcut Bryant "Big Country" Reeves is moseying through the paint. Both men watch the kid stop on a dime, all doughboy seven feet of him, pivot-step back for the pass from Andre Owens, then he's floating, up and away from a late-breaking Wildcat defender, unloosing the ball just before that crash landing back to court for an unlikely, ungainly two points.

"Kid makes you believe anyone deserves to play this game," Wolfman says.

"My black clients trash-talk him unreservedly. They call him the *great white hope*."

"It's a mystery he's so smooth."

"I know."

"Just look."

"I know."

"The love handles."

"The flushed cheeks."

"Why great white hope?"

"If he was black and seven feet tall, they say, we wouldn't be making such a fuss. Rutherford's on track to break some kind of three-point scoring record, they say, so why aren't we hearing more about Randy?"

"That's the skin thinking."

"You can't exactly blame them."

"I can do anything I like." Wolfman sips his whiskey, grimaces, chugs a Bud chaser. "I'm off the clock." They watch Big Country on the bigger screen. Without looking away from the game Wolfman says, "Something else is on your mind, Tonto."

Dean doesn't answer.

"You're not sleeping so good. Maybe you're contemplating a career change."

"Sam wants to have a kid."

"*Sam* wants."

"She's driving it."

"What about you?"

Dean doesn't answer.

A denim-skirted barmaid clomps by in red cowboy boots, serving tray balanced above her blonde hairdo, big breasts straining against a too-tight T-shirt. Dean calls for a 7-Up but she doesn't hear him for all the caterwauling small talk.

"Not finding the parents is sloppy work," Wolfman says. "The parents are the key. Most of them don't know what they're getting into. They think these kids come with a 90-day trial period. They don't understand parenting is a life goddamn sentence."

"I'm tired, Trent."

"Let me tell you the secret of Dean. See, Dean's a fighter. I've watched him go to work. And not just a fighter. Dean has that killer instinct. It's why he's so good at the job. It takes one to know one, right? To defend one?"

"Your point is fucking taken."

"Remember what you told me in that parking lot?"

"The truth?"

Wolfman is looking at him now.

"First time we meet. I'm out having a night on the town. Stumble out of that honky-tonk to find Tonto pounding snot out of some poor shit-kicker. Both of them drunk as Irishmen. Being the good, upstanding citizen I am, I pull Tonto off the guy. Save both of their lives. So I'm giving him a ride home after this and Tonto says something to me. I'll never forget it. *To account for the have-nots,* our wannabe killer says to me, *and to hold the haves accountable.* This is what Dean tells me he wants to do with his life. Right after I stop him from beating a bigot poseur cowboy to death for making fun of his heritage. Or his hair. I can't remember which it was. Doesn't matter. Because *that* is a mission statement worth getting in line behind. The mission statement of a man who'll always be itching for the next big fight. A true believer. And there are far too few of those in circulation."

"What's your attack plan for Carl Jefferson?"

"That's for Dragnet to worry about." Wolfman looks surprised. "Don't worry about it."

"It's not your regular kind of tired, Trent."

"There's no walking away, Tonto. This is the only fight out there worth showing up for. We're like Easter Islanders, you and me, the last of a dying breed. The way I see it, you owe me every extra hour of freedom since that dustup in the parking lot. So my answer is not just no. But hell no. You can't quit. I won't allow it."

Wolfman manages to stand but begins listing into the table. He rests the meat of his hand on Dean's shoulder, steadying himself.

"Now. Go. Find Grimes's parents. Keep your receipts, I'll see what I can do. Do your mind-trip thing. Your vision quest or whatever. Then come back here and tell me how to argue the mitigation piece of this case. Take a few days off after and go clear your head somewhere. Hell," Wolfman winks, "maybe Macy will grant your wish and throw us an innocent one next time."

"Let me give you a lift."

"I need the air."

Dean's boss stands there, sizing him up.

"Fatherhood might polish down some of your rougher edges, Tonto. It could look good on you." He shrugs into his coat and turns to go.

The barmaid is circling back. She bends down to clink the empties onto her tray.

"What's your poison?" she shouts at Dean.

He watches Wolfman maneuver carefully through the confusion for the street.

43. AURA

Opal is convinced she's just been dancing. Why else should her legs feel so sapped? And this being a Saturday night and all.

Help me to bed, child, I's tired.

Never mind that Sunday's just begun, that church is starting soon. And there won't be any reasoning with the woman. The more dramatic the lapse, these days, the more aggressive is Opal's investment in it. Aura spent a good deal of last weekend answering to the name of Irene, a long-gone friend of Grams's. Until that moment of shared clarity when Opal resurfaced into the present, her absent eyes going blessedly, bashfully wise.

The main thing now is getting control of the narrative. Aura takes two dresses from Opal's closet and exits the bedroom. Counts ten in the den. No . . . better make it thirty. The television is on, it's always on, that or the radio, wherever Aura goes, and Johnny Cochran is in it, looking indignant.

"O.J. wants to tell his fans to keep those letters coming," Cochran is saying. "Anyone who knows O.J. knows O.J. didn't do this thing. Those letters are making him strong. He's been reading his Bible in prison. This is a molehill next to Job's trials."

And on and on and on. Aura turns away from the news, suddenly queasy. Strange. She always admired O.J.'s chiller-than-thou disposition. But now the guy's being tried for double murder that same self-possession seems self-serving, almost obscene.

They'll be starting the sermon soon. But first Aura needs some air. That or a stiff drink. Even a few months back she might have let Opal stay home from church altogether. There will be other Sundays. But skipping today would mean admitting something Aura isn't ready to face.

Two big breaths, then she's holding both dresses aloft, walking quickly into Opal's bedroom and announcing, in as cheerful a tone as she can muster, "You're right, Grams. I was thinking green but you've brought me round to the purple."

Aura stands there behind the dresses, assessing Opal. Grams has been caught off guard. Trying her best to recall the conversation.

"Well . . ." Keep smiling. Let the lie take hold. Remember to sell it with the eyes. "I did, didn't I? Of course I's right, child."

Gotcha. "You look fit to paint the town red, Grams." Agreeably disagree, this is the key. Use the new illusion to her advantage. "Maybe we'll go dancing after church."

"Oh no, child. These legs are too tired for dancing. Church is excitement enough for one day."

The dress is buttoned, the face is in place, the hair is almost there. Good enough. Aura guides both grandmother and walker out to the car. And though Aura gets them to the church on time, though she still can't bring herself to sing, though she's heard some version of this same sermon twice before, it's a comfort to be going through the motions, at least, among friends. By the end of the service Aura has talked herself off the ledge, is feeling more or less hopeful. Opal looks just fine over there, after all, squalling that off-key contralto of hers. She really does.

Doesn't she?

ᴄᐁᴐ

After the sermon, once Opal has been installed inside the community room with her circle of friends, Nate finds Aura meditating amongst the pews, clutching a hymnal and gazing up at the knotted plywood wale where the stained glass window used to be.

"Aura Jefferson, you have made a Presbyterian of me," the preacher announces.

Aura hides her smile, waiting for the punchline.

"First time I saw you, I knew we would end up together. It's predestination."

"*There* it is," she laughs.

"No use in going against God's plan."

Nate reclines into the row before Aura, rests an arm upon the pew back, that handsome chin upon the arm.

"How you holding up?" he asks.

"Just fine."

"We tend to frown upon lying in here."

"Opal's getting worse."

"I know it."

"I've been treating her more like a patient."

"Well, so your grandmother is in good hands."

Aura shakes her head and grips tighter to the hymnal. "I don't know what to do."

"You probably don't want to hear this," Nate starts, "but there were two men snooping around town a few weeks back. Asking after you. After Opal."

"I know."

"Opal was in church, thank goodness, playing bingo with her crew."

"I'm glad she wasn't home."

"Looked like these two may have been police."

"Not quite. They're defending that . . . the boy who . . . who's accused of . . . it has to do with Carl's case."

"Ah. I see."

"If they come looking again, Nate, would you mind calling me? Call me right away and I'll come sort it out."

"It would be my great pleasure."

"And Nate? Don't let them bother Opal?"

"They'll get more than pastor Nate's wrath, they do that."

"Thank you."

"If you'd like, I can drop in on Opal every now and again. Once a day or so during the week? Whenever I'm making the rounds about town. It's not any trouble at all."

"It would mean a lot, Nate."

"I know it would."

"Just until I can figure what to do."

"What say let's try and paint another smile on that pretty face of yours? I might have seen a slice of pie in the kitchen."

44. BEN

". . . till now I've . . . impressive individual performances. But . . . them start to come together as a team . . . lose a few . . . understandable, at this point in . . . still high hopes for . . . before all's said and . . . turning point but . . . (laughter) . . . body knows how I hate a loss . . . to keep moving forward . . ."

"What in Sam Hill'd he say?" Cecil asks Ben.

"He said quiet down now, big brother, so we can *hear* what he's saying. That's what he said."

They're huddled around the radio in Cecil's living area, head-to-head, like metal shavings drawn tangent to a magnet. But something's wrong with the transmission. A storm somewhere between here and East Lansing has snowed the signal, obliging them to try and parse the post-game show from garbled parts of speech.

". . . boys finally . . . their true colors . . . whatnot . . ."

Ben's been wanting to visit Cecil since before Christmas, three cheerless drawn-out weeks ago. But that snafu with Chambliss had him near pie-eyed with anxiety. Odd because Ben's no stranger to the art of the graft. But all the ways this kickback might go sour. All the lies he's told, and especially to Becca, getting that stake together. It has him seeing things. Like the way, all the sudden, Becca seems too busy for him. All those takeout dinners and afternoon trips to the mall.

He knows this is all in his head. Of course it is. Even so, Ben's not sleeping.

". . . keep communicating on the court like . . . Big Country stepped up . . ."

Today's away game against Michigan State gave him a reason to relax, to make an appearance at big brother's, and the Cowboys rewarded them with another loss.

Nevertheless Cecil seems much improved since Ben's last visit. Dressed in nothing but a robe and his lucky Tony Lamas, big brother sits back in his rig, crushes his beer can and surrenders a profligate, blustering belch. He lobs the spent tallboy into the trash basket, where it lands with a papery *swish!*, and fishes another silver bullet from the cooler on the floor.

"Eddie's just spinning damage control," says Cecil.

Big brother tabs open the can and slurps a fizzling pull of happy water off the top.

"Two losses," he says. "Back-to-back. Stead of glib-glabbing on 'bout Lord-knows-what Sutton ought to just own it. Swallow his pride and tell the Pokes start giving Big Country the ball t'every opportunity."

"I can tell you exactly what he's saying," Ben says.

"How's that?"

"Winning's a tricky, a downright deceptive thing. The Cowboys score the most points it's nothing but blue skies for everyone."

Cecil swigs and listens.

"But you learn more about a team when it's losing," says Ben. "Right now Eddie's telling Teegins those last couple games showed him this team's got what it takes. Mettle and whatnot."

"True grit."

"There you go."

"Team's only tough s'its big man," Cecil says.

"Are you tight?"

Cecil straightens in his wheelchair. "So what if I am?"

"Pull your horns in. I won't tell on you."

"Two in a row. Out-hustled. Out-shot. Out-classed."

"But in-sync for the first time all season. You're too stewed to see this is a different kind of win."

Cecil responds with a dismissive and impressively protracted burp.

Ben says, "The Cowboys make it to the Final Four, it will be every boy on the team who's responsible for getting them there. But just one selfish player can bring it all crashing down. There's something for you to think on."

Cecil fixes on Ben. "You've been missing games, brother. What've you gotten into?"

"It's this construction deal I'm working on."

"Big one, is it?"

Ben nods.

"Seeing as how you're playing hooky, I was wondering if you'd let me have your seat at that Kansas game."

"Not if you're planning to scalp it."

"I've got this friend . . ."

"Since when has Cecil got a friend?"

"There we have it," another terse burp. "Big Ben and that piss-ant last word of his."

"I wonder if you've had one too many tallboys."

"You know what I wonder about? I wonder why a man who seems t'have everything wants to keep hiding behind his big brother."

Ben tries chuckling this off.

"It's time for last call, brother." He stands, scavenging the seat cushion for his belongings, and starts tossing empties into the cooler. "I should've cut you off twenty minutes ago."

"I wonder about Becca."

"Careful now."

"Why does someone run away from a woman like that every chance he gets? And for what? Just to ass around with a broken-down old cripple?"

"You old mule. You have it exactly backward. I'm trying to help you . . ."

"Help less."

"Said the man wearing the eight-hundred-dollar cowboy boots I bought him. Can't you see I'm only wanting to get you back on your feet?"

But soon as he says it Ben wishes he could take the words back.

Cecil chuckles.

"About time a foot was put in big Ben Porter's mouth. What about all this hellabaloo regarding communication and teamwork and gettin' along?"

"Conversation's not a team sport. The rules are different."

"Conversation's not a competition."

"That's what the loser always says." Ben walks out, shouting over his shoulder. "I'll mail the Kansas ticket."

"Drive safe now, baby brother."

45. BECCA

First Church's antediluvian secretary, Blanche something-or-other—
it dawns on Becca she's never learned the woman's surname—holds
the manila folder to her bird cage of a breastbone as if it wanted
suckling.

"You sure about this, dearie? In my experience, needing a notary
leads to the kind of drastic, legal-type action that can't be taken back.
Even a Methodist Jesus dislikes divorce."

Becca's laugh comes out sounding more like a sneeze.

"It not like that, Blanche. But, if you don't mind, let's keep this
just between you and me."

A puritanical scowl.

"Me and you and the good Lord too. That's the best I can do."

Becca pats the secretary's vein-strangled hands, but then when
she goes for the folder a perfunctory tug-of-war breaks out. Little
old Blanche is scrappier than her size suggests, though eventually she
surrenders the affidavit without malice, smoothing her blouse and
even cheerfully offering her services should Becca need anything else.

"Anything at all, m'dear, you hear?"

It's an enlightening though admittedly disingenuous experience,
preparing for judgment. Sifting the good bits of your life from the bad
in an attempt to uncover the true, the best and most representative,
you. Take this affidavit, which states that Becca and Benjamin Porter
have been members, in good standing, of the First United Methodist
Church for the past thirty-three-odd years or whatever it is. It should
also, Becca hopes, make mention of their time spent teaching Sunday
school, the sort of pseudo-philanthropic extracurricular an adoption
judge looks favorably upon. When viewed alongside the rest of it,
the paper trail Becca's been so busy blazing, the inference should be
that she and Ben are a couple of sane, capable, God-fearing parents

and citizens who are united in their desire to raise a special-needs child like Caleb Grimes, who Abigail says will probably need therapy throughout adolescence, if not the rest of his life.

What it doesn't say is that Ben hasn't the first clue about what's going on. That Becca's been sneaking around on him for months, lying straight to his face whenever it suited her purposes, even going so far as to secure his signature—under, again, false pretenses—on the forms the judge will want to see in their initial petition to family court.

It was Abigail who gave Becca the attorney's business card—*Tobias Gomez J.D., Family Advocate and Attorney at Law*—and Abigail who, after Mr. Gomez told Becca to gather as much evidence as she could about Caleb's uniquely bleak circumstances, had tried recruiting Mr. Goodnight to her cause. But Dean wouldn't return their phone calls, Abigail's or Becca's, and the bubbly Choctaw translator finally admitted that he was probably too preoccupied, and rightly so, with saving Caleb's father from the death penalty.

"Maybe this should wait until after the trial," Abigail said. "Dean will help you after that. I'm sure of it. Who knows, maybe helping now is a conflict of interest."

But something won't let Becca wait.

After Abigail convinced Child Protective Services to allow Becca to sit in on Caleb's weekly play and language therapy, ninety miserly minutes a week under the disinterested supervision of a state-appointed advocate, Becca even went so far as to transcribe snippets of the translator's lessons with Caleb. The lawyer has her gathering a tome of paperwork: affidavits and transcripts and tax returns and background checks and character references. And at almost every turn someone's tried nosing into her affairs. It's not as if Gomez didn't warn her.

"Put yourself in a judge's shoes," he'd said, without condescension at least. "You're just a good-intentioned wildcard to him. Foster care's a known quantity. An unfortunate and half-assed and often less than good-intentioned known quantity but still. So if you and your husband," Becca's heart skipped with the mention of Ben, "really want to adopt Caleb, you'll be asked to open your entire lives to the state. The whole kimono."

Becca was taking notes. But she didn't understand the kimono reference and said so.

"Meaning until the powers that be hand down a decision you, Mrs. Porter, may as well be naked. Anything the state or the Choctaw Nation asks for, they get. So stick to the straight and narrow. If you get the parents to go along—a big if, if you want my professional opinion, I don't care they're both incarcerated, there's still a thing we call parental rights—your chances are still pretty slim. Caleb's not enrolled in the tribe. Nor is the mother. But his father is. So the Choctaw Nation could very well claim concurrent jurisdiction over any future custody proceedings. It doesn't look like they were consulted during the boy's foster home placement but that might have been an oversight," Gomez said, fingering through the pile of papers on his desk. "This will be different. It would help if you and Mr. Porter talked to a tribal lawyer, as well."

At the mention of Ben, she couldn't help herself; Becca squirmed.

"I'm not saying it's impossible. Not quite saying it, anyway. But if you get so much as a speeding ticket in the next few months the odds fall to just that. *Nada.*"

Only two more hurdles to jump—and these are the doozies, the make-or-break sit-downs with Caleb's imprisoned parents—and she'll be ready to approach Ben. But Becca knows her husband. He'll mire her in minutiae, challenging all the ways and means—how is this whole adoption process going to work and where is Caleb sleeping and how are we introducing him into the family (what is he, a cat?) and oh by the way how will his care and feeding and education impact our retirement plans—and in the process he'll end up worming out from under the one question she needs him to answer, which is do you, Benjamin Abraham Porter, consent to take this poor abandoned soul not just under your wing but more importantly into your heart, with me, Rebecca Haislip Cain-Porter, your wife, alongside to help love and raise and cherish the boy like we did our own children?

Ben is the biggest if. With him at her side, anything is possible. Becca's been anticipating his objections the way Mr. Gomez might prepare for cross-examination, writing her rebuttals down on legal paper, bracing for what feels like the most important conversation of their marriage.

Stepping out onto the church steps she sees a queue of rain-slickered toddlers skipping through a seriously bright, what's it called, sun-shower, one of these freakish meteorological uncertainties where the rain seems to fall straight down out of the sun, like smelted silver. Bracketed by two appropriately uptight daycare teachers the kids waddle and squawk along the sidewalk, cute distractible little ducklings, at once carefree and mindful of their handlers.

She's putting up her umbrella when a woman's voice calls out: "Becca!"

Gloria—keeping-it-real-Gloria, from the Teamsters—is toiling up the church steps through the downpour. Swallowed by the colorless frump of an afghan sweater, her kinky black afro tied into a slapdash bun, the woman's normally warm gaze has cooled to permafrost. She crowds under Becca's umbrella, honking her nose into a balled-up Kleenex, and tries to make small talk. But the poor dear looks miserable.

"How are things going, Gloria?" she asks.

Gloria fakes a brave face. But the tremor in her cheeks tells the real story.

"He left me. Lazy old gadabout finally got off the couch and tells me he wants a *divorce*. Skipped the trial separation and went straight to *big-D!* Says he's met another woman. A *younger* woman. A *white* woman! Says he can *talk* to her? Says he's tired of me *riding* him? Says they're going to live a *fuller life* than the one I can give. Like it's my job to keep him entertained, on top of the cooking and the budgeting and the caring for the kids?"

Gloria blots her watering eyes with the wad of Kleenex and in the sniffly silence that follows, Becca watches the caravan of baby ducklings dogleg right onto Robinson Avenue, headed for the Murrah center daycare, maybe, down the way?

Now a massive storm cloud is steamrolling across the sun, glooming the church steps in a skewbald darkness while spotlighting the children with a single column of fair weather. Aunt Mabel called this postcard type of light Jacob's Ladder, and for some obscure reason the sight of it floods Becca's heart with a complex cocktail of emotion: guilt and fear and wonder and foreboding, yes, but most of all hope and even joy, joy all out of proportion to her recent double-dealings.

Gloria resumes her abstracted daze. She's talking, but you get the sense it's only to put off going inside the church.

". . . might be he had a point about the communication. The two of us weren't even speaking in complete sentences toward the end." A quick shake of her head; Gloria's doing her best to come up for air.

Becca wants to offer some bit of wisdom, something to help the poor woman through her troubles. But the thing she should say isn't true, probably, or not nearly true enough. And the true thing, she's realizing, shouldn't always be said.

"So why are you here, Becca, on a Tuesday afternoon? And in this weather?"

Becca hugs the manila folder more tightly to her side.

"I'm just getting ready for next Sunday's class. You'll be there?"

A humorless, rasping laugh.

"Looks like I'll be S.O.S. for a while."

That freshet of hope in Becca's chest has frozen over with the lie. As Gloria makes her way into the church the last of the children disappears around the corner, leaving Becca all alone in the cold mizzling half-light to wonder: *is this how it feels, being a criminal?*

46. CECIL

The Eagle has landed in his bathroom. Some high-speed electronic swing set to lug him in and out of the tub. Aura ordered it, insurance paid for it, and when that truck delivered the device earlier today Cecil expected they'd leave a rocket scientist behind and launch the thing into orbit.

Cecil rolls round the bathroom, a safe distance from the apparatus.

"This the right appliance?"

"It is," Aura confirms.

"That one you ordered?"

"The same one."

"Looks like Sputnik to me."

"Well tomorrow, after the manufacturer has finished his installation, it's going to make your life a whole lot easier."

"We'll see about that."

Cecil finds and lights a Marlboro and with his stubby pencil makes a notation inside the flip-top lid of the cardboard pack.

"We agreed you'd quit."

"I am quitting."

"This is quitting."

"It's a process."

Aura crosses her arms and adopts an accusatory, hip-cocked stance.

Cecil drags deep and damn does this feel right, indulging his only livelong vice.

"Nipping a pack-a-day habit in the bud takes some noodling," he says. "So I made a plan."

"Well why don't you explain it to me, Mr. Porter."

"Don't get sore now, missy. I'm quitting gradual. Every week I smoke one less per day, down from a pack. So after twenty weeks I'll of kicked it."

He shows her the scribbled sums inside the pack lid.

"I'm keeping count. That's five so far today. Means I get eight more before lights out."

"You've been tapering for seven weeks now?"

"Yes ma'am I have."

"You want to know the truth?"

"I expect not."

"I never imagined you'd live up to your end of the bet."

"A man's got nothing without his word."

Aura straightens her spine, a smile brightening her face.

"Good for you, Cecil."

"I'm full of surprises."

"I guess you are."

"Listen, I was thinking . . ." Cecil starts.

"Don't go hurting yourself again."

". . . my brother loaned me his tickets to that Kansas match, in February. It's a home game. What do you think about going and see Big Country with me?"

"What about Rutherford?"

"I expect Randy will be there too."

"You're feeling strong enough for a road trip?"

"Yes ma'am I am."

"Looks like my work here is almost done."

As he spins his rig and rolls smoking into the kitchen Cecil can feel the color coming into his face.

"It's a date," she calls after him.

"Let's don't get ahead of ourselves."

47. DEAN

"What would you think about going on a road trip?" Dean asks Sam.

"Where to?"

"To meet my dad."

"I thought you'd never ask."

∾

Abigail labors toward Dean's car with the adaptive swagger of the truly, unabashedly fat, in perilous, halting stumbles and pendular, arm-swinging recoveries, as if casting for and then reeling in her far destination on some invisible fishing line. When the colorful translator finally settles into the shotgun seat the Oldsmobile's suspension yields an arthritic-sounding squeal.

"Did you hear about our friend Mrs. Porter?" Abigail breathes.

"Hear what?"

The dome light flickers dimly while Abigail struggles against the seatbelt. "This thing must be broken. Oh, *hello* there! You're the girlfriend. Samantha?"

"Hi Abigail," Sam says from the backseat.

"What about Becca?"

"She's thinking about adopting the Grimes boy. She wants to talk to you about talking to the parents."

"Let me help," Sam says, handing the shoulder restraint to Abigail. "Here."

"And then the extended family," Dean says. "Then the tribe. Does she have a lawyer?"

"She might by now."

"From the Nation?"

"You should call her."

"After the trial."

"I'm not sure she's in a waiting state of mind." Abigail turns to Sam.

"I'll see what I can do."

"How did Mr. Goodnight manage to catch a girl with legs as long as *those*? It's Samantha, right?"

"Just call me Sam."

"Thanks for doing this," Dean says.

When he asked Abigail to tag along this weekend she told him every Indian they encountered would speak English. But Abigail spends quite a bit of time in these parts, and if she can help Dean catch a break on this case, he wants her at his side.

Billy hasn't exactly been forthcoming about his childhood. Grimes was born in Idabel, near the heart of the Choctaw Nation, to an unmarried woman named Peggy Grimes. Peggy gave a Wright City mailing address but didn't list Billy's father on the birth certificate. Eleven years later they moved to Oklahoma City, where Peggy left Billy with a southside aunt before falling off the edge of the earth. And now, after more than four months of phone calls, letters, faxes, voice mails, and records requests, Dean still hasn't found another Grimes in the state willing to claim Billy as kin.

Dean has arranged to use his dad George's place in Pushmataha County as a kind of basecamp, convenient as it is to both Wright City and Idabel. They'll be canvassing the area for a few days at least, maybe more, and Dean needs to go easy on Wolfman's expenses. You can't get much cheaper than free.

He accelerates onto the interstate, sliding the Oldsmobile into light traffic. A wintry mix has been drizzling down since yesterday, and the cars slush by with the muffled regularity of crashing surf.

Pulling and tying her blonde curls back into a ponytail, Sam asks Abigail what the Choctaw reservation is like. The translator explains about the Nation's tenuous, inter-municipal sovereignty betwixt and between the state and federal governments. There is no reservation.

"Are you still in touch with Caleb?" Dean asks.

"Becca's paying me to draw him out of his shell. So, yes. Twice a week at a neutral meeting place."

"How is he?"

"The foster parents mean well. And the more English Caleb speaks, the more he forgets. But the more he forgets, the more aggressive he becomes."

"Go faster," says Sam.

"You see this is my problem with English. It's a language best suited for fighting and forgetting. Sometimes I wonder if this is how the tongue evolved. If the fighting *necessitates* the forgetting. Why should we be surprised that the world is governed by a language this simple, this aggressive, this . . . *optimistic?*"

Abigail articulates this last word awkwardly, as if trying to dislodge a piece of gristle from between her teeth.

"Faster, pussycat," Sam says again.

"I'm going the limit."

"Faster faster."

"Who's driving here?"

"But optimistic isn't really the right word, is it?" says Abigail. "It occurs to me, right now it does . . ."

"It's *occurring.*"

"It *is* occurring—thank you, Sam. That this optimism cannot be genuine. Because fighting, at its most extreme, eventually it leads to dying. Kill or be killed, right? And forgetting. Forgetting is a kind of dying, isn't it? So this optimism is masking a more sinister process. Which is that the language engages us with our mortality. Every time we speak, we are brushing against the hem of our imminent, our inevitable, death."

Dean says, "You're exaggerating."

"I'm trying to say something true in a language that tends to hyperbole. Exaggeration is the beauty and the curse of this tongue. It's too crude for real specificity."

"Ding ding ding ding," Sam says from the back, "I call hyperbole!"

Abigail throws up her hands.

"*Ak akostinincho.*"

"By the way, don't do that tonight at my dad's."

"Do what?"

"Talk in Choctaw."

Abigail grimaces, waggling a finger at Dean. "Speak English!"

"You have it. You have it exactly."

The translator laughs. "Those schools may have done more damage than good."

Dean feels a fingernail strumming his left shoulder—*tap-tap-tap . . . tap-tap-tap*. This is a private code Sam developed for situations such as this, places like libraries and museums and movie theaters, where conversation might be inconvenient: *tap-tap-tap*, Sam is saying, *I love you.*

Abigail opens her mouth. Then shuts it. The translator seems engaged in an animated internal debate. When she does speak, it is with a certain plodding caution, like a woman walking across a frozen lake.

"Lacking specificity, flexibility, *imagination*," Abigail begins, "English resorts to metaphor. But what is metaphor? It is an illusion, pulled like a curtain across the natural world. And we love this illusion. More specifically, we love the process involved in creating this illusion. Because the creative act is akin to giving birth. And what is giving birth if not a protest against the idea of death? This is the tension, the false optimism, I sense running under the tongue. This language is at war with reality."

"But you seem so happy," Sam says.

"I am happy."

"Despite this glass-half-empty philosophy."

"Half empty or half full assumes a rule not recognized by nature," Abigail answers. "There is just a glass. If it has been raining, maybe there's also some water."

Sam is strumming surreptitious sweet nothings on Dean's neck.

Dean drums his own thumb on the steering wheel: *Tap-tap-tap-tap . . . I love you back.*

48. AURA

Aura and Cecil are sitting floorside in Gallagher-Iba Arena, one standing-room-only row off the Oklahoma State bench, watching colorful squads of basketballers run pre-game warm-ups over the polished maple-wood court. The Cowboys are taller than she thought they'd be, this close to the action, leaner and meaner than the team as seen on TV.

The Pokes in white are playing fellow Big Eight rival Kansas tonight, and the blue-jerseyed Jayhawks braid through their half-court weave-and-shoot drills with the relaxed, cocksure swagger you'd expect from an honest-to-goodness basketball powerhouse. Ranked second in today's AP poll, with a lineage harking back to both Naismith and Phog Allen, KU is heavily favored to win the contest.

"I bet these boys can stretch a rubber band silly," Cecil says.

If Aura's patient saw that poll, he's not letting on. Parked in an empty slot to her right, Cecil and his wheelchair intrude into the aisle but only just. A portable AM/FM radio is slung from one of the chair's handle grips; a pair of cushioned, aviator-style headphones are cradled in the big man's lap. What with the audio equipment, those fancy orange and black cowboy boots, the white Stetson, and that pumpkin-colored button-down, Cecil certainly stands out. No small feat in this capacity crowd.

Overhead, a behemoth, four-sided scoreboard flashes advertisements and twangs country-and-western music. Suddenly a jovial, disembodied voice introduces the manic-aggressive play-by-play announcer Dick Vitale, here to call the game for ESPN.

Aura points to the announcer's table and shouts above the racket.

"Dick Vitale's here!"

"Vitale's too . . . effervescent. You can't attach any credence to such militant affability." He pats his radio. "I like Teegins."

The powers that be have billed the evening as *Big Monday*, and word is the Cowboys booster club has planned a secret, halftime surprise. Whatever that might be, the OSU Cowgirls cheerleading squad will be on hand to ensure everyone is suitably titillated. Shrink-wrapped into black, long-sleeved midriff tops and skimpy, pleated skirts, the cheerleaders jitterbug pertly along the Cowboys' end line, inciting further fervor from the already boisterous student section assembled there.

Sufficiently loose, both teams retreat to the benches. But as the KU starters are introduced a disapproving hush, even a catcall or two, condescends from the stands. Aura watches Kansas coach Roy Williams watching the crowd. Surely he hadn't forgotten about the fans, that sixth man his Jayhawks would need to defeat here in Stillwater? Gallagher-Iba is one of maybe two venues in the country offering a demonstrable, statistical advantage to its home team, and when the Pokes start high-fiving their own way onto center court Aura sees—or rather hears—why that is. Everyone is contributing to the commotion, even the nosebleeders in the upper decks. There are air horns and bongo drums and war cries and primal, cinematic screams, every sound underscored by the polyphonic stylings of the Cowboys marching band, who in their black western hats and shirts welcome each OSU player with a rhythmic, attitudinal blast.

A baritone announcement booms from the scoreboard speakers:

"Ladies and gentlemen . . . geeeeeeeeeeet ready for a high plains basketball shooooootout!"

Everyone but Cecil rises for the national anthem, necks craning toward the star-spangled flag hung from the girders. Hands over hearts, *land of the free, home of the brave*, then both ball clubs are elbowing into position for the tip-off.

The horn honks once—a curt, skull-panging *hwwaaaaaaamp!*— and we're off.

The night's been hyped as a showdown between big men, OSU's Big Country versus his KU doppelganger Greg Ostertag, two white boys towering a razored head or more above everyone else on campus. When Big Country is fouled during his first lay-up attempt he nets both sides of a one-and-one to get OSU on the scoreboard. Fresh off a six-game winning streak, Kansas has the deeper bench and the wind at their backs, and from the moment the Jayhawks take possession they start prodding the Pokes into an up-tempo shooting match.

Everyone remains on their feet, tennis-necking side-to-side as the teams run-and-gun the court.

"Can you even see?" Aura yells down at Cecil.

But her patient has removed his cowboy hat and clapped those giant headphones around both ears and is now fiddling the dial in search of the Cowboys radio network.

Big Country with a lay-up for two. Ostertag for two. Rutherford from the field for three. KU turns it over. Big Country for two more.

Vitale's words scrolling across the hovering Adzillatron: *IT'S JAM CITY BABY!!!*

And so it goes. Fouled on a drive to the basket, Big Country converts two more free throws. KU's LaFrentz for two. Big Country with a put-back for two. OSU's Chianti Roberts dunking for two.

Vitale wants us all to know: *CHIANTI'S SWEET AS WINE BABY!!!*

The crowd can't get enough of Big Country. Whenever Reeves scores, the baseline bleachers practically seethe with teen spirit, an orange crush of hooting, hollering fans, all of them mugging for the network camera crews. There are faces smeared in greasepaint, naked male torsos brindled with orange and black, homemade posters thrust toward the championship banners dangling overhead: *Everyone Shout Pokes Now!*

Vitale's astounded: *IT'S CAMERON INDOOR STADIUM WEST BABY!!!*

Aura watches the student mascots play-act a silent argument along the opposite sideline. KU's Big Jay flaps a blue, feathered wing before the enormous fiberglass face of OSU's Pistol Pete, a frontier lawman done up in orange leather boots and chaps and hat. He's even got a silver star pinned on his vest. Pete's stubble-cheeked, lantern-jawed headpiece bobbles down at the upstart Jayhawk. The skinny cowboy hikes a pipe-stem arm, tickles one of the six-shooters holstered at his hip. But Pete doesn't draw on the bird, choosing instead to assault the mascot with the cowbell clutched in his other hand: *clonk-clonk-clonk-clonk-clank!*

A corn-fed coed in an atomic orange wig waves a poster that simply reads: *NOISE.*

Aura is beginning to grasp the reasoning for Cecil's audio equipment. With life dialed to this volume there's no point in chatting up your neighbor, much less trying to think. Closing her eyes, she tries grokking the game's chaotic, coded undersong:

. . . awright awright awright

get BAAAACK!

pass pass PASS!

shotclock shotclock SHOOOOTit take the SHOT!

s'not ebonics its

DEEEEEEE-fense!

be ready   alley alley drive the alley

look UP!

stay DOWN stay

no no nooOOO NO NO!

OOOOOOOOOOOOOHHH

ion the ball, ion the BALL

light it UP!

ESSSSSSSSSSSSSSSSSS

get that man   Just *trust* him

'TACK THE BASKET!

goddammit boy face-*UP*

s'ugleee

YOUUUUUUUUUUUUUUUUUUUU

GO GO GO

cocksucker call

high-low bring it down DEEP and sit up on

TIME!

Aura opens her eyes.

The game clock is paused. An avuncular Sutton confers urgently with his dripping giants. Three fresh bodies rotating in for Kansas. But Sutton stands mostly pat; he's working his seniors hard tonight. The horn honks and Rutherford snags the inbound ball and darts by a KU screen for three more from the elbow. The handsome black guard jogs backward downcourt, bald head and shoulders jiving, a celebratory sort of moonwalk. Then KU's Scot Pollard throws a brick and OSU's Owens brings it in low, dribbling six inches or so off the ground. Trapped into a corner, Owens improvises an underhanded shovel-pass over to Big Country, who's already stuffing the dunk for two.

Vitale emoting from above: *LOVING THIS GREAT BIG COUNTRY BABY!!!*

Pistol Pete rattles his cowbell beneath the Pokes' basket: *clonk-clonk-clonk-clonk-clank!*

KU takes possession. Haase skips a pass to LaFrentz inside. LaFrentz back to Pearson in the wing. The Jayhawks move the ball inside and back out, inside and back out, hoping to free up some leeway on the perimeter. But OSU won't take the bait and, with one eye on the shot clock, Haase tosses off a halfhearted prayer that clips the rim's back iron with a metallic *bwanggggg!*

Big Country with what Vitale trumpets as his one-thousandth career rebound.

More cowbell. Pistol Pete unholsters a replica Colt cap-gun and fires twice into the ceiling—*crackity-crack!* The mascot dances a confrontational little heel-toe jig through the ensuing gun smoke.

At halftime it's OSU doing the swaggering: the Cowboys lead the Jayhawks, 37-30.

While the teams amble off-court Cecil removes his headphones and points to Pistol Pete.

"My brother and I knew him."

Before Aura can answer, the man sitting directly in front of Cecil, a fellow Aggies fan upholstered into a bright orange cardigan, turns around to ask, "What was he like?"

"That old boy was a fibber, and almost as short as his temper."

Two pint-sized towel boys are swabbing up for the halftime show, pushing plush dry mops over the hardwoods in a practiced, headland zigzag. Several fans maneuver by Cecil's wheelchair, headed for the bathrooms or the feed trough or both.

"If only that camera added IQ points instead of pounds," says a deep, reassuring voice.

"I thought you were sitting this one out, brother," to Cecil replies, without turning to acknowledge the huge man standing behind him.

Big Ben Porter drops into a recently vacated seat adjacent to Cecil and says, "I came with a potential client."

Cecil's cheeks are burning.

Ben extends a hefty hand to Aura.

"I'm Ben."

Aura shakes his hand.

"Aura Jefferson."

"Let me in on a little secret, Aura. How do you get this one to do what you tell him?"

"I don't give him a choice."

"So? What'd I miss?" Ben asks. "Did the twin towers resort to violence yet? Any fisticuffs? The word I keep hearing on everyone's lips is *upset*."

"It's a war," Cecil answers. "Game like this, it's only the last two minutes that really count."

A posse of golfer types is taking the floor. One of them puts the microphone to his spray-tanned face and says, "Ladies and gentlemen, please direct your attention to center court. We're honored this evening to welcome some very special alumni back to Stillwater. Fifty years ago, in 1945, representing what was then Oklahoma Agricultural and Mechanical College and playing under the tutelage of legendary coach Henry Iba, these men defeated NYU in Madison Square Garden to win OSU's first NCAA national basketball title. That next year, in 1946, many of them returned to play on the team that won the whole thing all over again. It was the first dynasty in college hoops history. So let's give it up for the 1945 national champions . . . the Oklahoma A&M . . . *AGGIES!*"

Excepting the mammoth, silver-haired Bob Kurland, who even at seventy still stands nearly seven feet tall, the stoop-shouldered group of oldsters don't seem so supersized as today's players. Or as diverse.

"Quite a homogenized lineup they had," says Ben, as if reading Aura's thoughts.

"Did you ever play?" she asks him.

"Only vicariously. Through Cecil. There was one game I remember particularly well. Cecil gets singled out for the halftime show. It was a shooting contest against . . ."

"Stow it, Ben," Cecil snaps.

The memorial ceremony is nearly concluded. Having been given plaques commemorating their accomplishment, the brittle alums are escorted back to their seats. The emcee turns the mike over to one of his cohorts, a beet-faced car dealer calling himself Mitchell "Mac" Hogan. Mac's voice has a singsong, reedy quality that seems to come from anywhere but that squat, pork-and-beans physique. He's sponsoring a shooting contest this very night, Mac trills, and after he tells us about this new Ford dealership he's erected off Country Club Road—*qualified buyers can get zero-down, four-year financing, folks, at four-and-three-quarters-percent . . . that's almost same as cash!*—three members of the audience will get the chance to win a brand new Ford Mustang, courtesy of Mac Hogan's Country Club Ford—*all they hafta do is make a few buckets!*

Ben regards the car dealer with glazed disdain.

"I know this guy. Biggest decision Mac makes any given day is whether to decorate his parking lot with the giant, inflatable King-Kong or the two-story Godzilla." Cecil's little brother uncorks himself from the narrow seatback, laboring to his feet. "Cecil tells me you're quite the basketball player, Aura."

"I hold my own."

"Ben . . ." Cecil says.

But Ben has already stolen the cowboy hat from Cecil's lap, his distant expression giving way to a diabolical twinkle. He curtsies his big head into the Stetson and grabs Aura's hand.

"Come with me."

Before Aura can object Ben has beelined her out to mid-court, grinning all the way, like he's the real reason we're all gathered here today. Mac Hogan's almost done spelling out the rules for his shootout—*three shots from three different locales on the court for a graaaand total of nine balls fer'eeevery lucky contestant and all you gotta-do folks to drive home in that candy-apple Mustang tonight is sink one little ole basket from each of these three spots and otherwise the contestant with the most baskets wins this sizeable gift certificate here and it just don't get any easier than this*—and when Ben moseys up underneath Cecil's cowboy hat Mac doesn't miss a beat. The car dealer greets them as if Ben's visit was scripted.

"Looks like we have our first volunteer! What's your name, missy?"

"Aura."

"I like that name," Mac turns back to the arena and sings a silvery, rising arpeggio, stretching Aura's name into four—better make it five—syllables: "*Au-hah-hah-au-raaaaa!* Now. I need two more shooters besides her. So who's it gonna be?"

Next comes a dark-skinned teen with a scissor-cut fade named Jahleemah Wallace—*check that wingspan, ladies and gentlemen, this Jellyman might have my number!*—and a red-headed, freckle-nosed schoolgirl too shy to tell us her name, that's who.

Aura, Jahleemah, and Freckles queue beside a basketball cart parked beside the free-throw line where, yukking it up all the while with Ben, Mac allows each contestant to attempt three free throws in a sequential, round-robin format. Aura's feeling limber enough—Cecil's physical therapy has honed her set shot—and she swishes three good frees. Jahleemah sinks two. But when Freckles air-balls all three attempts Mac informs the poor kid she's through. The little girl walks away stiff-lipped while the car dealer escorts Aura and Jahleemah to the three-point line, Ben close behind.

It's been a while since Aura's played before a crowd of any size. Look at all these bodies. There must be, what, five or six thousand watching? Aura can sense them pulling for her, hoping that she or Jahleemah would get over on this huckster Ford dealer. The expectation, while familiar, has her rattled. It's the opposite of the calm she gets from a Saturday night pick-up game.

Jahleemah goes one-for-three from the field and then she's dribbling the ball, spinning it on her palm, psyching up for that first perimeter shot. She looks to Cecil for encouragement. There he is behind the OSU bench, he's talking with that man in the cardigan again, licking his lips now, watching with all of his being . . .

. . . saw that tic of his a few weeks ago and then conveniently forgot. The way Cecil licks his lips before shooting. Just like Carl. Her little brother was always trying to be like Mike. They'd play in the church parking lot and he'd soar like some new species of bird before the big blue . . .

She misses one three-pointer before snapping out of it.

Remember to breathe. *Slow your breath, slow your heart*, her coach would say. The next attempt circles the rim, hesitates, drains uncertainly into the hoop. But her third three sails cleanly through the net with a satisfying swoosh.

Mac relocates the show to half-court. But when she and Jahleemah both miss all three half-court shots, Aura is handed a fifty-dollar gift certificate to Blockbuster Video, never mind she doesn't own a VCR.

Ben removes Cecil's hat, he's whispering something at Mac Hogan.

The car dealer muffles his microphone and whispers back, "We square now, Ben?"

But Cecil's brother won't give the poor emcee a thing. He hands the hat to Aura.

"Give that to Cecil for me, I'm going and say hi to Boone."

Aura moseys back to the stands. She's thinking it could feel good, finally, to talk with someone about her brother Carl. And why not start tonight, with her new, sort-of-friend, Cecil Porter?

The contest having run its course, a student in an orange zoot suit, top hat, and sunglasses is now prowling the floor. Equipped with a bazooka-sized pneumatic air cannon, he begins mortaring the cheap seats with balled-up T-shirts. *Thhhhhhhhhhhhooomp!* A cheerleader broom-handles another shirtball into Zoot Suit's cannon: *Thhhhhhhhhhhhooomp!*

Cecil's still gabbing with the gentleman in the cardigan.

The Cowgirls drill team is mobilizing into a taut chorus line at center court where, to the sound of a squealing rap beat, they urge everyone to stand and jump-jump-jump around, hip-popping their black-sequined booty shorts and thrashing their orange-papered pom-poms.

Aura flips the cowboy hat onto her head and strikes a Pistol Pete pose before Cecil, both arms scarecrowed above an imaginary holster.

"I coulda' been a cowboy," she drawls.

But her patient is distracted, breathing hard, mumbling to the man sitting in front of him. When Aura takes her seat Cecil is saying, ". . . these *niggers* getting back to *Africa* with their long-ass names and these *haircuts* in your face . . ."

Wait, Aura is floored. *What?*

"I mean . . ." Cecil continues, unaware, ". . . these names don't even fit a jersey. Mutumbo. Olajuwan. Anikulapo-Kuti? *Jahleemah?* I mean. Come on."

Thhhhhhhhhhhhhhooomp!

The rappers bragging about the gauge of their shotguns and the upper deckers stretching for those bindles of incoming spirit wear. Another amplified voice is addressing the arena. But she can't make out the words. There's an urgent pulse in her ears, a slow-drumming no-sound which nullifies the surrounding din.

Breathless again. Somehow she's standing, has apparently taken two steps toward the aisle, around and away from her patient, and in the process almost fallen over Cecil's bemused neighbor, whose orange sweater is now dandruffed with popcorn kernels.

Excuse me.

"Aura, I . . ." Cecil is stammering, he has finally made eye contact and is now trying to explain: ". . . I mean, if you're going to move here, be *here*. Don't expect me to pronounce a string-a-foreign consonants like this . . ."

He wants to make it better but they both know it's only getting worse. Cecil can't seem to shut himself up: the lips keep moving. A look of actual fear pinches his face until finally, weakly, he says: "Takes all kinds, I guess."

Aura is beset by a passionate desire to hide. She considers fleeing. Away from Cecil, along the length of the cramped row, maybe? But people are staring, staring at *her*, smiling now and pointing, too. The game has become a circus, and Aura at center ring.

What's going on here?

Aura wills herself around Cecil's wheelchair and runs quickly from the arena.

She changed this man's diaper, for Christ's sake! Wiped his emaciated little ass-crack! And he calls her a nigger? Well. That cracker can go beg another ride home tonight. She's done.

It's not until she has crossed the wind-chilled parking lot—the night so cold her eyes are leaking freely down chapped cheeks—not until she sees the reflection in her car window, that Aura understands all the finger-pointing. Cecil's Stetson is still on her head. Folks aren't used to the sight of a big angry black woman wearing a white man's cowboy hat.

Honky wants his hat back, she guns the engine and tosses the Stetson into her backseat, *he'll have to come get it.*

49. BEN

"She wouldn't take him home?"

"Left him high and dry."

"What did he *say* to her?"

Becca and Ben have just climbed into the king-sized bed and are reclined into a pile of body and throw pillows, pretending to read. Ben frictions his feet playfully under the goose-down comforter, trying to heat the sheets.

"I don't know that he said a thing. Maybe he was just being himself. You know how Cecil is. Though he was pretty well worked up. Wouldn't talk about it. Aura, this is his nurse, she was sitting right there next to him . . ."

"Like a proper date."

"I hadn't thought of that. Maybe this tripped his wire. Plus, she's black."

"Oh no," Becca hides behind her *People* magazine, the cover of which features Nicole Simpson's battered face under a headline shouting: *WHY NOBODY HELPED NICOLE.*

"Oh dear goodness. He didn't . . ."

"Who knows. I was out on the floor with Mac and the Amazon for that shooting contest. Boy has Mac gotten fat, he . . ."

"She has a name, Ben."

"I know it."

"What *is* her name?"

"Aura."

"Aura!" Becca reappears, her brow beetled with loving tenderness. "I love love *love* this name!"

"I had to give Cecil a ride home after the game."

"It's lucky for him you were there."

Ben clamps his book shut and turns to Becca. He can't believe how good she looks right now: sans makeup, hair falling lush and dusky about those dainty, pajama'd shoulders.

"What's the secret to your beauty, missus Porter? True love? Vitamin B? Fountain of youth?"

Becca retreats back into her magazine and herself.

"Moisturizer."

"What did *I* do?"

"Why does it always have to be about *you?*"

"It should be about someone else?"

"Cecil needs you," Becca says, in a tone she typically reserves for disciplinary action.

"I know that. Look . . . I do. But he doesn't. Or does and won't admit it. I went over there again on Sunday and they'd already dispatched his new nurse, some namby-pamby white boy looks like he hasn't even graduated Perkins High."

"It's good Aura found a replacement so quickly."

"Good? She abandoned him, Becca."

"What could he have *said?*"

"Any old thing at all. Sometimes tip-toeing around those moods of his is like having a toddler-bomb strapped to your back. Remember when Sarah was three? How she'd get at bedtime? There just wasn't any reasoning with her."

Becca abandons her magazine and burrows closer, spooning her hips into Ben with sudden urgency.

"Thank God those days are over."

"You don't miss it? Not even a little?"

"Not even a bit."

"Really?"

"I always thought I was a pretty decent father . . ."

"You are a . . ."

". . . until Sarah and Reese left the house."

"What does that mean?"

"Twenty-four years we surrendered to those two," Ben explains. "Fretting about naptimes and carpools and extracurricular activities and how best to micromanage their little lives. What should they eat and who should they be friends with and where should they go to sleepaway camp and then college and what career will make them happy and then one day it's all over—*poof!*—just like a dream. And all I felt, if I'm honest, in that moment, was freedom. Relief. *Free at last*, I'm thinking, *free at last!*"

"*We?*"

"Okay, you. You were doing most of this work."

"*Most?*"

"Okay. You were doing *all* of this work. I had the business to run. But we never had much time for . . . just *this*. Us. And now we do."

"I can't believe what I'm hearing. We have all of this time, you say. So why don't you spend more of yours with me?"

"You don't believe me."

"I don't believe *you* believe you."

After a considerable silence, a silence that tempts Ben to think he could still get lucky this evening, she says, "You really don't think you're a good father?"

"I don't think I'm a bad one. But if I was good, or at least better, wouldn't the kids be coming home? Wouldn't they be calling?"

Becca can't, or won't, argue with this. Ben nuzzles her hair.

"I need a favor," she says.

"Anything for you, m'dear," he agrees immediately, hugging her closer.

"There's this thing I'm doing with the kids down at the shelter. They need me to submit a background check."

"You can't be too careful around kids, I guess."

"They'll want one from you."

"Don't worry, honey. I am pure as the driven snow."

Becca laughs.

"Is this about the deaf and dumb one? The little—whatshisface—Mexican boy of yours?"

Becca scootches back to her side of the bed, cold-shouldering Ben's advances.

"His name is *Caleb*. And he's not a Mexican, he's a Choctaw Indian. And yes. It is about him."

"What did I do *now?*"

"Nothing."

"You're not a very good liar."

Becca switches off the lamp on her bedside table.

"Lucky for you."

"Becca! I'm just . . ."

"Being yourself. I know."

50. BECCA

Willa Busby is angry.

"It's not right incinerating, I mean incarcerating, me like this is what I'm learning. Because it's a disease I've got and not a conscious choice to keep fucking up. Like, get this, would you sanction locking cancer patients away just because they've taken ill?"

Dressed in robin's-egg-blue inmate scrubs, Willa Busby paradiddles her fingers on the tin-topped table, *tappity-tap*, pulling a theatrical suck from her cigarette and waiting for this insight to work its inevitable magic upon Becca.

"I don't think so, missus Porter," she says from behind a white scrim of smoke. "It'd be barbaric treating an invalid that way. And you're way too nice for putting in with the barbarians."

They're sitting on cheap, plastic-backed chairs inside the Mabel Bassett Correctional Center's visiting area, a steel and concrete box with all the colorless, besieged appeal of an underground bomb shelter. Bars on the windows, deadbolts on the doors, ashtrays smoldering on every flat surface. Becca wound up waiting outside for more than an hour before the desk clerk called her name, feeling outright garish in her houndstooth pantsuit, and by the time she submitted to the prison's brusque security protocol—first the metal detector, then the confiscation of her lipsticks, finally a humiliating pat-down (during which some eager-beaver guard just had to poke her fingers in Becca's *hair)*—even Becca felt, if not quite criminal, then at least suspect.

"How are you holding up?"

A flagrant delight comes into Willa's face.

"I've got a joke for you, missus Porter. Who's the biggest thief ever?"

Becca shrugs. Willa's been fast-talking at her like this for almost twenty minutes.

"It's Atlas, because he held up the whole world."

Willa slaps her knee, mashes another cigarette into the ashtray, leans back and war-whoops into the fluorescent lighting.

"Ha!"

There is a curious lack of chatter happening in the room. Not a few prisoners have retreated to the rabbit-eared television set in the corner to watch the O.J. Simpson trial.

It's time to start the hard discussion, the one she's been avoiding since that mannish female guard slammed the door shut behind her.

"Have you noticed, Willa, that in all the time we've been talking you've never once asked me about your son Caleb?"

Willa lights another cigarette.

"How's Caleb?"

"Well, for now, both of his parents are in prison. So he's a ward of the state, which has him in foster care. And he's scared to speak. The only time I see Caleb is during his speech therapy, which thank God he's still showing up for. So I'd say he's having a lot of trouble dealing with things, with the things he saw in that hotel room. With things in general."

"Things in general are hard to deal with," Willa says, watching the television where, live from Los Angeles, Simpson's limousine driver is saying: ". . . and O.J. told me, night after Nicole was murdered, told me he'd been having these dreams. Said he dreamed of killing her. Like he knew it was going to happen even before it did happen."

Simpson stares bullets at the witness, shaking that big handsome head of his, furious. Attorney Robert Shapiro places a tentative hand on his client's arm and whispers urgently into his ear.

"Have they let you see Caleb?"

"My D.O. says I've got to work the program first. Piss three months of clean samples. Get enrolled in a class or two. Make progress towards being a productive member of society."

Becca caresses Willa's fisted hand with her own.

"I did some looking into those classes. They have some really good ones. I've heard they can help you learn to cope. With things.

With all of the stress you must be feeling. That if you do well, graduating can even reduce your sentence."

Willa regards Becca's fingers with something akin to pity but doesn't pull away.

"That D.A. ain't reducing a thing till Billy's in the boneyard. While this trial's going, he's got me right where he wants."

"What if he didn't, though? What if you were released right now? Or next week or next month? Could you clean up, if it meant getting Caleb back?"

That same guard—Ben would call her *butch*—rattles the doorway grating with her nightstick.

"No touching."

Becca releases her hold on Willa but doesn't otherwise acknowledge the guard.

"The thing is, missus Porter, is this. Jail's the worst place you can put a person like me. It's almost as easy getting high inside as out. Hell, easier sometimes. Everything is. They feed me, they wash my clothes, they put me to bed on time. And the security system can't be beat."

"Parenting's the hardest thing there is, Willa. The hardest thing. Especially for someone in your situation. There's no shame in being overwhelmed by it."

Willa's head swivels back to the trial. "I used to think it was me caring for Caleb. Like, that's the expected pattern, isn't it? But truth be told, it straightened me out for a time, having him. Billy and I playing grownup for our baby. I remember we bought a crib one time, it was secondhand but still. I felt like . . . this is it. This is the purchase gets my life back on track. And for good, I'm thinking this time. And meaning it. But it never took."

"What would you say if . . ."

"Isn't it weird how I ended up needing more from my son than he needed from me? Doesn't that sound like some kind of upside-down just . . . wrong, to you? You know, though . . ."

". . . what if I were to . . ."

". . . Caleb's tough, missus Porter. He'll pull through all this just fine."

". . . adopt your son?" Becca blurts. "My husband and I have raised two happy, successful kids of our own and we'd be the ones making the decisions about Caleb's education and upbringing. Not the state. He'd have the best of everything, which isn't to say he'd be spoiled because we don't believe in spoiling a child. What I mean is that he wouldn't want for anything. Anything at all. We'd make sure to find a good therapist and tutors, if he needs it, and if you agreed to all of this, if you signed some papers transferring your parental rights to us—Ben is my husband's name, by the way, Benjamin Porter—Caleb could be out of foster care inside of a few months, at most. Right now he's stuck there until you're freed from prison. Maybe until you've served out parole. And who knows how long that could last? Not that you *have* to agree to this, Willa. Only if you thought it would help your son. But if you did think that, that I could, that *we* could, help Caleb or even just relieve the pressure off you, then we could talk more about it . . ."

Willa's eyes are bright, still glued to the television. O.J. looks coiled, the muscles of his face seizing on seven separate frequencies, as if he might actually leap across the courtroom and strangle this limousine driver, who is clearly uncomfortable testifying against his former friend.

"Come on O.J.," the witness pleads. "Why you got to be like that? I'm just telling them how it went down."

"I'll tell you the truth, missus Porter," says Willa. "I love Caleb. I do. But the first place I'm going when they set me free is southside and get well."

"So, but, Willa . . ."

"I think you'd be a real good mom. Better than me, that's for sure. Better for Caleb. But it doesn't matter what I think." A pained, edgewise glimpse at Becca. "'Cause Billy would admit murder before giving Caleb away. He'd die first."

51. CECIL

Wheel into the lavatory and park before the tub and disrobe and haul that flabby ass into the swing set. Hold tight to the handlebars and double-check the legs are unimpeded. Everything looks to be clear, so push the rig away and punch a button on the machine's remote. An earnest mechanical hum and now he's being air-lifted in for a bath. The gadget is supposed to make the morning routine easier on Cecil's shoulders and he supposes it does. Mounted into the wall studs beside the toilet, the thing acts like one of those Chair-O-Plane rides you see at the state fair, swinging him up and over the lip of the bathtub before lowering him slowly down into it for washing.

He's thinking about that summer Dad had them build a fence around a five-acre plot he'd bought for growing soy and mung beans on. Cecil and Ben digging postholes and sinking stumps and stringing barbwire through the brain-boiling heat. Like to have lasted forever though it was probably only a couple-three weeks. But they did finally finish and when Ben runs to fetch him Dad moseys out and stands frowning down one measly corner of their new fence line.

"You'll want to do it over," he says, shaking that head under his hat. "And this time, make it straight." Then turns on his boot heel and strolls back up to the house without another word.

It was one of Papa Porter's more ruthless life lessons and it taught Cecil two things. One was to work, but to do it smart. The other was to fix your mistakes straightaway.

Cecil lathers up, feeling every part of his skin for bumps or scratches.

He didn't know how to right this particular fuckup with Aura, but Cecil could still work. He got back to cracking on his stained glasses, comforted by the kaleidoscopic lilt of light across the workshop curtain, whistling through the finishing touches on that

Sitting Bull pattern in under a day. Next morning though, when time came to decide his next design, Cecil drew a blank and it was the indecision that did him in. He started drinking too much. But he'd had no prior experience with true blue debauchery and there followed a spell where he couldn't tell what was real and what wasn't. A train would whistle him awake and the booze would keep him that way and he'd lay there in the sheets, tangled up in funk, waiting for her to arrive. Then the train harps again, a bent bluesy warble, and he remembers what he's done and spends the rest of that night and next day trifling about house, trying to forget.

He tried phoning the service but Aura wouldn't take his calls, and that's when he understood she wasn't coming back. Not today not tomorrow not ever. They sent a limp-wrist nurse in her stead but Cecil doesn't trust him yet. The kid's name is Ronald and he has a plump saggy face resembling a bulldog's and can't be very proficient at being a queer.

The inebriate lifestyle requires a powerful strong bladder and Cecil doesn't have it. He doesn't much cotton to the smell of his own piss whenever the catheter spills over, either, so partway into his three-day drunk Cecil decides to give Sputnik here a test drive. Clean as he'll be, Cecil presses a different button on the remote control and the robot cranes him up from the bathtub. But his ride is only partially over when the machine starts squealing, a syncopated riff of *chuck-chuck-uh-skrikk-uh-skreeeeing!* There follows a polite *poof* of white smoke from the machine's motor, then the lift gives out lifting altogether and now he's stuck.

He's perched a good three feet above ground. The rig is too far away to reach, and it's not safe to try and lower down from on high. Not in this state. That new nurse should be here soon and so Cecil just waits there in the swing set, pitiful as a pluck-bird. Somehow he achieved sixty-three years, more than half of it living alone. He grew two more inches after the accident, in his rig. Yet now a day can't go by without he needs someone's assistance. He tries not to see his reflection in the vanity but it's an unavoidable spectacle: nothing reflected in the mirror but the shriveled twist of his cock and the battle-scarred dangle of his legs. Look like empty britches strung drying from a clothesline.

Stark ball naked and toilet-ridden yet again, he hangs around patiently waiting for Ronald the roly-poly homosexual to come set him free.

52. DEAN

They've been here nearly a week, Dean and Abigail, trolling local schools or hospitals for any sign of Billy's passing. Sam stays behind at the house getting to know Dean's dad, good old George.

Dean's only new lead is the mother's birth certificate. Peggy Grimes was born in 1953 to a Choctaw couple from Mississippi who had recently relocated to Broken Bow. But both of her parents are now buried in Holly Creek Cemetery west of that town. Peggy dropped out of school in tenth grade and moved away. And though they find a few people in Broken Bow who remember Peggy and her parents, nobody knows anything about a baby named Billy.

On the sixth day they split up. Dean drops Abigail off in Wright City and drives to Idabel, where he spends an airless afternoon in the hospital records room, transcribing the names and addresses of nurses who might have been working the delivery unit in December of 1972, when Billy was born.

Sam has to get back to work soon. But Abigail says if Dean will call that volunteer from the shelter, Becca Porter, and hear the woman out, she'll give Dean four or five more days of her time. Dean caves, makes some calls, and arranges for Becca Porter to have one hour, and not one minute more, alone with Billy Grimes in the county jail.

He's running out of ideas.

Tomorrow they start knocking on doors.

∞

"Pack-a-coyotes is the smartest animal which lives," says George Goodnight. "I seen 'em flush a whitetail into yonder field once. Deviled that poor doe in shifts till her legs gave under from the fright. Little shits'll mount anything on four legs, too, so most mutts hereabouts have got the varmint in 'em somewhere back in the line. And a coyote half-breed can go mean in a heartbeat. It got to where mother and me was worried for little Deanie's safety."

Abigail raises an eyebrow. "*Little* Deanie?"

Sam slaps Dean's thigh from her place beside him on the couch. "Little Deanie! I love it! It's like an Elton John song."

"I've got so much love," Dean says, closing the photo album. He hasn't been home in almost four years. Hard ones, apparently, on Dad.

Rum-tummied George Goodnight tells stories backward, beginning disturbingly close to the climax and then circling back on his unsuspecting listener in ever-widening digressions, hoping to tease out the maximal amount of context. The bit of backstory he is now circumnavigating began when Sam asked about a photo frame resting upon the fireplace mantel, a washed-out snapshot taken two years before Dean's mother died.

Dean hands the photo album to Sam, lifting the print in question from her lap: little Deanie kneeling at the feet of his parents in the overexposed past, hugging a quizzical, sickly-seeming puppy of distinctly lupine origins. Everyone is smiling—George and Dean and his mother, Veree—though the right side of Dean's face is swollen by a freshly-minted black eye.

"You were hardly four foot above snakes when Veree found that whelp. Hadn't yet hit your spurt."

"What about the black eye?" Sam says, worried.

The women are spellbound by Dean's dad, who relaxes back into his easy chair with a gray and grizzled grin. Drawing on his cocktail. Drawing out the moment. Old George has them hooked and knows it.

"See round these parts coyote don't ever go out of season. You can kill 'em whenever you like. We had a neighbor up the lane. Clyde. He'd run 'em down with greyhounds. Made his nest egg taking citified people out hunting with those dogs."

The dog had been soft, Dean remembers, fawn-colored. A-wiggle with life. You could feel the ribs beneath its fur. There was a single dark kiss mark above its left eye.

"What happened was this pup starts skinking about old Clyde's henhouse. So one a Clyde's boys, I forget . . ."

"Toby."

"Toby. Right. Toby ties Dean's mutt up in Clyde's back pasture. Then when Dean goes over and try to fetch it home, little Toby claims the dog's been his all along."

"Toby stole your dog," Abigail says.

"Toby stole my dog."

"I always thought that-un had another face hid under his hat," George says.

Sam squeezes Dean's hand in sympathetic triplicate: *clasp-clasp-clasp*.

"Dean's begging me to go get his pup. But I want nothing to do with it. Go steal the dog back fair-n-square, I tell him. But little Deanie's still just a runt himself. Soon as he started at school the kids there set to whaling him . . ."

"Get to the point, George."

"Oh cool your jets. The telling is the point. I'd already been teaching him how to fight, see, on account of his fragility. But this Toby, he's got a few years and a few more inches on our boy. So I shows Dean some things I picked up in the infantry. How to kick a kid in the nutsack. How to go for the throat."

George jumps up from his chair and, to everyone's surprise, crouches into a bare-knuckled, southpaw boxing stance.

"I don't care how big a man is," he says, shadow-boxing, "poke him in his upper-glottis, he'll drop like Goliath."

"You're left-handed?" Abigail asks George.

Some heavy-hoofed footwork, a palooka duck-and-cover, and George has rolled back into a normal stance, his left foot now forward. He sucker-punches an imaginary antagonist.

"Ambi-dextrous."

George lowers his fists and sits back down, winded.

"Government teachers wouldn't abide by lefties. So I learned penmanship with my hand tied behind my back. Relearned pret' near everything else, too."

Sam pinches Dean's chin, turning his cheek this way and that, scanning for scars.

"Anyway. Little Deanie here marches over and calls that Toby out into Clyde's drive. *I'm taking my dog back,* he says. Toby doesn't much like him reappropriating the pup, though. Chases after him. They square up. Toby throws a jab and . . . okay. Dean takes it straight in the blinker. So now Toby's feeling good. Bulls-eye! Get it? Hahahahaha! Toby tosses off a right cross. But Dean's ready for him. Ducks down, comes up flailing haymakers. Winds up clocking that boy in the snot locker. Just breaks his nose wide open."

The elder Goodnight is having trouble keeping up with his breath.

"Might be it was the . . . proudest day of my life . . . had just acquired this camera . . . set the tripod up . . . to commemorate the occasion," George breathes.

"What was the puppy's name?" asks Sam.

"Uno," Dean answers.

"There's more," Abigail says. "I can feel it."

Dean stands up, into a long and yawning stretch, ready for bed.

"Eventually Uno ended up breaking into Clyde's henhouse."

"You two ladies ever seen a . . . greyhound going full-tilt for prey?" George asks.

Neither woman has.

"Poor pup didn't stand a chance. Had to been part coyote, way those hounds tore into him."

"They killed Uno?" Sam cries.

"Killed him deader'n disco." George appraises his son. "What's it like, would you say, watching those hounds on the hunt?"

"It is . . ." Dean starts, remembering. He wants to say something about cool and ferocious motion. Something about a lethal, waking dream. He wants to say it is like seeing the piebald wrath of God being loosed into the world.

"Nonnegotiable."

53. AURA

The car had been idling, with Aura inside of it, for one-going-on-two hours when he finally got home. When he recovered from the shell shock of her unannounced, late-night visit, Nate tried to speak but she shut him up quick with a slow, deep kiss that announced her intentions. They stumble-stepped inside and before he even had a chance to flip the entryway light switch Aura was grabbling for his belt buckle, so urgent was her need for the man under those clothes. She took him there on the carpeted hallway floor in an almost predatory way, and whenever the preacher threatened speech she suckled him with a tongue or a chin or a nipple to his lips. It was a right kind of wordless violence she was doing, and there would be complications to come but she would handle those later. They were so perfectly balanced on the knife-edge of that moment, his smooth beautiful cock moving inside of her, that words could only circumscribe Aura's rough and boundless hunger for this. It. Him.

54. BEN

Popping in at the lunch spot Ben feels exactly like he's got needles in his blood. He follows the hostess to a favorite corner booth and orders a forbidden gin gimlet. Something's up with Becca—he knows this absolutely, knows it bodily—and the knowing has him at sixes and sevens. When the gimlet arrives Ben drinks his medicine quick, can't afford to be so scattered with Terry, and orders another.

The restaurant is appointed in the chrome-and-wood-paneled veneers of a Depression-era soda counter. Frequented by judges, cops, city councilmen, state and federal prosecutors, even the occasional shopworn public defender, the Oyster Bar is the go-to feeding ground for a certain set of up-and-comer, a kind of free-range K Street where, every weekday, mossback conservatives and limousine liberals declare détente just long enough to drink lunch over shellfish flown in fresh from the Gulf.

Ben takes the second gimlet slow while watching the temperamental picture on the TV mounted above the backbar. A pugnacious Newt Gingrich is soapboxing with a C-SPAN reporter. The Speaker and his principled colleagues in the House are waging a battle—actually, *Ms. Liberal-Media-News-Anchorwoman,* it's a war, a veritable *crusade*—against a corrupt, entrenched Washington bureaucracy. They're joined every morning by pro-family, pro-liberty, pro-industry private citizens who dare to challenge the status quo. Big government's a cynical machine, and the Republicans have a divine duty to dismantle it before the heart and soul of these United States of America has been forever poisoned. A duty to our children, our children's children, our . . . *gabbity-gobbity-blobbity-blah . . .*

Here's Giffords now, a fashionable-but-forgivable ten minutes late, seeming trimmer than normal in his made-to-measure mayor's uniform: navy blue Brooks Brothers suit, cardboard-collared Oxford shirt, nonpartisan pewter necktie. On the short trip to Ben's booth Terry pinballs from one table to the next, wrestling palms with no fewer than seven of his constituents, including Macy's eager-beaver assistant district attorney, Robert something-or-other. Granger. When the mayor finally slides into the leather bucket seat across from Ben a white-aproned waitress is already standing by to take his order. Terry has his eye on the shrimp po-boy, no surprise there, with iced tea and a half-dozen raw oysters to start.

Ben will have the same. As the waitress scurries off to place their order he says, "You're more popular in here than a debutante at a bachelor party."

"Popularity's part of the job description these days, unfortunately."

Ben tries not to laugh too loud.

"Unfortunately. I love it."

Replying doesn't gain him anything, so Giffords just grins this one off. His great gray head owls around the dining room until it lands on the television.

"Newt's not using his optimistic governing words this afternoon," says Giffords.

"I'll say this for Clinton," Ben says. "He's given Newt plenty of rope to hang himself with. Staying out of the Speaker's way, let the Contract succeed or fail on its own merits, it's the smart play."

"Though the liberals had better start playing ball on the budget. Less than a month into the new term and Gingrich is talking shutdown."

"D.C.'s already paralyzed, if you ask me."

Giffords fixes Ben with a soulful stare.

"Everything I'm hearing translates to hurry up and wait," the mayor says. "Newt's serious about these cuts. It will be awhile before we know who our friends are on the Hill."

First person plural. Ben can work with that.

"Meantime we've got work to do here in cowtown," Ben says. "I've got some ideas about our riverwalk. Wanted to . . ."

Terry is playing with his fork.

"I've been meaning to tell you, Ben . . ." Giffords puts a tiny violin in his voice, ". . . and I really mean this. Congratulations on the M.A.P.S. coordinator appointment. It's a big accomplishment. You and me are finally teed up to do some good. About damn time, if you ask me."

"Why do I get the feeling my favorite debutante is about to stand me up before we've even had the chance to dance?"

"Nothing could be farther from the truth. I just . . ."

"Good."

". . . want to introduce you to a new friend of mine. Of ours."

"I've got all the friends I need, Terry."

"Play nice when he gets here."

"When *who* gets here?"

The waitress chooses this moment to deliver Terry's tea and two silver serving platters. The oysters are fanned out on the half shell, bedded down in ice shavings and garnished with green splashes of parsley, yellow wedges of lemon, ramekins of red cocktail sauce. Ben squeezes hell out of a lemon slice—he's not having any fun trying to read Giffords this afternoon—and gulps down an oyster in one swift slurp. His sphincter has squinched tighter than an O-ring.

The mayor is talking again: ". . . like a witch hunt. I've never seen anything like it. There's a lot of pressure to conform. A lot of rat-fucking going on. M.A.P.S. is a tax, after all. Never mind the sunset provision. And until I can hold it up as a proven, twenty-four-carat example of *pro-business* ingenuity . . . well. I'm a target, aren't I? I've got to distance myself from the day-to-day minutiae. So I've brought in this new fellow to handle logistics. The two of you will get along just fine. You'll liase with him, he'll report back to me. Just until things are golden again, mind you."

"You're in permanent campaign mode, Terry. Don't you read the papers? The ugly season's over. Election's finished. You won it, mister mayor. Won it fair and square."

"Campaigns don't ever die nowadays, they just go broke a spell."

"I have a new boss, is what you're saying."

"Here he comes now."

An oily little fellow in shirtsleeves and suspenders is approaching the table. He has the hypervigilant manner of the teacher's pet, of the striver who's too smart for his own good. Or thinks he is.

No stranger, this one.

"Ben, this is my new chief of staff, Gary Chambliss," says the mayor. "Gary . . . Ben Porter."

Shaking Chambliss's hand, Ben murders an impulse to crush the man's metacarpals. Chambliss shows his teeth and says, "Nice to meet you, Ben. I think you and me are gonna make a first-rate team."

Ben takes what he hopes looks like a casual dose of gimlet. He swallows a second oyster, whatever might be left of his pride, and tries to play nice.

55. BECCA

After Abigail called in a favor from Mr. Goodnight, Dean arranged for Becca to use one of the jail's private interview rooms for today's visit. But from the way this Billy boy is acting, Becca is afraid the conversation could be short lived.

"Lady, I don't know you," he says. "You come to talk about me you'll want to take my lawyer's card. You come to talk about anything else you'll want to take a flying fuck 'cause there's no future here in dropping dime."

From his chair opposite Becca the prisoner, in orange jumpsuit and flip-flops, lifts both handcuffs to scratch at an acne-scarred forehead. The guards have chained Billy to the floor, like a dog, and the chains rattle against the concrete whenever the boy moves. Becca waits for him to finish with his itching. Willa was right to warn about Caleb's father; he's no pushover. Billy has the disinterested demeanor of a truant teenager, with wrists so thick it's a wonder they found handcuffs that fit.

But Becca knows all about dealing with difficult teens.

"I came to talk about Caleb."

Billy goes calm as a pillar of salt. She has every bit of the prisoner's attention.

"I want to adopt him."

He laughs for almost a full minute, big shoulders bouncing.

"Do you know where Caleb is now, Mr. Grimes?" She's careful not to say *your son*. "He's in foster care. I check in on him once a week."

Billy does a kind of yawn, showing Becca his teeth before puckering his lips tightly shut.

"How's he doing?"

"He's not communicating with us much. Not in English, anyway. We have a Choctaw speech therapist working with him . . ."

"I taught him that. Taught him Choctaw."

"And you did a good job with it. But Caleb is going to be a handful. He has a lot of problems. The translator costs money, and he's going to need speech therapy, which also costs money. Right now my husband and I are paying for it. I'd like to adopt him, to get him speaking English, to teach him about caring for himself. The future isn't something to be scared of and I want Caleb to know that. I want to equip him with the tools he needs to believe in himself."

Billy is nodding.

"Willa can do all that."

"From prison? You do know, right, that she violated her parole?"

"I'll do it then. Once I beat this rap I'll do it myself."

"Do you think the jury is going to find you innocent?"

He watches her with a cold, a carnivorous, confidence.

"What would you teach Caleb, if they did set you free?"

"How to be a man."

"And what does that involve?"

"How to fight. How to make money. You know, how to get by. How to survive."

"Okay. But what sort of values would you teach him?"

"Values like, sums?"

She could laugh at the absurdity of her situation but it would ruin everything. Because Becca and Billy are speaking two different languages. She says one thing, he hears another. Caleb's father hasn't the first clue how to teach a child the difference between right and wrong.

What was it Willa said?

Billy will admit murder before giving Caleb away.

So be it.

"I've been teaching Sunday school lessons for years now," Becca begins. "And if there's anything I've learned from that experience, Mr. Grimes, it's that the best teachers are failures. They have failed at everything they've tried."

He snorts.

"They got any openings at that school?"

She bluffs a chuckle.

"The most important thing about teaching, I think, the most difficult thing, is stubbornness. Failure's a great teaching experience. You need a stubborn streak to keep picking yourself up and attacking a problem from some other angle. A teacher does that enough times, eventually he'll get through."

"What does any of this have to do with my son?"

"Children don't trust a teacher who can't admit to his mistakes. They have an innate sense of fairness, Billy. Of honor."

The killer does some more scratching.

"Mr. Goodnight tells me you're on trial for first degree murder. He seems to think you'll be found guilty, though Dean's doing his best to avoid that. But regardless of what happens with your trial, if you hope to step back into the role of Caleb's father—his life teacher—then you need to be honest with yourself. Admit that what happened in that motel room was a failure on your part. That this thing didn't happen how you planned it. This is the only way you'll learn from the experience. And it's the only way you'll ever teach Caleb something useful about . . . about regret. Otherwise, I hate to say this, Billy, but I really do believe it, Caleb will probably carry this horror around with him for the rest of his life."

"I'm not copping. Not to murder one."

"I'm not asking you to. But you do have to tell the truth, even if it's just to yourself. It doesn't need to leave this room. But the truth's the only chance you have of getting your son back. Really getting him back. Do you understand? Even if you never get out of here, you could still get him back in a significant way. You could still have a relationship with him."

Having made her play, Becca sits back and waits.

For the longest while, Billy says nothing. Minutes pass by— five, ten, fifteen of them—in a silence broken only by the pounding of her own pulse, Billy's slow and heavy breathing, the recurrent mechanical sounds of the prison beyond the interview room door. Then, just when she thinks it might be time to leave, Billy starts sobbing. Quietly at first. But as the crying continues it assumes an out-of-breath, almost childlike, quality.

It takes every ounce of her self-control, not consoling him.

When he does finally speak it is like seeing someone drown. Between wet raggedy breaths and deep choking sobs, Billy Grimes confesses to Becca.

"That nigger shows up at our motel all he has is a *taste* of crystal. I'm expecting a suitcase, right? Supposed to meet my connect right after. So what am I gonna do now? I can't fence a fucking envelope. Didn't have any cash, either. I was planning to liberate the product from homeboy and bid him good evening, you know? Then this guy starts stepping to me. Wants his dough, you know? Wants to show me how hard he is. But I knew he had to have the stash close by. So I tied that nigger down and proceeded to lose my temper. I'd been drinking a few days, you know, so I wound up beating him pretty nice. Willa went and searched his car but the nigger just laughed even louder. He wasn't backing down. Called us white trash, said he wasn't ever going to forget this. Said we were good as dead if I didn't let him go free. Caleb was there. This dude says his buddies would take care of us, all three of us. So now I'm in a bind. I can't think right, can't see right. Like I was on auto-pilot or something. Just doing, no thinking at all. Caleb made us bring this cat everywhere we went . . . it had this litter box? Always full of shit and piss? Stank to high heaven. So I took this dealer into the bathroom and shoved his face in the mess. Nigger was scared but wouldn't break. Then I filled the litter box up with booze and held him under it for a minute or so. After a couple-three times he stopped fighting back. He knew it was coming but still wouldn't tell where the drugs were. So I put him under once more. I couldn't stop. After that he didn't come up again."

"Did Caleb see you kill Carl Jefferson?"

Billy blinks at his handcuffs, nods: *Yes.*

"Do you think he'll ever forget it?"

A distressed shake of his head: *No*.

Becca is sweating through her clothes. She knows Billy will never repeat what he's just told her, especially in front of a judge. But his admission has charged the air in the interview room, and the oversized boy sitting across from her, with an electric kind of possibility.

"I'm proud of you, Billy. You do know what comes next, don't you?"

"Fucking . . ."

"You need to discuss this with Caleb. To let him know how sorry . . ."

". . . cunt this a trick? Someshit like . . ."

Becca tries pressing her case. "Sorry for what you've done. Sorry for what it's done to Caleb's life. Otherwise you'll always be the killer to him and not . . ."

"Get out."

Billy dismisses Becca, the backsides of his shackled hands flapping like wings. He mouths a single word: *Go*.

She's so close! Becca opens her mouth to protest but Billy is shouting now, a primal, an ear-splitting scream. A squat burly guard peeks in from a window in the interview room door, looking panicked. Then Billy is on his feet, he's trying to climb across the table but the chains yank him erect, stop him from getting too far. Becca is standing, backpedaling quickly. With his forehead the boy butts the metal tabletop. Another head butt. Another. With the third or fourth butt the prisoner's scalp splits, splattering the table with a red mess of blood and Becca finds herself backed against the wall, as the guard with his nightstick rushes inside to wrap Billy into a chokehold from behind.

A second guard is already shepherding her to safety. Down the long dark stretch of the prison hallway Billy's wailing echoes like the mewling of a dying or injured animal, a godforsaken death rattle.

It's a sound sure to haunt the rest of her days.

56. CECIL

Baby brother is carrying a sackful of groceries when he lets himself panting into the place. He comes slow-stepping through the workshop and up the ramp into the debauched wasteland of Cecil's living area.

"Cecil? It's Ben," Ben has one free hand cupped across his nose. "You home? Brother? You alright?"

Cecil's still in pajamas, soiled ones, propped against the partial wall behind his mattress and smoking a Marlboro with rapacious concentration. On the bedside table are partly empty or overturned beer bottles and two wide-mouthed mason jars junked with his cigarette leavings: charred rolling papers and still-smoking butts mashed into a fine black scree of sedimentary ash.

Ben sets his sack on Cecil's couch, steadying himself against the doorjamb and the smell.

"Brother . . ."

Cecil holds up a hand, buying some time, drawing his cigarette down in one last crackling drag.

"What's . . ." Ben interrupts himself with a burp. "What are you doing?"

Cecil coughs out a blustery white cloud of smoke.

"Quitting."

He drops what's left of the cigarette into a mason jar, takes a pencil and his pack of Marlboros and makes his notation in the lid.

"That makes six today. I get three more."

"Three more what?"

"Cigarettes, idjit."

The idea was they'd grill a few steaks, watch today's away game against Iowa State. But Cecil forgot Ben was coming by, and the house reflects his tatterdemalion state. The kitchen's even meaner than the living room, days-old dish plates shellacked with dried oatmeal and refried beans and peanut butter paste and curdled milk. Banana peels rotting in the sink. There's plenty of room in his fridge for the groceries but nothing Ben would deem fit for consumption.

Ben finds some pink rubber gloves under the garbage disposal and snaps them over his shirt cuffs. He starts running hot soapy water for the cleanup.

"Get yourself a shit, a shave, and a shower," Ben shouts from the kitchen. "Game starts in a half hour and you smell like a pigpen, if you want to know the truth."

From his side of the knee-wall Cecil mutters some wiseacre incoherence under his breath.

"This place needs some sunshine," Ben says, cracking the mullion windows over the sink. He walks into the living room and throws the screen door wide. Even with the cold breeze Cecil doesn't budge. Ben makes a move for the mason jars, intent on dumping the offending ashtrays into the wastebasket.

"Leave off."

"Oh my God, Cecil. The smell . . ."

"The sight, too. Reminds me why I'm quitting."

Another inadvertent burp from Ben.

Cecil smiles.

"You're looking a little green around the gills yourself."

"I was up late last night."

"Meditating over a bottle of hooch?"

"Something like that. You have any Pepto in the house?"

"Bathroom. Behind the vanity."

Cecil hears baby brother searching through his medicine cabinet.

"This crap tastes like microwaved chalk," Ben says, coming back to the living room with the Pepto. "But I sure do like your new toy in there."

"Must have been made in Taiwan because it's already broken."

"Let's get you washed up."

Cecil shakes his head.

"What?"

"I can't."

"Why?"

Cecil massages his right shoulder.

"Gimped my shoulder again. Now I can't get back out of the tub. The other morning I was stranded two hours almost in that thing."

"What about your toilet?"

Cecil picks at his sheets.

"Brother . . ."

"It's been a couple days."

"Jesus, Cecil. How do you get this bad and not call?"

Baby brother undresses Cecil, helps him insert an ass bullet, a humiliation Cecil hasn't endured for at least two decades and one that he wouldn't mind avoiding for two more after today, then lifts him into the empty rig and wheels him into the bathroom and hugs him grunting onto the toilet.

While Cecil's bowels are emptying he can hear Ben finishing the dishes, stripping the mattress, starting a load of laundry.

Getting into the tub is tougher than it ought to be, but they finally accomplish it without major mishap. Once Cecil is installed in the water Ben mixes two shandygaffs in the kitchen. Cecil doesn't have any lemonade so baby brother improvises with Coors and orange Kool-Aid, dials up the game on television and punches the volume so they can catch the color commentary from the bathroom. Ben delivers Cecil's shandy to the bathtub and then lowers his bulk, both hands clamped about his own beer, carefully into Cecil's empty rig, which is parked beside the tub.

Cecil drinks the entire beer in one go, licking an orange, powdered moustache from his whiskered upper lip. He hoses his lopsided body with the handheld showerhead, soaping his skeletal legs—they're thinner than Ben's wrists—with arms that are starting to fail him.

He can tell that the serrated sight of this latest scar has Ben's stomach spinning cartwheels.

"Where's that new boy nurse?"

"I told him I was healed."

"I'm calling the service and get him back starting tomorrow."

Cecil doesn't answer. But he's not arguing.

Ben touches Sputnik and says, "How long before they fix this thing?"

"Insurance wants more paperwork before they'll fix it. I hadn't yet filled out the warranty."

"Give me the forms and I'll get it done." Ben finds something on the checkerboard tile worth looking at. "Have you ever thought about moving in with me and Becca?"

"As often as I think about rolling off a bridge."

"We've got the room. Or will have it, once the new addition is built. And I've already told the contractor to build one of these swing sets for the shower. For when you visit."

"Hand me that razor and that shaving cream, will you?"

Cecil beards his face in white foam and shaves without a mirror, the fingers of his left hand doing advance work for the blade. The individual noises of the basketball game soothe his scraggled nerves: the squeal of a shoe, the breathy grunts from a dead-ball brawl, the lonesome shrill of a whistle.

"There'll come a time when you won't be able to live like this any longer. Alone, I mean."

With the showerhead Cecil spritzes first the razor and then his clean-shaven cheeks. He's developed a talent for turning silence back on Ben and is flexing it now. Eventually he says, "I can see how from where you're sitting, my life here might not seem like a whole helluva lot to write home about . . ."

"What are you . . ."

"Don't interrupt! It's mine and I made it. Made it out of nothing. Capital-M made it. It's the only life I got and I tend to like it. So stop worrying that fat little head because I'm fine. I will be fine."

"You're fine."

"Capital-F fine. Now hand me the fucking shampoo."

"What you are is well down the road to another pressure sore and surgery, possibly traction . . . that's capital-T traction, brother . . . if you remember . . ."

"The only thing I can't do is get back out of this tub. Go fetch me another beer, then help me up so we can see the goddamn game already."

Ben eyes him awhile.

"I'm going to interpret this conniption as a good omen."

After bringing a second pair of Kool-Aid shandygaffs in from the kitchen baby brother lifts Cecil's naked and dripping proportions into the rig. While Cecil performs his skincare check Ben sits on the toilet. The brothers sip their fruit-flavored beers and try to avoid the touchy topic of home healthcare.

He's wearing flannel pajamas and his lucky game-day boots when Ben finally gets him tucked back into the living room. The bed has been remade with a fresh waterproof slipcover, crisp cotton sheets, and a comforter. The Cowboys are neck and neck with the Cyclones, the scoring's tit for tat. Nevertheless Ben takes a break to broil the steaks and pan-sear some mushrooms. Ben serves him dinner in bed and, despite Cecil's protestations, manages to swipe the giant ashtrays, hiding them out of sight in the garage while they eat. Two beers and Cecil's steel-wool world has blurred to blessed velveteen. He hoovers the steak like he hasn't eaten in weeks and, after his plate is cleaned, lights another Marlboro.

"Nothing like a smoke after a good meal," he sighs, leaning back into the pillow.

"Okay Blondie."

"Bring me one of those ashtrays."

"Nope."

"Where'm I gonna ash?"

"It's not my problem. I'm still eating."

Cecil resumes that shut-eyed rapture Ben walked in on earlier.

"You think Mother and Dad were happy?" Ben asks.

"Why?"

"No reason."

His eyes are still closed.

"It was different between them after I went into the hospital. Dad was different. He'd been riding me so hard for so long. I'd push back sometimes but he'd push back even harder. Back and forth like that was how we talked. Then I was hurt and he couldn't push anymore. Mother wouldn't allow it. Dad was beside himself. He couldn't figure out how to be around me. Couldn't talk to me the way he would a normal person. There was always this . . ." Cecil's eyes have opened, ". . . pity."

"I was mad at you after the accident."

"Mad."

"Jealous maybe. Mother and Dad were always gone to visit you in the hospital. I had to make my own breakfast, lunch, and dinners. Do the chores on my own. Walk to school on my own."

"Dad rode you twice as hard. I'm sorry."

"What are you sorry about? I'm sorry. Sorry for being mad. Sorry about my . . ."

"Ben," Cecil taps an ash into the steak sauce on his plate, *hisssss* . . . , "you were twelve."

Ben looks grateful for the interruption. In almost fifty years, this is as close as they've come to discussing the accident.

"I remember one fight in particular. It was right in my hospital room. I'm strung up in traction, pretending to sleep. And they're carrying on about the farm. Back and forth. Really going for the other's soft tissues. Dad was expecting I'd work the harvest and now he's having to hire someone instead. I guess you were too little to pick up the slack. Mother's saying to him how you mustn't be neglected. How he needs to see our new circumstances in a more positive light. But she puts it a little plainer than this. So then he digs in. You know how he'd get. But she stays on him. Badgers him just speechless. Finally he's had it. Storms out. But I hear him stopping at the door. 'Well,' he says. 'I love you Ida.' Then he huffs it out the door and on back home, I guess."

"I wish I'd seen that."

"The thing I remember is the way he said it. He really drew out the 'well.' Then he spit out the other part like it was spoilt milk. I mean he couldn't get it out fast enough. You could tell it cost him, saying that."

Halftime's almost over. Ben clears their plates into the kitchen and when he retrieves the ash-blackened mason jars from Cecil's workshop he comes back carrying a big gift-wrapped box, which he presents to Cecil without commentary.

Cecil opens the present in similar silence.

"What's a Toshiba . . . Satellite . . . P-R-O?"

"It's a notebook-type computer. You're supposed to be able to plug it into the wall and get the time and temperature, the news and whatnot, right from the phone line."

"I'd just as leave keep the phone line free for dialing time and temperature."

"This is different. There's more. It's called the worldwide web. They're saying it's the next big thing."

"Looks to me like the next big thing in Japanese paperweights." Cecil squints around what's left of the cigarette, turning his head sideways. "Are you catting around on Becca?"

"What?"

"Why are you so interested in Mother and Dad all the sudden?"

"No reason."

"I find out you're leaving Becca I'll get up out of this bed and open some whoop-ass on you right here."

Ben falls into the couch cushions with an overblown groan.

"I think . . ."

"What?"

"I think Becca might be . . . could be thinking about . . . leaving me. Maybe. I don't know."

Cecil opens his mouth but then promptly shuts it. A beat as he reconsiders.

"Can't blame her, really." He's trying hard not to smirk. "You find yourself living all alone, think about putting up in my spare bedroom. I'll take real good care of you, baby brother."

Ben's snigger gives Cecil permission to do the same and soon they're cackling like hyenas.

"Asshat," Ben laughs.

57. DEAN

Sam has to get back to work, so Dean takes her into the city and drops her off and barrels back to help Abigail canvas the area. He's had his fill of empty stares. A few more days, Dean is thinking, after chasing pavement all morning and afternoon, a few more days and they'll have given it the old college try.

He parks outside the Wright City burger palace where he left Abigail this morning and the translator is already waiting for him, here she is tap-dancing up to the driver's-side mirror, happy-go-lucky, a Styrofoam go-cup in hand. She curtsies down level with the window frame, a shit-eating grin weaseling across her face.

Abigail has found something.

"What do you think you have?"

She slips him a folded piece of notepaper.

"This is the grandmother's address. Billy's father's mother. I just spoke to her on the payphone. She's expecting us for lunch tomorrow in Antlers. Her name is Caroline Amos."

Dean leans out and kisses her full on the lips.

∾

In her starched blue jeans, polished cowboy boots, snap-fastened western shirt and bolo tie, it would be easy to mistake Caroline Amos for a man. But the silvering braid of hair falling down her back gives the woman away. A mixed-blood Choctaw Indian, Caroline's wiry, expressive hands compensate for a careful, pidgined diction.

"My Grammy claimed she could be seeing the *future*." Caroline Amos puppets all ten fingers before her face in a jokey kind of jazz-hands *taa-daaa!*

"She was always saying about some big troubles that was coming. How the earth was getting too heavy for all these people. How the buildings are going to break apart and fall into fire and things like that. She repeat this over and over but I never did believe it."

Now the fingers are making flame.

"But then I hear about those fires burning in Los Angeles two years ago. Then there are the earthquakes in California. And that mountain that was exploding there in Oregon. So all that's coming about now, just like Grammy said it would."

They are sitting in a cozy sunroom overlooking the quiet street where Caroline has lived her entire life. Dean on the couch, Caroline in the rocking chair, Abigail in the love seat beside her. Cold cheese sandwiches and hot tea on the coffee table. Spread flat on Dean's lap is a family tree resembling a basketball tournament bracket. Billy's name is penciled in the center.

Dean tries getting Caroline back on task.

"You were born and raised here in Antlers? Raised by your mother and grandmother?"

Caroline smiles innocently back at him, gently rocking.

Dean looks to Abigail for help. As the translator explains, Caroline's eyes light up. "Mammy and Grammy are come from *Mississippi*," she clarifies, pointing east, "before here."

"But you were born here . . ." Dean double-checks his notes, "to Tuesday Amos."

"That's right."

"In 1940. When was Tuesday born?"

"Don't know. Though Grammy was always saying Mammy is too young to be birthing babies."

Dean scratches two question marks next to Tuesday Amos's name. "Tuesday dies in 1979. You have your son Joseph with this . . . Hiram Deek?"

"Joe."

"Joe Amos, right. Born in 1956. Then Joe and Peggy Grimes have Billy in 1972."

Caroline is nodding, smiling, rocking.

"Billy takes Peggy's name," says Dean. "Joe takes your name. You take your mother's name."

The smile fades, the fingers clench. When Caroline suddenly stands and walks from the room her chair rocks audibly on the hardwood floor behind her. Dean looks to Abigail, puzzled. But the translator doesn't have any answers for him so Dean stares outside. Careful now, she's about to give you something. Beyond the sunroom window, a middle-aged man is sauntering somewhat idly along the sidewalk, casting hooded glances at the strange Oldsmobile parked before Caroline's house. A concerned neighbor.

Caroline returns clutching a turquoise leather photo album. She sits beside Dean on the couch, caressing the album.

"You are right in this. I wish I could be saying it was because of the old ways, but it was mostly being on account of shame. When I was born, my daddy was already married to another white woman over there. Though Mammy didn't care. Daddy was more handsome even than my Hiram, if the truth is told. Just look in those pictures."

Caroline surrenders the album to Dean. It begins with a single pinhole portrait of a beautiful Indian girl, no way she's older than fifteen or sixteen, and a skinny white kid with a five o'clock shadow. Caroline's mother and father.

"What was your father's name?" Dean asks.

"Eli Cain. Like that brother in the white Bible. Daddy was living here in Antlers while he did live. But he and his white wife die right before I was born. So Grammy raise me up there in the Choctaw ways because Mammy was too distress to do it herself. She wasn't wanting people to know I was a bastard child. Just like my Joe and his Billy."

Dean scratches in Billy's bracket: *Eli Cain (b: ??) (d: ~1940 - Antlers)*.

The rest of the album is filled with more recent shots of Caroline in her youth: Caroline and Tuesday, Caroline and her full-blooded Choctaw grandmother, Caroline and this Hiram fellow. Other pictures too, color Polaroids of a chubby brown boy and his haggard mother. There are birthday parties and picnics, swimming holes and yellowed summer Sundays lazing around the television set.

"These are of Billy?"

"Billy and Peggy. She give them to me before she move to the city. All in a tizzy, like."

The neighbor outside is looking straight at Dean, unseeing. From the way the man shields his face Dean can tell that a sun flare caught in Caroline's window has him blinded. Dean is briefly reminded of the observation room at Passages.

"Can you tell us more about Joe and Peggy?"

"Peggy was being Choctaw like Grammy. She was out on the carpet ready for marrying Joe. But he started getting the church ways into him, that white church over there. Joe was getting Jesufied just in time for Peggy to be pregnant with Billy in her belly. So he leave on a mission like they do it. Never did come back. Peggy raised Billy in the Choctaw ways just like Grammy did me. But one day she give it up for a white man from Tennessee. She give me these things and take Billy into the city over there to live with her sister. Never did come back, too."

"Did you ever visit Billy in Oklahoma City?"

Caroline waves Dean's question away.

"I don't like to be remove from my home. That is happen so much in the past. That is coming again soon enough, too."

"What's coming?"

"Grammy was always saying to us about a third removal is coming. The first removal to Mississippi. The second removal to Oklahoma. Then the white man is going to push us out into the forever and things like that. I start thinking that that can happen. Like her other seeings, that this can be coming true now. We don't disappear all in one sudden but bit by bit till the days are finish. Now we have the white man and the Choctaw being all mixed together in one blood. Grammy was always saying she think I will come out spotted, way Mammy got the hankering for white boys like that." A curt, crooked laugh. "That I got it from her, too. All this loving is thinning the blood. This makes me kind of wondering if that is the third removal."

Abigail is transfixed.

"So the third removal is love," the translator says.

"Yes. But even if it isn't always lasting, love is nothing to be scared of. Grammy was saying it will happen when there is no difference between inside," Caroline presses a palm into her breastbone, "and out." The other hand waves wide, an invitational flourish, indicating this chair, that desk, the noontime light outside. "Saying how scared I should be for these things, the end of time, like. When the night comes twice in one day, she said, then I will know it is true. But here it is. Here you are. And I think things are not so bad."

"I'm not tracking this," Dean says to Abigail.

Abigail opens her mouth to translate but Caroline rests a hand on Dean's left knee, way ahead of her.

"You were saying your name is night," she continues, squeezing softly. "So night will come twice today. You are bringing word of my grandson, my great-grandson. *Alla nakni.* Blood of my heart beating free in the world."

Not so free, Dean thinks.

"Would you mind terribly if we borrowed the photo album?" Abigail asks. "It could help your grandson, Billy."

"We'd make copies of the pictures and have it back to you within the week."

"*Okeh.*"

"What does this mean about the end of time?" asks Abigail.

"Nothing means nothing while it's meaning. It only means something once it's meant." Caroline cackles. "'Course by then the time for changing is going past."

58. AURA

Pastor Nate is still waiting when Aura curbs the car next to Opal's mailbox, crouched into a hunter's squat in his orange-knit beanie and dark woolen overcoat and smoking, if you can believe it, on her grandmother's front porch. It's early enough that even the roosters haven't started crowing, an icy drizzle spittling her windshield, so Aura blazes the high beams but leaves the engine running. Nate assumes his full height, makes a show of trampling the cigarette, and walks stiffly over to let himself into Aura's passenger-side door.

"I'm sorry it took so long to get here," Aura says. "I just got your message."

"She finally went down." Nate extends both palms to rub his fingers before the dashboard vent. "You ought to be there when she wakes up."

"I don't know how to thank you."

"I think you did that the other night."

Aura kills the headlights and cranks the heater, ignoring this, not ready to go there. "What set her off?"

Nate takes a business card from his pocket and slides it across the seat. It reads:

Ethan Podesta
Investigator
Oklahoma County Public Defender's Office

Aura gasps. Nate is bleeding from four parallel gashes cat-scratched into his cheek. She reaches out to touch the wound but he shies away.

"Grams did that?"

"She thought I was your brother. You two should talk about that, by the way. About him."

"I know."

"What if I'm not around next time, Aura? Someone could get hurt. Opal could."

"I know."

"Decisions like this don't come easy. But like it or not, it's time this one was made. Opal needs a full-time caregiver. And soon."

"Let me give you a ride home at least."

"It's only a few blocks. The walk will get the blood flowing." He slaps his cheeks, goes startle-eyed, shakes himself awake. "It's almost time for my first pot of coffee, anyhow."

"Thank you. Again. Thank you."

Nate smiles. "Eventually we're going to talk about the other night."

"I know."

"It was beautiful, Aura. A pure and uncorrupted thing."

"I know."

Inside, Opal is snugged under a homemade quilt on the couch, her breath heavy with sleep. A broom and dustpan in the kitchen, several broken dishes in the wastebasket; looks like Nate tried to clean up after the confusion. Aura sighs into the armchair and waits for her grandmother to stir. The television is on, of course, its vivid test pattern throbbing like the proud flag of some unmapped, colorblind country. A country of the future. The screen tricks Opal's furniture out in gossamer blues and sad, saccharine pinks. She should probably turn it off, but Aura can't summon the requisite activation energy.

"Devil take that boy," Opal whispers. "Where'd that Carl run off to?"

"Who, Grams?"

"Carl! Your brother! He's just here, Aura! They's looking for him! Those policemen from the city, trying to know where he's hiding. They want me to . . ."

"No, Grams," Aura takes Opal's hand. "Carl's dead."

"Why your hands so warm?" Opal tries to sit but Aura gentles her back to horizontal. "I won't have that talk in my house, child.

Hear me? A mistake's been made. Case of false identification!" Grams is getting worked up again, her eyes hungering about the living room. "You've got to help me find Carl, Aura! You've got to help me protect him."

Aura could use a little make-believe, right now, in her life. She kneels beside the couch and tucks Opal back under the quilt.

"I will Grams, just shut your eyes. We'll find Carl in the morning. Wait till the sun comes up. Right now we need rest."

"Promise me Aura, you'll help me find your brother. Promise me."

"I promise."

Opal turns against the couch cushions, comforted, and it's not long before her grandmother is spooned into a fetal curl and snoring lightly. Aura closes her own eyes. Time to regroup, to sleep if she can. But her worries are already working overtime from the tube-lit shadows.

Opal is losing her mind. Carl has lost his life. Aura's lost her trust in Cecil. And she just about lost her head over Nate.

She has never been one of these moon-eyed stargazers who believed that the world should, or even could, be fair or balanced. But Aura's been working hard and playing by the rules, as Clinton is so fond of saying, for such a very, very long time now. So why can't fate cut her a little slack?

She swats this thought away the moment it registers. Anyway it's the wrong question. *You're doing better than some*, she thinks, *worse than others. Just like everyone else you know*. No wallowing.

Another day will be starting soon, sooner than she'd like it to, and the best she's going to get before sunup is a shallow imitation of sleep.

Whatever. She'll take it.

59. BEN

"Pull!"

Ben sidearms an orange disc up into the dun-colored morning with a handheld skeet launcher. The trap Frisbees quickly out over the fog-wrapped field, it's really moving, as beside him Gary Chambliss tries drawing down on the target. The clay pigeon flies right, describing a lazy arc back to earth, then . . .

BOOOOM!

The disc splits into two distinct halves, each pinwheeling into the mist on opposite, wounded vectors. Ben slides the safety muffs down from his ears, necklacing them at his throat.

"Winged it."

Still holding the double-barreled shotgun, Chambliss lifts one of his own earmuffs.

"What's that?"

"You need to lead the target more. Don't aim for where it's already been, but for where it's going to be. That's why the bird's getting away from you."

Chambliss levers open the twelve-gauge and two spent shells pop from the breech with a hollow *thoomp!* to fall black and smoking into the trample of dead grass at his feet. He slides a fresh cartridge into each barrel and snaps the gun shut. Ben fits another clay disc into the thrower, wrestling with the spring-action arm until it has clicked into position.

"My turn."

The mayor's new chief of staff relinquishes the shotgun with care. Ben hands the awkward launcher to Chambliss and the man gives the contraption an experimental, slow-motion bounce, testing the heft of the thing in his hand. He indulges in a full-body shiver for warmth.

"Thanks, by the way, for making good on the . . . and for doing it so quickly too, Ben . . . on the second installment of our agreement from before. And for taking this meeting today. You've been real accommodating so far, what with this new role over at the mayor's office."

Ben smiles blankly and waits for the ask.

"You know the mayor thinks, and I think it too, that this M.A.P.S. effort is the future of the city. Of the whole state, even. It's big. And I want to make sure you and I are in lockstep as things start happening. I gotta be honest with you, Ben, when I say I don't know the construction business from Adam's mother-in-law. But I do know you'll be dealing with a lot of moving parts, a lot of contingencies. You'll have a whole mess of things on your plate trying to bring this project off. So I want you to think of me as your silent partner. Someone who can grease the gears, so to speak, and make things happen. Or even put a little sand in them, case you need to buy a little time with Terry or the oversight committee."

"Sort of an all-purpose, industrial lubricant."

Chambliss actually snorts.

"Funny. An effort big as this one, though . . . on occasion you're liable to find yourself in a rough spot. And I can help smooth things out. This is all I'm saying."

"Well I certainly do appreciate it Gary. Thanks a mil."

"Of course there needs to be a little something in it for me."

"You're acquiring a taste for the honeypot."

"I don't hafta tell you Terry doesn't like surprises."

Ben cracks the action on the shotgun, double-checking it's been properly loaded.

"God I love this gun."

"It's a beautiful firearm. Twelve gauge?"

Ben nods.

"Antique?"

"Nineteen-oh-two. A Parker Brothers VH-grade side-by-side with a satin black walnut stock. In the fifties someone had it refinished at the Remington factory."

Ben steps to Chambliss, balancing the break-action over his forearm while hugging the gun butt with his elbow.

"See these rainbow-looking swirligigs on the casing? To get that pattern they had to take the gun apart and bake the metal in cyanide. It's hard to do well, but it makes the thing worth a fucking fortune." He snaps the weapon shut and the briefest of vibrations steels through his forearms. This is a deadly-type tremor known mostly to hunters and target shooters and it has a palliative effect on his current temper. "Now why do you suppose they'd cook a gun casing like that? With poison?"

He can see the message registering in the lard behind Gary's stare. Chambliss stands his ground. But his gaze has fallen to Ben's trigger finger.

"To harden the metal. See, these old guns were made of alloys that were just a bit more malleable than today's. Not enough carbon. They needed some method to toughen the outer shell while leaving that softer inner core to absorb the everyday stresses. All that shooting can tax a gun's constitution." Ben bends his knees, bobbing and weaving his head until he's recaptured Chambliss's gaze.

"Boom!"

The man's face bleeds white with distemper but, to his credit, Gary barely flinches.

"It'd be a shame," Gary whispers, "watching you fail."

"And you right along with me. Terry's staying as far away from M.A.P.S. as he can. At least until you and me prove to him it's a slam-dunk. You've quit the city council, Gary, so if it all goes to Gomorrah he's only got you, Gary-Goddamn-Chambliss, for blaming. And in this town, quitters and losers don't move up, in business or in politics."

"Don't push me."

Ben mimics the man's earlier snort and a faint nebula of dragon breath curls from his nostrils.

"Didn't Terry warn you? Working for the mayor involves all kinds of unforeseeable stresses. It doesn't do to be too soft. Terry thinks, and I think it too Gary, that for a marshmallow like you it's the best move there is. Might just toughen your exterior up a bit."

Chambliss starts squabbling but Ben has already slid the safety muffs over his ears. He turns back to the tree line.

"Pull, you rat-fink motherfuck."

∽

He pictures life without Becca and feels like Dorothy's tin man, his heart hollowed to nothing but echoes. She's hiding some secret and he needs to know what it's all about. But he'll want to be a better man, or at least try to be, in order to deserve the knowing.

This break with Chambliss is a step in the proper direction but just the first one. He'll have to tell it all, all the petty bribes and cheats Ben has doled out over the years to get ahead. She won't like what he's been holding back. That he's a phony and a cheat and a backbreaker to boot. Ben has never told Becca about the night Cecil was hurt, how he was the one who caused the accident. She won't like any of it. But this is the only way he can think to get close to her again and he'll gladly suffer the consequences.

He's fretting like how a woman might but so damn what. Long as she doesn't leave him.

This is where his head is at when Ben walks into the kitchen later that evening. It's time for a reset. He'll do it soon. Tonight. Hell, he'll do it right now. Better to rip the Band-Aid off quick. Except Becca's already waiting for him at the dining table, her fingernails tap-tap-tapping the handle of a coffee mug and her face writ with worry.

She beats him to the punch.

"We need to talk."

60. BECCA

"About?"

"Why don't you set the gun down first, honey."

He has just walked in from a hunting trip and Ben has brought the fields in with him, that damp delicious smell of mud and buckshot and unshaven husband. He props his shotgun against the corner wall and takes the seat beside Becca at the kitchen table, exhaling in an almost meditative way as he settles into the chair.

She *tring-a-lings* two fingernails against her coffee mug.

"I haven't been entirely honest with you lately."

"How long is lately?" Ben asks.

"A few months."

There is a thick manila file folder on the placemat between them and Ben is doing everything he can not to see it.

"Don't do this babe," he pleads.

"What?"

"There's someone else."

"First of all don't *babe* me and second there is no one else. *No one.* Well, hold on, actually there is but it's not like that. It's not what you think. Thirdly . . ." This isn't at all how she imagined things would go. All of that preparation, all of that *practice*, and already she's lousing it up. Isn't it, what did Willa say . . . *upside-down* . . . she's so nervous? After visiting two prisons, after coaxing a jailhouse confession, Becca's more frightened of this little chat with Ben.

"We can fix this, Becca. I can . . ."

"Ben . . ."

". . . don't tell me any more about it. I don't care. I'll, I . . ."

". . . be quiet a second . . ."

". . . can change. I will . . ."

". . . I have something to say."

She takes his hand in hers and it's shaking, both of them are shaking, and this is when she understands: *he's scared.* For the first time in perhaps her life Becca feels more powerful than her husband. And she likes it. Likes it maybe just a little too much.

"I want to adopt Caleb, that little boy from the shelter."

Calmly now, she's no longer trembling, Becca tells all about the last two months, everything she knows. Opening the file folder, she shows him the poor boy's photograph, that sad lost soul—*it's an old soul, don't you think?*—shows him the transcripts from Abigail's language lessons, Caleb talking about the house of horrors he called home; shows him the parental release she has prepared for Willa—the girl hasn't agreed to this yet but she will, you'll see—the background checks they'll need to submit and the petition they can make to the family court, they can file it next week, all she needs is Ben's approval. His approval and his signature.

"Caleb's father is a Choctaw Indian, so it could get complicated," she says. "But we could start by fostering the boy. Billy hasn't agreed to any of this yet but I believe he will. And if he doesn't, take a look at the birth certificate. Willa never put the father's name on the form. So Mr. Gomez, the attorney I told you about, he says we can make Billy prove his paternity. There's a chance Billy might not even be Caleb's biological father. If he's found guilty, and he will be, the whole thing should go more smoothly."

"This is the kid being tried for murder?" he asks.

Becca nods.

"What if he gets out?"

"He won't get out."

"You can't know that."

"He did it."

"And you know this how?"

"Billy told me."

"You went to see him?" Carefully now. "In the county jail?"

"A few weeks ago."

"He knows your *name?* He knows what you *look like?*"

"And yours too. He has to meet us, Ben, if we're going to raise his child."

"I'm . . . I . . ."

"You're speechless." She laughs. "It's about time."

Ben shrugs out from beneath his DayGlo orange hunting vest, restless now, pulling at his undershirt collar.

"This isn't what I thought . . ."

She leans across the table, caressing her husband's hot chubby cheeks, leans in to kiss him deeply on the lips. It's a long, passionate kiss and when she pulls away Ben is better.

"I don't think I can do this without you."

"But . . ."

"But I will."

"It's funny because at the office I'm always wishing kids on my worst enemies. Hoping it will throw them off their game."

"But you don't mean it."

"I don't mean most of it. What about our retirement?"

"What about it? We could retire five times over and you know it."

"I need to understand why. Why this kid? Why now? Isn't the volunteering enough?"

"Whatever time we have left I want it to count."

"Becca, I haven't even met the kid."

"I can fix that."

"I'm not saying yes."

"You're not saying no."

"I don't know what I'm saying."

61. CECIL

After Ben dropped by and got him sobered and that foreign-made swing set repaired and that queer jowly nurse returned, Cecil's world slid slowly back into something like focus.

He decided to make good with Aura, or to try. Dialed every Jefferson in the book hoping to find her number. But only part of them answered and the other part wouldn't or couldn't help. Then he gets the bright idea of phoning the nursing service and pretending to be someone else—a made-up city doctor checking in on a made-up country patient—and this is how he learns about the regular church services in Langston and it's why he's driving there today, the last Sunday in winter, to try and see her and apologize.

He hasn't dedicated any thought to what he'll say. Just praying the words come out right when it's time.

The parking lot is empty when Cecil pulls into the handicap spot outside Gracefield Baptist Church. Figured to arrive as services were letting out, but Cecil must have misjudged. Nobody here but a tall, muscled, dandied-out Negro, clean-shaven dome slick as chrome under the noonday sun.

"Help you?" He's giving Cecil the stink-eye.

Cecil opens the truck door and rattles the rig down to the asphalt. He nods at the man's bright orange tie.

"I like that neckcloth."

He scootches across the bucket seat and out into the chair and the postcard-perfect weather, restless trees and hedges already coloring with the early buds of spring.

"You're an Aggie?" asks Cecil.

"Not quite. But I do know my audience. Mister . . . ?"

"I'm trying to find a young woman named Aura Jefferson. Someone said she went to church here?"

"Someone."

"That's right."

Standing there in his Sunday-go-to-meeting clothes, Nate sizes Cecil up. Has to be an ex-athlete, way he stretches out those pinstripes. When his power silence has finished the man grins, wipes both hands on his pants, and strolls over with one of them extended.

"I'm Nate Franklin, Aura's pastor here."

"I thought you looked like the preacher type." Cecil shakes an aggressively muscled hand. "Cecil Porter."

"Mr. Porter, I sure could *eat* right about now. Could you eat?"

"I could last I checked."

"I have some *diabolical* chicken salad sandwiches in the kitchen. Best blasted chicken salad you'll ever *have*. Blow those taste buds right off your *tongue*. Mrs. Thurston down the way makes them for me just about every Sunday. She's worried I'm wasting away." The preacher's big grin biggering as he claps hands upon his paunch. "But I think that's just wishful thinking on her part. Come on inside and we'll have us a little chat."

"I appreciate it."

"Can I give you a push up the ramp?"

"I'll manage."

The church is a modest sandstone saltbox with a ten-foot steeple and a cat-slide roof pitched higher away from the street. A pair of well-tended redbuds planted out front just itching to blossom. There is a switchback ramp hugging one side of the building and as Cecil navigates the too-narrow affair he's mindful of the ornery shoulder, hairpinning once at the landing before finally achieving the patio, where pastor Franklin is holding one of the front doors ajar, a puzzled expression on his face.

Inside, past a small sunlit vestibule, is the high shadowed hush of a sanctuary.

Cecil wasn't sure what to expect from an all-black church. But other than the tall gothic window frame someone's boarded over with plywood there doesn't seem to be anything particularly noteworthy about the interior of this one, just some oaken pews and lectern and a choir box with a little patch-quilt electronic organ in one corner.

"Renovating?" Arching an eyebrow at the window hole.

A wrinkle in the preacher's smile.

"I wish it were that. Some pack of vandals ruined our stained glass a few months back. The congregation tell me I should be putting a storm window up, some curtains at least, until we get the money to replace it. But I'm not on board yet. I think that hole reminds us of something."

"Of what?"

"That's the million-dollar question, isn't it? I think it's different for everyone. Speaking strictly for myself, the sight of where that window used to be lights *hellfire* in my belly. Makes me preach with *feeling*. I swear if I ever catch those goddamn kids . . ."

"I thought you weren't supposed to say that in here."

With one hand the man holds a finger to his lips. Then he points to the sloped ceiling and says, "I'll let you in on a little secret about our *creator*, Mr. Porter. He knows when we don't mean it." The smile is recovering. "Come on into the kitchen and let's break some bread."

This pastor has a voice like a thunderstorm, deep and undulant and biblical, and it makes you want to sit straighter in your chair.

The kitchen looks equipped to serve half-a-hundred people or more and has a vaguely institutional aroma, bacon or some other type of grease cut with lemon-scented bleach. Freestanding deep-fryer, gas-heated griddle, a couple of industrial-sized refrigerators.

Franklin pours two mugs of coffee.

"We've always got a fresh pot going. I swear sometimes people show up more for the caffeine than anything else, good word included." The preacher laughs. "But I'll pack the pews any way I can." He serves two chicken salad sandwiches wrapped in wax paper and they both eat slowly, eyeing one another from opposite ends of the aluminum island and sipping loudly at their coffees.

When his sandwich is gone the preacher wipes noisily at the corners of his mouth with the wax paper.

"What's your denomination, Mr. Porter?"

"Oh, I don't go to church anymore. But it used to be Church of Christ."

"Church of Christ. Over there in Perkins?"

"That's right."

"So you were under pastor Bynum?"

"Not quite. Bynum's new, past ten years or so."

"What happened?"

"I guess I just stopped seeing the point in all of it."

"I meant with your wheelchair there."

"Oh. Farming accident," Cecil lies.

"Looks to have been a pretty nasty one."

"Could have been worse."

"How old were you?"

"Sixteen."

"Sixteen. Hadn't even gotten started yet."

His cup is empty so Cecil sets it aside, wishing they could talk about something else.

The preacher obliges.

"Aura tells me you're a basketball player."

"Was."

"Did you ever see her brother play?"

"Her brother?"

"That boy was a *rocketman* on the court. I watched him dunk all the way back from the free-throw line one time. I was still in seminary then. Carl must have been oh, about fifteen or thereabouts. He sails through the air like he's just grown *wings*. Could have been the best ballplayer ever came out of Langston, better maybe than our Globetrotter, Mr. Marques Haynes, if he'd kept at it."

"Carl Jefferson. From Langston."

"It's a shame about what happened."

"Of course. Listen, I thank you for the sandwich. Tell this Mrs. Thurston it was the best chicken salad I've ever had."

"She wouldn't be happy with anything less."

"You think you could point me in Aura's direction?"

"You'll need to drive into the city to see her."

"She's moved?"

"Lord no. She's meeting with the district attorneys today about the trial."

"The trial."

"Aura and her grandmother have been asked to testify in the killer's trial, if it comes to that."

"The trial of the man who killed her brother."

"Yes."

"That has got to be tough on a person."

"I'd have you leave me a note to give her," says the preacher, rising to clear coffee cups and toss trash, "but my guess is you'll want to speak to her in person."

"You're a good guesser."

The preacher offers Cecil a toothpick, saying, "I'll show you out." Then, as they're rolling through the darkened sanctuary, "You make sure and come back now, Mr. Porter. We takes all *kinds* here."

Cecil brakes beneath the boarded-up window. He's driven all this way to eat crow and shouldn't take the bait. But Franklin is too forward to be completely in the dark.

"I get the feeling you know all about who I am and why I'm here."

"Aura did relay a few of the juicier bloopers."

"It's . . . listen, this is just how we talk. How my father talked."

"*Listen*," chides the preacher. "*We. My father.* This doesn't sound like someone who's taking responsibility."

"It's how I talk. Always have. I never saw any real malice in it."

Franklin is pulling a frown, unconvinced. Rather than make eye contact, they are both looking up to where the stained glass used to be, the preacher standing perpendicular to Cecil's rig, a crosspiece of sun honeying thinly through the church despite the plywood protecting the window hole.

Cecil chews his toothpick and admits, "But now I do."

Franklin claps him on the good shoulder.

"Don't punish yourself too much, Mr. Porter. This might be the first time you've been caught saying the great unsayable *n-word* but I can guarantee you it's not the first time Aura's heard it. The fact remains you're here and you're sorry. That's all that counts in my book. And it gladdens my heart. Gives me a reason to hope."

"I lost my head at that game," Cecil says, fascinated by the missing window. "When I said it? Watching those kids on center court, watching Aura. She moves with such . . . grace. And I got to thinking she was as good or better at handling that basketball than I had ever been. Or ever would be again. I was jealous of it, of that freedom I used to feel on the court. I have to find her. To tell her."

"Tell her what?"

"That I'm sorry."

"Yes you do. But she's juggling too much right now as it stands. You might give her some space."

"I will." Cecil is nodding. "You know, I'm not accustomed to thinking of myself as a racist."

The pastor's laugh is seconded by a ghostly murmur from the echo-chambered chancel.

"I wouldn't say you were that."

"You wouldn't."

Outside, a flock of birds rockets pell-mell past the window hole, strobing the sanctuary with glimmer-ball bursts of light and darkness.

"It takes power to make a racist, Mr. Porter. Clout. A racist is someone who can change my fate. Someone who denies me a job or railroads me into jail or out of town or takes away my vote or my wife or my life. But you'd have trouble standing up to swat a fly, wouldn't you? I'd say this makes you just a harmless little bigot. And not a very good one at that, all the trouble you're taking to make amends."

"You're enjoying this."

"Yessir I am. And not ashamed to say it."

"I'm making your day."

The pastor appears merely as a massive shadow among the scanter shadows deepening the sanctuary, but when he smiles those white teeth surface suddenly, brilliantly, from the depths.

"Old man, you are making my entire *month*."

⌁

Later that same evening Cecil is bent into his workbench and sketching a pattern, inspired. There are reference books strewn atop the desk, ornithology manuals and *Birds of North America* and various encyclopedias and his Holy Bible and among them is a brittle hardback volume titled *Pistol Pete: Veteran of the Old West*, broken open at the spine to a passage that reads:

Wah-ken-tucka, the Great Indian Spirit, said to the wise men, 'I will put a curtain in front of the future to hide all the evils that frighten you, for know you not that you live only in the present moment? When the night comes dream of the future and see if your dream comes true.'

Since that day we cannot tell what may happen, for the curtain is before us. But we can paint on it beautiful pictures, not with our hands but with our spirit, and ask the Great Indian Spirit to help us make them come true. But the curtain rolls up and we cannot see beyond the present. We can only ask Wah-ken-tucka to look after us, for he alone knows the future.

You go your whole life blinded to a truth and then one day it becomes self-evident, though of course it's been there all along, just waiting for you to get wise, and now it's all you can see, now it's the only thing under heaven worth knowing.

He dials Ben and after four rings baby brother picks up, chuffing hard into the receiver.

"You're up awful early."

"I'll say . . . it's . . . whewsh . . . goddamn brother it's . . . not even light out? What's this about? You okay?"

"Everything's fine," says Cecil. "But I need your help."

THE CURTAIN OF
THE FUTURE

SPRING 1995

62. DEAN

"There is magic in the blood," Dean is saying. "Magic and power. *Kallo*. Without the power I am nothing. The laws were written to dilute the blood and so I do not recognize them. The laws were written in a language of the past. *Illinaha*. But the past is dead and the future is a lie. There is only now. And so the laws do not apply. The only law is survival, survival and the blood and the magic and the now."

Seated Indian-style on the conference room floor, the small of his back pressed into a wall. His eyes are closed. There are others here; he can sense the indulgent rhythms in their listening: the airy rustle from Staples's paperwork, the wet smoker's sough under Dragnet's sigh, the heavy steady tread of Wolfman's shoes across the carpet piling. Whatever that is Dr. Kevorkian's chewing on.

"The woman is tolerated. I care for her only so long as she can sustain the blood. The boy I care for instinctively, as I do myself. It is both a burden and a form of self-preservation. Because the boy is a successor to the blood, though the woman has diluted its power, and whenever I find myself without him I am reduced, vulnerable, *kallo keyu*."

"Timeout."

"Hear-hear."

"Methinks Tonto should lay off the peace pipe."

"Everyone *shuddup*."

"This is some hoodoo horseshit if you ask me."

"Well I didn't goddamn ask you," says Wolfman. "Tonto, if you would be so kind."

Every data point the team has uncovered about Billy Grimes is noted on a four-foot length of butcher paper unfolded on the floor before Dean. There are dates and times and places and names, hospital stays and days home sick from school and arrests and truancy reports and more, all of it footnoted in chronological order using an obscure shorthand Wolfman developed, years ago, for this specific purpose. They call this document a lifeline and Dean lays hands on it now, on Billy's lifeline.

"You might see these incidents as some sort of cry for help but you will be wrong. These collisions with the law are a testing of its jurisdiction." Opening his eyes, he points to a particularly severe concussion indicated on the lifeline. "I should have died here but I did not." He points to a fractured vertebrae when Billy was seventeen. "I should have been paralyzed here but I was not." An emergency room visit. "And here I should have overdosed but, again, I did not. Every time, the magic held. Confirming its power." Dean looks to Wolfman. "I have them cut the boy's hair short because I do not want him to appear different. But he is different, as I am. Different because of the blood. I teach the boy the language, *anumpa isht okchaya*, as a means of discovering the magic in the blood. I teach him the language as a protest against the dead and dying laws."

"Time. Fucking. Out." It's Dragnet.

"I do not understand these rules intellectually but they are nevertheless understood. Felt. And though I do not know it, this philosophy dictates my every action. This is . . ."

"I'm not feeling it," Kevorkian says.

". . . both a burden and a form of self-preservation."

"I can help you with that, sugar."

"Objection," Staples says. "Blatant sexism."

"The witness can't . . ."

Kevorkian bites into her cereal bar. "Sustained."

"There's more," Dean says.

"I'm not sure I can take any more," says Staples.

"That's what she said," Dragnet says.

"That's it," Kevorkian says through a mouthful of food. "I'm holding counsel in contempt."

"Honey, you can hold me any way you like," Dragnet says, doffing his straw cowboy hat and fondling the silver-plated cap gun wedged behind his belt buckle.

"Do I have to remind you nincompoops that a man's life is on the line here?"

"Who says *nincompoop* anymore?"

Wolfman swallows his answer, a vein bulging, blue and freakish, down the ridgeline of his forehead.

"Wait," Staples says, "are we live?"

They call it the Murder Board. Four men and a woman staging a fake trial in the boardroom. A few days ago Wolfman distributed a file folder containing the essentials of Billy's case to the attendees, and today everyone should have come prepared to poke holes in his argument. With the big cases they've been known to recruit law students as jurists, to rehearse for days, weeks even, pulling all-nighters if Wolfman's feeling jittery about his strategy for the cross. But the evidence against Grimes is so overwhelming, he'll get a handful of afternoons at most.

"Magic in the blood." Wolfman paces cagily about the mock courtroom. "An all-expenses-paid vacation to Indian territory for your vision quest or whatever it is. And you come back with magic in the blood." Fanning the air with a forearm, as if fending off an unpleasant smell, he says, "Let's get back to Willa. Staples, you're on."

"Let me get into character." Staples tosses back his head, alternately pursing and distending his lips, a gargled sort of *waawaawaawaa* warbling from his throat. "Okay shoot."

They've moved the conference table flush with the windows, Wolfman at one end of it arguing against district attorney Dragnet at the other. In preparation for his role as Bob Macy, Dragnet has worn a bolo tie around his neck, a child's straw cowboy hat on his head, a silver-plated cap gun at his waist. Judge Kevorkian presiding behind an aluminum file cabinet someone dragged in from the graveyard of closed case files down the hallway. Seated beside her at the card-table witness stand is Staples, playing whichever role they require, which right now is Willa Busby.

". . . do you remember, Willa, what Mr. Jefferson said," Wolfman is saying, "when Mr. Grimes admitted he didn't have the money?"

Assuming the punchy, semi-hostile attitude Willa is expected to take on the stand, Staples scratches his forearms and says, "Oh he said lots of things but I'd heard them all before. 'Cause Billy never had *any* money, know what I'm saying?"

"Did Mr. Jefferson threaten you or Mr. Grimes or Caleb?"

"I'll say he did."

"What exactly did Mr. Jefferson say?"

Staples consults his notes. "He said and I quote: '*You best git that money right quick or I'm gone lose my temper on yo' cracker ass.*'"

"Were you scared?"

"Damn straight I was scared," Staples snorts. "Not, like, *Exorcism*-style scared but still."

As Wolfman cross-examines the fake witness, as fake district attorney Macy objects or doesn't, as fake judge Kevorkian overrules or sustains or chews absently at her breakfast, Dean observes from the sidelines, dissecting his boss's eye contact, body language, word choice, inflection. From the way Wolfman equivocates, Dean can tell he's already thinking about the penalty phase, future appeals, the outside chance he could score a mistrial.

After exhausting his line of questioning with Willa, the public defender switches off his courtroom voice, seeming to shrink into his suit.

"Lay it on me."

"You're good to go," Dragnet says. "Basically ready for trial."

Kevorkian is nodding. "I think basically you're good."

"This is a tough one," Staples offers.

"I want to hear what Tonto thinks."

"You nailed Willa," Dean says to Staples.

"It wasn't too white trashey?"

"Not a bit."

Proud of his interpretation, Staples does a little bow from his chair.

"She'll try to crack jokes in the courtroom," Dean says to Wolfman. "The lighter it gets when we're talking about Billy, the better. When you're asking about their relationship, let her have the spotlight. If we can laugh at Billy, he seems less intimidating. But we can't afford for the jury to start laughing when you're asking about Carl Jefferson, so shorten her leash for that testimony." Dean imitates Wolfman's drill-sergeant demeanor, "'What I'm about to ask you, Miss Busby, this is a very important part of the trial. If you don't mind, let's just keep your answers to yes or no for a little stretch here, okay?' Like that."

"What else?"

"We want them thinking of Billy Grimes as a child and of Carl Jefferson as a threat. And 'mister' means I'm a full-grown adult, responsible for my actions. Let everyone else in the courtroom but Billy be responsible. So Willa is 'Miss Busby,' Carl is 'Mister Jefferson.' But Billy is always Billy. Just Billy."

"What else?"

"Stop pulling your punches. It's not lost yet."

"Maybe you want to argue this one?"

"You're the one getting paid to talk."

Wolfman laughs.

"If only they paid me by the word."

Kevorkian raises her hand.

"This isn't elementary school," Wolfman says.

"Excuse me . . . but . . . we want them thinking of this guy as a child? What kind of legal strategy *is* that?"

Dean closes his eyes and runs his fingers over Billy's lifeline. There's an entire life here, elided into a single sheet of paper. When he begins to talk it is in the same zombified monotone as before. It was important to get the words right. The order and the cadence and that stupid, impenetrable logic. He's repeating himself but only to resume the flow.

"I do not understand these rules intellectually but they are nevertheless understood. Felt. And though I do not know it, this philosophy dictates my every action. This is both a burden and a form of self-preservation. For like a child I believe in magic. I believe this magic has the power to protect me. To save me. I am a child in a man's body and I meet existential threats with a man's violence. Tit for tat but tenfold. But I am not responsible because, like a child, I live only for the here and now. There is no past, and the future is a lie. Only this man threatening me and the boy and thus our magic, so he must be dealt with."

Dean opens his eyes. This is as close to Billy Grimes as he will ever be.

"Protect me."

"I'm sorry, Wolfman," Kevorkian says, crushing her cereal bar's wrapper and sucking at her teeth, "but this doesn't make any fucking sense."

"It doesn't need to make fucking sense, Lindsey," Wolfman says. "It just needs to help."

63. AURA

Opal won't come out of her coat. They checked into the Wellspring Assisted Living facility over an hour ago and ever since unpacking her grandmother's suitcase Aura has been trying unsuccessfully to get Grams to relax.

"Look at that. There's a little pond outside your window."

Opal hugs deeper into her peacoat.

"When we leaving for home?"

"We're already there."

"This no home, child. This a *hotel*."

"It's an apartment. It's *your* apartment. There are people here to cook for you, to clean for you, to help care for you."

"I expect they'll be wanting a tip."

"Everything's already been paid for. There's no reason to tip. It might actually offend them."

Opal scopes out the one-room studio. There's a sofa, half a fridge puttering under the kitchenette sink, a dresser and a little end table and a big-screen TV. Last night, hoping to make today's transition easier on the both of them, Aura dropped by to hang a few of Grams's most treasured pictures. Also made up the bed, draped a familiar quilt over the sofa back, unwrapped a bar of scented soap for the private bathroom. But it was all so silly, she's realizing.

Because how could you expect this to be anything but the most awkward kind of awful?

"Where's the rest of it at?"

Aura indicates the door. A polished brass peephole and throwbolt both contribute to an illusion of privacy. But the nurses—check that, she won't call them nurses, the *caretakers*—all carry a skeleton key should they need access to Grams in an emergency.

"The dining room and game room and television are all out there, remember? You want to go take another look?"

Grams disappears deeper into her collar. She's not so sure about this faux front door—*what kind of people paint an inside door blue, Aura, anyhow?*—but just then a *knock-knock-knocking* comes from the other side of it.

It's Tahira, the intake nur . . . no—*caretaker*—holding a bouquet of wildflowers she's gathered from the footpath surrounding the Wellspring grounds.

"How are we settling in, Opal?"

Tahira is a tall, graceful Indian woman with a dancer's taut posture and soft, sympathetic eyes. Inviting herself inside, she places the bouquet in an empty vase beside the television set and beams beatifically down at Grams.

"It is much too warm to be wearing this coat in here, Opal! Let us get you out of it then. It will be time to take the tour. Simon will be setting out the lunch by now. Today we will be having the chicken and the dumplings, with a nice pecan pie for dessert. And trust me Opal, you will not want to miss Simon's dumplings."

Opal is more pliant with this stranger and gives up her coat without a struggle.

Tahira escorts Grams past the threshold but Aura hangs back a bit, bracing herself for the lunch to come. Look at them already. Chatting like long-lost friends. Grams hanging on her new handler's every word, hanging on to her elbow for support. Aura wanders, alone, along the hallway after the two women. It's a nice place, Wellspring, equal almost to the rosy picture painted in the official literature. Professional. Clean. Friendly. Just five minutes' drive from Aura's apartment in downtown Stillwater. They might even see more of one another.

For better or worse, though, Grams is here to stay. Here to live out the remainder of her days. Or Aura's savings, whichever comes first. Selling Opal's car, selling the house, these things would help. A lot. But for how long?

Of course it's for the better.

So why this sense of abandonment or loss? That same runaway train churning her stomach, like this was the first day of grade school?

The dining room is buzzing with news of Opal's arrival, a capacity crowd of blue-haired old ladies and liver-spotted old gentlemen—mostly it's blue-haired old ladies—everyone seemingly eager to meet the new neighbor. Offering to sit with Opal and Aura, Tahira begins dishing dirt on their tablemates.

"Opal, you must keep your eyes on Bennie here." Tahira touches Grams above the elbow. "He will rob you blind in the bridge game. Personally I think he has found a way to cheat. But do not get too pleased with yourself, Bennie. We are wise to you."

"They got the blacks and the whites equal," Opal says. "Everyone sitting together now."

"We all get along here," Tahira assures Grams before introducing Roseanne McGuire, the Irish widow whose auburn hair won't ever go gray: "I hear rumors," Tahira whispers when Roseanne isn't listening, "that Roseanne owns at least one dozen wigs." And wheelchair-bound Pauline Hobson, the oldest woman on the wing at ninety-seven or ninety-eight, Pauline can never remember: "Pauline will say she has met Ulysses Grant. But I believe she is joking."

It's comforting to see Grams in a different context. Next to Mrs. Hobson here, Opal seems spry as a prizefighter. Aura can't help but feel Tahira's giving them some special sort of treatment. But she's worked with enough geriatric specialists to know that making people feel special is this woman's job.

Sensing Aura's mood, perhaps, Tahira blinks a good-humored wink—*everything's going to be just fine here*, the gesture promises, *your Grams is in good hands*—and Aura is immobilized by a boundless rush of love for this beautiful, this wonderful caretaker.

Aura has never been good at goodbye. But after lunch is over, after two games of bingo, okay make it three, and one of dominoes, after showing Opal back to the new apartment, Aura hears herself saying it.

"I've got to go, Grams. I'll see you tomorrow, okay? Tomorrow after work."

"Aura, don't put me in this hidey-hole too long. These people so *old!*"

64. CECIL

Remembering he's forgotten to curtain the workshop, Cecil rolls for his garage only to find Ben there, pondering several stained glass windows and sipping from a bottle of Pepto-Bismol. Must have missed him coming in. Cecil watches his little brother for a moment. Standing quietly before the window, haloed by a last flame of dusk burning through the clouds outside, Ben looks to have lost all definition.

Cecil glides down the ramp, slowing to a stop beside Ben and the workbench.

"Lost?"

"You made this?"

Ben's free hand floats above the newest window, air-tracing the pattern. Cecil has been working day and night to complete it and is about ready to start soldering panes.

"I'm still making it. That one's not quite finished. But yes. It's what I called you about."

"You do the rest of these windows too?"

Cecil fishes in his shirt pocket for a cigarette, nodding.

"I thought you were quitting."

"I keep telling people," Cecil sighs. "It's a process."

"Cecil these are . . . I mean, really. I never thought you were capable of something so . . . beautiful."

Cecil lights his cigarette.

"What's on your mind, Ben?"

Ben ignores the question.

"You never told me about the windows."

"It's just a hobby. Calms me down some."

From where he's standing next to Cecil's rig Ben bends down to attempt a sort of sideways, bumbling hug. There are pronounced, lamp-black-looking shadows under baby brother's eyes and he's wearing an absent grin, like he's lost some of his marbles.

"What was it you wanted to ask?" Ben says.

"Are you drunk?"

"The answer to that one, right now at least, is no. I should be feeling fitter than a fighting cock. You probably haven't heard."

"Heard what?"

"I'm about to be a father again."

Cecil tries to swallow his reaction but all he winds up getting is a mouthful of smoke.

"I was worried Becca was about to leave," Ben blurts. "I thought she was hiding something from me. Well this was it. She wants to adopt a five year-old boy. Caleb. The kid's a Choctaw Indian, has trouble speaking English, both parents in jail. Emotional problems. Personality disorder probably. Most likely he'll grow up to be violent."

"I think I saw a Hallmark card the other day for this exact situation."

"You don't ever turn it off do you?"

"Sorry."

"If I say no she actually might leave me."

Cecil draws some more smoke into his lungs and exhales slowly, savoring that illicit taste. Eventually he turns his rig to face baby brother.

"Look here, Ben. You've got all the money a man could want. You've got a good-looking woman who can stand to be around you long enough to raise two smart, good-looking kids. She's even saying she wants to do the parenting thing all over again. That's some kind of commitment. That's love, brother. Most people would pay to have these problems."

"You're right."

"I know it."

Ben swigs on his Pepto-Bismol.

"You needed my help with something."

"Later."

"Out with it."

"Remember that nurse I took to the Kansas game?"

"The basketball player. The black woman."

"Aura. I might have . . . no. I did. I messed up. I hurt her. And I'm trying to make amends. She goes to church in . . ."

"Hurt her how?"

Cecil lets the cigarette drop to the garage floor, extinguishes it with his tire.

"I called her a nigger."

"Oh Cecil. Oh no."

"Well I . . . I mean . . . it . . . I . . ." Cecil stutters, "I said it just generally. I wasn't talking about Aura."

"Jesus Christ. This doesn't make it any better."

"I know it. I do know it. I said it about someone else and she happened to overhear. We were getting to be friends. But after this happened Aura broke it off. Now I'm trying to fix it."

Ben tilts his Pepto bottle at the unfinished window, liquid sloshing thick and pink inside the plastic container.

"This fixes it?"

"Who the hell knows, I'm making this up as I go along."

"What would she want a window for? Especially one shaped like this?"

"She goes to church in Langston, so I drove over there looking for her. I was trying to apologize in person but wound up talking with Aura's preacher instead. Her church used to have a big stained glass window hanging over the chapel. But some kids smashed it last winter and this preacher, he's been saving to replace the thing ever since."

"So you're going to step in and . . ."

"That's right," Cecil interrupts. "My thought was I could donate this one to Aura's church. I've already arranged everything with the preacher. Nate's his name. I don't want Nate having to pay a dime, though, if I can get away with it. I owe Aura that much. I owe her more. She helped me, not just with the injury but helped me see some things. And I was wondering if you would ask one of your guys to come over and pack this window up after I'm done. Maybe help me truck it over to Langston and then take care of the installation? I can build the window but there's not a chance in hell I'll be able to secure it, waterproof it, insulate it, frame it. Flash it. The jamb's at least ten feet off the ground. You know someone who could do that? It would mean a lot to me. It would mean everything."

"You haven't strung that many sentences together since I've known you."

"Don't make fun."

"I'm only joking."

"This isn't a joke."

"Okay, okay, I know it isn't. And the answer is yes. I can positively handle the installation for you. Give me the pastor's name and I'll send a contractor over next week to take measurements."

"You can see it's a nonstandard frame, this octagon shape here. Your guy will need to cut an outside storm window to keep the moisture away."

"Consider it done. But there's something else you need to think about."

"Which is?"

"Which is what you'll say to Aura when you see her next."

Cecil tucks his shirttail tighter under his belt. "I was hoping those words would just reveal themselves to me over the fullness of time."

"They won't."

"What would you say then? You're the spin doctor in the family."

"Sorry can't be spun, brother."

"Maybe this is a bad idea."

"It's the best idea I can remember you having. But you'll need to practice. Here," Ben says, leaning back against Cecil's worktable, "pretend I'm her."

"Pretend you're Aura?"

"That's right. I'm Aura." Ben is pulling back his shoulder blades, pushing out his chest, pretending to pretty up an imaginary hairdo. "Now, Cecil Porter. Apologize."

"Well, I'd say to her, I'm sorry . . ."

"Start with her name. 'Aura,' you would say to her, 'I'm sorry for being such a bigoted old broken-down wrongheaded codger who will cut off his nose to spite his own face.' Something in that vein."

"Aura. I'm sorry."

"And . . ."

"Stop needling me. This isn't easy."

"You think it will go any easier with her? Or that it will be any easier *for* her, hearing it? Trust me, Cecil. Practicing will help. Just say how you feel."

"Trust you," Cecil says. "Alright. Aura. I am sorry about saying what I said. I know it's hurt your feelings and that's the last thing I wanted. I grew up saying this word. Don't take that wrong, it's not an excuse, I'm just trying to explain. My father said it, his father said it, it's not something I ever thought much about. It's a reflex. It wasn't until the other day, I was thinking about how people look at you when you're crippled, that I started to understand a little about how it works. See there's a fear in people's faces when they look at me, like they believe being crippled is something that rubs off on a person. There was always this little stab of fear I'd get around black people. Fear because you're different. Maybe it's not fear. But it's something. And saying 'nigger' made me feel superior, helped push that feeling down. I don't know, Aura, I don't quite understand the mechanics of it. But I hope this is getting across. What I'm saying is that I considered, I still consider, you as a friend. You helped me see this blind spot in my heart and . . ."

Cecil trails off, unsure what comes next.

"Finish the thought," Ben says.

Drawing a deep chestful of breath.

"I'm not even wanting you to forgive me right now. That would be too much to ask of a person. It took me sixty-three years to understand how black people and me are so similar. You've had to cope with this look all your life. I've only been dealing with it since my accident. I'm a slow learner. But I am learning, Aura. I'm still quitting the smoking. And if you'll just give me the chance, I can prove to you it won't ever happen again. I can . . . wait . . ." Cecil slaps Ben on the leg. "Are you blubbering?"

Ben thumbs a tear from the corner of one eye.

"Big Ben Porter doesn't blubber. This is Aura Jefferson you're talking to, remember?"

"So how was that?"

"It was fine. It was better than fine," Ben says. "What do you think she'll say?"

"I wish I knew."

The brothers are silent for what feels like forever.

"Listen, Cecil. I've been wrestling with this adoption thing for a little stretch of time now. And it's got me thinking, you know, since we're saying our sorries, about making some changes of my own. I wanted to . . . about your accident."

Cecil goes fishing for another cigarette, but then realizes with a sad and hungry feeling that he has already smoked the day's allotment.

"I've always felt responsible," Ben says. "I knew you'd let me drive it home. I knew you'd know it was wrong, too. That Dad wouldn't approve. But I knew you'd let me do it and so I asked. You were going places. But then by trying to drive that truck I stranded you here in Perkins. It's all my fault. And then you saved my hide, lying to Mother and Dad like that."

"Somehow I doubt Aura will say any of that."

"I'm sorry. I love you Cecil and I'm so sorry. I feel like we need to start over from that night. With everything."

"It's okay. It's nothing."

"It's everything. You were my hero, brother. If I'm honest, you still are. I couldn't have lasted as long as you have in this town, in that chair. I don't know how . . ."

"It's getting late." Cecil aims his rig at the ramp. "Let's go inside."

"Alright."

"And Ben?"

"What?"

"Thanks."

65. BECCA

She is rereading the nearly completed adoption paperwork when Ben gets home. Back from another visit with Cecil. He has been spending quite a bit of time in Perkins. And why not? There has always been some scabbed-over tension between the Porter brothers. These visits can only do them good.

Before she can deliver this packet to Gomez, though, Becca needs Ben's signature on one final document—Willa has finally agreed to relinquish her parental rights to Caleb—so when he walks into the kitchen Becca waylays her husband, pen in hand.

"I need your autograph."

Ben signs the paper without looking at it.

"There's something I should say," he starts.

"Say it."

"First off, I love you."

"You should say that more often."

"There's a background check in there."

"Spotless," she smiles. "Just like you promised."

"Character witnesses. Driving records. Affidavits and whatnot. Oaths we've made about being law-abiding citizens who can, who will, set a good example for this boy."

"Caleb."

"I was about to say his name."

"You were."

Ben is looking at his shoes.

"Why am I not liking the sound of this, Ben?"

"There's a not insignificant chance I could get indicted someday."

Becca actually backs two steps away from her husband.

"For bribery. I did it so we'd get ahead. And I did it more than once. Kickbacks, little things at first, to win a big contract or a city council vote or a zoning resolution."

She's having trouble staying on her feet.

"Why would you tell me this now?"

Ben finally looks her in the eye.

"Because I love you and I want you to be happy. And let's adopt Caleb, if it's what you want. But if anyone ever finds out about these things it would . . . well, a judge wouldn't allow the adoption to go forward. And I wanted you to know that this was a risk. Some. A slight one. Before we go any further."

"This is just like you. Doing this. And now."

"There's one more thing . . ."

"Oh spare me the sour grapes Ben!"

"I thought you'd want to know."

The pen, when she hurls it at him, clatters from Ben's pant leg, provoking from her husband a quick but satisfying flinch.

"Well I don't."

66. DEAN

There is a moment there where Dean thinks they have a fighting chance. The jury selection has been completed, the actual trial has finally started, and Wolfman calls Aura up to the stand, intent on charging hard after her dead brother.

"Miss Jefferson," Wolfman says, "when was the last time you spoke with your brother?"

"The night he was killed," Aura says.

"He called you."

"Yes."

"You spoke for almost half an hour."

"Yes."

"Did Carl talk about his plans for that evening?"

"No."

"What did you talk about?"

"About the NCAA tournament."

"So about basketball."

"Yes."

"What about it?"

"Last year Arkansas beat Duke. Carl was happy," Aura says. "We both hate Duke."

"Any particular reason?"

"It was just a thing between us."

"Miss Jefferson," says Wolfman, "were you aware that your brother Carl Jefferson was a drug dealer?"

"Objection," says Bob Macy.

"Sustained."

"Let me rephrase. Miss Jefferson, were you aware that your brother Carl Jefferson sold drugs?"

"Yes."

"And are you aware that selling drugs is a crime in the state of Oklahoma?"

"Yes."

"Why didn't you turn Mr. Jefferson in to the police?"

"Carl promised me he was going to stop."

"And did Mr. Jefferson keep his promise?"

"No."

"So Mr. Jefferson kept selling drugs."

"Yes."

"Are you aware that selling or even possessing drugs, specifically methamphetamine, a class one controlled dangerous substance, is a felony under Oklahoma state law and punishable by anywhere from two to twenty years in state prison?"

"No."

"But you are aware that selling or even possessing drugs, specifically methamphetamine, is a crime under Oklahoma state law, correct?"

"Yes."

"And that this crime is punishable by some indeterminate amount of time spent in a state prison facility?"

"Yes."

"So would it be reasonable to speculate that if you had turned Mr. Jefferson in to the police for selling methamphetamine . . ."

"Objection!" says Bob Macy. "Speculation."

"Sustained."

"Would it be reasonable for someone to say that if you had turned Mr. Jefferson in to the police for selling drugs, that he might be alive in prison right now rather than dead?"

"Objection!" Bob Macy is standing now.

"Sustained," says the judge. "Counsel, you're on thin ice."

"Would it be fair to say that you share some responsibility for the terrible incident that led to Mr. Jefferson's death?"

Macy is coming around from behind the prosecutor's table.

"Objection! Your honor, this is . . ."

Dean can see the district attorney is actually reaching for the gun holstered under his blazer. Actually laying a palm on the pistol grip there.

Aura says, "No I . . ."

"Sustained."

". . . an outrage!"

Dean leans forward, hoping. If Macy pulls out his heater in court it's a mistrial, and Wolfman wins.

"Bob,"—Granger is standing now, purple with fury, hissing at his boss—"sit!"

"No further questions."

". . . wouldn't say that was fair."

67. AURA

The trial and the basketball tournament started the same week. March madness, sadness, what's the difference? Maddest, saddest March in memory. Every morning she drives in to the city, sits listening, in the wood-paneled courtroom, to the horrors visited upon Carl in his last seconds of life. A week ekes by, interminable, during which she testifies two whole hateful afternoons, hating Dean Goodnight and hating his boss Paxton even harder and hating this Billy Grimes boy with a quiet, boiling passion.

Then cleaning out Opal's garage one night Aura finds Carl's old basketball. Forgotten, deflated, its hide scuffed smooth from years of overuse. Holding it in her hands, Aura senses the whole belligerent history of her brother stirring under her fingertips. Every summer afternoon spent sweating on that blacktop court outside church, every frigid winter night spent dribbling inside the Langston University gym. The endless repetitive drilling. Their shared fears and hopes and private confidences. All those silly squabbles. All those teachable moments Carl got so good at forgetting.

It was all still there, even now, flashing hypnotically by her mind's eye like a parlor trick.

She inflates the basketball and takes it with her to see Nate. It's Thursday night and she finds him inside the church doing minor repair work, dressed in jeans and a *Fat Albert* T-shirt and hammering something inside the choir box.

"Hey-hey-hey," Aura says.

Nate does his best Bill Cosby imitation.

"It's Aaaauuuura Jefferson!"

"Want to play?"

"Abso-tootin-lutely."

"Go easy on me now."

"Please. We're both too old for false modesty."

The preacher lays his hammer in the pews and points up to the planks where the stained glass window once was.

"We're getting a new window soon. Maybe a couple of weeks and we'll have the unveiling."

"You've been fundraising."

"Not at all." A devilish splendor in the preacher's eye. "But the donor wishes to remain anonymous."

Outside, the basketball court is illuminated by a single streetlamp. The evening blows brief cold blasts of wind in their faces as Aura and the pastor are warming up.

"How's Opal?"

"She's been better," Aura says, shooting and missing. "But she's settling in alright."

The ball bounces off the backboard and a metallic crack rifles across the deserted parking lot. Pastor Nate snags the rebound.

"This ball has seen better days."

"It was Carl's."

"Ah."

"I'm still so . . . damned *mad* at him, Nate."

Letting the basketball fall to his feet, the preacher strides over to blanket Aura in a hug.

"I want to show you something." Releasing Aura, though she wishes he wouldn't, Nate works down to his hands and knees, first scrabbling below the basketball net, then scribbling with a twig in the dirt there. "This, Aura Jefferson, is you."

"Thank heavens I'm not a square."

Nate laughs.

"I've always thought you were well rounded. So if this circle represents Aura Jefferson, answer me this. Where is Aura Jefferson's past?"

"I didn't come here tonight for Sunday school."

"It is exactly why you came here. It's why you all come. So. Is it out there?" He pokes the dirt outside the perimeter of the circle. Aura draws breath to answer but before she can speak the preacher touches the earth inside of the circle. "Or in here?"

"What's the difference?"

"Freedom is the difference. I'm always telling people they should take control of their past, you see, because . . ."

"You mean future."

"The future's as good a place as any to get started. But if you control your future," drawing an X inside the circle, "then it must sit here inside of the circle. And if that's true," scratching a second X in the circle, "then so does the past. And if the past is *inside* of you, Aura, that means you control it. You can change your understanding of it, your feelings about it, your relationship with it. Anytime you decide to. Anger, hate, resentment . . . these things are a prison." Now he's drawing a box around the circle, scraping a cage of parallel lines in the ground. "People assume that the past and the future are out here beyond their control. But it doesn't need to be that way. All it takes is the smallest shift in perspective and everything starts to get better."

"That's all it takes, Nate?"

"You're angry with Carl because he fell from grace. Fell hard. You may even believe, on some level, that when he embraced that life of crime your brother deserved whatever punishment God chose to dole out. And maybe that's true. I don't believe it's true but maybe it is. The point, though, is that it no longer matters. Because the worst crimes aren't the ones committed against us by others. The worst, the most violent crimes, Aura, are those we commit against ourselves."

68. BEN

He drives through Guthrie and Langston and then Coyle under a thin cold sky sown with fat little lead-bellied puffclouds that shadow the gullies and creeks and cattle wallows with somber, Holstein-looking spots and generally reflect Ben's wretched state of mind, which is irredeemably hung over. The road snakes alongside and then over and beyond the Cimarron River, the mud-brown shove of the water beneath the bridge bringing back countless lazy summer afternoons spent tending trotlines with Cecil before he was broken, the two of them chawing on bittersweet plugs of Red Man tobacco and doing their damnedest to master the casual craft of spitting into a soup can, an art that must have required more habitual practice than they were putting in because neither brother ever quite got the hang of it.

He finds Cecil flaunting his gaudy game-day boots, corn chips and guacamole spread out on the coffee table, tallboys cooling in the fridge, the Final Four playing on the TV.

"Sutton's wearing his Cheshire-cat tie," Cecil announces as Ben wilts into the couch cushions. "Grab a cold one."

But Ben's too tired for drinking and says so.

"Oklahoma State has some momentum heading into this match," Dick Enberg is saying in that paternal television patter of his. "Eddie Sutton's team is coming off of a seven-game winning streak. But these Bruins are so good at execution. Coach Harrick has assembled a deep bench of players who can handle the ball well and drive for the basket. If the Cowboys aren't careful, UCLA will bounce them right out of the tournament tonight."

Tip-off's any second now. Bryant Reeves and UCLA's big man George Zidek are both moseying toward center court. A Czech immigrant, Zidek appears to be at least as talented as Reeves. An infographic appears onscreen, BIG COUNTRY vs. FOREIGN

COUNTRY, comparing their stats. The Bruins are wearing white, the Pokes in black. Then the referee is tooting on his whistle and their boys are scrambling for the rock and now here it is, the biggest game since just about ever, and Ben has lost all interest in seeing it.

Ben reaches for the remote and mutes the set.

"Hey now!" says Cecil.

"What do you think Dad would have done if he'd known the truth about who was driving?"

"I don't expect you'd of lived through the night."

"Remember how sometimes they'd try and curse?"

"Mother and Dad?"

Cecil chuckles.

Ben summons a smile.

"Oh . . . *my*," Cecil tries to sing, a splintery smoker's falsetto.

"*Land sakes*," Ben coos, imitating Mother.

"Oh . . . *sugar*."

"Shinola."

"Boy, I'm fixin' to beat *tarnation* out of you."

"Gosh-a-livin's!"

"Those slow-as-molasses accents."

"You're one to talk about accents."

Making fun of Mother and Dad has always been out of bounds. But once the brothers get started, neither of them wants to stop.

"Blast you son!" Cecil roars.

"By ginger!"

"Ding you, boy!"

"Lawdy me!"

"We're missing the game, brother," Cecil says.

"Didn't you say it's only the last two minutes that count?"

"Remember when you ran over that milk cow with the tractor?"

Now his shirt is tickling him and no matter which way Ben wiggles it won't let up.

In an elaborate and theatrical gesture Cecil frames the past with those big hands.

"Let me paint the scene."

"Please," Ben tries to say above his giggling, "don't."

"The baler's knocking along behind that tractor like an anchor. That dadgum dairy cow just standing there, stupid-faced, directly in your path. But you don't see her until it's too late."

"You said . . ." Ben cackles, "*dadgum*."

"By the time you finally stop the tractor me and Dad are clipping across the field to see what's what. We only had three milk cows, if you'll remember. And now this one's leg is broken. So dad unfolds his buck knife and slits open the animal's throat and we lift that poor cow into the truck bed and haul it cross-lots for slaughtering. The butcher carves the carcass into what cuts he can salvage."

"And we eat grass-fed Holstein for a month."

"The fat on it was *green*, Ben. All thanks to you."

"Dad was mad. He never mentioned it to me again. Not once."

"I remember your kids used to read *Green Eggs and Ham* when they were staying over. Aloud, Ben. To me. Whenever Sarah started in on that story I'd taste my lunch coming up."

It goes on like this for hours, the Porter brothers so busy talking, laughing and giggling so eagerly about the past and the accident that changed everything, their hopes and their regrets and their women and whatever cork it was that had bunged up in their Dad's ass, that when the Cowboys ultimately lose to the Bruins and drop out of the tournament altogether, at first neither of them takes any notice whatsoever.

69. CECIL

Cecil is sitting in his Chevy outside Aura's church, both wrists balanced atop the steering wheel, twirling a box of Marlboros between his thumb and middle finger in the way you might measure dice.

The windows are rolled down. It was getting to be a pleasant afternoon. Peaceful, quiet, one of those lazy natural lulls you kept expecting to be broken by the distant gong of a church bell or the bark of some stray dog. But it was Tuesday, not a Sunday, and the dogcatcher must be earning his paycheck because the only thing to be heard is the bumble and churn of the ever-turning world: meadowlarks twirpelling, horseflies droning, breezes huffing through the wind tunnel of his truck's cab.

Earlier, inside, he'd rolled around the sanctuary watching the guys work. Baby brother couldn't make it today, but Ben sent three crackerjack contractors who could obviously handle this gig blindfolded. The preacher called last week wondering if Cecil could come, supposedly to supervise the installation but Cecil gets the impression Nate just wants him here to witness the window in its rightful environment. When he slipped back out to the pickup for a catnap Cecil found the Marlboros, still in the cellophane, stuffed behind the driver's seat. Some rainy-day stash squirrelled away by his old pack-a-day self.

He begins to understand why Nate asked him here when Aura's car pulls into the parking lot. She slows to a stop on Cecil's side of the truck, ratchets the parking brake into place and sits there staring at him, her face a puzzle of emotions too private for Cecil to parse.

Cecil tries to smile but it doesn't quite come off and so he just waves.

Aura leans over to roll down the passenger-side window, her car still idling.

"Need a light?"

"Oh no. I smoked the last cigarette of my life on Sunday after lunch."

"So that's just for the new car smell then."

"Honest to God. I haven't had a craving since."

"Good for you. You seem a little less gray around the edges."

"I've been looking for you."

"I've been busy."

"I heard about your brother."

"You heard that."

"I've been trying to find you a while now, called the service and . . ."

"I know."

". . . so then your preacher let it slip when I came here hunting you. I think he thought I already knew."

Aura's eyes go slack. She kills the engine and says, "Pastor Nate watches out for me."

"It's good somebody does."

"He called last night, said he had a surprise. I thought it had something to do with the trial."

"I'm so sorry about that, Aura. About your little brother. I'm sorry about everything else, too. I wanted to speak with you a minute, if you'd let me, about . . ."

"What's the surprise?"

"Let's go inside and I'll show you."

Cecil pulls his rig from the cab and inchworms down into the seat, taking the Marlboros along with. But then pushing up that impossible switchback alongside the church, hoping to hell she's in tow but too afraid to peek over his shoulder and see, a back tire snags on the ramp's lower rail and here he is stranded all over again.

"Want some help?" Aura is wearing his white Stetson and trying not to smile.

"Please."

She takes the cowboy hat—Cecil had forgotten all about the Stetson—and places it on his head. His rear tire is wedged under one of the ramp's horizontal railings, the rubber really jammed in there tight, so she kneels to tug at the axle until the rig rolls free. He starts pushing up the ramp again. But Aura says let her help, she can push him, and he's already feeling puny anyway, so Cecil allows it. There is a trash basket just inside the church vestibule and as Aura pops him over the threshold Cecil hooks the pack of cigarettes at the bin.

The box flies wide and caroms off the wall.

She walks over to complete the shot for him.

"Nice assist."

"I see you haven't been practicing."

They hear pastor Nate approaching, that deep rich voice imploring.

"Aura Jefferson, don't you step one more foot into this church! Cecil, you stop that lady from going any further, now, we're not quite ready for the two of you."

"You had better take that hat off," Aura says. "Nate won't like it inside."

Cecil does, putting the Stetson in his lap. Looking for someplace else to put his eyes.

They can hear the preacher inside the sanctuary, pleading with Ben's workers, cajoling, telling them come down and take a little coffee break.

"I've got a hot pot of coffee in the kitchen here. Our guests of honor have arrived and we want this to be just perfect as can be. So get down off that tower why don't you and sit a spell? . . . There we are. Thank you. Thank you kindly, this won't take long, I appreciate your efforts. You're doing a bang-up job . . . coffee's in here. Just make yourselves at home."

When all the hubbub is complete pastor Nate jogs into the vestibule to greet them. He's wearing jeans and sneakers and a white

T-shirt and smiling like a simpleton, breathless as an asthmatic but beckoning now.

"Come in, Aura. Come in and see it. Cecil."

They follow the preacher into the sanctuary. The workers have erected a scaffolding just under the window, tools and power saws and paint buckets and drop cloths spread haphazardly about the chancel, but the stained glass is finally sitting in its frame above the pulpit, bathing the sanctuary in blues and oranges and reds and greens, a sieve for the springtime sunlight. The window is shaped like an octagon, a smidge over four feet across, and it depicts a simple pastoral setting bordered by a patchwork tapestry or quilt woven with every exotic color and texture of glass Cecil could lay hands on. An oversized sun is rising up above the rolling prairielands, looks to be autumn, with a few clouds advancing in along the yellowing horizon and a flock of birds, Cecil likes to think they're geese, ascending crossways before the orange sunrise, stringing up into clear blue sky.

"You said something once about flying," Cecil explains. "I was hurt and you were working on my shoulder and you said pretend you're in flight."

The colors shift like liquid along the walls of the sanctuary.

"You built this?" Aura asks.

Cecil nods.

"Is that a curtain along the side?"

"I imagine it like this," Cecil explains. "We've gathered here to watch a play or a performance. We've been waiting awhile, here in the pews, listening to the sniffles and the coughs and the maybe creaking of the church, waiting for the players to appear. And now someone has suddenly pulled the curtain aside and it's time to get started."

Aura tilts her head to one side.

"And is that a, that sun, it could also be a . . . is that right? A basketball?"

"If you want it to be."

"I don't see that," Nate says, also tilting his head. "That looks just like a sunset to me."

"It's a sunrise," Aura says.

"It's one of those things you have to decide for yourself," Cecil says.

The men watch Aura, her face rainbowed with light. Waiting.

No time like now.

"Aura, I'm sorry about saying what I did," Cecil starts. "I know I've hurt your feelings. It's the last thing I wanted. I . . ."

"Later." Aura rests her hand on Cecil's bad shoulder. "Right now I need to feel something pretty in my life. Let's just look. We'll do this later, Cecil. I promise."

Pastor Nate claps both palms together and bounces from toe to toe.

"You've nailed it, Aura. This window, it isn't something you *see*, now is it? This window is something that has to be *felt*. The whole place feels different in this light. Don't you think?"

Aura is nodding.

Pastor Nate steps around behind Cecil's rig, leans down to hug him up fiercely from behind.

"Careful, Nate," Aura says.

"Can you feel the difference, Mr. Porter?" Nate is saying. "Can you feel it?"

Cecil shuts his eyes. The colors are dancing across his closed eyelids.

"I can," he says. "I can feel it."

70. DEAN

The sousetrap north of the courthouse is one of those expensive, contrived places doing its best to look like a dive—sawdust on the floor, animal pelts on the walls, microbrews on tap—and its patrons have the long-suffering air of parolees waiting out a sentence. Ingrid, the bartender, is a waifish hipster with an obvious piercing problem and a Wile E. Coyote tattoo peek-a-booing from her shirtsleeves, the once purple dye-job in her pageboy haircut paled partway to gray. When Dean bellies up to the bar she takes one look at him and pours off two shots of well whiskey, casually clinking the glasses onto a cocktail napkin placed under his nose.

"On the house."

"I'm good."

She turns back to the television balanced on the bar flap. "If you could see your face."

"Really, I'm okay. Just waiting for someone."

"Trust me mister, the one thing you are *not* right now is okay. Those two'll get you closer to fine."

Posted behind the carefully antiqued liquor display, tacked amongst the handbills wallpapering the corkboard paneling, is an oversized poster of a puckish Crash Lambeau in three-quarter profile, one eyebrow arched conspiratorially into the camera:

BIG GOVERNMENT IS WATCHING
. . . ARE YOU LISTENING?
WEEKDAYS, KTOK—AM 1000

Dean shouldn't be here. There are rules about interacting with a witness once the trial has started. Some people might say this is tampering. But there is a thread he has yet to pull all the way through. And it has to do with more than just this case. In what feels like an ancient gesture he cradles one of the whiskeys, rolling it slowly between his palms.

The first two whiskeys burn going down. Dean orders two more.

While Ingrid preps the shots she says, "From here on out you pay your own way."

There is an empty booth nearby and as he carries the drinks over to it Lambeau's eyes seem to follow, tracking Dean's every movement. The TV is tuned, just like every third set in town, to the O.J. Simpson spectacle in Los Angeles. A week or so ago, in what has turned out to be that trial's most captivating exchange to date, LAPD detective Mark Fuhrman denied using the dreaded *n-word*. And now, whenever the networks have dead air that needs filling, footage of Fuhrman's testimony can be seen looping as split-screen accompaniment to the pundit of the moment.

When Aura arrives she stands silhouetted in the doorway, as though bent on some official or even malignant business. Dean waves her over. She has just come from court and looks great in her gray suit and heels. She slides into the seat across from his.

"What are we drinking?"

"Bourbon." He nudges a drink across the tabletop. "I'm sorry about how Wolfman treated you up there last week."

"Wolfman?"

"Sorry. Paxton. We all have nicknames in the office."

She lifts her glass. "To surviving this trial."

"To surviving."

They drink. Aura hides her grimace with the back of a hand, eyes shining. "Still running?"

"Every day."

"I don't know anybody who does that anymore."

"I might be burning out. I used to get into this zone, a kind of endorphin dream . . ."

"I know all about the zone."

". . . where I'd picture this invisible-type barrier between myself and the finish. Or the world, the future. Whatever."

"It doesn't have to compute. You were in the zone."

"Right, so you get it. Well for the rest of that run, my job was to push through the barrier. To see what was on the other side."

"What was it?"

"That's the thing. I never broke through."

"I hope you haven't asked me here to decipher your dreams."

He chuckles. "You did a good job against Wolfman."

"I thought the D.A. was about to shoot your boss."

"We'd have some hope of winning if he'd gone ahead and done it." Dean flashes the high sign to Ingrid and she pours two more whiskeys but makes him fetch them himself, which he does. Walking back from the bar he can hear F. Lee Bailey grilling detective Mark Fuhrman: *". . . use the word BLEEEEP! in describing people?"*

He's settling back into the booth when she says, "What's yours?"

"What's my what?"

"Your nickname."

"Tonto."

Her disappointed face.

"I know," he winces.

They hear *". . . Not that I recall, no."*

"Carl wasn't a monster," Aura says.

"Neither is Billy."

"You mean if you called someone a BLEEEEP! you have forgotten it?"

Aura is trying hard to ignore the television.

"The way you talk about Carl, the way your boss does. It isn't the Carl I remember. This isn't the truth of him."

"A trial has very little to do with truth."

"There are these things called facts."

"Facts aren't sufficient for getting at the truth. We're about to see a whole boatload of facts in the next few weeks. And in a perfect world they would all be true. But we don't live in a perfect world. If Wolfman wanted to, or if Macy did, he could hire an expert witness to testify that two plus two equals five. And everyone, basically, would believe him."

"You're exaggerating."

"In my experience, the argument with the least amount of untruth in it is usually the winner. And that's the best anybody can hope for."

"The least amount of untruth. Wow."

"I want you to assume that perhaps at some time since 1984 or 1985, you addressed a member of the African American race as a BLEEEEP! Is it possible that you have forgotten that act on your part?"

"They can't execute Billy Grimes without you," says Dean. "If a family member asks the jury for mercy, most times they'll grant it."

"Your boss tells me I'm responsible for Carl's death. You say I'm responsible for this Billy kid's life. You two give me too much credit."

"Answer me this. If Billy gets the death chamber, who's responsible?"

"How about Billy is?"

"Nice. But it's out of his hands now."

"So the district attorney."

"No. First he has to present the evidence. Then he needs a jury to decide the case."

"So the jury then."

"All twelve of them?"

"Sure."

"Okay. But no. Someone has to carry out the sentence."

"So the warden."

"No. He needs someone to administer the injection."

"So the executioner or doctor or whoever."

"Which one?"

"What?"

Dean holds up three fingers. "There are three executioners."

". . . you say under oath that you have not addressed any black person as a BLEEEEP! or spoken about black people as BLEEEEP! in the past ten years, Detective Fuhrman?"

"Each of them stands behind a cinder-block wall, finger on a button. They wear Halloween masks to hide their faces. And after Billy's last words everyone will push his button and head happily back home for dinner, secure in the knowledge that he probably wasn't the one who killed the prisoner."

"So nobody is responsible," Aura says.

"This is the genius of capital punishment. Nobody feels responsible because the responsibility is spread so thin. But the genius has a weakness. They can't do it without you, Aura. During the victim impact testimony you don't just speak for Carl. As far as the jury is concerned, you *are* Carl."

"Stop saying my brother's name, Tonto."

"Billy has a son. A son who loves him."

"I heard," she sighs. "Are they going to make him testify?"

"There'll be no point. After Willa has testified, after Billy's cellmate does . . ."

"So that anyone who comes to this court and quotes you as using that word in dealing with African Americans would be a liar, would they not, Detective Fuhrman?"

Without warning Aura slides out of the booth.

"Yes, they would."

"Wait, just hear me out . . ."

But Aura is already strolling casually over to the television set, where she bends down to tug briefly at the power cord, killing the broadcast. An enormous silence quiets the bar. For what feels like an eternity—five, eight, nine seconds—she stands there, hands on hips, staring down the patrons. She's the only African American in the place and, aside from Ingrid, the only woman.

As she makes her way back to the booth Aura's heels clap a hollow clop upon the sawdusted hardwoods. She falls back into her seat.

"Do you believe in evil?"

"I think evil is a failure of understanding," Dean says.

"I didn't ask what you think."

Dean pulls at his neck, loosening the tension clamped along his spine.

"I believe in . . . no. I believe there are evil acts. I believe they happen when people focus on their differences instead of their similarities. But I don't believe there are evil, inherently, people."

"Well I sure as hell do. And I want to hear how evil people are reconciled into this kinder, gentler worldview of yours."

"In, again, a perfect world . . ."

"Jesus Christ, Dean. You sound like a trailer for a B movie."

"Let me finish. Because in a perfect world I could justify killing Billy. In a place where nobody lied and we understood not just the facts but the truth of every case beyond a shadow of a doubt. Because what this kid has done is horrible, Aura."

The bar banter is picking back up.

"But people are people," Dean says, "and people aren't perfect. Evidence gets manufactured. Eyewitnesses make mistakes, prosecutors bend the rules because they're just absolutely certain *this* guy is their killer. People lie to get on a jury, people lie from the witness stand, people lie to seem smarter or stronger or better than they really are. They lie to themselves about their biases, which is the most insidious kind of lying there is. And innocent men die for crimes they haven't done."

"Billy Grimes isn't innocent."

"It doesn't matter."

"It matters," she pokes herself violently in the chest, "to me."

"You're trusting a bunch of guys who put on masks when they get dressed for work in the morning. A man wears a mask because he has something to hide. I know a little about this, Aura. A bank robber wears a mask. A rapist wears a mask. The KKK . . ."

"Did you really just say KKK?"

"There's a double standard at work here. You'll see, what, hundreds of pictures in this trial? Pictures of Carl's dead and bloated body. Pictures of discrete wounds. Bloodstains and bodily fluids and weapons and hemorrhages. But you'll never see a picture of someone gasping for air in the death chamber. You won't see a picture of the guy that swallows his tongue or shits himself or takes forty-seven horrible moaning minutes to die because they punched through a vein and injected the poison into his soft tissue. The guy whose head explodes because one of the executioners was drunk and forgot to wet the sponge in his electric chair. Oops. The guy who's allergic to the cocktail, his convulsions so intense he snaps his spine like a twig, even with the restraints."

Aura begins clapping. Slowly, ironically.

"You talk as though you have it all figured out. Righteous Mr. Goodnight against the whole jury-rigged system. Everybody and nobody is responsible."

"The court wants you to believe the responsibility for Carl's murder lies solely with Billy Grimes. But it won't own up to the murder it's about to commit. It wants you to believe this is as routine as putting the kids down for a nap. But it's a premeditated, a cold-blooded, a deceptive kind of killing. And you're being recruited into it."

"There's a big glaring error in your logic, Tonto. If everyone is responsible on the other side, who's responsible on yours?"

"My boss."

Aura jabs the tabletop with her index finger. "One person."

"He's the one making the argument."

"And why is that? You aren't smart enough? You're an Indian, just like this Grimes guy. You apparently understand him better than this Wolfman fellow. Sound pretty convincing to me. So why hasn't Dean taken the trouble to get that law degree? Find out if he has the chops to save some of these poor wayward souls?"

She has caught him out, seen into Dean, the way he does his clients.

"I'll tell you why." She points the finger at his chest. "Because you're too scared to argue one of these cases."

"Don't get back in that witness box with an agenda, Aura. Or . . ."

"You don't want the responsibility that comes with losing."

His hands are shaking under the table.

"What are you going to do?"

"You keep asking me that."

"You keep not answering."

She lifts her shot glass. "To answers."

They toast.

"Answers come cheap," Dean says. "To understanding."

∽

He flees the bar a drink or four too late, legs leaded with liquor, dragging north on Walker Avenue for home. Too drunk to drive. Running could clear his head but Dean's feet won't cooperate. A fire engine plows howling through the nearest intersection, a terrible trajectile of chrome and light and whiplash noise, stunning traffic to a standstill, and before the dazed motorists have regained their courage three different police cruisers come screaming around the corner in its wake. The night shift, punching in.

So heavy. So deeply, deathly, tired and heavy.

They built this city in a day. The founding fathers were claim jumpers and boomers and criminals and thieves, desperate men who crept in from Texas or Arkansas or the Indian tribes out west to get the jump on their fellow land-runners. Those same men later designed the schools and the courts, the prisons and the laws to keep them filled. Bricked these streets down over the prairie in a pattern plain as graph paper.

Dean plods along. He hears bulldozers leveling a lot east of the railroad tracks. Some ruined teardown tenement, probably. Making way for the new restaurant or condominium complex or hotel franchise. Every shuffled step away from downtown takes him that much further from this case. That brief connection with Billy already falling away, sloughing off like a second skin. Nothing to be done now but wait.

He'd pray if it would help but it won't. It's all down to Aura now.

He hurdles a curb and stumbles, falling, down into a park. Familiar. Goodholm Park. Crawls across the clammy grass to a rusted swing set. He should continue on up to the apartment. Sam will be sleeping. No reason to be sitting here, kicking dirt, swinging up and back into the airy evening chill.

Doesn't know why he's dawdling.

But he does.

Because Aura was right. Right about everything. He saw past the end of himself that night in the parking lot and he's been running ever since. Running from Sam, from fatherhood, from anything resembling a responsibility.

Dean closes his eyes. It's warm enough again for the crickets to be chirruping. There's a peculiar humming coming from the highway and a whispering between the treetops and the kick drum of his heart thumping under his chest. The night roaring quietly down.

He stands, steadies, walks slowly through the park and on up to his apartment. Climbs the staircase and stealths past the threshold, slips sighing into bed with Sam. Turns into her small and snoring body to slide one hand over her warm tight belly.

It would be important to get the words right, when he asked her. The order and the cadence and that strange, lovely logic. *Marry me.* Because he was going to be a father. A father and husband and a lawyer if it was possible. He could do these things. Could and would and wanted to.

Need to sleep. To sleep and dream and one day, someday, die.

But first, finally, to live.

71. AURA

Nate phones her late that night, after Aura has just returned from meeting Dean in some bar near the courthouse.

"I woke you up."

Aura stretches under her nightshirt, her head still swirling with bourbon. She's in her Stillwater apartment, he's in Langston; nevertheless, her heart starts at the apparent proximity of his voice.

She closes both eyes and imagines him here, beside her, in the bed.

"What time is it?"

"Late."

"I'm back in court tomorrow."

"I know it."

"It's almost over. Will you come?"

"Absolutely."

"I feel sick, Nate. Cancerous. Being in that courtroom? Staring at this kid, listening to what he's done? It's like sipping a slow poison."

"I'm here for you."

"You're in Langston."

"I'm not going anywhere is what I mean."

"Nate?"

"I'm here."

"Nothing."

"Aura?"

"What?"

"I love you."

The world might not be perfect. But there are a few perfect things in it and this beat between lovers is one of them, a not-quite-uncomfortable silence conveying everything she'd like to say: I love you too, love you and want you and need you, need you more than you can know, but give me some space because I'm not quite ready for this conversation, not tonight, not now, not over the phone. But soon.

Another trembling feline stretch.

"So we'll pick this up after the trial."

"Okay."

"Nate?"

"I'm here."

"I'm not going anywhere, either."

It took the jury just two hours to find Billy Grimes guilty of killing Carl. Murder in the first degree. It was the third week in April, a drowsy, deaf-mute spring afternoon, and as the foreman read the jury's verdict the courtroom assumed a sacramental sort of surreality. The experience was not unlike a wedding or a funeral.

Nate drove Aura home after and when the penalty phase got under way the next day he sat clasping Aura's hand as the district attorney adopted the first stage evidence to prove aggravating circumstances in the case.

Considering the amount of bourbon in Carl's lungs, a medical examiner had sworn that he must have suffered unspeakable pain while drowning.

Hoping for a big tear-jerking finish, Macy saved Aura's impact statement for last. She held Nate's hand, waiting to say her piece, trying all that time to breathe through the lump choking her throat. The district attorney wanted to send Opal up onto the witness stand but Aura wouldn't hear of it.

And then it was time. There she was with her palm on the Bible swearing to tell the truth the whole truth and nothing but the truth but still having no earthly clue what to tell, she wasn't prepared, isn't prepared, but it's too late because when she's done speaking Macy will rest his case and then Dean's boss Paxton and pretty soon after that the men and women of the jury will be filing quietly down out of the jury box to decide whether Billy Grimes will live or die.

She hasn't brought notes. Aura just starts talking.

"The first time I saw Carl he was just a few hours old. I was almost seven and thought he looked a little like a boiled Mr. Potato Head. I'd never seen anything so ugly. What an ugly duckling, I remember saying. Mom told me to be nice. She said all babies look like that. We brought him home from the hospital the next morning. First thing Mom showed me was how to change the nappies and swaddle him so he'd sleep. Carl liked to be swaddled tight. Mom worked at the university in Langston as a secretary of sorts. It was a good job and they were offering to give her a month of maternity leave but she wanted to go back sooner. There was a nice daycare at the university and Mom would walk over there to feed Carl every few hours, take a long lunch break and rock him to sleep. I would come after school to play with him when I could. Dad was useless, just angry and sullen and stewing around the house all the time. Carl was the opposite, a perpetual motion machine. He grew like milkweed. I remember Mom coming home from the pediatrician's once, she's wearing a pretty blue strapless dress and has rouged up her face because the doctor's office is in Stillwater. But the mascara is dripping like India ink down Mom's cheeks because she's been crying the whole ride home. 'That doctor says I'm not feeding him enough,' she says, Mom's really sobbing by now, 'but he eats all the time! My nipples are bleeding he eats so much!' Carl might have looked skinny but he grew so fast and so, so tall. Once he started walking it was the first thing anyone noticed about him. Their eyes would open wider, they'd sort of step back and study him a spell. 'My Lord,' they'd finally say, this is to Mom, 'look how big that boy of yours is getting! Got some ball in his future,' they'd say or, 'Got some hoops in his future!' It ended up being hoops for Carl. I was already playing at the junior high by then, then the high school and later at Langston

University. Once he was mature enough not to embarrass me, I used to let Carl tag along to practice. He was already scissor dribbling on me by the time he was seven. This is about the time Mom died. She had pancreatic cancer and after we found out the illness progressed pretty fast, about four or five months. She didn't do the chemotherapy, Mom said the cancer was too far advanced. She just wanted to enjoy the time we had left. Everyone was there when she died, Carl and me and Dad and our grandmother Opal, Mom kind of hiccupped or gasped and then she was gone. It just tore Carl apart. Dad couldn't deal with it, either. One night after the funeral he left Carl and me with Opal. Never did come back to get us. So we started living with Grams. She had different ideas about leisure time. Grams said free time wasn't free, you had to earn it and bettering yourself was the way to do that. Grams made us listen to gospel music and read the Bible or the encyclopedia. By the time he turned ten my little brother was six feet tall. I was a senior in high school, starting at shooting guard or sometimes point. Carl had already learned everything I could think to teach him and was doing it better than me. That was the year he started beating me in games of pick-up or twenty-one. He was a hellion on defense. Sharp-elbowed, stuck to you like superglue. Knew when the ref wasn't looking so he could foul you on the sly. Carl loved to steal the ball and did it every chance that came along. He loved everything about the game but loved winning most. Liked gloating about how good he was, bragging and trash talking and especially the compliments he'd get around town. That hungry look all the girls started to give him. You were supposed to be modest in our family, Grams was always telling us that the greatest men are willing to be little, but when it came to basketball Carl saw he was the best kid in town, maybe in the county or even the state, and he wanted everyone else to see it, too. If you could have seen his face when he lost. When Carl lost I think he felt like a loser. He was afraid of losing more than he wanted to win, if that's possible, and he spent every second of every day trying to improve himself on the court. He liked to challenge himself to some longshot goal and then obsess until he'd achieved it. He'd say things like I'm going to make fifty free throws in a row and not miss one shot . . . no cheating, no mulligans . . . then he'd do everything in his power to make it happen. Anyway, Carl was like that. He'd set a goal and one week later he'd have accomplished it. Set a harder goal, accomplish that. Set, achieve, repeat, over and over and over again. He just kept getting better. Soon there were scouts coming to Opal's house. Billy Tubbs came to watch him play but Carl had set his sights on Oklahoma State. We'd spent our entire lives within fifteen minutes' drive of Stillwater and going to OU would have been like betraying everyone in town. Eddie Sutton wasn't yet at OSU but during Carl's senior year in high school the Cowboys hired a new head coach, Leonard Hamilton, and Hamilton wanted Carl. He came by Opal's house a few times, explained about how he was building this team from scratch and how the Pokes were done losing now that he was onboard and how Carl was going to be an integral part of them turning the team around. He'd been an assistant coach on the Kentucky squad that went to the Final Four in 1984 and when Hamilton started talking about the hype surrounding those games Carl's eyes would get real big, you could see him seeing himself making that last clutch shot to win the national championship. In the fall of 1986 Carl moved to Stillwater and enrolled at Oklahoma State. They gave him a full ride but he had to keep his grades up to keep the scholarship and stay on the team. But the effort it took for Carl to be on that campus, the discipline it took, to study and practice and eat right and get to bed on time. You can't imagine. If any of you remember the Cowboys in 1986? It was just a disastrous season. Carl's first year playing college ball the Cowboys only won something like eight games. I think at first Carl thought he could singlehandedly turn the season around for the whole team. But all that losing just wore him down. He was already having trouble making his grades, first semester he was barely eligible. Hamilton got him studying with a tutor but then when winter came and the team started losing . . . and losing, and losing . . . grades and schoolwork just became a lot less important. I've always thought this was when he started doing drugs, partway through that first basketball season. Carl got introduced to speed or whatever it was so he could stay up and study. And at first I think it did help him. He was studying and practicing and had more energy. But you all know how these stories go. It caught up with him. Carl missed a few practices and Hamilton found out about the drugs and told him to get clean. But Carl couldn't. And after that season was over Carl left school and never came back. He was living in Oklahoma City with some friends he'd met. I'd hear about what he was doing but just kind of hoped it was a phase. I had graduated from nursing school and was working in Stillwater by now and volunteering at this midnight basketball league. I'd have Carl come by to show the kids some things, get them inspired, you know, and sometimes it would seem like he was on the edge of snapping out of it. But he never did. He started dealing, or this is what I heard. I never knew too much about that part of his life. I didn't want to know. Seemed like every time he came close to cleaning himself up there was this part of Carl that would sabotage it all. It was like, he failed at the only thing he loved to do and so Carl thought he didn't deserve to succeed at anything else, ever again. He was so full of life. I wish I could make that real for you all. Make you see how alive he was. I remember there was a song Opal liked to play on the record player, some spiritual-sounding tune. She just loved it, so of course Carl had to pretend to hate it when Grams was around. But when the two of us were alone he would sing, sing like he meant it, like he was trying out for the band. The song had a refrain running through it and I can see my little brother with his eyes closed, we're goofing around the kitchen one Sunday afternoon while Opal's out at the grocery store or something, and Carl, he's really putting his whole body into it, you know, his throat for example it's working like a baby bird's, that perfect voice booming out of him like a trumpet, the blood pumping along the big artery of his neck and he's singing, stretching out those notes as long as he can, his whole torso moving side-to-side like Stevie Wonder's, like a snake charmer's, swaying and singing:

"I got wings, you got wings, all of God's children got wings . . ."

Did she, is she really . . . *singing?*

". . . when I get to Heaven gonna put on my wings, gonna fly all over God's Heaven, Heaven, Heaven . . ."

Ignoring that whisper in her head that says quit it, Aura, stop it now, stop it right this second because nobody wants to hear this, you're making an ass out of yourself—this is the same voice saying stay angry at your baby brother and Aura has already listened to it for far too long—Aura sings, the song ringing clear and pure and true throughout the vaulted courtroom.

". . . everybody talkin' bout Heaven ain't goin' there . . . Heaven, Heaven, Heaven . . . gonna fly all over God's Heaven . . ."

Aura stops to catch her breath. Nate is sitting in the benches behind the bar, smiling up at her and nodding, that steadfast calming presence of his giving her the strength to go on.

"That's how I want to remember him," she says, "singing that song, an imperfect human cup running over with hope and laughter and joy."

She can hear the buses groaning along the avenue outside. She looks at Bob Macy, at the jury, at the indecipherable mask of Dean Goodnight's face.

Aura turns to Billy Grimes and addresses him directly.

"Someone told me that when I stood up here today I'd be speaking for Carl. There's a court reporter over there, writing down every word, and I want to think this means Carl's story will be read a hundred times over in the years to come, by lawyers and court clerks and legal assistants and Lord knows who else. I want all of those people to hear this but most of all I want the jury to hear it. Had my little brother lived to see thirty I believe he would have changed. Eventually he'd have learned that losing doesn't make you a loser.

I'm not so sure he'd want this loser here, the one you've found guilty of killing him, put to death. But I've decided I definitely don't want that. Executing Billy Grimes doesn't change a thing. It won't bring Carl back. I've been so mad at my brother for so long. For dying like this, for finally orphaning me in this world. But it hasn't helped. I don't think staying angry with his killer will help anything, either. So if you all want to execute Billy Grimes, that's fine with me. It's your decision. But know this, know that it's *your* decision . . . it's what you want, not me. And not my little brother."

Her eyes are dry. There is no sadness, no fear, only this lighter-than-air feeling of release or freedom.

"Billy, I forgive you for killing Carl," Aura says. "You've been caught and you'll be punished. I won't waste another day of life worrying about it. And that's all I came to say."

72. BECCA

Becca has decided to forgive him but Ben doesn't yet know it. She would curse the man if she didn't love him this much. They can talk about it tomorrow.

73. BEN

It was the second anniversary of Reno's final assault on Waco and the drive-time deejays all had David Koresh on the brain. But there was nothing new to say about Waco so Ben switches off the car stereo and guzzles another gritty pull of Pepto-Bismol. His stomach has been engaged in active rebellion for at least three weeks. And though this morning he's feeling somewhat better about his recent revelations to Becca, their discussion hasn't helped with his indigestion.

He has told her everything, or almost all of it. All but the bit about Cecil. He tried not to make excuses. But Ben didn't beg, either. And after he came clean Becca was too stunned to say much of anything at all. She's been shutting him out for almost three weeks now. But then, when Ben was leaving the house this morning, Becca said maybe they could talk tonight.

Everything would be alright. They would work this out and everything would be alright. He would be a better husband, a better lover. A better father. A better man.

The clock radio glows 9:01.

He's running late. Killing time at a stoplight on Robinson, admiring a deep ice-blue sky. A WhisperJet slicing slowly through the heavens and not a wisp of cloud in its flight path. First Church just down the road a stretch. There's a yellow Ryder truck double-parked in front of the Murrah building and after the stoplight winks over to green and Ben is accelerating along Robinson for the city center, only then does he remember that the Ryder's cab had been filling with white smoke.

Radiator trouble, he thinks. *Bad break.*

This is when everything falls apart.

He does not hear it so much as see it, a rippling, first in the air and then along the sidewalk. Then the windshield itself waving like

353

a flag and then crackling glass cutting his face and Ben is on fire, a thunderclap clapping crashing clamping *CRACK!* and then silence as with a great rushing of wings or water. The asphalt buckling skidding sidewise into the curb then the ricochet whipcurling him round into a tailspin and he's working the brakes but the brakes won't work he's cursing *fuckall* pink Pepto-Bismol spilling every which way the SUV crashing mercifully to a rest, tossed rearward into the queue of cars parked parallel outside First Church.

He is looking the wrong way down a one-way street through what used to be his windshield. A fist of smoke is clenched horribly above the city. There has been a plane crash somewhere north of the Murrah building. A gas leak maybe. The cars along Fifth Street have all been incinerated, some of the cars on Robinson too.

Pat yourself down, make sure you're not a human torch.

His left arm is throbbing, as though it's been branded or dipped in acid, but Ben is not actually on fire.

Stop drop and roll, he says out loud, joking, trying to minimize the moment. But then doesn't hear his voice. It is oddly quiet. Touches his ears, they're bleeding freely. Just as well. If he could hear anything he might have reason to be scared. But the only noise is an amniotic sort of bloodbuzz cottoning his senses, a gentle hum resounding above the ever-burning world, and it has a pleasant sedative effect upon his emotions.

Put the car in park and open the door and step down into the street.

He can't see the site of the accident from where he's standing. Middle of the road. South, southeast of impact. But this is going to be bad. The mushroom cloud looked to be a pale gray color before but now the cloud is blowing black with smoke and ash, pillaring thickly skyward.

Come down to the water, he thinks.

Moving toward the cloud he can feel the building still coming down, feel it but can't hear. The earth trembling beneath his feet. At the corner of Fifth and Robinson Ben looks west. The bottom floors of the Murrah Building are gone. Desks and whole hallways and paperwork collapsing into the crater below. As Ben watches, the columns supporting the fourth floor shear clear of the building, an avalanche of material cataracting from the superstructure and into the blast site. A large portion of that floor tumbling soundlessly down and out into where Fifth Street used to be.

Inferno.

He coughs.

The smoke is.

Fucking hell his *arm*.

The Ryder truck vaporized.

And the crater.

A cruise missile, then. A misfire. Or a bomb. Of course. A bomb inside the truck.

Ben watches the columns supporting the fifth floor give way. Another avalanche sliding into the crater, concrete scree caroming into the street. These collapses will keep happening until every floor has crumbled.

The ammoniacal air skunking his tongue like bad booze.

There is something else he ought to but Ben can't.

The crater is bigger than Ben and Becca's first house. In the immediate, cauterized perimeter, objects have reverted to their constituent parts. There are no cars but there are tires. Fenders and radiator grilles and steering columns and cracked rearview mirrors. Twist-tied ribbons of burnt and burning wrack. Not much left of the building but bricks, girders and computers and wall calendars and rebar worming into what's left of the street. Buckled sections of sidewalk. And dust, dust everywhere, on the windows and his clothes and most of all in the air, dust and ash falling like snow in the soundless morning light.

The shade tree in the parking lot across the street is nothing but twigs, most of its branches and all of its leaves have been shorn away. The surrounding cars have all caught fire. The Murrah Building itself has gone dark but you can still see into it. A sense of shame, shame or voyeurism, peeking inside a building's private spaces like this. Not supposed to see this. Without walls and the scale is all wrong. Everything seems so small. Almost intimate.

The sixth floor calving off. It has become an object lesson in structural mechanics. They built the place to be impregnable, it was a federal building after all. But take out the bottom floors and the rest collapses under its own weight. Three more to go, then possibly the ceiling.

There will be people up there.

That a building comes down this easy.

Just imagine if.

Near the place where the sidewalk ends there is a single white shoe, spotless, its laces still tied. An infant's shoe.

Ben bends over and empties his stomach into the street, vomit splattering pink and noxious onto his calfskin wingtips.

Someone taps his shoulder.

A woman. Blue-eyed. Maybe green but he'll go with blue. A blonde. Talking at him.

I can't hear you says Ben.

Still talking, gesticulating.

Ben points to his ears, wipes his mouth dry with a sleeve.

The woman pulls Ben by the arm, the good one, leads him south along Robinson, away from the street corner. She's talking, looking back over her shoulder and up into the sky. Wants him to follow. He does. Follows the blonde around to the south side of the building. There is what looks to be a loading dock here. Several doors, one dangling loose from its upper hinges, with smoke streaming out.

Infernal.

A tall tough-looking guy comes running up, an Indian. He's sprinted here from downtown, must have been working nearby. The blonde she's talking to him, apparently the Indian can hear. Now they are both gesturing, gesturing and ignoring Ben.

The woman starts for the doorway.

Ben and the big Indian stay behind, unsure what to do. Watching her go.

Ben remembers about the daycare, something Becca told him once, told him recently. There are children inside. Probably dead. Dead or dying. But maybe not. Maybe trapped.

Yellow rubber duckies, he thinks, apropos of nothing.

They could help.

The woman stepping through the doorway and the smoke spiraling out of it.

Ben looks at the Indian. The Indian looks back. Neither of them is sure. Go in there and you might not come back out. But there's something about this woman. Steels your nerves, doesn't it? Maybe she has some training. Seems to know what she's doing. Fearless. Filled with a fearless purpose.

Ben points at his ears.

To the Indian he says: *I can't hear. We need to see if we can help. Help her bring the people outside. But we have to stay together.*

Ben's throat hurts. He realizes then that he's shouting.

Ben says, a little quieter this time: *Do you understand?*

The Indian is bobbing his head.

Good. He's getting it.

Ben and the Indian follow the woman into the building.

They went into the building with the smoke and the bedlam and the darkness and apparently it had just rained. Sprinkler system. You could see all the way through to the naked tree across the street. You could see the sky. But they couldn't see the blonde woman. She was busy elsewhere. People were beginning to stir. Crawling out from under desks or trying to climb down from the upper floors. Ben thought he smelled gas. But then a breeze blew through the building and he couldn't. The Indian was in front of him. The Indian pointed to the ceiling, pointed to his head. Concrete and drywall, still falling.

There was a stairwell. The big Indian tried to open the stairwell door but couldn't. Then a desk moved. Ben went over to it. He shouted at the Indian.

Help me!

There was a man under there. He was coated head to foot in dust and blood. Ben thought he looked tarred and feathered. The Indian put his shoulder under the desk and he lifted. The desk moved a few feet. The man was screaming. Ben was glad he couldn't hear it. The man's foot was pinned under a slab of concrete. Ben bent down and lifted the slab. It was about the size of a television. The man pulled his leg out from under it and then his eyes rolled back in his head and then he fainted. Ben set the slab back down.

That was when he started to hear things again.

Moans. Screams. A furious hissing *fssssssssssssst!* The graveled rush of things falling and that hollow *thud!* of impact. This was the building's death rattle but there was nothing natural about it. When his hearing returned so did the fear.

Ben said we have to get him out of here. The Indian was nodding again. Then a file cabinet fell on the Indian. The Indian tried to jump out of the way but the impact came full on his calf and buckled his left knee. The Indian was screaming now and this time Ben had no choice but to listen. Ben shoved the file cabinet off of the Indian's leg. They were going to die in this place. Ben was having trouble breathing. He had a strong desire to urinate.

We have to go, Ben said to the Indian. *Can you walk?*

The Indian grimaced. *I don't know.*

The leg didn't appear to be broken. Ben wrapped his hands around the unconscious man's torso, lifted him up from behind.

Can you get his feet? Ben said to the Indian.

The Indian took the unconscious man by the ankles and they began sidestepping toward the doorway. The Indian had a severe limp. You could see the outside world through the doorway. Policemen. A firetruck. Red and blue lights twirling. Firemen. Help was on the way. And then they were outside in the parking lot. They laid the man out on the asphalt. A fireman came over. He was wearing a helmet and he began tending to the man.

Ben started back for the building.

But another fireman was in his face now.

It's not safe inside sir.

There are children in there, Ben said.

I can't let you go in there sir. It just means more work for us, trying to get you back out. Please. Stay here. It's safer for everyone if you stay out here.

Dear God his arm hurt.

Ben saw the blonde woman wandering the parking lot. She was bleeding profusely from the head and wandering purposeless circles in the parking lot.

Ben went over to the Indian. The Indian was leaning against the hood of a car and talking to a very tall black woman. She was bent double, trying to examine his knee. Every time she touched his pant leg the Indian winced.

I don't feel right, Ben said.

The black woman looked at him.

The black woman. This was Cecil's nurse. Aura.

What she was doing.

"Dean," Aura said, "I know this man."

The air was too thick.

Another fireman came over and told them to evacuate the area. Aura asked him for a defibrillator machine. I'm a nurse she said. The fireman looked at Ben. He ran over and fetched one and handed it to Aura and then headed for the building. Aura told Ben to lay on the ground and he was relieved that someone was finally telling him what to do. She tore his shirt open, buttons were flying, and put her fingers to his neck and asked him how he felt, asked him where he was, but the world was going dreamy and Ben couldn't manage an answer.

She hooked him up to the machine and there was a beeping noise and a jolt of pain and Ben cried out. He started to weep. He was lying supine on the asphalt and his clothes were ruined with blood and antacid and his flab was hanging out of his shirt and he was sobbing like an orphan.

"Dean," Aura said, "your car. He needs an emergency room."

Dean stood upright.

"Let's go."

Ben was helped up. He could hardly stand. But he did manage to stop crying. He put his arm around Aura's shoulder. She was helping him down the street. She was still holding the defibrillator machine but it was no longer stuck to his chest. Ben's shirt was open. His belly was exposed and he felt embarrassed because he was fat. Obesity. One of his life's great failings. One of many.

They were walking south. The Indian was too injured to help. Aura was surprisingly strong. Two blocks from the explosion, an SUV was parked in the center of the street. Men in sunglasses and combat boots were establishing a perimeter. Everyone carried an assault rifle and sported big block-lettered initials on his shirt or baseball cap.

FBI. ATF. OCPD. DEA. POLICE. U.S. MARSHAL. SWAT.

There was a clean-shaven kid, younger than Ben's son Reese, wearing a bulletproof vest and pointing a machine gun at the sky. His eyes were scanning everywhere and he looked absolutely scared out of his wits.

Then they were in Dean's car. Aura was in the backseat with Ben, and Dean was driving. There were barriers and sawhorses obstructing the road. The city had become a maze. Everyone was fleeing work for home. Not even lunch and it's gridlocked. Horns honking. People frenzied, hypervigilant.

Tire rubber squealing.

Sirens harrying.

Ben was trying to talk with Aura about Cecil. He was trying to apologize for his big brother but Aura told him save your breath. I saw him yesterday and it was beautiful. Save your breath.

"Dean," said the black woman, Ben remembered the black woman's name was Aura and she was saying, "go faster."

They were on the highway. They slow but was alright.

This was the what is it. He'd been preparing for and. Every other had been prelude. There had clues. Signs. But he had been too living to see. It was probably for the best but. So many things wanted be done. Said. But he wasn't ready. Hurt. Hurts. Closed them but no yet. Opened. Becca. Eyes slippy-sliding. Outside in the deep time.

74. CECIL

Baby brother wanted anything but a church funeral so they're gathered in Knipe Cemetery, less than a half mile from Cecil's place, in Perkins, to send him off. Folding chairs and picnic tables arranged in the caliche lane between graves. It's an overcast Tuesday in April and when the breeze chills through him Cecil is glad he only partly feels it. Only partly feels anything.

Wheel up to that casket gripping his little book and look to that mob of vacant faces. Everyone alone in the crowd, all the blissfully ignorant grandkids and family and those others Cecil doesn't know and doesn't care to, Ben's high society set. Hell everyone in America has got that same look blanking his face of late. Even the party-crashers, those who hardly knew Ben. Hardly knew him but were there in those last minutes, when things really mattered. Aura and her preacherman beau, that Nate Franklin. That big Indian fellow Dean and his woman, the lovely girl with her ugly man's name. Sam.

Becca's still too stunned for living, as are her kids, peripatetic Sarah and the sleep-deprived Reese. So it's down to Cecil to try and talk Ben up into Heaven.

"I guess this is the only way anybody ever gets the last word over Ben," Cecil starts.

But when the distant backfire of a car punctuates his opening shtick Cecil flinches.

"Little runt probably arranged for that ahead of time."

Sheepish titters from several of the assembled mourners.

Cecil points his book at a granite headstone catty-corner to Ben's plot.

"That there is Pistol Pete's grave. For those of you who don't know, Pete was a minor celebrity round these parts. Lived just south of town. He was a little sawed-off runt of a lawman but Pete could cow any man who stepped to him. Ben and me got to meet Pete a couple-few times. Came and talked at our grade school, even. Recited some yarns from this book about his life I'm holding here in my hand. It got so scatological our teacher had to ask Pete if he'd leave early. We saw him address the crowd at an Aggies game, too, in nineteen forty-eight. It was some kind of fun. Anyway I remember Pete said something that night and it stuck with me. He said the hardest part of being a lawman was figuring how to talk with the aggrieved. I never quite grasped what he meant. But if any of you are hurting like me, then we're all in a pretty sorry way right about now. So I'm starting to understand it."

Swallow that lump and keep on jawing.

"After that basketball game, when we saw Pete, well on that car ride home my back was broken in a wreck. The doctors said I'd live six months, maybe a year at the outside. That's been almost fifty years ago now. Shows you all that schooling don't make a person much smarter than the rest of us. But the truth is I always expected Ben would be the one talking at my funeral. No doubt about it, that would have been a better speech. Ben had more hot air in him than a sauna after a chili cook-off. But I can't say I'm overly sorry it's gone the other way."

Now everyone is laughing.

"I was headed places before I got broken. I was going to be a bigtime basketball star. Make a trailerful of money, marry the prettiest girl, drive the fastest car. But the car crash changed all that. For both of us. Ben went from looking up to me—hell, everybody did, there's a lot about me to admire—to caring for me. And the change never sat well. I was hard on little Benjamin. Angry at him for getting out of here. I never left Perkins, though for a long while I wanted to. But baby brother went on to do some great things in the city. He was an important man. A good one. He might have had a few more notches in his belt than anyone I see standing here, but Ben's heart was even bigger than his waistband.

"None of you probably knows this, but the night I was hurt it was Ben that was driving our truck. He was twelve, which was plenty old for plowing back then. But not for highway driving. I was just a smidge older. If our dad had found out, well, Ben's funeral would have happened a long time ago. So when the sheriff came asking, we lied. Said I'd been at the wheel. And until just a few weeks back we never spoke about it. Not ever. It got so I'd remember the accident and it would be me behind the wheel, not Ben. That little fib we told, it turned into a kind of truth between us. I've been thinking quite a lot about that, last couple days. About the past. About memory. How Ben wound up sharing my fate once I was paralyzed. It was a heavy weight to carry, all that success he had. And that secret responsibility for . . ." and here Cecil looks down at his useless limbs, ". . . all this. For me. Even though it wasn't his fault. Not a bit of it. Sometimes I'll imagine going back to that night, after the game. I'll wonder what it would have been like if we'd switched our lives. How would things have worked out, if it was Ben's back that was broken, and not mine?"

Cecil takes a moment to fix the flutter in his chin.

"I don't like what I see, imagining it. I don't expect I'd have handled success as gracefully as Ben did. Not that he couldn't have done better. But I don't expect I would have come back to Perkins, practically every Sunday, to check up on a quick-tempered invalid. And I don't expect I'd have come to love Ben with as much conviction as I do today. With as much certainty. And I did love my little brother. For that. For everything."

From the front row Becca begins to glow. She's muttering something too, unintelligible, lost under the whispering weather.

"God rest his great big jelly-belly soul."

THANKSGIVING

FALL 1996

75. BECCA

Becca is sitting alone at her dining room table, staring out the window again. If she turns her head just so, the sugar maple outside seems to ignite, torching orange and red in the dreamy afternoon light. The proverbial burning bush.

The kitchen is filled to bursting with grub, there are four pies and two types of stuffing and collard greens and mashed potatoes and a turkey baking in the oven, she can smell it's almost done, with all the fixings. There's even a batch of homemade fudge cooling on the rack. But the house is empty, neither Sarah nor Reese could make it home this year, and she hasn't bothered to set the table.

Her reflection in the windowpane looking infinitely older and sadder than it should.

In the days after the bombing a spring storm blew through, thunderheads wailing thick and wet above the city, water puddling in the yards and ditches and gutters and gusting down slantwise with the wild north wind. Rainsplash popping up off the earth like muzzle fire. Becca remembers thinking the heat needed turning down, the world was about to boil over. It was a strange, a portentous, weather. And once the sky and the smoke had cleared Becca watched as everyone came back to work, and to life, again.

History—that's History with a capital H, the kind of collective trauma with the capacity for paralyzing an entire nation, and the bombing accomplished that, it crippled us all, even if only briefly, even if it did nothing else—when it does finally happen, History has a way of subsuming individual grief into the bigger picture. Minimizing it, in every sense of the word.

What was her loss when compared to the woman who had had her leg amputated with a pocket knife? She was visiting the social security office with her family when the building came down on top of them, tumbling to a stop right atop her knee, and the recovery team needed to get her out of there, and to do it quickly, because she's bleeding to death and the structure is still collapsing all around them. But the only tool at hand is a pocket knife. This poor soul is awake during the entire ghastly operation. She's screaming for the doctor to stop, living isn't worth this pain. Then she does finally survive the ordeal only to discover that her grandmother and *both* of her children, both of her *infants*, have perished in the blast.

What was any one person's loss next to a story like this?

One hour and eighteen minutes after the blast, Timothy McVeigh was pulled over by a state trooper for a routine traffic violation. And three days later, when the boy's mugshot began circulating, McVeigh was already locked up in the Noble County jail, in Perry, for carrying an unlicensed handgun. The banality of the boy's getaway plan, the simplicity of his capture, standing as one last insult atop the mountain of hurt he'd already wrought.

Becca tells people how Ben passed and they summon an outsized empathy into their faces, a grief sufficient for mourning one hundred sixty-eight others, and strangely enough it does seem to help. To minimize her pain. Ben died in the backseat of Dean Goodnight's car. Cardiac arrest. He was in Aura Jefferson's arms when it happened. They were just two blocks from the emergency room. He was never part of the official record, wasn't recognized as a hero. Not like that nurse Dean told her about, the one who inspired them to try to help.

Rebecca. Rebecca Anderson.

Same name as her own. Becca likes to imagine that there are others out there—undocumented, whether by choice or mere oversight—other invisibles who wound up losing their lives or their mobility or their sanity or their conceptions of God and country and themselves, and who find that they are lost, now, and wandering.

There have to be others. Don't there?

Wondering.

Outside, Cecil's truck is pulling into Becca's circular front driveway.

She blows a loud raspberry, *enough with the woolgathering, Mrs. Porter*, and gets up to open the front door. Becca knows better than to offer Cecil any assistance getting out of his pickup. Though when Ben's big brother rolls up to the front porch, an overnight bag and his precious laptop computer balanced upon his lap, Cecil does allow her to walk around behind his wheelchair and pop him over and up onto her slab-stone porch.

He scowls at the cardboard boxes stacked inside the foyer. "I see you saved some of the work for me."

She has never appreciated the man's humor. But during Ben's funeral, when Cecil ended up cracking self-deprecating, off-color jokes for the good part of fifteen minutes, she started to understand it. These men of hers, they talk tough in order to hide how utterly frightened they are of their own emotions. To the Porter brothers, making fun of someone is the socially acceptable way of saying: "I love you." By the time Cecil had finished with his farewell speech everyone at the funeral was laughing. Everyone but Cecil.

Ben couldn't have asked for a more touching sendoff.

"I have something to show you," she says to Cecil.

He follows her outside. Becca has had a ramp installed in the garage, and another ramp connected to the guest quarters. After pushing through the front door (she painted it Ben's favorite color in the end, sky blue) and into the living room Cecil whispers, "Lord-amighty."

Just before he died Ben had the builder make some modifications to the granny flat, so the Neverending Remodel From Hell stretched on for another six months after he was buried. And though Cecil has never yet set tread inside, the apartment has been complete for a little over a year now. It's a bright, airy, two-story living space: two bedrooms, two baths, a kitchenette, a loft overlooking the main sitting area. Either a cast-iron spiral staircase or the elevator will take you up to the second floor.

Becca opens the door into the main bedroom.

"This is where you'll be staying."

Cecil tosses his things onto the bed and wheels into the master bathroom. She has installed an electronic lift, handicap railings, two extra-wide benches in the shower. The vanity has also been elevated—four inches, room enough for the extra-large wheelchair—and an array of articulated mirrors are capable of swinging several feet out from the wall so Cecil can tend to his skin.

"Let's go upstairs," she says.

Cecil follows Becca into the great glass-walled elevator, which whisks them on up to the second floor. When he lays eyes on the workshop Cecil says, "Oh my God. Becca."

"Ben came home after one of your basketball dates," she explains. "He was talking nonstop about your stained glass windows. He was . . . you could say Ben was emotional about it. We'd been talking about asking you to move in with us, into the granny flat when it was done. I guess he thought this space might seal the deal."

The studio sports an open floorplan with plenty of natural light: twelve-foot ceilings, more than enough storage space, windows spanning all four walls. Any direction you look there's a flare of fall color to be seen. Tree leaves seething in the crisp November breeze. Cecil pushes over to the supersized island—it's large enough he can construct nearly any size stained glass window he wants to—and bends to examine the vertical storage slots built into the shelving there.

"A lathe," he says, touching the tool. "Cubbyholes for the glass."

"There's a desk and printer over here. And over there are the phone and an Internet connection for filling your orders. A packaging station. This, what's it called, this worldwide website storefront? Where you've set up shop?"

"eBay."

"Yes. Well eBay should work just fine up here. How's business, by the way?"

"I wish I could grow two more hands," Cecil laughs. "Who knew everyone and his mother would be willing to send money to an absolute stranger for a stained glass window?"

"Well if you would agree to move in with me, I know someone who'd love to help. And I could use *your* help. My hands are full, Mr. Porter, if you'll remember."

Cecil doesn't answer but he's nodding, thinking and nodding.

"Are you still going to that church in Langston?" Becca asks.

"Every Sunday."

"I have a theory. That you just go to watch people admire that window."

"That's as good a reason as any, I guess."

A car horn is honking outside—three abbreviated bleats—so Becca excuses herself, leaving Cecil to explore the apartment. She hopes he'll stay longer than overnight. If not this visit, then maybe the next one.

You stubborn old coot, she thinks, quick-walking back through the garage for the house, *I'll wear you down yet.*

Back downstairs, in the kitchen, Dean Goodnight and a very pregnant Samantha Goodnight are unloading the sacks of ice Becca sent them to fetch. She'll be churning homemade ice cream later and wanted to be sure they wouldn't run out.

"That was quick."

"There was nobody on the road," Samantha says.

It's Sam, Becca keeps reminding herself, *not Samantha.* Though why a woman would want a boy's nickname Becca will never know. Especially a woman as gorgeous as this one. With that big round belly, that pale creamy skin, she looks so soft and maternal and *exquisite.* Like a lost or forgotten sculpture you might stumble upon in the Louvre. The Goodnights are going to have an absolutely beautiful baby.

Sam starts to kneel down before the freezer but Becca waves her away.

"Save your energy, dear. I won't be responsible for that back going out two weeks before your due date."

While Becca is replenishing the ice Dean limps back out to his car. When he returns the big Indian is carrying a sack of groceries under one arm and Caleb Grimes under the other, the boy wiggling and giggling, trying not-so-desperately to break free.

"Look what I found." Dean drops the boy on the floor and the paper sack on the marble countertop, groaning overloudly for effect. After three knee surgeries Mr. Goodnight is moving a little slower than before, he's even gained a little weight. But Becca thinks he carries it well. She might even like to fatten him up a tad more.

"*Yakoke*," Caleb says to Dean.

"*Ome*," Dean answers.

Caleb skips up to Becca—she's on her knees in front of the freezer door, down at his level—and takes her face into his hands, forcing her to look him in the eyes. "Momma," he says to her, very seriously, he is touching her cheeks and he says, "where's Uncle Cecil?"

"He's up in the apartment."

Caleb wiggles a finger, correcting her. "He's in the *tree house*."

"The tree house, then." Becca smiles. She can't help it, she can't ever stop smiling, it seems like, around this adorable little boy. Seven years old going on thirteen.

"Momma. When are we unhiding the Christmas decorations from the cardboard?"

"After dinner. And after you help Uncle Cecil unpack his suitcase."

Caleb drops his hands, darting for the garage.

"Caleb! You be careful in that tree house! There are power tools and saws and sharp pointies every place you look. Don't touch anything unless Uncle Cecil says it's okay."

"*Okeh*."

Both Dean and Sam are watching Becca.

"Are you two ready for this?" she asks.

Sam says "Yes" at the same time that Dean is saying "No," so she punches playfully at his arm.

"Ouch."

"Listen," Becca announces. "I have a favor to ask."

"Anything," Dean says.

"Come into the study a minute."

Inside the office, there is a red file folder lying on Ben's old mahogany desk. Becca gives it to Dean. The lawyer delivered the paperwork this morning. She had asked him to stay for dinner but of course Gomez already had plans.

"It's a living trust," she explains. "I'm fifty-five years older than Caleb, so if anything were to happen, God forbid, to me, this document basically states that the two of you have agreed to step in as his legal guardian. To raise him like you would your own. There will be money. Plenty of money. But I wanted you to read it over. Think on it awhile. And then let me know."

Dean sits in Ben's plush leather chair, rubbing on his knee and scanning through the document. He's studying tribal and criminal law now, at Oklahoma City University's law school, working toward a legal degree, and in Becca's experience a lawyer's ears don't start working until he has absorbed every word of an official document.

"This work you're doing with Caleb," Becca says to Dean. "Teaching him Choctaw. He loves it. He loves you. Both of you. And I want to make sure he's taken care of. No matter what happens."

"Can I take this home?"

"Of course."

"Alright. We'll call you this weekend and talk more about it."

"That's fine."

"Becca," Sam says, "I've always wanted to ask, and I hope this isn't off limits, just let me know if it is and I'll shut up. But when you were adopting Caleb? When Dean let you read Billy's case file and you found out that Caleb's great-great-grandfather, Billy's great-grandfather, what was his name?"

Dean looks at Becca and says, "Eli."

"Eli Cain," Becca says, nodding.

"Right," Sam says. "Dean, well. He told me Eli was *your* father?"

"Yes."

"Well, I know how this helped with the adoption. Dean said it made things go so much smoother, having the blood relation and everything. But what I really wanted to ask was, how did you feel? When you found out? What was that, you know, *like?*"

Becca sighs. The truth is she still can't believe it.

"I felt, I guess, everything. Everything all at once. Aunt Mabel told me dad was catting around on my mother. So I shouldn't have been too surprised. But I was. Surprised and shocked and sad. At least initially. Sad for my mother. To know that the man she loved was hiding something like that. But happy, too. Happy for Caleb. Happy for me. Because I'm able to give him something I didn't have much of at his age. Stability, security. A home. A routine. Love, basically."

"Has Caleb visited Billy?" Dean asks.

Becca is shaking her head no.

"After the trial, once Billy realized he wasn't going to be executed, he signed away his parental rights almost immediately. But then he stopped taking my calls. Just like that. Anyway it was a big help, especially with Willa. Someday, I'd like Caleb to have something to do with his parents. To be able to talk with them. Someday. I'm just not sure, yet, how that would work. Caleb's great-grandmother, Caroline, she wants to see him. But Caroline says she is too old to care for a child."

"Willa," Dean almost spits the name.

"Give her just a small break, Dean," Sam says. "She's . . ."

"She's back inside, is what she is. Two months out of jail. All she has to do is not screw up. And she's sent up on a possession charge.

Five years mandatory minimum. Nothing the judge or Wolfman or any of us could do to save her. I will not give that damn woman a fucking break."

"Dean," says Sam, shielding her tummy with both arms, "we talked about the cursing."

"I'm sorry."

"Will you stay in the public defender's office?" Becca asks. "After you graduate?"

Dean leans back into Ben's chair, composing himself.

"I think so."

"Would you have taken Timothy McVeigh's case?"

Becca's not even thinking when it comes out of her mouth.

Dean looks stunned to be hearing the question.

"It wouldn't have been allowed. I was a witness. I was on scene. I saw . . . people die. I saw . . ."

"But hypothetically. Say you weren't. Would you want McVeigh to be executed?"

What's come over her?

But Dean won't answer. He's standing, excusing himself from the room, limping outside to watch the leaves.

"I'm sorry," Becca says to Sam. "I'm so sorry. I don't know what . . ."

"Don't worry about it," Sam says, hugging Becca. "He's fine. He still gets worked up about it sometimes."

Sam steps out into the yard to talk with Dean.

Becca sits in Ben's chair, the leather sighing softly as she settles, and watches the two of them through the office window. They're doing a great job with the marriage, judging from what Becca has witnessed over the last year and a half. They are as communicative as she and Ben ever were.

More so, even.

What did she know about communication, after all? Becca couldn't even claim to know her own husband. Not really.

But say what you want about Big Ben Porter—and people, they most certainly do—he was *real*. Bigger than life itself. With colossal appetites and flaws, but also enormous virtues.

The way he used to make her laugh.

Becca's big bad Ben.

There is a freestanding basketball hoop planted beside the driveway. Ben had it built when Reese was about Caleb's age, and Becca can see Cecil and Caleb are out there under it, bouncing the basketball on the concrete, talking trash as they shoot. She doesn't really approve of this whole trash-talking thing. But Caleb can't get enough of it. Sometimes he'll start speaking Choctaw words to Cecil and the old man gets so flummoxed—he can't understand a word of what the boy is saying and imagines the worst, of course—and Caleb will just laugh and laugh.

A buzzing sound in the kitchen. Turkey's done. As Becca is pulling the bird from the oven she hears another horn honking in the front yard. The Franklins have arrived, Aura and pastor Nate. After putting the groceries away she steps outside, leaving the front door open, to stand watching from the porch.

Everyone is here.

Caleb is talking them all into a game of basketball. Soon it's three-on-three, Caleb and Cecil and Nate against Aura and Sam and Dean. Sam is dribbling awkwardly toward the basket, trying to waddle around Cecil's chair, but the old man steals the ball—those arms of his are so *long*—and tries breaking for the basket. But Aura's in his face now, she's not giving him any ground, so Cecil passes the ball off to Caleb, who dribbles toward the goal only to be blocked by the twin towers of Dean and Aura. Caleb passes the ball back to Cecil and he shoots, the ball dropping through the basket with a *whoosh!*

"Nothing but net!" Cecil crows, spinning his chair in a little celebration dance.

And everyone is laughing.

But Caleb is hurt. He's come down hard on a knee and his eyes are tearing up, then he's crying. Becca steps down from the porch, jogging for her little boy, but by the time she gets there everyone has converged on the child, huddled with concern around him, and he's already looking better.

"Umbrella," Cecil says, smiling at Aura.

Aura is smiling back, smiling and nodding her head.

"Yes."

"What's umbrella?" Becca asks.

"It means we're a team," says Aura.

And they are. A team, Becca thinks, and a family.

Caleb is loving the surplus of attention. He's hamming it up for Cecil.

"Next time let me make the shot, Uncle Cecil! Don't be such a big fat ball pig."

Everyone is laughing again, Aura whispering in Cecil's ear, Sam making eyes at Dean. In a little while, Becca knows, it will be time to make the gravy, to set the table and call them all inside for dinner, where they'll suffer Cecil's inappropriate stories and laugh at Caleb's insatiable questioning and speculate about the imminent arrival of the Goodnight baby, maybe a Franklin baby, too. It might be Becca's wishful thinking, but is that a baby bump under Aura's jacket? Becca keeps hoping she'll hear the Franklins are pregnant. They'll unbox the Christmas decorations while Dean and Nate lie on the carpet before the fireplace, watching the football game, bellyaching about how much they've eaten.

But first Becca just wants to enjoy this moment. There's another game going. She can hear the ball *slip-slapping* on the concrete and the pleasant babble of these now-familiar voices and laughter—Caleb's laughter, Aura's and Dean's and Cecil's too—rising through it like a bell.

When Becca was a child, Aunt Mabel taught her that a prayer should always begin with some form of thank you. And so the prayer she finds herself saying is at once a thanksgiving and a plea, an invocation and a benediction. It is a celebration of life, of this strange new family she has found, of this eternal, this blessed and powerful *Now*, and of laughter.

Laughter ever after amen.

Amen.

ACKNOWLEDGMENTS

My wife and best friend, Lisa Remedios, and our two crazy daughters, Cadence Tomlinson and Laurel Tomlinson.

Eleanor Jackson, Ben LeRoy, Alan Rinzler.

Josh Jefferson, Gary Peterson.

Mel Freilicher, Austin Sarat, Rilla Askew, Matthew Hefti, Dave White, Matthew Dicks, Joe Milazzo, Eddie Sutton and family.

The Peripatetic Old East Dallas Book Club: Laura Freeland, Kelly Gordon, Lisa Remedios, Caroline Terry, Stephanie Woolley.

The Tomlinson Family: Bob, Sandi, Steven, Carol, Phil, Larry, Sid, Tracy Kienitz, Christy Doering.

Christopher Hill, Steve Freeland, Christopher Dvorak, Arthur Remedios, Janet "Query Shark" Reid, Mary Bisbee-Beek, Bethany Carland-Adams, Kate Petrella, Ashley Myers.

Phil Jackson's *Sacred Hoops* and Bill Bradley's *Life on the Run* taught me about basketball and the wider world in which it is played.

Both the novel's structure and Caroline Amos's speech patterns were influenced by Tom Mould's excellent *Choctaw Prophecy*.

Austin Sarat's insightful *When the State Kills: Capital Punishment and the American Condition* opened my eyes to the moral contradictions inherent in the administration of the death penalty in this country, and inspired Aura's victim impact testimony.

Al Franken's *Rush Limbaugh Is a Big Fat Idiot and Other Observations* was essential to understanding how politicians and the media manipulate language to shape public opinion.

Jeffrey Toobin's *The Run of His Life* was instrumental in getting a sense for how the O.J. Simpson trial unfolded over time, and for illuminating how race was a complicating factor for both sides, often in ways you wouldn't expect.

Ben Fountain's *Billy Lynn's Long Halftime Walk* taught me how to convey the sensory overload of a live sporting event, and inspired the word cloud in Chapter 48.

Don DeLillo's *Underworld* showed me how the techniques of film-making—establishing shots, cross-cutting, ellipsis—can be applied to literature. Its opening section contains the best sports writing I've had the pleasure to read, and the first scenes of my novel owe a heavy debt to Mr. DeLillo's.

BOOK CLUB DISCUSSION GUIDE

Author David Eric Tomlinson is available to discuss *THE MIDNIGHT MAN* with your book club. To arrange a Q&A with the author, visit www.daviderictomlinson.com.

1. Over the course of this novel, each of the five main characters changes in some dramatic way. Cecil Porter, for example, comes to terms with his bigotry, and learns to ask for help from his friends and loved ones. As the story progresses, in what ways do the other characters grow? Do they do it alone, or does someone else facilitate the evolution?

2. Becca Porter volunteers at a battered women's shelter. How do the other characters involve themselves within the community? What are they hoping to achieve? Which of these contributions has the most impact? Did you agree or disagree with the ways in which the characters attempt to influence matters of business, politics, or faith? Why?

3. Consider the theme of forgiveness. "If the past is *inside* of you, Aura, that means you control it," Nate says. "You can change your understanding of it, your feelings about it, your relationship with it. Anytime you decide to. Anger, hate, resentment . . . these things are a prison." Do you think pastor Nate is correct? Is true forgiveness possible? And is the act of forgiveness more beneficial to the perpetrator, or the victim, of a crime? Why?

4. Billy Grimes isn't the only criminal in this novel. How are Billy's crimes different from those committed by O.J.

Simpson, Mark Fuhrman, Bob Macy, Jane Barrett, Willa Busby, Timothy McVeigh, Carl Jefferson, Ben Porter, or even Dean Goodnight? How did you feel about capital punishment before reading this novel? Did you learn anything new about the death penalty? Did your opinions change? If a prosecutor is absolutely positive that a defendant is guilty, do you believe that manufacturing evidence or lying under oath, to ensure a conviction, is ever justified? Do you think Dean Goodnight would want to see Timothy McVeigh put to death?

5. "Conversation's not a competition," Cecil says to his brother. "That's what the loser always says," Ben replies. How do the characters in this novel use language to achieve specific goals? Identify instances of nonverbal communication between characters. Is it effective? How is persuasion different from communication? What is the point of the "I spy" competition between the father and his daughter in Chapter 33?

6. "'It [umbrella] means we're a team,' says Aura. And they are. A team, Becca thinks, and a family." How are the themes of teamwork and family juxtaposed throughout this novel? What do you think the author is trying to say? Can you identify other paired themes within the text?

7. Becca has a recurring daydream about a red door, closing. What do you think doors symbolize in this story? Identify other symbols and discuss the scenes in which they appear.

8. Not all of these characters are sympathetic. Both Ben and Cecil Porter, for example, use emotionally-charged racial slurs in casual conversation. Does this make it more difficult to empathize with their personal or moral struggles? Does a character need to be sympathetic to be interesting? Or heroic? Why?

9. Imagine that someone is writing a novel about your life. Describe your character arc. What are the main obstacles between you and your goal? Are these obstacles financial, psychological, physical, intellectual, philosophical? How might your character need to adapt in order to overcome them? Have you ever changed your mind about a strongly-held belief or bias? If not, imagine and describe the circumstances which might cause you to reevaluate one of your core principles.

10. Choctaw storytelling involves stepping back in time and telling a kind of forward-looking prophecy, reconciling the past with the present moment. Consider the novel's four-part structure and eventual climax. Identify clues or motifs which connect the earlier chapters of the story to its ending. What do you think the author is trying to say about the political or social circumstances that give rise to domestic terrorism?

11. Discuss the portrayal of the various ethnicities in this novel. How did the author convey race or class differences? What stereotypes did he rely on? Should a novelist's ethnicity limit what he or she can write? How would Aura answer that same question? How would Becca, Dean, or Cecil?

12. "Amen doesn't have to mean we've reached the end," pastor Nate says to Opal Jefferson. "Sometimes it means we're just getting started." Consider the ending of THE MIDNIGHT MAN. What do you think will happen to these characters five, ten, or even twenty years later? How would Cecil Porter and Aura Jefferson, for example, react to witnessing a black man become president of the United States, or to current tensions between the police and people of color? How might contemporary political developments affect the beliefs, motivations, and relationships of the characters?